THE PRINCE AND THE SILVER PLATTER

EMILIA LEE

For everyone who came back for seconds.

1

It was amazing how different things could look in the dark. Dom traveled the road out of Hindry hundreds of times before, but now the headlights of his uncle's old jalopy struggled against the gloom as the car plodded up the hill, turning the trees and signposts Dom knew well into lurking shadows.

Dom usually liked to be home early on the night of the annual Elmmond House party. He ate alone, drowning his frustration in whiskey and half-imagined fantasies of bursting through the large front doors of Elmmond House and...

And what?

Nothing. Because he wouldn't. And even if he did, it was impossible to rescue people who didn't want to be rescued.

Elmmond House, the large, ancient manor that loomed over the town, sparkled in front of Dom as he finally crested the hill. It seemed luminous, somehow, in spite of the heavy dark; lights glittered temptingly from every window and open door, impossibly bright. If Dom squinted, he could see movement. Dozens upon dozens of guests flitted back and forth between the windows, moth-like, strange silhouettes against the ethereal glow.

Elmmond House was the last place Dom's brother Ares had ever been seen, and Dom was captivated by its strangeness.

The car bumped as Dom accidentally drove into the grass. He gripped the wheel tighter, gritting his teeth, and tore his gaze away from the house.

There had always been rumors that the house was magic. Or magic people lived there. People who weren't exactly human. His mother had laughed it off when Dom had asked. But, she vanished when Dom was thirteen, and Dom's uncle, Hector, had warned both Dom and Ares away from Elmmond House. 'It's dangerous,' had been Hector's constant refrain for all of Dom's teen years. And Dom had no reason not to believe him. Six years after their mother's disappearance, Ares had gone too. Dom was no detective, but he wasn't sure he needed to be. It all added up: Elmmond House, and the magic that everyone rumored the house was full of, was as dangerous as anyone said.

Except.

Except, Elmmond House's caretaker, Jonas Rookwood, was a frequent, friendly customer of the diner Dom owned in Hindry.

Jonas didn't live at Elmmond House, just in the small cottage beside it, but still, Dom had never gotten up the courage to ask him about the house. He and Jonas chatted, maybe flirted a little here and there over the years, but that was all. They weren't sociable outside of the diner. Dom wasn't exactly social with anyone outside of the diner. But when Dom's motorcycle had popped a tire a day ago, Jonas had been driving by, and he stopped to give Dom a hand.

And Jonas hadn't seen fit, that fateful evening, to hide the fact that he was not a human, but was, in fact, a very tall, very large demon.

It was strange, but then Hindry was a strange place. There were always customers with accents that were unrecognizable even to the well-traveled sailors who frequented the diner;

townsfolk who aged too slowly, like the local vicar whose appearance hadn't changed in Dom's twenty-some years of knowing him. Little things. Oddities that could be ignored if one was inclined to ignore them, which Dom definitely was. But what was stranger, was that on the drive to Dom's house, his motorcycle safely tucked in the back of Jonas' truck, Jonas and Dom had been startlingly honest with each other. And Jonas had said that he thought he might be able to find Ares.

And Dom hadn't stopped thinking about it since.

Dom parked in the lot of Bittergate Chapel, on the far side of the hill from Elmmond House. He tried to focus on pies and deliveries and not on what Jonas Rookwood may or may not know.

"Sorry I'm late." Dom climbed out of the car, closing the door carefully, always worried it would fall off its hinges. Father Michaels, the ageless vicar, with his dark brown skin and halo of white hair, chuckled, his footsteps crunching in the gravel.

"It's alright. Your aunt and Mrs. Byrne will be at it for another hour yet." Father Michaels shoved his hands in his pockets as Dom fumbled with the keys to the trunk. Dom was late because he'd burned two cherry pies and had to start them over from scratch, thinking about Ares. Wondering for the thousandth time what would happen if he went into Elmmond House and demanded answers from whomever he found inside.

"How've you been, son?" Father Michaels' voice was gentle, but Dom still startled.

"Good. Fine. Busy." He *was* busy at least. The Silver Platter, Dom's restaurant, always lost good waitstaff to the Elmmond House Party. Dom gathered up the pies from the trunk and straightened up, handing a stack of boxes to Father Michaels, who was watching him closely.

"How've you been?" Dom reached into the trunk for the remaining desserts to avoid Father Michaels' eye.

"I've been well. I need to get some of the pews refinished in the church. Your aunt told me you're a wonder with wood-stain. I was hoping you might be willing to take a look."

Dom hesitated. He shouldn't have hesitated, because it was rude, but he didn't like being at the chapel any more than he needed to be. But Ree would be disappointed if he didn't help. Aside from the small beauty salon she ran in town, the church was her world. He only had his aunt and uncle left, and Dom couldn't bear to let her down.

"Sure." Dom let the trunk fall closed behind him. "I'd be happy to."

"Not tonight, of course," Father Michaels said, as they started across the parking lot together. "Maybe before the holidays." The vicar kept talking and Dom nodded along, thinking of all the things he'd already committed to getting done 'before the holidays.' One of the sinks in Aunt Ree's salon was leaking. The local Fisherman's Lodge had contacted him about catering their Thanksgiving meal. There was the LeClaire's anniversary cake, and the desserts for the town council potluck, and the book return slot at the library was bound to get stuck again sometime in the next two weeks. In a small town, it was hard not to be neighborly, but Dom wasn't sure when he'd become the only neighbor who knew how to work a wrench or a screwdriver or an oven. He told himself he didn't mind. Most of the time he didn't. At the very least, it kept him busy.

"Are you sure everything's alright, Dominic?" They'd stopped at the door to the hall. How long had they been standing there? Dom fumbled, ignoring the heat of embarrassment on the back of his neck.

"Here, I can take those pies. If you can—" The door swung open before either of them could reach for it, and Aunt Ree poked her head out, looking between the vicar and her nephew with a wrinkled nose.

"What are you two doing? Come in out of the dark!"

Ree was a petite woman with light brown skin, a softly rounded face and bright blue eyes. She marched into the parish hall like she was leading an army, and not two men with a dozen pies between them. Ree could have led an army if she'd wanted to. She had more confidence in her little finger than Dom had in his entire body.

"Look who I found outside!" She exclaimed to Mrs. Byrne, who was on a ladder, twisting streamers along a windowsill. "Better late than never, I suppose. You could have called."

"Hello Dominic!" Mrs. Byrne chirped over her shoulder.

"Hello, Mrs. Byrne." Dom set his stack of pies in the empty space his aunt had left for them.

"What do I owe you for the pies, Dom?" Father Michaels asked. It must have been an even year if they were doing this old song and dance. Dom dusted off his script.

"They're a donation, Father," Dom said. Aunt Ree nodded proudly without looking up, still adjusting the placement of pie boxes on the table. "I'm happy to do it." Father Michaels would say thank you. Dom would ask if they needed help getting out the tables, and then Mrs. Byrne would say how strong he was in the exact same way that she had when he was sixteen, and then—

"Take a walk with me, Dom," Father Michaels said. Dom jerked in surprise, as though he'd taken too long a stride and stumbled off a sidewalk. His eyes darted to his aunt, which should have been embarrassing since he was twenty-nine and not twelve, but what was he supposed to do? Aunt Ree shrugged, her own gaze sliding questioningly to Father Michaels, clearly not anticipating the change in their routine any more than Dom had. Dom still half expected to hear Mrs. Byrne saying, 'How often do you go to the gym?' as Father Michaels led him back out to the parking lot.

"I'm happy to stay and help, if you need me." Dom began to offer, but Father Michaels shook his head, slowing as they arrived at the car.

"Can I ask you something? A personal question. And you don't have to answer."

"Of course."

"Do you know Jonas Rookwood?" Did he mean the Jonas Rookwood that Dom had spent the bulk of the drive to the chapel thinking about? Dom turned over the keys in his pocket nervously. It was just a coincidence.

"I know him."

"And have you seen him recently. In the last day or two?" It was hard to miss a man who was nearly seven feet tall with red skin and big black horns. Dom nodded.

"He gave me a lift back to my place last night when the tire on my bike blew out."

"But not today?" Dom had seen him that morning, early at the diner, but the line of questions was making him uncomfortable. He paused, and the vicar changed course. "You're not going to Elmmond House after this, are you?"

"No," Dom said, because he wasn't. Even if that was the most likely place for him to find answers about his brother's disappearance. The only place he'd never dared to look. He frowned at Father Michaels, puzzled. "Did you... want me to?"

"No, it's alright. I just assumed that a young man like you might be attending the..." Michaels trailed off. "I just needed to speak to Rookwood, and I thought he might be there. I'd go myself, but..." he trailed off, gesturing to the parish hall.

It was a better excuse to go to Elmmond House than any Dom had ever been offered before. Not that he'd wanted one.

It was dangerous. Everyone said it was.

Dom *knew* that it was.

"I'll stop by. If I find Jonas, I should tell him to get in touch with you?" Dom asked.

"It's alright." Father Michaels shook his head. "I'll take care of it."

"It's on my way back." Dom shrugged, as though this was nothing. "I don't mind." He was just being helpful. Michaels had known Dom since he was a child. He was Ree's favorite member of the clergy. He wouldn't knowingly put Dom in danger. And Dom wanted to talk to Jonas again. Badly. "If I can't find him, I'll leave a message with someone."

"Only if you're sure it's not an imposition. If he's there, just have him come up and see me. It's... not urgent, exactly. But it is important."

"Alright," Dom said with a nod. "I'll tell him if I see him."

2

O n the last night of his life, Asterion lay alone in a giant, uncomfortable bed. He was in the ugliest bedroom it had ever been his privilege to sleep in. All the furniture was gilded and shining and hideous, and even though he had just woken up from a nap, he was still exhausted.

The sounds of a string quintet seeped up through the floorboards. If the band was playing, then cocktail service had started. He could loll about for at least another half hour before anyone missed him. Likely longer than that.

Asterion kept the time of a minuet he could barely hear, tapping his fingers on the bare skin of his chest, and staring at the cloud mural that adorned the ceiling. He could tell the cellist was already drunk; the sheer volume of dropped notes was appalling.

"Asterion?" Ellery rapped her knuckles sharply on the other side of the bedroom door. Asterion sighed and let his eyes fall closed.

"Yes?"

The door creaked and Asterion looked over to see Ellery

sticking her head in sideways, two bespangled antlers poking out of her moss green hair.

"Are you with someone?" she asked.

"No." Ellery pushed open the door and stepped into the room, frowning. She looked him over, hands on her hip. Her gown was a shimmering russet silk, her ample peachy cleavage stunningly dotted with white fawn speckles.

"What are you doing?"

"I was resting, Ellery. Am I not allowed to rest?"

"Not when you're supposed to be hosting the biggest costume party in the nine realms, no." As though he didn't know that. It was childish, but he didn't respond, and after a moment, Ellery groaned and strode across the bedroom, flinging open the armoire with more force than was required.

"Be careful with that," Asterion said, though he didn't really care. "I'm sure it's an antique."

"Everything in this house is an antique," Ellery grumbled. He could hear her shifting his clothes around and couldn't be bothered to look at what she was picking out for him. He'd brought several costumes, but none of them suited his current malaise. "Get up," Ellery said to him over her shoulder.

"I don't think you're allowed to speak to me that way. Especially tonight." He did sit up, though. He knew better than to sass Ellery Van Ahlberg. Even if he was, technically, her boss.

"Why should tonight be different than any other night?" Her tone was forcibly airy. Asterion rolled his eyes.

"Because everything is about to change."

"Wrong," Ellery said. She spun around with a pile of dark blue fabric in her arms. The diamonds stitched along the seams of the cape glittered. "Nothing changes tonight. Tonight is the same as any other night."

"Except that it's followed by tomorrow." Asterion leaned

back, his hands pressed against the lumpy mattress. "When I cease to exist." Ellery huffed.

"That's overdramatic, even from you."

"You have a horrible bedside manner."

"You're not dying." Ellery tossed the costume onto his legs. "Nor will you die tomorrow. Get dressed."

Asterion kicked the fabric off his legs and climbed out of bed. Maybe he was being overdramatic. But if he was, it was because he didn't know how else he ought to be. Asterion wasn't afraid of the change he was about to undergo. Nor was he grieving everything he was going to lose. He was pretending to be dejected because he knew he ought to be dejected, but really he just felt numb. It led to overacting.

Without another word to Ellery, he gathered up the blue costume from the foot of his bed and swept into the adjoining bathroom. A velvet jumpsuit, dotted with diamond stars, and sheer fabric across the chest. Asterion pulled it on, adjusting the fit here and there. It looked striking against his fair skin, although his chest was dotted with honey-colored freckles that he'd always hated. The easiest way to hide them was to shift his whole complexion, so he drew up the tannish gold tones of his freckles, letting a swell of morphological magic pulse softly across his skin. Asterion's magic was warm and settled on him with a practiced grace. He threaded his fingers through his hair, drawing magic down through the strands, taking a moment to cup the ends of his pointed ears and shrink them down to a more subtle curve. His natural hair was the color of a robin's egg, but tonight he needed something closer to the sky at dusk, a moonlit dark blue.

Magic straightened his shoulders and smoothed the lines of his waist. People expected perfection from Asterion. Elegance and sex appeal, and not a moping sad sack who didn't want to get out of his bed. Asterion stared at himself in the wide silver mirror above the bathroom sink. He looked beautiful, but it was a prosaic sort of beauty. Predictable. Anticipated. Boring.

Before he could think too hard about it, he raised his hands to his hair. With a sharp slice of magic, he cut his shoulder-length locks, watching as the first blue tresses fell into the sink.

The cut he settled on was more in line with earthly human appearance, where shorter hair had become the preference for male-presenting people over the past hundred years. He'd be just like a human tomorrow anyway. Might as well prepare for it.

Asterion closed his eyes, marrying magic and intention together, sweeping his hands over and against his scalp, momentarily relieved by the difference in sensation, as the bulk of his hair drifted down onto the floor.

When he was done, he straightened up, sweeping the midnight blue locks off his forehead, where they lay perfectly coiffed, the picture of earthbound elegance.

He still didn't feel right, but he was calmer, the perception of control somewhat restored. Asterion strode back into the bedroom, cape sweeping out behind him as he walked over to the bed to where Ellery had laid out a large mother-of-pearl moon on a dark blue velvet band. He'd just finished affixing it around his head when Ellery returned and stopped short at the sight of him.

"That good?" He tried to ignore the twist of anxiety in the pit of his stomach telling him he'd done wrong. Ellery, very briefly, pursed her lips in a clear expression of pity.

"Of course it looks good."

"I thought you were a better liar than that."

"You always look very handsome." She grabbed a jewelry box off the foot of the bed as she walked over to him.

"But you don't like it."

"Do *you* like it?" Ellery asked, flipping open the case in her hands.

"Well, I *did*."

Ellery smirked as she took him by the shoulders and turned him around. Across from the foot of the bed was a wide mirror mounted on the back of the dresser. The dresser was barren on top, a reminder, almost, that this was a space no one lived in. Empty, though it was full of gilded furniture.

"I like your hair," Ellery said, as she draped the necklace around his neck. "But it doesn't look like you."

Asterion snorted. He changed his appearance regularly, so what did that even mean? Yes, he usually kept his hair long, but so what?

Before he could ask what she meant, Ellery stepped back, and Asterion glanced down at his chest and at the silver necklace that she'd slipped beneath the sheer fabric. Small, green emeralds made the shapes of ivy leaves on a silver crescent; his sigil in the royal houses of Andurnei. Asterion frowned.

"It doesn't exactly fit the theme," he said, pressing the necklace against his skin with the palm of his hand, letting the stones dig into his flesh.

"Say it's night blooming jasmine, if anyone asks." They both knew no one would. Asterion caught Ellery's eye in the mirror and arched an eyebrow at her. "Humor me," she said. "I don't ask you for much." That was true. And after tomorrow, Ellery might be out of a job.

"Anything for you," he said. She smiled, and then took him by the arm.

"Come on, or we'll miss the second round of canapés."

3

Dom parked the car at the edge of the long, circular driveway, leaning forward to look at the partygoers who drifted in and out of the open door onto the wide front porch.

He bit the tip of his tongue, trying to decide if he was afraid. Nothing that was happening seemed particularly scary, but he'd been told for so many years that he ought to be afraid that the feeling lingered anyway. People disappeared in this place. People he loved. And now he was going to what? Go inside? Follow them?

Dom didn't understand magic. What it was, or how it worked. He'd never tried to, even though now, as he stepped out of his car, he could nearly taste a strange energy in the air. But Father Michaels had asked Dom to stop by the place like he'd asked for any other favor. So it couldn't have been dangerous.

Luckily, he wasn't going to have inside to find out if Jonas Rookwood was there. There were enough people on the front porch, milling around, drinking and smoking and laughing, that it wouldn't be hard to just ask someone. Dom couldn't imagine a world where Jonas Rookwood wasn't a memorable figure.

But then, maybe he should have tried imagining a little

harder. A man with wings as wide and bright as a monarch butterfly's at a human size walked past him down the driveway. A woman swept across the porch wearing sparkles somehow, and very little else hanging off her dark brown skin, mauve hair spiraling down over her shoulders. She was followed by two women and a man who looked enthralled just to be near her. One of the women carried a tray of drinks, and Dom thought he recognized the man from town.

But no one seemed distressed. No one seemed like they were there under any sort of compulsion or like they couldn't leave if they wanted. Dom hesitated, unsure if he could bring himself to put a foot on the bottom stair.

Two men stumbled out the door, doubled over in hysterics. The first was swathed in blue velvet, a shade lighter than his deep blue hair, iridescent golden skin shining in the twinkling lights that were strung around the porch. The second wore a small black mask held on by a string. Otherwise, his costume was barely a costume at all: a well-tailored black suit, a black bowler hat, bright red lily in his lapel. Dom immediately recognized him as The Spectre, a detective character from one of Dom's favorite radio shows; the red lily gave it away.

"Excuse me," Dom called, his shoes firmly on the pavement. The men glanced in his direction, the blue-haired one immediately distracted by a woman in a rose-covered headdress who followed them out, lighting a cigarette as she walked.

"Sorry," The Spectre replied. "D'you mean me?" His brown eyes narrowed beneath the mask, and then widened as he straightened up. "Wait, I know you!" He came halfway down the dozen steps, smile wide beneath a bent, previously broken nose. "The man from the diner in town. Best omelet I've ever had! Come in, won't you? Join us! Evie!" He turned back to where the woman in the rose headdress was leaning on the arm of the blue-haired man. "This is the—well, he's not the diner. He *works* at the diner I was telling you and Paul about this afternoon!"

Dom tried to speak, but before he could manage a word, the man had come close enough to grab Dom by the hand and pulled him up onto the porch. Dom stumbled, barely catching himself on the banister. The Spectre was short, but considerably stronger than the cut of his suit had let on. Dom racked his brain, trying to think back to the customers he'd served that morning. Who'd ordered omelets? In his distraction, Dom tripped over the top step. The Spectre caught him, a firm arm around his waist.

"This is Evie Corning and Asterion..." he stalled, his hand outstretched toward the man with blue hair, who shrugged.

"Just Asterion," he said without affectation, placing a cigarette at the center of his lips as he gave Dom a once-over, eyebrow arched.

"Nice to meet you," Dom swallowed nervously. "I'm Dom Silva. I own the diner. I'm looking for Jonas Rookwood."

"Rookwood?" The Spectre sounded surprised.

"Are you a friend of his?" Asterion asked. Dom made his most non-committal sound, the one he trotted out when customers were sharing bad opinions that they assumed he would agree with. After all, he and Jonas weren't *not* friends.

"I was just hoping to speak to him."

"Good Gods," Asterion murmured, blowing a line of smoke above everyone's heads. "Has he thrown you over too?"

"Now, Asterion," The Spectre began. "I hardly think—"

"Ignore them." Evie Corning's soothing voice managed to make it to Dom over the beginnings of Asterion and The Spectre's argument. "They're ridiculously drunk. Come in." She put a hand on his arm. "We'll see if we can find who you're looking for." And with that, Dom was drawn into Elmmond House.

It was exactly as grand as he'd imagined it would be. Waiters and cigarette smoke drifted in between people draped in the most elaborate costumes Dom had ever seen. Feathers and furs, thick around some bodies and strategically thin on others. Music seemed to come from everywhere and nowhere at once, every person swaying and shifting in a way that threatened to make Dom seasick. It was warm in the house, plush carpet sinking beneath the worn-out soles of his short boots. Ms. Corning handed Dom a drink off a passing tray and guided him halfway up the grand staircase that dominated the foyer.

"That's a much better vantage point. Now, what does this Rookwood fellow look like?" What a very good question. Dom gripped the banister with the hand that wasn't holding the coupe glass and looked down. There was more than one person milling around with horns. One twisted upward like a gazelle's, another pair were so wide that they nearly curled together at the back. None were Jonas' rams' horns. In this context, they almost seemed plain.

"He's got black horns," Dom said. "Red skin. Or, reddish—" Dom hesitated, stepping closer to the railing as a man and a creature began to descend the stairs from the upper landing. But Ms. Corning cooed in delight, and the next thing Dom knew, the human was kissing her cheek, trailing his fingers along the nape of her neck.

"Evie, this is Indigo." Clearly the being, who didn't seem to fit any concept of gender that Dom had ever understood, had been named for the color of their skin. Iridescent tresses curled around a sharply angled jaw and their eyes were as bright as their canine teeth, which angled sharply into what Dom could only think of as fangs.

"Pleasure," Indigo hissed, their eyes finding Dom over Ms. Corning's head. Dom realized too late that he was white knuckling the railing and took a sip of his drink for something to do. The cocktail tasted as though a basket of strawberries and a mint bush had birthed a beverage. He turned away to splutter into his shoulder, when a body pressed against his back.

"Believe me, Mr. Silva. That is not a row you want any part in hoeing," Asterion's voice was smooth and low, his fingers digging into Dom's elbow. Before Dom understood what was happening, The Spectre, Ms. Corning, Indigo and the man who had come down with them were all moving toward the landing at the stop of the stairs. Indigo's eyes flitted over Dom's face. Then his body. Dom knew he was blushing, terrified and weirdly aroused. The pit of nerves in his stomach had become a void.

"Are you coming?" Indigo hissed.

"Mr. Silva is on something of a mission, I'm afraid. What kind of host would I be if I didn't assist him?" Asterion replied easily. Up close, his smile seemed strained. Tense. "Feel free to get started without me." The Spectre laughed, and then Dom was turned and ushered back down the stairs.

"Is Indigo—?" Dom faltered, even though he'd kept his voice down. There wasn't an end to the question that actually made sense in his mind.

"A vampire. Likely attempting to hypnotize you, though he'd never admit it. Come this way," Asterion said flatly.

While Dom and Ms. Corning had had to thread their way through the throng, the opposite was true of walking with Asterion. People made way for him, crowds and groups parted, and then he and Dom were in a quieter, longer hall. Dom could almost breathe again, though he was reeling over the idea of having just encountered a vampire. Asterion led him into a small study, deep green walls lined with built-in shelves, filled with books and trinkets. Asterion left the door ajar, and when he turned to face Dom, his shoulders sagged as he exhaled. He was still handsome, but out of the glistening lights, away from the beating pulse of the crowd, he seemed tired.

"Why are you looking for Jonas?" Asterion asked. Dom was uncomfortably warm.

"Father Michaels is looking for him." Asterion took a half a step back and frowned. Then he crossed his arms over his chest.

"That's it?"

"Should there be anything else?" There were, of course, a dozen other things. What was this party? How did people go missing here? Could Dom conceivably find someone who had?

"You own The Silver Plate? That diner in town?"

"The Silver *Platter*," Dom corrected. "And yes."

"And you're here because Michaels sent you to find Jonas?"

"Yes?"

"Not because Jonas has run off with some other human?"

"Run off with a—? Wait, do you mean Sidney?"

"That's the one." Dom had seen them together on a few occasions, at least one of which had clearly been a date. Sidney and Jonas had been together that morning, in fact. Along with the man Sidney had introduced as his brother. Who had ordered an omelet.

"Oh! The Spectre," Dom nodded toward the stairs where The Spectre had left them. That was why he looked familiar; he'd been with Sidney and Jonas that morning.

"The Spectre?" Asterion frowned.

"His costume. The whole," Dom touched his chest where a lily would have been on his lapel, if he'd had either a lily or a lapel. "From *Nocturne Mystery Theatre*. The show."

"What?" Asterion asked in an exasperated breath. How did anyone *not* know about Nocturne Mystery Theatre? Dom was momentarily offended and had to shove the feeling aside.

"Nothing. Never mind. So, Jonas is here, then?" It stood to reason anyway, since Sidney's brother was in attendance. But Asterion pursed his lips.

"Jonas has been telling me about your diner for years."

"Oh," Dom said. "Okay." If he hadn't been so confused, he might have been flattered.

"And now I meet you. And you are..." Asterion trailed off, gesturing at Dom with widespread palms, as though there was something significant about him.

"I don't—" What did *he* have to do with anything? "Sorry. Is Jonas here? Or is he not here?"

"Have you been sleeping with Jonas Rookwood?" Asterion asked. Dom was so shocked he took a step back and knocked into a chair.

"What? No!"

"No." Asterion's eyebrow was nearly to his hairline, his head at a skeptical angle. "Really?"

"Of course not." What the hell was going on? Asterion's eyebrow had lowered, but now he was shaking his head, one hand cradling his forehead.

"I think he might be the stupidest man alive."

"What?"

"Nothing." Asterion snorted and dropped his hand. "Not a thing. Jonas isn't here. He never comes to these parties, and Father Michaels should've known that. Though, now that I say it, I suppose I'm not surprised he didn't."

"Okay," Dom said slowly. "Well, when you see Jonas..." Dom paused, waiting for any indication that Asterion might not see Jonas. None came. "When you see him, Father Michaels is looking for him. He says it's important but not urgent."

"Probably trying to get blood splatter off the pews," Asterion muttered. Dom blinked.

"What?"

"I'll pass the message along." Asterion smiled, thin and insincere. Maybe he was the sort of person who never really smiled, in which case, what a waste of a pretty face. "Was there anything else?"

"People disappear here," Dom said, because now that he wasn't being pelted with bizarre questions and accusations, his brother was, again, forefront in his mind. One corner of Asterion's mouth quirked up slightly.

"All the time. Though it's never the ones you want to leave who actually go, is it?"

"How?" Dom asked. Asterion huffed.

"How, what? How do they leave? There are half a dozen portals wide open upstairs. Get marked and go through any one you like."

"Marked?" Dom frowned. Asterion looked him over slowly, and then shook his head.

"Jonas ought to start offering lessons to you people. A primer for humans."

"I'm not sure—"

Asterion's hand was almost on the doorknob when the door swung inward so aggressively that Dom and Asterion both stepped back. In the doorway were two imposing figures, light shining in off their shaved heads, their bodies blocking the exit. Asterion sighed.

"Oh, shit."

4

Asterion decided to take comfort in the small sense of vindication he felt. He had known this was going to be the worst night of his life, and it was good to be right about something.

He hadn't realized that the clock had ticked over. It was midnight, or just past, in Andurnei. The clocks were never exactly the same earthside, but Assembly Bailiffs were never late. His time was up.

He took a step back to let them in. The first was a woman with brown skin and dark eyes. The man was extremely pale, and his entire eyeball was a shade of purple that reminded Asterion of grape jam.

"Uh, what's going on?" Dom Silva, the diner owner, was standing slightly further back, his shoulders squared as though he was going to fight. Ridiculous. Asterion shook his head.

"Don't worry about it. You should go."

"Nonsense," a lilting voice trilled from the hall. "We do need a witness, after all." Desdemona. Of course. The night could get worse still.

Desdemona Briarthorne was beautiful and absurd, but

mostly beautiful. Her skin was bright pink, dusted with snow-white freckles across the bridge of her round nose. Her eyes were mauve, and her hair the same vibrant shade as her skin, though tinted lavender beneath a sheer scarf that exactly matched the sheer robe with white feather trim that barely obscured any part of her all the way to the floor. Heeled slippers matched the clinging lavender silk negligee beneath. What the hell kind of costume was that supposed to be? Asterion supposed it didn't matter. Desdemona cocked her head to the side, grinning, and ran her tongue over the tip of one fang.

"Hello Desdemona," Asterion said.

"Hello Asterion, dear. Who's this?" She gestured to poor Mr. Silva, who began to stutter out protestations. "Should I be jealous?" Asterion only stared at her blankly, the joke at his expense, and almost painfully unfunny besides.

"I hate you," he said. Desdemona laughed, and then pulled her mouth into an over-exaggerated pout. The female bailiff stepped forward, holding out a thick, gold amulet the size of a tea saucer, and a golden bracelet, like a single handcuff.

"Prince Asterion, are these the terms you agreed to?" Asterion looked down at the words etched into the gold. He'd replayed his argument with Desdemona so many times in his head, that he could almost hear it. Her line first: *I bet you couldn't get someone to fall in love with you if you tried.* His response, stupid, arrogant: *I bet you all my magic that I'll be in love within a year.*

Well, he wasn't in love. And now his magic was forfeit.

"That's correct," Asterion said. "Those are the terms." The bailiff snapped the cuff around his wrist, and he could see an identical one glinting off her belt. Some kind of holding spell. Like he'd be stupid enough to try and run. The bailiff gestured for Desdemona to step forward.

"Madame Briarthorne, if you'd be so kind as to align your fingers with your debtor's."

"Sorry." Silva finally managed to speak. "What the hell is going on right now?"

"Asterion is paying a debt," Desdemona said. She smelled overwhelmingly of patchouli. Asterion was going to have to sneeze. "You don't mind being a witness, do you, sweet? It's a simple legal matter. It'll only be another minute."

"I..." Silva trailed off, and when Asterion glanced over his shoulder, Silva was staring at him with wide eyes, looking to Asterion, of all people, for an answer. He'd never had fewer.

"Mr. Silva doesn't know what any of this is," Asterion said, primarily to the bailiffs.

"He doesn't have to," the purple-eyed bailiff said, and in the following silence, the soft snick of metal sliding against metal echoed in the room. A silver bladed casting knife appeared in the bailiff's hand, and all thoughts of the diner owner's discomfort vanished from Asterion's mind. He had spent the last several months trying not to think about what this process would be like. The magic involved was largely a secret, but it hadn't been a far stretch to guess that blood would be at least one of the necessary components.

"Hey! Wait a second!" Suddenly, Silva was at Asterion's side and then was trying to elbow his way between Asterion and the bailiff. Gallant, but Asterion certainly wasn't interested in enduring Jonas' wrath when what might have been his second favorite human got stabbed. Asterion held Silva back.

"Stop. It's fine."

"He has a knife!"

"Just—" Silva jerked out of Asterion's hands. "You don't have to be a part of this. You can go."

"I'm not letting him stab you!"

"It's not a stab," Desdemona chirped. "More like a slice." Asterion ignored her.

"It's all fine, Mr. Silva, I promise you." Silva grimaced, his eyes darting around the room as though he was looking for some other option. The door was wide open, but he didn't seem to be inclined to exit. And then, perhaps even more shockingly, he took a step closer to Asterion again, his wide bicep brushing against Asterion's velvet sleeve. Asterion blinked up at him. "What are you doing?"

"I'm being a witness," Silva replied stubbornly.

"Fine." Asterion wasn't in the mood to argue. He wanted this over. "Just don't get in the way." Silva made a sound of derision in the back of his throat, and Asterion found he appreciated it, no matter how misplaced it was. Asterion had made his bed. It was time to lie in it.

Asterion held out his hand, and Desdemona put her fingers on top of his, the tip of her middle claw almost reaching to the center of his palm. The female bailiff held the amulet to the back of Asterion's hand, and the male bailiff pressed the tip of his knife against the highest crease of Asterion's wrist. Silva drew an audible breath, as the blade bit into Asterion's flesh. Blood seeped up over Asterion's palm as the bailiff drew a deep line to the base of Asterion's thumb. He traced the cut back across Asterion's hand with the knife, and when Asterion flinched, Silva's wide, warm fingers pressed against the base of his spine.

Asterion leaned into Silva's touch, head starting to swim as a thin silver light began to slide out of the cut. Magic. His own. It followed the stream of Asterion's blood down the back of his hand.

When his magic hit the gold amulet, nausea overwhelmed him. Asterion lurched forward and Silva's heavy, strong arms caught him around his waist. One bailiff twisted the amulet, the other's blade pinned Asterion's hand to the gold. He bit his tongue to keep from vomiting, vision blurring as all his magic flooded up at once, surging out of him in vibrant thin tendrils, burning his flesh.

"And if you find—" Desdemona began. The bailiff jerked his hand away at once, taking the knife with it, but it was no use. Magic was pouring out of Asterion now. No change of terms would stop it. "If you manage to find it without magic, your magic will be returned to you."

What a horrible person. Changing the terms of their deal just to rub salt in the wound. No one loved him when he had magic. How would anyone ever love him without it? How had he ever slept with her? Before he could say any of that, the bailiff was back at it with the knife, and it really was more like a stab that time. Asterion groaned, his knees buckling with the pain.

"Whoa! Hey—Asterion! Asterion." And Dom Silva's unfamiliar voice was the last thing Asterion heard before he passed out.

5

D om's heart raced as he sank to his knees, cradling a stranger in his arms. Asterion was bleeding a lot. His hand was bleeding on Dom's trousers. His nose was dripping blood onto Dom's arm. It seemed like he'd gone pale all over, and even his hair had lost its deep blue-black shine. That wasn't possible, though. Was it?

Without speaking, the female bailiff bent down and stroked the golden cuff on Asterion's wrist with the one she'd taken from her belt. They both popped open, and she slid the bracelet off Asterion's hand before turning and walking out of the room.

"Wait!" Dom looked up, shocked that they were both already gone. The pink woman with the ice-white horns was looking down at him, a serious frown drawing down the corners of her plush lips. "What just happened?" Dom forced himself to take a shaking breath.

"He cheated on me," she said, with a slight air of haughtiness that didn't sound real.

"So you killed him?"

"Don't be dramatic," she scoffed. "He's not dead. Just... indisposed. You ought to get him out of here," she added. "It'll be an absolute spectacle if anyone sees him like this. And they'll probably blame you."

"What?" She made a small 'hmph,' sound and left, pulling the door closed behind her. Dom sat back on his haunches, a half-dead magic man lying across his legs. "Asterion." Nothing. "Asterion!" Still nothing. Shit.

Shit.

What was he going to do?

He could leave Asterion behind. That would be easy. Maybe. Even though Dom had just been given proof that the people in this house were just as barbaric as he'd always imagined. If magic existed, this was what people did with it. What *had* they done to him? Why was he so pale?

Dom shifted Asterion in his arms and found the man easier to move than he'd thought. He was smaller somehow. Like he'd lost body mass, along with his coloring. Everything about him was fading. Was *this* how people vanished in Elmmond House? If Dom left him, would he just fade into nothingness before anyone found him? Blood trickled in thick rivulets over the peachy bow of Asterion's upper lip. Dom didn't have it in him to abandon the man. It wouldn't be right.

Every day, Dom lifted sacks of flour and slabs of meat that weighed more than Asterion. It took less than a moment to haul Asterion up into his arms. Dom nudged the door open with the toe of his shoe and glanced into the hallway. The party continued in the distance. The hall to the left led further into the house. On the right, a french door opened onto the side of the wraparound porch.

No one stopped Dom. No one even gave him a second glance as he carried Asterion across the porch and down the driveway. Halfway back to the car, Asterion curled into Dom's chest, fingers tightening for a moment against Dom's bicep, and Dom froze.

"Asterion?" But then Asterion was limp again, as though it had never happened.

The backseat of the car was wide enough that it was easy for Dom to slide him into it. When Dom got into the driver's seat, he sat for a moment and tried to breathe. Tried to ignore the way his hands were shaking. He didn't know what he had just witnessed. He didn't know what he was doing. But he wanted to get away from Elmmond House.

So, he did.

Dom pulled into the alley behind the duplex where he lived, the unpaved road crunching loudly enough to wake the dead. But not enough to wake Asterion. Navigating the back staircase would have been easier if a light rain hadn't started, making everything slick. There was a spare apartment on the upper floor, but Dom had just about run out of steam by the time he reached his own back-landing. Asterion could have Dom's bed. Dom would sleep on the couch.

Exhaustion numbed the panic that was prickling at the edges of Dom's thoughts. He got Asterion into bed, the velvet jumpsuit sagging off him at the waist and shoulders. It looked like it would be hot. Maybe he wouldn't need a blanket? Dom got him a blanket anyway, just in case.

Then he stumbled into the hallway and almost immediately forgot what he was doing. He locked the back door, turned on the kitchen light, remembered he needed a blanket for himself and got halfway to the hall closet before he thought about bandages. Asterion was still bloody. Maybe bleeding. It was hard to tell. There was gauze and tape beneath the sink in the bathroom, and Dom gathered it up along with a first aid kit and went back to the bedroom.

Gingerly, Dom sat on the mattress beside Asterion's injured

hand. The man didn't wake as Dom cleaned his wounds. The cuts weren't as deep as he'd thought, which was good. He'd seen his share of nasty knife wounds working in the kitchen, so while he wasn't exactly a whiz at first-aid, Dom felt pretty confident that Asterion would heal alright without stitches.

As Dom wound gauze around Asterion's palm, Asterion stirred again. A deep breath and a full body shudder. Again, Dom froze, waiting for more. Waiting for anything. Asterion wrinkled his nose, his eyes opening barely. He squinted at Dom, his good hand flexing in the bedsheets.

"Asterion?"

"Mm?" Asterion moved his mouth, as though he was trying to speak. Fingers twitched against Dom's wrist, and Dom stared. He should have wiped the blood from Asterion's face minutes ago; it was drying now. Asterion's fingertips dug into Dom's skin. Barely. Just a little. But enough that Dom felt like he needed to press back.

"I'm here," he said, unaware if that would be any comfort at all. Asterion dropped back into unconsciousness with a small sigh.

Dom thrived in routine. Everything in his life followed steps, prescribed and methodical. It was why he was such a good baker, and how he managed to squeeze more hours out of his days than anyone else. He relied on sequence to keep himself moving. Happiness, distress, loneliness, strong emotion of any kind could be stifled by the adoption of an order of operations that didn't leave time to dwell on much else. Dom pushed himself to that place now. He cleaned up Asterion as best he could. Found another old, knitted blanket in the hall closet and draped it over Asterion's lower half. Put a glass of water on the bedside table and closed the door. Done.

Dom showered in the hall, dried off, and had to duck back into his bedroom for his pajamas. Asterion didn't move. Dom dressed in the hall bathroom, got a set of blankets for himself and proceeded to the living room. He made up a bed on the couch. He turned on the radio and made a cup of tea, his normal bedtime routine. Mentally, he prepared his to-do list for the next day, leaving a sort of middle-sized blank space for "dealing with Asterion" and whatever that would entail. Even that gentle vagueness made unease settle on his shoulders again, and Dom tried to shake it off. He had the early shift at the diner tomorrow. It wouldn't do to go in tired. Dom emptied his half-drunk tea into the sink, turned off the radio and the lights, and crawled beneath the blanket he'd draped over the couch cushions.

But in the dark, it was impossible to turn off his mind. He should have brought a book out of his bedroom with him. What was he going to do? Where had Jonas gone? What had Asterion been insinuating about him? Was any of this going to help him find Ares? Or had he gotten himself into a bigger mess somehow?

He couldn't have left Asterion in that house, wasting away on the floor. What if Dom went to check on him in the morning and Asterion had vanished? It would maybe solve some problems. Though it might create some too. And that was what Dom was still turning over in his mind when his exhaustion finally got the better of him, and he fell asleep.

6

"Order up!" Nina's voice and the sharp ring of the bell jerked Dom back into awareness.

Dom had slept poorly, and when he had gone into his bedroom that morning to find his clothes for work, Asterion was almost exactly where Dom had left him. He'd curled onto his side at some point in the night, but he didn't stir as Dom got his things out of his closet and his hairbrush off his dresser. The longer Asterion slept, the more Dom began to wonder if magic was turning the whole thing into a sort of Snow White situation. Maybe Asterion would sleep for a thousand years unless he was awakened by true love's kiss. Not that that was how magic really worked. Was it? And even if it was, it absolutely wasn't Dom's responsibility to find Asterion's true love, should they exist. If he had to choose between a quest for a stranger's true love or having a comatose prince in his apartment for a thousand years, he'd better start putting personal ads in the paper. *Nice to look at. Terrible conversationalist.*

"Dom!" Nina, his line cook, the only other staff member aside from his uncle who had showed up that morning, dinged the bell twice more for emphasis. Dom swung around, nearly running into Hector who was carrying a tray of hot coffee around the edge of the counter.

"Sorry! Sorry," Dom said to both of them in turn, as he scooped up a steaming plate of scrambled eggs and bacon and rested it on his arm, catching the next two dishes, toast and an omelet as Nina shoved them through the window. A line of sweat trickled out of the shaved side of her close-cropped black hair.

"Where's your head today, boss?" No one could make his technical job title sound more like a joke than Nina.

"Be nice to him," Hector called, already returning with an empty tray. "Ree had him up at the parish hall until after midnight, I'm sure."

"It couldn't have taken you that long to hoist their cornucopia up onto the table." Nina's long straight nose wrinkled as Dom made a face at her through the pass.

Nina and Dom had been friends since high school. Aside from Ares, she might have been his only friend, and that was probably because they worked together. Dom had never been good at making time to socialize, and he didn't know if pity or affection was the reason that on nights Dom stayed late to bake, Nina usually stayed with him.

"I went out," Dom said. Nina laughed heartily, like he'd told a very good joke, shaking her head as she turned to go back to the griddle.

Dom delivered the plates to the couple of fishermen who were seated in the corner. The diner's clientele was mostly fishermen and dockworkers on rainy mornings like this. It made the events of the night before feel even more like some kind of bizarre fever dream. None of the folks currently seated in the cracked old booths of The Silver Platter had been within a mile of Elmmond House last night. There was nothing glamorous or magical going on. It was just life. Routine. Entirely normal.

Until Sidney Quince walked in about fifteen minutes later. The man was as thin as seaweed and as academic as Dom had ever seen, a threadbare sweater pulled on over a button-down shirt. His black hair was thoroughly ruffled and paired with the lively flush on his cheeks, looked a little obscene. He came up to the counter, swiping his hair out of his eyes, beaming up at the Specials board like he'd just drifted down from cloud nine. It took Dom a whole minute to realize that if Sidney were here, then it was likely Jonas Rookwood was close by.

"Is Jonas with you?" Dom asked, immediately depositing the cup of coffee he'd just poured for someone else in front of Sidney. He grabbed the nearest sugar shaker, placing it next to Sidney's hand before Sidney could ask for it.

"Uh, yes. He's out in the truck." Sidney frowned, picking up his mug as Dom scooted around the edge of the counter. "Is everything okay?"

"Fine," Dom said over his shoulder as he swung out the door.

Jonas' red truck was idling across the parking lot, and Dom jogged over, rain prickling against his face and bare arms. Jonas must have seen him coming in the rearview, because by the time Dom was at his window, it was rolled down.

Jonas leaned out, one curved black horn getting speckled with raindrops. Several tattoos, delicate black lines of ink, looked like lace poking out from beneath his cuffs.

"I haven't found anything out about Ares yet," Jonas said, his deep voice firm. "It'll take me a couple of days, and I—"

"It's not about that," Dom said hurriedly. Jonas' eyes were as bright as new copper, and they narrowed as they looked over Dom.

"What happened?"

"Do you know someone named Asterion?"

~

ASTERION WOKE UP IN AN UNFAMILIAR BED, FEELING LIKE ABSOLUTE shit. Once, in his younger years, he'd been out riding and had gotten thrown from the back of a horse, and his current state reminded him of that. His body ached, head throbbed, and it wasn't until he raised one heavy arm to his temple to cast a sobriety spell, that the events of the night before came rushing back.

No magic.

Shit.

He dropped his hand over his face and groaned. At least this mattress was better than the one at Elmmond House. And the walls were a calm, deep forest green. Maybe that handsome man, Jonas' friend, would be gone all day, and Asterion could just lay in this quiet room and mope until he felt better. Asterion looked up to see a glass of water on the nightstand. Water would be good. He reached for it, the weight of his stupid velvet cape dragging his shoulder down. Shitting Hell.

The water did clear his head, though it did little else. Rain pattered against the window, and Asterion rolled onto his back, trying to give himself over to melting into the extremely comfortable mattress. Would Ellery be looking for him by now? Neither of them had known what to anticipate from the Assembly Bailiffs, and Asterion had forbade her from looking into it. He had hoped the contract wouldn't be sealed until they'd gone to an Assembly tower for sentencing. It was doubtful that Ellery had been so optimistic, but then he never could tell with her. And he wasn't her problem anymore anyway. She was probably glad to be rid of him.

Asterion looked down at himself and was a little surprised to find his costume sagging off his chest like an elephant skin. The vacancy in his body was tangible, but he hadn't quite expected it to be manifested physically. Which had been stupid of him. The magic that had broadened his shoulders was gone. He reached up to find that his ears had returned to their true shape. Long, pointed. So much for fitting in in the human world.

And his outfit was no help either. It had always looked stupid, but suddenly, he hated it. He rolled off the bed, ignoring his aching limbs and the pain in his hand, and slid himself out of the dark blue velvet, diamonds tapping as they knocked together on their way to the floor.

Judging by the clothes in the dresser and Asterion's vague recollection of Mr. Silva from the night before, the man was several inches wider than Asterion in every dimension that mattered, except for height, where they seemed to be of a size. Eventually, Asterion managed to find a pair of wide legged denim pants at the back of the bottom drawer, two sizes smaller. Someone else's, likely left behind. Asterion hummed mock-judgmentally, as he slid them on, thinking only that it made sense that a man *that* good-looking had someone else's clothes in his house. A t-shirt, too big, would do fine for the time being. Asterion pulled it on, tucking it into the denim as he wandered into the bathroom to assess the damage.

He looked as garbage as he felt. His hair had settled at something of a middle length, just below his chin, not all the way to his shoulders, and a lapis shade, nowhere near as rich as the midnight blue it had been. Freckles were eking up across his nose. It was only going to get worse as the last of his magic ebbed away, too little left to replenish itself. Asterion shivered, and told himself it was because he was cold and not verging on the edge of panic. He turned off the light in the bathroom and went back into the bedroom to root around for a sweater.

A dark grey, beautifully soft, wool cardigan had been erroneously stashed in the back of the closet, and Asterion tugged it on with a sigh of pleasure. His stomach grumbled as he tucked his hands into his pockets. He needed coffee. Coffee was easy, wasn't it? Beans and paper filter thing? Hot water? Espresso needed a machine. He spent enough time in the human world to know how machines worked, surely. Though generally he conjured a double shot with fingers curled just so around an empty cup.

Before he could leave the room to seek out the potentially elusive coffee, a distant door opened. Asterion stilled at the sound of a voice.

"At the end of the hall." He was at the end of the hall, wasn't he? Probably. Did he need a weapon? No. That was silly. The people who wanted to hurt him already had.

"Asterion?" And then the bedroom door swung open, and Jonas Rookwood ducked inside.

Jonas' mouth crumpled, his shoulders tense, as he strode across the room and pulled Asterion into his arms in one solid yank. Asterion tried to breathe, but Jonas had cracked something in him. A rib, probably, but also something that Asterion had been clinging to in a desperate attempt to hold himself together. Tears sprung up in his eyes, and he had to take several deep, perhaps shaking, gasps before he could manage to speak.

"I can't breathe, you massive brute," Asterion mumbled into the soft lapel of Jonas' coat. Jonas pushed him back, an oversized hand curling over each of Asterion's newly slender shoulders. He looked a little bit furious, and a fresh wave of guilt washed over Asterion.

"What the hell happened?"

"I'm sorry," Asterion said immediately.

"I'm not mad at you!"

"Well, you look mad."

"Gods, Asterion. I wonder why. Are you hurt?"

"Only my pride," Asterion lied, shifting his injured hand behind his back. Jonas pursed his lips.

"That's not what Dom said."

"He's a human," Asterion sniffed. "What does he know?"

"He said you owed Desdemona a debt." Damn. Dom Silva had been paying better attention than Asterion had hoped.

"We made a wager," Asterion said. Jonas made a grunt of disapproval. "I lost."

"What was the wager? Why didn't you tell me?"

"Never mind all that." Asterion waved his good hand weakly. He didn't want to rehash it just now.

"Asterion," Jonas warned. Asterion rolled his eyes.

"Jonas. What's done is done."

"That's rarely true, and even less so with you," Jonas replied. Asterion snorted.

"Not this time, I'm afraid."

"What was it?" Could Asterion tell him? Could he admit that he'd been so stupidly overconfident. People loved him; one of them had to be truly *in* love with him. He'd thought it would be easy. He'd been so arrogant. So stupid. And at the end, when he was just about out of time, he'd thought Jonas, out of all Asterion's legions of paramours, had been a sure thing. Jonas did love him. Just not the way Asterion needed him to.

"Coffee, first. And if you insist on bullying me—"

"Asterion." Jonas' voice was still stiff, but it wasn't a warning anymore. There was a plea in it, soft and undeniable. A knot emerged in Asterion's throat that he couldn't seem to swallow down.

"It's not important."

"You know better than to toy with Desdemona."

"It seemed like an easy bet to win." Asterion shrugged. Jonas cocked an eyebrow, and Asterion sighed. "I bet Desdemona that I could get someone to fall in love with me in a year." His voice was little more than a whisper. Jonas' eyes widened, and Asterion closed his in response. "Do not look at me like that."

"Your eyes are closed."

"I can stomach pity from Ellery, but I won't have it from you."

"I don't pity you. I think you're an idiot. But we'll figure this out." Asterion opened his eyes.

"You don't even know the worst part yet."

"I don't?"

"Edmund's involved," Asterion said. Jonas took a deep breath.

"You never do anything by halves, do you?" It was true enough. Asterion frowned.

"I said I was sorry."

"I should have killed him when I had the chance," Jonas said, his hands dropping to his sides.

"I don't think that would have changed anything," Asterion smiled. "But it would have gone a long way to making me feel better."

7

They made a brief stop at a silver-sided building with a parking lot full of cars. The infamous Silver Platter diner. Dom Silva had spent the short trip in silence, and began fumbling with his seatbelt as Jonas maneuvered the truck into a spot.

"Thank you again for the clothes," Asterion said, staring down between their hips as Silva's sturdy fingers released the latch. "Take some of the diamonds off that cape I left on your floor, if you like. They're all real." Silva turned an interesting shade of red, and mumbled his thanks to Jonas for the ride before climbing out of the truck. When Asterion looked up at Jonas, Jonas was making a face as though he'd smelled something bad. "What?" Asterion asked after Silva closed the door.

"Nothing."

"He helped me. I'm paying him back."

"You probably traumatized him, and then you told him to pull some diamonds off your cape to pay for a pair of old dungarees."

"Oh, do humans not like diamonds now?"

"I don't think he helped you to get diamonds. I think he helped you because he thought you were dying."

"Well..."

"You're not dying, Asterion."

"That's what Ellery said too." Asterion sniffed, watching as Silva's silhouette disappeared amongst the other diners. "You didn't sleep with him?"

"What?" Jonas spluttered.

"I know he's not exactly your type, but he's nice looking. And too kind for his own good. You know something about that."

"He's a friend, Asterion." Asterion sniffed. A small, jealous part of him preferred when he was Jonas' only friend. But that was primarily because Jonas had notoriously bad taste in friends. Before Asterion could say so, Sidney appeared, looking hale, hearty and disgustingly comfortable in his own skin. A white apron was cinched around his narrow waist and he was carrying two paper cups, little streams of steam seeping out the tops. He went to Jonas' window.

"Hello," he said cheerily, handing in the cups. "This one's yours," he said, tapping one of the lids and looking at Jonas. "The other one's for him. I foamed the milk."

"What about for you?"

"I'm going to stay and help, I think. They're awfully short-staffed. Dom said he could give me a ride back this afternoon. Unless you need me for something." Jonas' expression softened, his mouth turning up at the corner. Asterion rolled his eyes and forced himself to look out the opposite window without retching.

"I'll be alright. Asterion will have to make himself useful."

"Is everything alright, Asterion?" Sidney asked. Jonas elbowed Asterion, and Asterion glanced back at Sidney, and his permanently mussed hair and the genuine concern he was leveling at Asterion. By every metric, Sidney should have hated him. Both as Jonas' ex and because Asterion had very recently thrown himself at Jonas, a last-ditch attempt at making someone fall in love with him. Instead, Sidney brought Asterion coffee. It was all really quite intolerable.

"I'm very well. Thank you."

It didn't last long. As soon as Sidney had disappeared back inside, Jonas began to question Asterion about his dealings with Desdemona. Luckily, the coffee was quite fortifying, and as Asterion sipped it, the whole sordid tale began tumbling out.

He recounted the affair, from the early days of his dalliance with Desdemona Briarthorne, to the accidental encounter with her cousin, and the less accidental but adjacent tryst with the cousin's half-brother at last year's Ascension. It had all riled some already strained bad blood between the demonic and fae families that Asterion had truly had no idea about, until Desdemona was berating him for it, loudly and in the receiving hall of his own palace no less! What was he to do but call her bluff?

"Literally anything else," Jonas sighed heavily, as Elmmond House appeared above the crest of the hill. "You've known Desdemona for years. You had to guess she wasn't likely to back down." Asterion shrugged.

"A mere lover's spat," he said, sipping his coffee. "At least, until Edmund got wind of it. I know he's the one who convinced her to file it with the Assembly as a binding wager. I got the summons six months ago when it happened."

"You've known about this for six months and didn't think to come to me?"

"So, you could, what? Fall madly in love with me?" Asterion rolled his eyes. "And if you'd so kindly remember, I did come to you. But you were already smitten with some little professorial tart. Obviously, I was bereft."

"You *were* behaving a little strangely," Jonas smirked. "And I won't pretend I'm not hurt that I was absolutely last on your list of possible true loves." Asterion picked at the seam of his paper cup with his thumbnail. There were layers to that, weren't there? He had about a half-dozen reasons he'd waited so long to come to Jonas, and all of them made him feel vulnerable and stupid. The easiest one to admit was the only one he managed.

"After everything you went through with Edmund, I didn't want to get you involved."

"I would have," Jonas said softly. That damned knot rose in Asterion's throat again, and he forced himself to take a gulp of coffee.

"I know you would have. Which is why I didn't."

Jonas pulled the truck to a stop along the side of his cottage and turned to look at Asterion.

"You could always go to the Assembly and contest."

"Contest what?" Asterion sniffed. "A wager was made and filed."

"You didn't agree to its filing."

"You know as well as I do that the words of a wager are binding," Asterion sighed. Jonas hummed unhappily.

"And you rather put your foot in it when you gave a date, didn't you?" Asterion nodded, despair settling on his shoulders in the comfortable place it had dug for itself over the weeks before the Ascension party. When he was no closer to anyone truly loving him than he was to sprouting wings and flying to the moon. It was a rather disgusting situation, but at least one he had grown used to. "Well," Jonas exhaled, "you'll just have to fall in love the old-fashioned way, I suppose." That was hilarious. Or it would have been, if it wasn't also impossible.

Asterion wasn't unlikable. In fact, Asterion was preeminently likable. One of the most charming, affable people anyone could have the pleasure of spending an evening with. Asterion was built for courtly intrigue and cocktail parties. He'd shunned depth of emotions with a firm hand; hurt feelings and serious conversations were the antithesis of a good time, after all. Even when Jonas had tried, decades ago now, at something like a serious relationship, Asterion had kept him at a distance. Asterion constructed walls laced with intricate, thin discordance: the difference in their rank and their interests; Jonas' introversion and Asterion's courtly duties. Asterion was a master craftsman in the art of being so precisely unlovable, that any jilted paramour could be convinced that it was all for the best, really. And before he could feel the sting of loss or regret, Asterion made sure to be warming some other partner's bed. He'd never known how to be anything else. He'd been told that he wouldn't like it if he tried, so he'd never tried. And then when he did try, it didn't work. He thought he might have to step outside and vomit.

Thankfully, he was rescued from a discussion of his sickly pallor by a figure walking along the drive. Ellery's green hair draped flat over her shoulders, wide, dark rimmed spectacles perched on the narrow bridge of her nose. Asterion handed his coffee to Jonas and got out of the truck to greet her.

Asterion couldn't hear her stream of muffled curses until he was close enough to notice that her eyes were ringed in red, her normally perfect complexion blotchy. Asterion's chest tightened as she looked him over, and they drew close enough to speak.

It was worse when she didn't shout.

"So, I just finished speaking with your mother." Oh.

"Ellery, listen—"

"She's already found out, somehow."

"Who told her?" Asterion demanded, surprised more than anything else. It wasn't like his mother to take an interest in anything he'd done. Unless he'd embarrassed the family. Which, he supposed he probably had.

"I don't know. I'm working on it."

"It doesn't matter," Asterion conceded. Ellery clenched her fist and Asterion almost smirked. "Easy, Ellery."

"It matters to me," she snapped, rage barely concealed. Asterion blinked at her, his cheeks heating. Theirs was not a relationship that often entered into the realm of feelings. But aside from Jonas, she was his oldest friend.

"Well, look," Asterion tried to soothe, "when we get back—"

Ellery's lips drew into a thin line, her entire body stiffening. "What?"

"You can't go back."

"What?"

"Not for a few days. Your mother asked me to tell you. She's meeting with Cressida. She says they need to discuss your position in the family."

"The magic loss might not be permanent," Asterion said, meekly. "When they did the binding, Desdemona said that if I could find love without my magic, it would be returned to me, so..." he trailed off, as Ellery rolled her bottom lip beneath her top teeth. She didn't believe it. Or maybe she did, but he knew his mother wouldn't. Asterion's stomach sank.

"Stay with Jonas," Ellery said, and suddenly Asterion was a child again, being deposited at boarding school.

"Alright," he managed. Suddenly, Ellery was hugging him, the top of her head nestled under his chin as she squeezed him with an impressive strength. If he hadn't been near tears he would have wheezed. Before he could speak, she stepped back and nodded at him.

"Take care of yourself," she said. "I'll be back soon."

8

F ive minutes before shift change, one of Dom's evening servers stumbled into the diner. Dom would have wept in relief if he hadn't been so tired. He dipped into the kitchen, poured a glass of water into an old quart jar, drank the whole thing, and then leaned out the half open kitchen door into the cool November air to take a deep breath. The same misty drizzle had persisted all day, the sky grey for as far as the eye could see. Nina came over, pulling a flannel over her sweat-stained white t-shirt, cigarette already dangling off her bottom lip. A rucksack hung limp over one shoulder.

"Hey, take some of those eclairs from the walk-in with you. I made extra."

"You already pay me, Dom," she grinned. "You don't have to feed me."

"They're for Casey," Dom said. Invoking Nina's boyfriend was the only way to get her to take extra food home. Nina rolled her eyes and redirected her footsteps toward the walk-in.

"I like that new server. What's his name?"

"Sidney?" Dom asked. He glanced up through the window

pass, where he could see Sidney standing with Hector, wiping down menus.

"He's a hard worker. I don't think he's taken a break all day." And they'd needed the help. The diner had lost more people to the Elmmond House party than last year. Dom's current plan was to drop Sidney off at his house and then come back, send Hector home, and work through the night shift. Dom didn't have a house guest anymore, which meant he could eat at the restaurant; he'd throw something on the griddle for himself later. Nina stuck her head out of the fridge. "Should I make up a bag for him too?"

"I'll do it," Dom said, pushing himself off the door frame, letting the door swing closed behind him.

"That was great!" Sidney's enthusiasm was impressive for someone who had ended up staying half an hour past the shift change because he wanted to finish refilling sugar shakers. "There's something so satisfying about working with your hands, you know? I've been in the classroom too long." Dom smiled as he steered his uncle's car down the narrow side streets.

"It pays the bills. Speaking of, did you get your tips?"

"Yep," Sidney patted his pocket, leaning against the window.

"The bag's for you too," Dom said, elbowing the brown paper sack that sat on the bench seat between them. Sidney grabbed it and looked inside.

"Christ, Dom. That's a whole cake!"

"There are eclairs underneath. But they're frozen. I made them at the beginning of the week."

"What do I owe you?"

"Nothing." Dom snorted. He glanced over at Sidney and was surprised to see a frown. "Sidney, you saved my ass today. Multiple times. A cake is the least I can do."

"I had fun." Sidney said. Dom glanced over at the earnestness in his voice. "I mean it. My mom owns a general store. I grew up in it. I'm used to it. I like it. Felt like being at home." Dom agreed, though he wasn't sure he could say it aloud. Ever since his mother passed, the diner had been his home. First, his and Ares', and now, his alone. Most of the time that was a good thing. A safe thing. And he was glad it felt that way for someone else.

"Well, come back anytime."

"Do you think you'll need more help tomorrow, or do people, you know... come back?" Dom considered for a moment, twisting his hands on the steering wheel. He didn't know how connected Sidney was to whatever was happening with Elmmond House. With Jonas and the creatures like him. But the question seemed honest enough.

"People do come back. A lot of the time they don't stay long. They always seem a little different." Sidney nodded, his lips pursing, like he was trying to keep words inside his mouth. "What?"

"Oh, nothing. I was just thinking about why that might be. The mark, probably."

"The mark?" Asterion had said it to him the night before. *'Get marked and go through any one you like.'* Any portal, wasn't it? "What's a mark?"

"A mark," Sidney said, as he took a deep breath, "is basically a way for a creature, like a demon or fae or anything, to basically brand a human. Not unlike livestock, I suppose."

"Like livestock?" Dom grimaced. "Does it hurt?"

"Uh," Sidney coughed, his cheeks flushing, his attention suddenly fixed outside. "No. Or, I mean, I suppose that depends. It can happen different ways, and I don't think all of them are pleasant... Some of them are, though." Dom tried to understand what that meant without drawing any salacious conclusions and came up empty-handed. He pressed on anyway.

"So, they mark you, and what does it do?"

"It lets them know where you are. Makes you findable. Lets other creatures know that you're a part of their world. They can smell it on you, Jonas said."

"And it lets you travel into their world?"

"Worlds. And yes. It can do a lot of things."

"Have you been?" Dom asked, trying to contextualize every-thing he'd just learned. "Have you been to the other worlds?"

"No," Sidney shook his head. "But I've seen them."

Their conversation tapered off there as Dom's mind worked overtime trying to put all the disparate parts together. Ares had vanished through Elmmond House, which might mean that he'd been marked and gone through one of these portals. People could come back, but when they came back, they were different. Ares hadn't come back, but Jonas seemed to think there was some way to find out where Ares had gone. And someone who might know where Ares had gone *could* be the creature who marked him.

"Come inside and have a sandwich," Sidney said as Dom pulled up in front of the small cottage. "I'm sure you're starving."

"I'll eat back at the diner," Dom said. Sidney rolled his eyes.

"I have something that might help you though. It'll just be a second," he said, reaching for the door handle. "And Jonas will want to thank you for the cake."

Asterion had lost the ability to pretend like he was fine. His mother's disregard stung far more than it should have, considering he'd always very clearly been the spare child.

Asterion was the youngest of three, his birth a bandage that did little to close the weeping wound of his parents' failing marriage. He had done what he could to please his family, up to a point; though, he'd never managed to convince himself that what they wanted for him—a political marriage, a seat at the table in high Andurneian society—were things that he wanted. Eventually, truly making them happy had become an outright impossibility.

It hadn't been a stretch for Asterion to believe that his mother wouldn't find out. They didn't exactly run in the same circles. And if she did find out, what did it matter? She never approved of his choices anyway. But exile? Even if it was only a request that he not return *'for the time being,'* was like a knife in his chest. He didn't want to care, but he did. And that hurt worst of all.

Asterion and Jonas watched from the foot of the stairs as two under-butlers from the big house carried Asterion's trunks to

Jonas' guest room. The moment they left, Asterion feigned exhaustion, just needing a minute, several minutes, away from Jonas' concerned glances.

The desk in the guest room was covered edge to edge in notebooks and regular books, a half-full bag of dirty clothes and several moldering cups of tea. Asterion flopped onto the unmade bed, the scent of it unfamiliar. The wallpaper in the guest room was pale, faded stripes of tiny blue flowers. Not hideous but doing nothing for his burgeoning headache. He pressed his face into the pillow, wondering if suffocation was as easy as it sounded. Everything was fucked. His head hurt. So, Asterion let himself fall asleep.

When he woke, he felt worse. Groggy and hungry, he stumbled down the stairs to the kitchen. There was a bottle of wine on the counter alongside half a loaf of some kind of crusty bread. Asterion took both, then remembered he'd need a corkscrew, and shuffled through drawers until he found one. He returned to the bedroom, relieved that Jonas hadn't turned up to make sad faces at him in the interim. Then, Asterion set about the pleasant work of not feeling his emotions, hopefully to the point of forgetting he had any at all.

THE NEXT TIME HE REGAINED CONSCIOUSNESS, HE THOUGHT HE heard voices. Squeezing his eyes closed made his pulse pound in his temples, but it also helped him hear better somehow. Asterion rolled over, knocking the wine bottle off the edge of the mattress. It landed with a thud on the rug. Asterion winced knowing that a sound would bring attention, and he'd have rather stuck his head in a bucket of ice water than try to hold a conversation. A knock at the door made him shudder.

"Asterion?" Jonas' voice was gratingly gentle.

"No," Asterion said, reaching for covers that he'd never

pulled up in the first place. They were too far away and tangled around his feet. Great shitting hell.

"You need to eat something. Something that isn't just bread."

"What's wrong with bread?" Asterion demanded. He sat up to deal with the unruly blanket and his head spun. It was possible he'd never been this drunk before. Magic was a hindrance in many ways; apparently, it'd been keeping him from getting too drunk. Maybe he was glad to be rid of it.

"Come on. Sidney's made bacon." Asterion paused, hands gripping the edge of his blanket tightly. Bacon would be good. So good. And there was likely more wine downstairs as well.

With an almost embarrassing amount of effort, Asterion got to his feet. He yanked open the door and there was Jonas, looming over him. Asterion attempted to adjust his cardigan in a dignified manner.

"How're you doing?"

"You said there was bacon," Asterion muttered, pushing past Jonas and stumbling toward the stairs.

It was a miracle that Asterion made it to the kitchen without falling on his face, but just over the linoleum threshold, he stopped short. Dom Silva was sitting at the kitchen table with Sidney. In front of him was a notebook and an empty plate with crumbs. His hair was down. Not all of it; the crown of Silva's hair was tied up away from his handsome, light-brown face. The rest of his dark strands trailed over his square shoulders, framing a hard jaw that he drew his hand across. Silva's attention was locked onto Sidney who was nattering away about something irrelevant to Asterion's quest for bacon and wine.

But Dom Silva was distractingly handsome. The sort of good looking that made Asterion want to turn on his heel and go back upstairs at the injustice of it all. Asterion looked like shit, and Dom Silva looked like if Asterion were just a little more drunk, he would have tried to kiss him on the mouth.

Asterion didn't like Silva, he decided all at once. Or the wine decided. He didn't like that Dom Silva was pretty. That he was nice and strong and kind. That he'd seen Asterion at his worst. Was actively seeing Asterion at his worst. Not that it mattered anyway, because a man that looked like that was just as out of Asterion's league as anyone else. Everyone else. Now more than ever.

Asterion pulled out a chair at the end of the table and ignored that Sidney and Dom Silva looked over at him as he flopped into it. Silva seemed to flush, likely in second-hand shame for the general state of Asterion, and fuck nice people who pitied the poor and less fortunate. Asterion hated them. Jonas slid a bacon, egg, and cheese sandwich on a plate in front of Asterion, and Asterion was grateful for something else to give his attention to.

10

Asterion appeared, flopping heavily into a chair at the opposite end of the table, drawing Dom's attention away from Sidney's notebook. He couldn't help but notice how his old clothing fit the Asterion strangely, exposing collar bone and a narrow waist. Dom hadn't been able to squeeze into those trousers for at least fifteen years; he'd thought he'd gotten rid of them. Asterion pushed his hair out of his face, turning a handsome scowl in Dom's direction. He was thinner than he looked. Someone needed to feed him.

Dom knew he was staring, so he went back to examining Sidney's notebook, but it was basically gibberish. Scribbled notes covered drawings of constellations. Planetary orbits collided with paragraphs where words like "planes" and "portals" stood out among the rest. Dom knew Sidney was trying to be helpful, but Dom was fixated on who might have marked Ares. And why.

"There are nine realms," Sidney explained. "And he could have gone to any of them through Elmmond House."

"Not all of them are habitable for humans," Jonas added.

"And even some of the ones that are habitable aren't comfortable. What was he trying to do?"

Unfortunately, Dom didn't know what Ares had been trying to do. Whatever his goals were, he hadn't shared them with Dom. And that realization managed to hurt fresh every time he had it. The 'where' and the 'why' of Ares' disappearance had always been separate things in Dom's mind. He'd been so concerned with how to find Ares, that Dom had never given as much thought to why Ares left. In his most self-pitying moments, Dom had asked 'why did Ares leave *me*?' but that wasn't the same question as 'why did Ares go?' or 'what was he looking for?'

They began theorizing about what Ares might have been up to, but the possibilities were so vast and varied, that it didn't get them anywhere. Dom looked back at the notebook on the table and sighed.

"You seem frustrated," Sidney said. Dom nodded.

"It's hard knowing there are things he kept secret from me. He's my big brother. I told him everything. We were close," Dom admitted, hoping it would ease the ache in his chest. "Family meant a lot to Ares. Or, at least, I thought it did."

"Secrets are strange things," Sidney said kindly. "And you can't assume he was keeping it from you for a bad reason. Maybe he thought he was protecting you. That it would be safer to keep you away from magic."

"Maybe," Dom agreed. Magic *was* dangerous. But it was hard to feel like that was a good enough reason. "Finding out who marked him would be useful, though, right?" Dom posited. "They might be able to tell us where he was going, or what he was looking for?" Sidney nodded, and Jonas shrugged.

"Possibly, but not necessarily. Any mark will get you into a portal. And you don't have to explain why you want a mark to get one. It's not a contract."

"It can be," Sidney amended, glancing at Jonas for confirmation.

"It can be, but it doesn't have to be."

"Why does it matter?" Asterion asked, his mouth full of biscuit. Jonas raised an eyebrow, but before he could cut in, Asterion swallowed and kept going, his gaze settling on Dom. "Why does it matter where your brother's gone? He left. Why do you care?"

"He's my brother," Dom said. Asterion snorted.

"How noble. It doesn't change the fact that he left and you're still here."

"Asterion—" Jonas tried to interrupt.

"He abandoned you," Asterion snarled, his eyes bright with contempt. "And if he didn't want to be around you then you're better off without him. Don't go nosing where you're not wanted, Mr. Silva."

"If he's alive, I want to know."

"He doesn't care if you know or not. It doesn't sound like he cares about you at all."

"Asterion, that's enough." Jonas' voice was stern, but Asterion pinned Dom with his golden stare and didn't flinch.

"I want to know," Dom repeated. Dom had no idea what he'd done to piss Asterion off so badly, but somehow the rudeness didn't sting. It was too much anger, so much that it couldn't have really been about Dom. At least, not all of it. "I want to know where Ares is. If he's okay. And maybe that's selfish. But I still love my brother."

"Then you're a fool for loving someone who doesn't love you back." Asterion snapped.

It should have hurt. But Dom just felt bad for him.

"Are you alright?" Dom asked. Asterion made a choked sound and tried to turn it into a snort of derision. It might have been more believable if his eyes hadn't suddenly gone wide and damp. He snatched his plate up off the table and stormed out of the kitchen.

They listened in silence as he stomped up the stairs; no one breathed until a door slammed on the upper floor. Before Jonas or Sidney could speak, Dom got to his feet.

"I should go."

Jonas and Sidney exchanged a brief glance, and then their twin apologies nearly drowned each other out.

"I'm so sorry, Dom."

"He didn't mean it—"

"It's alright," Dom excused. It would be alright, once he got outside where he could take a breath. None of it was new. It was mostly kinder than the things Dom had told himself for years. His early twenties had been spent in a furious rage, driving too fast, breaking things, worrying Ree and Hector. It had just left him feeling horrible and hollow.

"It's not about you," Jonas said. "He got some bad news earlier." Dom couldn't imagine how things could get worse for Asterion than what Dom had already witnessed.

"It's fine," he said, ignoring his spark of curiosity about Asterion's situation. "But I do need to get back to the diner."

"I'll look into who Ares might have dealt with," Jonas said. "If he did enter into a contract, they'll have a record of that at the Assembly." Dom didn't know what the Assembly was, but it sounded promising. He nodded.

"Thank you."

"Don't thank me just yet," Jonas sighed, ushering Dom out into the foyer.

"What time do you want me to come in tomorrow?" Sidney spoke up. Dom glanced back at him.

"Are you sure?"

"I said I enjoyed it."

"Fair warning, you won't see him before ten," Jonas added, clearly teasing.

"Hush." Sidney rolled his eyes, looking pleased. "I can get up early. Is seven alright?"

"No, it's fine. I really can't ask you—" Dom said, though he shouldn't have been demurring. He needed help. And he couldn't remember the last time anyone in town, aside from Jonas and Sidney, had offered to help *him*. Usually, it was the other way around.

"Don't bother." Jonas nudged Dom into the foyer, before anyone, including Dom, could realize that Dom wasn't going to turn Sidney down again. "Sidney does as he pleases." Dom took a deep breath.

"Thank you," he said as he followed Jonas to the door.

"Like I said, I'll do my best. It can be complicated to unravel anything to do with the other worlds. Creatures aren't always inclined to talk about what they've done or why. But I don't want you to think— There are a lot of places he could be."

"I know," Dom said. "But this," Dom tried to let himself feel the hope that was struggling to bloom in his chest. "It's more than I've had for a long time. Even if it doesn't come to anything. So, thank you."

"Happy to help," Jonas said. "I'm sorry, again, about Asterion."

"Not your fault. I hope I wasn't too—"

"You had every right to be short with him."

"What happened?" Dom asked. He couldn't help himself. "Is he okay?"

"Let's just say he got left behind."

And maybe Dom was silly. Maybe he was just trying to avoid thinking about Ares. But on his drive back to the diner, Dom couldn't stop himself from wondering who had abandoned Asterion.

11

"Ah! Jonas—" The cry of pleasure was followed by a thud, likely a headboard hitting a wall, then the rhythmic creak of floorboards or bedsprings. Another shout of ecstasy. Insufferable.

Asterion lay flat on his back in the dim light of early morning, listening to Jonas and Sidney have vocal, prolonged, athletic sex. It would have been a horrible state of affairs even if Asterion's head hadn't been pounding, and his mouth hadn't felt like it was full of cotton twill.

After everyone had gone to bed the night before, Asterion had stupidly gone back downstairs and emptied another bottle of wine down his gullet. He felt hideous, and unsurprisingly the wine did not help.

Now, he had to get out of bed quickly, lest he be forced to listen to Jonas growling Sidney's name again like he was some sort of feral beast. Jonas had never sounded like that when he and Asterion—

No. Asterion could feel vomit inching up the back of his throat. His hand longed to reach up and twist a sobriety spell against his temple, but Asterion forced it to his side, rolling out of bed and staggering for the door. He grabbed a sweater off the hook and pulled it on as he stumbled down the stairs, sounds of vocal climax chasing him out of the foyer.

There was no coffee or tea in the kitchen because Asterion was the first one down. Asterion had never once been the first one awake in his entire life, and when he cast his eyes toward the small silver coffee pot on the hob, he realized why. He didn't know how to open the damn thing, let alone how to conjure coffee from it. The front lobe of his brain throbbed at the idea of having to sort anything out so early in the morning, and his chest felt tight. Being hungover was awful. How did humans manage it?

An echoing thud (Gods, had they collapsed the bed?) forced Asterion out the back door. The air was cold and still as he stepped off the mat without bothering to put on shoes. Grass, wet with frost, crumpled beneath his feet as Asterion strode purposefully across the lawn toward a small gazebo. It sat alone, overlooking the cliff. There, at least, it would be quiet.

Asterion folded his arms over his chest, wrapping the bulky wool of the sweater around himself to keep warm. The steps of the gazebo were damp and rough, and the cracked railing of the structure was enough to keep him from charging forward and flinging himself off the edge of the cliff. The frigid air cleared his head a little; pain was slowly being replaced by a searing cold that froze his sinuses.

His hair was longer this morning than it had been the day before, and paler. It whipped at his cheeks, tangling at the nape of his neck. He'd never needed to brush his hair before; he'd only done it for the feeling of it. The routine. Now that he had to make the effort, he resented the idea as much as he longed for the comfort of the sensation.

The thought of sensation, of sex, of Sidney and Jonas, left Asterion feeling uniquely empty. He wasn't jealous. Jealousy would have been easier, probably. But Asterion had determined long ago that no one would ever want him in a way that precluded them from wanting anyone else, and so he'd begun to unlearn jealousy. He forced himself not to care when lovers took on new paramours; the fact that Jonas had done the same was almost meaningless to him.

Except that Jonas and Sidney didn't just like each other. And they weren't just having sex. Jonas was happier than Asterion had seen him in centuries, and apparently that had quite a significant impact on the way his bedroom activities sounded. It sounded fun, sure. Asterion had fun in bed sometimes, though it didn't sound quite so fevered. Passionate. Asterion couldn't remember the last time he'd been intimate with someone and it had been either of those things. That sex had felt like anything other than work.

Thinking about it was only making him more depressed, and so he made a firm decision to stop thinking about it. He didn't need sex, and if he wanted sex, he could get it. And if he got it, he wouldn't enjoy it all that much, so none of it was worth thinking about.

If he leaned forward, Asterion could see that the sky wasn't lightening as much as the clouds were turning a slightly brighter shade of grey. The bay, as it stretched out into the distance, appeared to agree with the pallet of the morning. Silver capped waves churned angrily against the rocks far below. It was an unpleasant place, and the misery of it nicely mirrored Asterion's mood, which he greatly appreciated.

As he was trying to decide whether or not it was safe to go inside again, a door opened and closed somewhere behind him. Asterion refused to turn around. His toes were numb, his fingers clenched tightly around the weave of the sweater, which he now could see was a burgundy color, not unlike the wine that had so gracefully bestowed his current headache and terrible mood. It was also threadbare at the elbows.

The stairs of the gazebo creaked, and out of a sense of personal safety more than actual curiosity, Asterion turned. He wasn't sure if Sidney was the last person he wanted to see in the world, or just the second to last, but either way he wasn't pleased.

"Done enjoying my leftovers?" Asterion snipped on principle. Sidney arched an eyebrow, as he held a steaming mug out toward Asterion.

"Thought you might want some coffee." Shitting hell. Asterion exhaled out of his nose. He was in no condition to turn down coffee. He took the mug from Sidney and sipped it, willing the heat of it to sear his brain into action. It tasted lovely.

"Fuck you, Sidney," Asterion muttered, unable to inject a single ounce of sincerity into it.

"You're welcome. And you're welcome for the sweater."

"I don't like you," Asterion grumbled. "Or your sweater."

"I think you might."

"You're a cock-hungry lapdog with more brains than sense."

"I've been called worse," Sidney's tone was light, and he was barely hiding a smirk, damn him. "Enjoy the coffee," he added as he started down the stairs.

Asterion sighed. He drank half his coffee before he sank onto the small bench in the gazebo and let his head hang. There was no reason to be mean to Sidney and even if there had been, his heart wasn't in it. Asterion tucked one foot up on the bench and wrapped his arms around his leg, the mug of coffee warming his calf. He could hear birds over near the garden, but instead of turning toward them, he pressed his forehead to his knee, wishing he was unconscious again.

Asterion didn't hear Jonas approach until he was already in the gazebo. By the time Asterion looked up, Jonas was leaning against the cracked railing, staring at the beams that crossed above them. He looked up for so long that Asterion's eyes began to water in the cold.

"Don't speak to him like that again," Jonas said abruptly. It wasn't a request; it was a command, and it sent a chill down Asterion's spine. He swallowed a quip about pulling rank and nodded.

"I'm sorry," he said, meaning it, for whatever that was worth. "I'm not myself." Jonas hummed, but didn't respond. "Was he upset?"

"I think he thought it was amusing. *I* was upset."

"Oh." Asterion felt worse then than he had all morning. Disappointing Jonas was like disappointing an over-enthusiastic, rosy-cheeked child. "Jonas, I—"

"He's not a pet," Jonas said, his voice still stern. "You know how I feel about him." Asterion nodded.

"I know. I didn't mean—"

"I know what you meant to do," Jonas said quietly. He glanced over his shoulder at the bay, the faint sunlight glinting off the curve of his onyx horns. Asterion watched him for a long moment, trying to find a word to describe what had happened to his oldest, dearest, friend.

"You're devoted to him," Asterion said, finally resting his chin on his knee again, tension eking out of his shoulders. "I don't... I don't quite understand." Jonas huffed at that, and after a minute, he looked back at Asterion.

"Sidney brought me out of my stupor. Reminded me that there's a bigger world out there than me and my hurts." He took a deep breath. "Asterion, this isn't the end of the world. It can be a beginning."

"Well, of course you'd say that." Asterion rolled his eyes. "You came out of the whole thing ahead, didn't you?"

"I lost my house," Jonas smirked. Asterion huffed.

"As though you care about this bloody place."

"As though you care about the things you're leaving in Andurnei," Jonas said. Asterion pursed his lips. He wanted not to care about his family. His palace. His things. Maybe someday he would. "We just need to give you something else to focus on," Jonas said. "And get you out of this cottage," he added, straightening up.

"I like it here," Asterion said. "Aside from all the sex noises."

"There's no use in getting comfortable here. We're leaving soon." Jonas said.

"I can stay until then, though?" Asterion asked. Jonas shrugged.

"I mean, you can, but I think you'd be more comfortable somewhere else."

"You can't possibly have coitus that loud every morning," Asterion tried to joke.

"And twice in the afternoon," Jonas smirked. Asterion groaned, getting to his feet, weighing the effect that listening to Sidney and Jonas have loving, passionate sex every day would have on his sanity.

"Did you have somewhere else in mind for me?" he asked.

"I did."

"It better not be that fucking boat," Asterion warned, thinking unhappily of the one time he'd set foot on Jonas' second-hand fishing trawler and nearly slipped into the bay.

"First of all, my boat is lovely."

"It's smaller than a rowboat, and only half as comfortable."

"I wasn't going to put you on my boat," Jonas said. "The place I was thinking of comes with an opportunity for you to apologize for your horrible behavior. To Sidney and Dom both. Come on." Jonas nudged Asterion toward the steps of the gazebo. "Let's go have breakfast."

12

Asterion wore shame like an old scarf; it wasn't a piece he trotted out often, except when the weather required it, and when he put it on, he was always reminded how remarkably well it fit him.

Sidney accepted his apology with grace and a raised eyebrow at Jonas, who was seated next to Asterion at the counter in the long, narrow diner. Jonas sipped his coffee in response.

The diner was quiet that morning, a lull that was apparently quite normal for a Monday, which was the day it was. Dom Silva did not emerge from the kitchen for at least half an hour and, when he did, his apron, and much of the shirt beneath it, was white with flour. When he wiped his hands at the apron's hem, Asterion was sure he did nothing but move the mess around, hand to apron and apron to hand.

Dom opened his mouth to greet them, and seemed to think better of it, glancing over to where Sidney was pouring coffee for an older couple who were sitting by the far window at the curve of the wall.

"I'll get him for you," Dom said to Jonas who shook his head.

"He already stopped by."

"Oh." Dom's eyes briefly touched Asterion's face, frowning before he looked back at Jonas. "Did you... you didn't already find something?" Jonas shook his head, but before he could prompt Asterion to speak, Asterion cleared his throat.

"I wanted to apologize." Asterion straightened his back and gripped his coffee mug like the lifeline it was. "I was in poor form yesterday, and I've been reliably informed that I was rather rude. I'm sorry."

"Oh." Dom cleared his throat. "That's alright. It seems like things have been... rough."

"Indeed," Asterion agreed, his resolve faltering, his eyes dropping to his mug. It wasn't as good as the coffee Sidney had brought him that morning.

"Also, I have a favor to ask you," Jonas said to Dom. Dom nodded, wiping a hair off his forehead with the back of his hand, swiping a smear of flour over his smooth olive skin. The ease of his movements belied a unique self-assurance that Asterion admired and envied in equal measure.

"You're welcome to it," Dom was saying. Asterion hadn't been paying attention to their conversation, but Jonas had already explained on the drive into town that Dom Silva owned a duplex with a vacancy. "It's not much."

"It's better than nothing, and he'll happily pay for it." Jonas nudged Asterion's shoulder as Dom walked off to get a key. Asterion hadn't converted gold to human currency in some time, but likely that wouldn't matter in a place like Hindry.

Before they'd left the cottage, Asterion had slid several coins into the pocket of his narrow cut trousers. The trousers were the only part of his favorite suit he could bring himself to put on. He was still wearing Sidney's sweater and understood why Sidney was so fond of it. It was so oversized that it had the same soothing effect as being wrapped in a blanket. He needed one of his own, ideally one that was thicker.

He fished around in his pocket, finding a coin that felt like the right size, and then slid it across the counter, where it was waiting for Dom when he returned. His grey-brown eyes widened when they landed on the gold coin, and he stared at it for a long moment.

"You don't take gold?" Asterion asked. Dom's flour covered hand reached out and slowly picked up the coin, sliding it between his fingers. He arched an eyebrow at Asterion but couldn't seem to manage any words.

"We ought to stop by the bank," Jonas said.

"I'll go tomorrow," Asterion replied. Dom slid the coin into the pouch on his apron and handed Asterion the keys before turning to go back into the kitchen.

DOM SILVA'S HOUSE WAS A SMALL, BOXY WHITE CLAPBOARD AFFAIR, sandwiched between several others that were identical to it in size and design, the only noticeable difference being the color of the wood siding or how much the paint was chipping.

Jonas was kind enough to carry Asterion's trunks up the stairs into the bedroom of the small apartment. Then he left, citing chores that tickled Asterion's curiosity, but Asterion couldn't bring himself to ask about because he was tired of feeling like a hanger-on. Instead, Jonas left and Asterion unpacked his trunk of anything he thought he might wear now that he had no magic and was basically not a prince. With these parameters, his wardrobe was distressingly thin.

The apartment was bland, not as warm or well-decorated as Dom's downstairs. But that was fine. The blankness suited him at the moment. The large bay window in the living room let in a lot of natural light, which was sort of nice, even if it was the staid grey of a day that promised rain.

Asterion showered and then spent too long examining the

change in his coloring in the mirror. His skin was very freckled and naturally oatmeal colored. His hair, too, had shifted to a subdued aqua, almost powder blue, and his ears were back to their normal length and pointedness. Thankfully his stubble, which had never grown particularly fast, was still at least a day or two from needing tending. The change in coloring he might be able to stomach, but he hated the way his chin looked with a beard.

Once in his shorts and trousers, he slid into an undershirt and stared at the options that were left to him, trying to focus on anything that wasn't the creeping misery in his chest. Sidney's sweater looked particularly pathetic laying on the bed beside Asterion's exquisitely tailored navy jacket and waistcoat.

If he was going to be depressed, he at least wanted to look good doing it. He also wanted to be comfortable. So, he was going to go shopping.

13

D om ended up staying at the diner until just before the dinner rush, when one more waiter and a cook who'd been missing since the night of the party returned in good spirits and ready to work. One of them might have had a different eye color, but Dom thought it would have been rude to ask.

"Go home." Nina practically pushed Dom out of the back door. "Rest."

"I have one more thing to do," Dom sighed, scooping the to-go bag Jonas had paid for off the counter.

"I don't know that Asterion actually knows how to cook," Jonas had said.

"Oh." Dom accepted the fistful of actual dollars from Jonas with two hands. "Well, what does he like?"

"He'll eat anything." Based on what how thin Asterion was, Dom doubted it was true. Still, Jonas had paid for a spread, so Dom had boxed up several different options to take home.

The wind picked up as the evening turned to night, shuffling away the grey clouds that had lingered all day. Dom shivered as he stood on his own front porch and knocked on the door to the upstairs apartment. For a long moment, he heard nothing, and then footsteps. A figure appeared, blurred by leaded glass.

The Asterion who pulled open the door might have been a different man than the one Dom met at Elmmond House. He was pale and speckled, like someone had flecked his skin with honey. His hair was the color of a robin's egg, and his fine-boned features threw striking angles across his face. His high cheek-bones seemed to set the straightaway for the path of his long, pointed ears, like an elf from a story Dom vaguely remembered from childhood.

Asterion was wearing Dom's old jeans again, and beneath an unbuttoned cardigan, a cotton undershirt drew tight across the slant of his chest.

"Hello," he said, with a curious arch of his eyebrow. Dom was warm, suddenly, though there was no reason for it. He raised the bag of food.

"Jonas asked me to bring you some supper." A fond smile crossed Asterion's face before he sighed and shook his head. Then he stepped back and gestured toward the stairs.

Dom hadn't planned on going up. He was going to drop off the food and then go inside for a shower, a drink and whatever leftovers he could throw into a skillet while he waited for his favorite radio show to come on. Monday night at seven thirty was when the local station played *Nocturne Mystery Theatre*, and they were three weeks into a good story. But Asterion stood wait-ing, wafts of blue drifting down around his cheeks like spun sugar, and, because Dom felt bad for him, being left behind and all, he carried the bag up the stairs, Asterion following behind.

"Actually, while I have you," Asterion drifted into the kitchen as Dom set the bag of food on the counter, "could I get you to show me how the hob works? I was going to have tea earlier, but I couldn't get it sorted, so I had to settle for gin." Asterion grinned in a way that might have been sheepish or entirely false but wasn't unattractive. Dom waited for Asterion to laugh, and when he didn't, Dom heard the echo of Jonas in his head: *'He doesn't know how to cook.'*

"Right." Dom stepped past Asterion to the stove, where the black kettle was sitting on the back burner. "So, these knobs each correspond to one of the hobs, and it's marked here..." And like that, Dom explained how to turn on a stove to a fae prince.

"If it doesn't light, turn it off quick, because you don't want to fill the house with gas," Dom added at the end. Asterion had one arm wrapped around his narrow stomach, the other floating above, his fingers pressed against the pointed angle of his chin as he frowned at the stove and then at Dom.

"Gas is bad because... it's flammable?"

"Yes." Dom almost laughed, relieved that even if Asterion had understood nothing else, he got that neither of them wanted to be blown up in the middle of the night.

"It seems awfully dangerous just for tea."

"Well, you can cook things other than tea on a stove. Like soup." Asterion wrinkled his nose, and Dom did chuckle at that. "They don't have soup where you're from?"

"Soup is cooked in a big pot over a magically induced fire," Asterion said, as though he was explaining a fact of life. As though there were no other ways to prepare a soup.

"Well, if it helps, feel free to think of the stove as four smaller magically induced fires."

"Magic doesn't create invisible air that explodes when it comes in contact with heat," Asterion said, his eyes narrowing at the stove again. Dom snorted.

"As far as I can tell, magic *is* invisible air that does far worse things than make a house explode. And it doesn't need to come in contact with heat to do it." Asterion turned toward him, his gaze suddenly piercing. Dom regretted bringing up magic at all.

"Is that what you think?" Asterion asked. Dom shrugged. It

was what he thought, but he didn't want to argue. Asterion rolled his eyes and placed the kettle on the front burner. Dom watched as Asterion turned the appropriate knob.

"Magic is dangerous," Dom said, parroting what he'd always been told.

"This stove is dangerous," Asterion replied, patting the stovetop like it was a dog. "That doesn't mean you don't have one in your house." Dom had no response for that, as he'd never considered it like that before. He cleared his throat.

"Enjoy your dinner," he said, starting for the stairs.

"You're not staying?" Asterion's voice hitched slightly. Dom hesitated, spying Asterion's suddenly pink cheeks, as Asterion turned toward the bag of food. "I certainly can't eat everything in this bag on my own."

"You can put the leftovers in the icebox," Dom said. "And heat them up in the oven. There's a pilot light—"

"What's a pilot light?" Asterion asked, looking back, his face the absolute picture of innocence.

Dom exhaled. Then he looked at the bag of food where he knew he'd packed one of Nina's famous roast beef melts, which he could claim for himself if he stayed.

Asterion had been a prick. But he'd also been stripped of his magic, and, according to Jonas, abandoned. By who? Did it matter? Dom knew how jarring it was to suddenly find yourself alone.

"Alright, look," Dom conceded. "We'll eat and then I'll show you how the stove works. But while we eat, we're going to turn on the radio. My show is on at seven thirty."

"What sort of show?" Asterion began taking boxes out of the bag as though nothing had just happened. Dom shrugged off his coat and threw it over the back of the chair, as the kettle began to creak with heat.

"It's a play they broadcast on the radio. A mystery."

"A play? Like a theater play? Acting and such?"

"Exactly the same, but you can't see it." Asterion opened and spread out boxes on the counter, clearly eyeing the roast beef melt. Thankfully at the last moment he moved on to the pancakes and rashers.

"What's the point of theater you can't see?"

"What's the point of a book without pictures? You have an imagination, don't you?" Dom challenged lightly, scooping up the melt and taking it to the table. He skirted around the seat that faced the window, which had always been Ares', and put his container down so that his back would be against the wall. Then he walked over to the radio cabinet in the corner beside the window and bent down.

Ares' records tipped to one side as the doors opened, and Dom reached up to turn the dial. The tune that played at the end of the weather segment of the local news show filled the room. Dom turned the volume down, and when he stood, he saw Asterion was sitting in Ares' chair, his head cocked to the side as he listened to the announcer discuss the planned holiday festivities that would be starting in the next two weeks.

"I've never been here for your winter holidays," Asterion said. Dom came back to the table, deliberately not having any feelings about the seating arrangements. "What are they like?"

"You don't have holidays?" Dom asked, taking a bite of roast beef. It melted on his tongue, and he almost groaned in delight. Asterion shook his head.

"We have festivals and feast days. Solstice, which Jonas tells me some humans do celebrate, but not like we do."

"How do you celebrate solstice?"

"Feasting from dawn til dusk. Dancing and fornicating from dusk til dawn." Dom choked and reached for his water, which didn't exist. Asterion chuckled and got to his feet as the kettle began to whistle. "Sorry. I forget how prudish you all are."

"We're not prudish," Dom defended around the lump of roast beef caught in his throat.

"Yes, you are." Asterion's back was to Dom, as cups clinked together on the countertop. "Barely any intercourse laden rituals anymore."

"None that I can think of," Dom admitted, hoping that concession might cap the conversation. Asterion returned to the table with two steaming teacups, nudging one toward Dom.

"That's what I mean! I could name at least five that happen annually. No, wait," he paused, staring for a moment at the ceiling. "Six."

"Our holidays are generally more about giving and showing thankfulness—"

"Have you never had sex before?" Asterion asked, his expression as guileless as it had been when he asked how to use the stove. "Because I believe those are some key components." Dom knew that his face was doing something embarrassing, and there was nothing he could do to fix it. Sex was just not something Dom talked about with anyone, let alone a near stranger. Asterion burst into a pretty peal of laughter. "I'm sorry! That was unkind. It's simply the easiest thing to tease humans about. I'm sure you've had plentiful and varied satisfying sexual encounters." He glanced up at Dom from beneath his eyelashes as he lifted a forkful of pancake to his mouth. Dom forced himself to take a large gulp of very hot tea.

"I'm glad to see you're in a better mood."

"Isolation doesn't suit me, I'm afraid. I give all credit to the company, of course," he added, gesturing toward Dom. "I doubt Jonas has paid you enough for your patience." Dom might have gotten whiplash from the speed at which Asterion had gone from teasing to self-deprecating. Dom stopped eating to watch Asterion focus on cutting up one of his rashers.

"How are you feeling? I mean, your hand? And the..." he

trailed off. Asterion wasn't looking at Dom anymore. His gaze was trapped by the still surface of the cup of tea in front of him, a magenta hue. Dom may not have understood much about the man beside him, or about magic, but he understood grief. "I'm sorry," Dom said quickly. "Forget I asked."

"It hurts," Asterion's voice was quiet. "But there's nothing to do about it now, so I guess I'd better learn to live with it," he added with a finality that didn't make the smile on his face seem any more genuine. He took another bite of his pancakes and they both listened to a commercial on the radio for soap.

"Well," Dom said, grabbing the last bite of his roast beef melt and lifting it to his mouth. "I'd better explain to you what happened on *Nocturne Mystery Theatre* last week, or you won't be able to follow what's happening." It wasn't a graceful change of topic, but Asterion did finally lift his head.

"Alright," Asterion said. "I'm listening."

And he seemed to be, even though the first ten minutes of *Nocturne Mystery Theatre* were spent with Dom answering Asterion's questions about who was speaking and where they were going, and what the sound of the gunfire was supposed to be. But eventually Asterion settled in, curling catlike on the end of the couch closest to the radio. The program was an hour long, and by the time it was done, Asterion was asleep, slunk down on the pillow, his legs curled up beneath him so that he barely took up the space of a cushion.

Dom got up quietly from the armchair by the window. He went to the bedroom where he tugged one of the spare quilts down from the closet and returned to drape it over Asterion's thin frame. Because of their conversation more than habit, Dom checked the stove, put away the leftovers, and then crept down the stairs to his own apartment, only discovering once he was safely in the silence of his bedroom, that he was glad he'd gone up.

14

Asterion woke up just before noon, curled on the couch beneath a duvet. His limbs felt stiff as he sat and stretched slowly, his back popping in places that had certainly never popped before. Would he start aging more quickly now that his magic was gone? Jonas' magic was gone, and he hadn't withered in any noticeable ways. At least, not noticeable to Asterion. But then, Jonas had given up many of his bad habits before Asterion had. It was going to have to be beds for Asterion from here on out.

He got up and walked to the kitchen, looking askance at the kettle. He wished it was one of those silver coffee makers Jonas had, not that Asterion would know what to do with a silver coffee maker if he had one. Maybe he ought to start a list of things he needed from his new landlord. Unless coffee makers were a thing one was supposed to buy oneself.

Dom Silva bringing supper over had been very generous, even if Jonas had paid him to do it. Hopefully, Asterion's ability to remain civil and pleasant throughout that interaction would afford him this additional favor. They'd had a nice conversation, he'd thought, even if he had accidentally embarrassed Dom by talking about sex. He always forgot how humans were. Well, humans who weren't Sidney, apparently. And really, Asterion was better off not thinking of Dom Silva and 'sex' at the same time, if he was honest. The man was, he thought as he filled up the kettle at the sink, unreasonably handsome. And his kindness, even if it had been bought, only made Asterion like him more.

And then, the handsome, kind man appeared in the backyard below the window. Asterion leaned forward to watch as Dom walked across the narrow plot of grass to a large shed. He was dressed strangely, some kind of jumpsuit that Asterion couldn't identify, but more importantly, Dom carried a steaming mug in his hand. Coffee.

Asterion assumed Dom would be at work, as that was the place he seemed to always be, but there he was. And he'd already made coffee. Asterion's desire far outweighed practicality and decorum. Also, it seemed like coffee was a thing most people made in multiple cups, which meant it wouldn't be too much of a bother for Dom to let Asterion have some. He had splurged the day before on a very nice pair of leather house slippers with suede lining, and he hurried to the bedroom to find them before starting down the back staircase.

The grass was slimy and slick, and Asterion nearly landed on his backside twice, trying to mute his sounds of disgust. He tiptoed his way to the shed, fully prepared to beg for at least one cup of coffee and a lesson on how to make it so that he wouldn't have to debase himself like this again.

Asterion tucked his sweater around himself, realizing abruptly that he ought to have changed; this was the same rumpled outfit he'd fallen asleep in the night before! Then he remembered that he wasn't a prince anymore and Dom Silva wasn't likely to care about what Asterion was wearing whether it had been silks or an old sack. Which Asterion decided was going to be a comforting fact, instead of a disappointing one.

The shed door was open wide enough that Asterion wouldn't have to move it, thank Gods, because it looked very large and heavy. Inside, metal clanked against metal, and as Asterion stepped through the gap, he could smell oil and heat. His ankles were immediately toasted by a small, circular looking fan that sat on the ground by the door.

Dom Silva was also on the ground. His head was beneath the body of a silver and black motorcycle. The sleeves of his jumpsuit were rolled up to his elbows, and several lines of grease streaked his forearms as he clacked a wrench against something on the bottom of the vehicle. Beneath his jumpsuit was a smudged white shirt, stretched tight across his chest.

Asterion had several largely incoherent thoughts in quick succession. The first was simply, '*Oh.*' He had, mere minutes before, been telling himself that he was going to stop thinking about how handsome Dom Silva was, and now Dom Silva was lying in front of Asterion being extremely handsome. And since when had Asterion ever found the idea of laying in the dirt appealing? He had nothing against tradesmen, but also, he hadn't encountered many tradesmen in his life. Perhaps it was good that he hadn't, as the presence of this one was making him feel as though he might like to be pinned to a grimy floor with dirty hands. Perhaps giving up his silks would have some perks after all.

"Asterion?" Dom had lifted his head up at some point and was now looking up at Asterion with a curious raise of his eyebrow. Had Asterion been staring at his chest that whole time? Oh no. "Are you okay?"

"Coffee," Asterion said. He frowned as his brain struggled to recalibrate. This was a side-effect of his magic being gone, surely. He could feel himself blushing, and he never blushed.

"Coffee?" Dom smirked. "This is a machine shed."

"You had—" Asterion cleared his throat and forced himself to look around the small space. "I don't have a coffee maker in my apartment."

"You do. It's in the cabinet beneath the sink," Dom said, lying back down with a grunt that did not send a bright, stinging heat to the base of Asterion's spine. Something clanked, and Dom huffed, and Asterion glared at him, because he was certainly making those noises on purpose. But Dom wasn't actually paying attention to him. With the press of his heel against the floor, Dom lifted his hips with an ease that had Asterion's body tensing inappropriately.

"What are you doing down there?" Asterion demanded, his own arousal making him irritable. Gods, was this what a week without sex turned him into?

"Tuning up my bike." Dom pointed with his wrench to a table built into the far wall. "There's coffee over there, if you want it. I only had a sip." Asterion did, desperately, need coffee. Perhaps more than he ever had before in his life. He padded over to the table and picked up the mug. It was heavy ceramic, the logo of Dom's diner printed on the front. Dom's mouth had already touched the rim of this mug. Asterion ignored that and took a gulp.

Bitter, bright and hot, Asterion sighed in relief. He could feel his body relax as he studied the wall of hanging tools, the shelf of supplies above the workbench.

"Do you have an espresso machine?" Asterion asked. Dom laughed.

"I've got one at the diner."

"Uh huh. Is that something I could buy for myself?"

"You could," Dom said. He made a sound, and Asterion turned in time to see Dom on his feet, bent over, picking his tools up off the ground. There was dirt smudged across his ass. Asterion gave up trying to ignore his attraction and took another sip of coffee, staring openly while Dom's back was turned. When Dom straightened up, he was holding a dirty rag in one hand, wringing it between his fingers as he turned to face Asterion. Dexterous.

Gods. Asterion needed to get himself under control.

"I'll have to ask you to show me the coffee pot. And how it works."

"I'd be happy to." Dom glanced at a small, battered clock on the wall and frowned. "Unfortunately, I don't have much time at the moment. I need to shower and change for work. But I can leave the back door to my apartment unlocked, and you can help yourself to mine. You can use my oven as well, if you need it. Until I show you the pilot light on yours."

"Alright," Asterion nodded. The least he could do was be amenable to learning. Otherwise, he was going to have to find a sympathetic human to baby him very quickly, and that thought rankled. He didn't enjoy being helpless. He also hadn't been in a position to realize how helpless he was until now. It was embarrassing to think about, especially when he compared himself to landlord, mechanic, diner owner Dom Silva. "Thank you," Asterion added. Dom smiled and shrugged, as though it wasn't a bother at all.

IN THE KITCHEN, DOM DIRECTED ASTERION TO THE COFFEE, MUGS and a toaster before he went into his bedroom to shower and change. When he emerged twenty-five minutes later, tying his apron around his waist, Asterion was seated at the table, eating toast and reading a pulp novel from one of Dom's nearby shelves. Asterion was resting his cheek on his hand, long fingers running through soft-looking strands of blue, and glanced up at Dom with a smile.

"Are you off already?"

"I am," Dom said, ignoring the weird warmth blossoming on the back of his neck. "Do you want me to bring you anything back? I won't be home until late."

"No," Asterion shook his head. "I'll be fine. I think you brought me enough food yesterday to feed a small militia. Plus, I should practice with the stove."

"Alright," Dom nodded. "Well, if you change your mind, you know where to find me."

"Have a good day at work," Asterion said, turning back to his book.

Dom walked, hands in his pockets, thinking about Asterion the whole way to the diner. The interaction they'd had at Jonas' cottage seemed to be an outlier; Asterion's emotions had gotten the better of him. He was stuck, alone, in a world he knew very little about, and who wouldn't lash out after too many drinks paired with that level of bullshit? As far as Dom could tell, Asterion had accepted everything that had happened to him as though there was nothing to do but accept it, which was strange. But also brave in a way that Dom admired.

Asterion and Dom had both been left behind, and at least Dom had the advantage of living in his own world, where he knew how to make breakfast and could take care of himself. Asterion had been stripped of all that. Stripped of his magic, which was undoubtedly important to him. And now all he was asking was how to use the coffee pot. It wasn't an inconvenience to show him. Or to share.

And maybe it was a little nice, before he left, to have someone tell him to have a good day at work.

15

Asterion stole several more pulp novels off Dom's shelves and retreated to his own apartment. As he succeeded in only slightly burning the edges of a cheese sandwich (otherwise expertly reheated,) it began to rain aggressively. Asterion ate, listening to the percussive pattering of rain on the roof, and then gathered up his books and went back to bed.

He changed into the silk pajamas he'd purchased for himself, and then fluffed the pillows before climbing into bed and settling back against the headboard. The upstairs apartment was beginning to remind him of the horrible golden room at Elmmond House. Not that it was gaudy, but that it was empty. Unlived in, in an almost tangible way. He needed to get some things and spread them out across the dresser. The small stack of books he'd put on the nightstand was already making a world of difference.

There were also very few books in the upstairs apartment, and most of them looked too scholarly to be of any real interest, likely something Sidney or Jonas would want to read. On the other hand, Dom's collection of novels was expansive. It was one more thing Asterion was going to have to work to find unappealing about him. The one he'd selected at random that morning was called *The Kiss of Death* and the cover featured a disheveled and thoroughly kissed looking woman sitting on the center of an unmade bed. Dom Silva, you naughty boy.

Within the hour, Asterion reached the part of the book where the man who smoked a lot of cigarettes and was always looking out from under the brim of his hat arrived at the brunette's front door, his shirt stained in blood, and the woman nearly swooned, but didn't. Without much talking, she bravely took him inside, barely a fleeting mention of fear for her virtue.

It was delightful dreck, the sort of thing Asterion had to work much harder to get his hands on in the fae realms. Having copious amounts of sex and doing blood rituals was one thing, but reading about it was considered quite gauche. Even most of the theater Asterion had attended in recent years had become increasingly moralistic. Likely his sister Cressida's doing. She had only recently taken the throne and was certain the path to legitimacy would be found in austerity. If she wasn't careful, she'd follow too closely in their father's footsteps and end up loathed by the general populace. One reason, at least, he could be glad he was stuck earthside.

Asterion adjusted his back against the pillows and continued to read. Now it was the scene where the man stripped himself of his bloodied shirt, and the woman pushed his hair back from his forehead, and then began to undress. Asterion was riveted by the sensuousness of her movements, the ache of the man beneath her, the tenderness as she climbed aside his naked hips and lowered herself onto him. Asterion could feel himself getting hard, the descriptions just florid enough to be tantalizing. And, as his ridiculous thirst for his landlord in the shed had so rudely reminded him, he was firmly in the longest dry spell of his adult life. He bit his lip and tried to read on, one hand bending the spine of the small paperback, as he reached with his other beneath the waistband of his pajama pants.

As soon as he touched himself his eyelids fluttered closed, his back tightening in bliss at the first stroke of his thumb across his cockhead. Would he like to imagine himself as the man or woman in this scenario? Both. Either. He rocked his hips up and tried to picture the brunette woman on the cover of the book above him.

No, that didn't quite suit. The silk of his trousers against his hand could be the silk of the woman's slip against her thighs. He could grind down against the man, who was gruff but caring, his hand calloused but warm against the skin of her hips.

The book fell closed on his chest as Asterion gave up the obligatory appearance of reading so that he could work his other hand beneath him. He had no oil, no soft magic to ease the ache that would come from pressing inside himself. He decided to only tease, his breath catching at the sensation of it. He worked himself slowly, not realizing that the description of the man in the book had fallen away. Strong, muscled arms were now streaked with engine grease, long dark curls splayed over the ground, Dom Silva's gorgeous mouth twisting into an expression of pleasure as Asterion rode him on the floor of his machine shed.

Asterion came hard and fast, a guttural groan escaping his chest that was so feral it was almost humiliating. But he couldn't stop. He turned his head, muffling the sound with his pillow, grinding up into his fist.

His cheeks flushed in exertion and embarrassment as he collapsed back against the mattress. A fictional character was one thing. Dom Silva was not. Jonas' friend and Asterion's landlord was firmly off-limits, and likely attached. Although, a tiny voice reminded, Asterion had seen no indication of a partner of any kind in his few forays into Dom's apartment. Not that he'd been looking. Not that it was any of his business. Asterion hadn't pined for anyone in two centuries, and he certainly wasn't about to start now.

And aside from all that, Dom didn't like magic. After what had happened with Dom's brother, Asterion couldn't blame him. But still, Dom was less likely to fall in love with him than most, which meant Asterion's crush had to be put to bed, and not... well, whatever Asterion had just done.

Still, one little slip up was nothing to wring hands over. Perhaps it was out of him now, and he could move on. With that, he rooted the book out of his blankets, laid it on the bedside table, and got up to change. He was hungry again, and he wanted a snack before he kept reading.

"WHAT ARE YOU DOING?" NINA ASKED. DOM BACKED OUT OF THE lower cabinet he'd crawled halfway into and glanced up at her.

"Looking for the old french press. Have you seen it?"

"We didn't buy that Italian monstrosity on the back counter so that you could fish around for the french press less than a year later," Nina said, her hands on her hips. Dom chuckled.

"I was going to take it home. It's closer to espresso than what I can get out of the drip pot."

"You don't drink espresso."

That was true. But the press was easy to use and nearer to espresso than what Asterion could get otherwise, unless he was willing to come to the diner every morning. And it was just sitting in a cabinet somewhere. Asterion might as well have it.

"You haven't seen it?"

"It's on the high shelf in the pantry," Nina said, shaking her head as she walked away. "Also, one of the trawlers just came in. I'm going to fire up the griddle."

The town of Hindry was home to two small fisheries, and the trawlers they employed sailed north toward the deep, icy waters and would be gone for weeks at a time. When they returned, their crews were usually tired and always ravenous. Dom found the french press quickly, and then went out to help Hector move tables around.

Serving the fishermen was as rote to Dom as getting dressed in the morning. When he'd been young, he'd been intimidated by them. The oldest were grizzled and world-weary, to a teenaged Dom, they'd seemed unapproachable, unfriendly, even if they were close with his Uncle Hector, who'd worked with them for years before an injury had put him permanently ashore. For able-bodied young men of a certain age, not getting out of Hindry quickly enough after graduating high school meant the fisheries were your future, and Dom was an anomaly amongst his classmates. He hadn't wanted to stay in Hindry either, not at first. He'd gone to college for a year but dropped out after Ares' disappearance and never had time to look back. He was needed here, even if that meant he'd lost track of wanting something else for himself.

"Excuse me." A man with collar-length honey blonde hair and a face full of blonde stubble flagged Dom down. Dom didn't recognize him.

"Yes, sir? What can I get you?" The man's eyes narrowed. They were a startlingly bright shade of blue, and he stared at Dom with an intensity that he had only ever encountered with his mother, or Aunt Ree, when he was in trouble.

"Have you lived here long?" The man asked. His accent wasn't thick, but it was unusual enough that it took Dom several moments to parse what he'd said. And even then, the question still didn't make a lot of sense.

"I've lived here my whole life," Dom said.

"Is everything alright?" Hector appeared, as he always did

when a customer was acting strangely. He had a good sense for those sorts of things.

"I'm looking for a church," said the man. "Bittergate Chapel. Do you know it?" Hector took over, and Dom slid away to the kitchen to help Nina with plates.

"I think he's Scandinavian," Hector said later when they were bent over the sink. "Said his name is Anders. I guess he's new. Ron said they weren't exactly looking for anyone, but his references were so good, they couldn't not take him."

"Wonder how he ended up all the way out here." Nina came over, pulling off her apron. She hooked her thumbs into her pockets and made eye-contact with Dom over Hector's head. "Might be a story there."

"Everyone's got one." Dom shrugged.

"It's like you're working to avoid every handsome man that comes into town," Nina sighed. Not quite. He'd moved the last one he met into his spare apartment. The thought of Asterion made him blush, distracted, and he barely caught the tail end of what Hector was saying.

"He's gainfully employed. Goes to church." Hector nudged Dom with his elbow. "Your Aunt Ree would like that."

"Aunt Ree's the one who told me to never get involved with a fisherman." Dom stepped back from the sink, drying his hands as Hector chuckled and shook his head.

"You know," Nina said, twenty minutes later, as Dom walked her to her bicycle. "If you're hell bent on spending the rest of your life in this shit town, you could at least try to find someone to spend it with."

"I just want to keep my head down and get my work done."

"That's depressing." Nina climbed on her bike and offered Dom the cigarette she'd been taking a drag of. "And dull." Dom took the cigarette and inhaled, feeling the burn of tobacco in the back of his throat.

"It's fine. It's just life. We can't all be blissfully coupled up like you."

"Maybe," Nina said. "But you could at least try." Dom offered her back her cigarette, and Nina shook her head. "You keep it. Casey hates the smell."

"Tell him 'hi' for me."

"See you tomorrow, boss." And then she was gone.

Dom walked home, french press clacking on top of the carry-out boxes he'd filled with leftover cherry pie and turnovers. He finished Nina's cigarette, trying not to think too hard about what she'd said. He'd tried things before. He'd tried college. He'd tried to build something for himself outside of Hindry. But in Dom's experience, trying only led to disappointment. Having something, like a family or a dream, was just the first part of watching that thing vanish out from underneath you. He was tired of trying only to wake up alone.

When he came in through the front gate, Dom looked up to see the lights on in Ares' apartment. He smiled. At the very least, he couldn't deny that it was nice to come home to someone else. Even if it wasn't anything more than that.

16

A sterion woke to a distant knock on the door. It took
several moments to register that it was his own front door
being knocked on, and several more moments to remember that
there were no servants to answer it for him. By the time he
tumbled out of bed and put on his clothes and slippers, he was
half certain he'd imagined the sound. Curiosity got the better of
him anyway, and he stumbled down the stairs and he pulled
open the door. On the ground was a plate with four triangle
shaped pastries, oozing cherry red and glistening with crystal-
ized sugar. They were still warm.

Asterion took the plate upstairs, biting into the sweet pastry
and moaning in delight as he stepped into the living room. He
was going to have to find out where Dom was getting all these
remarkable desserts. Obviously, they were from the diner, but
the baker deserved a passionate kiss on the mouth for their
genius. He never would have thought that food in the earthly
realms could taste so good.

The only thing that would have made it better was a
steaming cup of espresso. He frowned at the silver coffee pot
which he had unearthed from beneath the sink the day before.

It had taken Asterion a little more than half an hour to make what was essentially a cup of sludge. He ate another cherry pastry and considered his options. They were few. Dom had still not taught him how to make coffee, but he could hardly be mad about that when his landlord was being so accommodating in every other imaginable way. Dom might have even left coffee downstairs for Asterion, if Asterion was brave enough to check.

Or Asterion could walk to the diner.

Spending another day in the apartment seemed dangerously self-indulgent. And he was curious about the much-lauded diner where Dom worked, having only been inside once himself, and that time with his tail between his legs. He hadn't really been paying attention.

Asterion went back into his bedroom and pulled a crew neck sweater on over his undershirt. The fashion was to wear sweaters over button-downs, but that seemed far too stuffy. Plus, the high neck of the button-down would hide his collarbones, so Asterion went without. Earthside clothes for men were so inconceivably dull, unless one was getting dressed up, which no one in Hindry ever seemed to, so Asterion was going to have to make his own fun. He put new earrings, which he'd had to go into the ladies' jewelry department to buy, and examined himself in the mirror. He was almost too pale, but that couldn't be helped at this point. He swept his hair back, put on a pair of penny loafers, and grabbed another pastry before heading out.

It was a crisp but surprisingly beautiful day, with so few clouds in the bright blue sky that it seemed inconceivable that yesterday had been nothing short of a monsoon. It was a nice walk to the diner, not far at all, but Asterion was still unduly pleased that he managed it without getting lost.

The bell above the door jangled as Asterion walked in. There were a few patrons at either side of the counter, and a couple of tables along the rounded edge of the building were occupied. In front of him, several chalkboard signs announced daily specials. On the wall was a rack of mugs and a shelf of salt, pepper, and sugar shakers, and other condiments Asterion didn't recognize. It smelled as good as he'd remembered.

Sidney was standing behind the counter, a mug of coffee in hand, and Asterion went over and took the empty stool in front of him. Sidney smiled and Asterion rolled his eyes on principle.

"I was wondering when I'd see you."

"Missing me already?" Asterion flirted. Sidney chuckled.

"Espresso?"

"Please." Asterion glanced toward the glass case of baked goods that sat beside the register. "And a slice of pie."

"Blueberry, apple, pumpkin, cherry—"

"Surprise me," he said.

Sidney moved comfortably in the space and Asterion watched him for a moment trying to not be annoyed again by Sidney's self-assurance, before the little window that led into the kitchen caught his eye. He leaned forward, trying to catch a glimpse of Dom. There were people back there. A broad-shouldered woman with close cropped black hair and brown skin. She was talking to someone, though Asterion couldn't hear her over the hissing of the giant, silver espresso machine.

"Jonas was getting worried about you," Sidney said, delivering a small steaming cup.

"He doesn't think I can stay out of trouble for a few days."

"I think he was worried you'd starve to death." Sidney fetched a pie from the other end of the counter.

"Dom's been taking good care of me," Asterion said. Sidney arched an eyebrow as he cut into the pie, and Asterion ignored it. Humans. So prudish, yet so eager to read into things! Asterion changed the subject, for both their sakes. "You work here now?"

"Just in the mornings. Jonas has been busy." Sidney delivered a slice of the pie and a fork. "A lot of writing letters and making calls. He managed to source everything to unbind the house. Got in touch with someone named Mae—"

"One of his old Alchemist friends." Asterion took a sip of espresso and then a forkful of pie and groaned. Twice in the same morning. Asterion wondered what planet he was on; he had never tasted anything so good in his life. "Oh, Gods. Sidney."

"I know. It's good, right?"

"What is it?" Asterion took another bite and clutched the counter to keep from falling off the stool.

"Shoo-fly pie," Sidney said. "One of Dom's specialties."

"Dom?" Asterion asked. Sidney nodded. Asterion nearly dropped his fork. "He's the baker? All the pastries?" Sidney nodded again. Ridiculous! Gods, was there anything Dom Silva couldn't do?

"You're blushing," Sidney said.

"Don't be a bastard," Asterion mumbled through a forkful of pie. "And go ahead and cut me another slice."

WHEN DOM ARRIVED AT THE DINER, IT WAS THE SOFT LULL OF THE post-lunch crowd. He'd had the morning off again and started his day, after dropping off pastries at Asterion's door, by going to the bank and the hardware store. Two hours had passed at Aunt Ree's salon, fixing wobbly chairs and getting his cheeks pinched by her clients, but he'd been gifted a box of her molasses cookies for his trouble, so it was all worth it in the end. Nina was outside taking her smoke break, and the kitchen was empty and quiet as Dom put down his bags and took a deep breath. Another day. Eight or nine more hours of work ahead of him. But that was fine. What else was he going to do?

Dom tied on his apron and walked through the wide

swinging door into the restaurant to find Sidney hanging clean mugs on the rack behind the counter.

"Please tell me it wasn't just you for lunch." Dom eyed the half empty coffee pot as he came up beside Sidney, trying to remember what had been on the schedule board he'd just walked past.

"Well, James was here to open, but he left around one. Kinsey and Nina were both in and out of the kitchen."

"No Hector?" Dom frowned. Sidney shook his head.

"I haven't seen him. But we were fine. Asterion helped, though he only served coffee, and I think only to tables he decided he liked."

"Asterion?" Dom must have misheard. But Sidney gestured to the corner booth, the one with the best view of the bay, where Asterion was sitting with Dierdre Buchanan and Maude Villante, two eighty-year-old women who drove to The Silver Platter twice a week for lunch. "Uhh..."

"He ate half a shoo-fly pie and forgot his wallet, so I put him to work to pay it off. I did try to explain customer service to him. And money. I don't really think he listened. But no one's thrown anything at him, and all the tickets have been paid." Dom tried to swallow. He was braced for something bad, his body tense because it knew that this was inherently wrong. Asterion was a prince, not a waiter. He should have been lounging on a throne, throwing lavish parties, being waited *on*.

But whatever Dierdre was telling Asterion was enough to make him tilt his head back and laugh. Three gold earrings dangled temptingly toward the line of his neck, drawing Dom's eye, unbidden. Asterion's light blue hair was tied in a small, messy knot at the back of his head, loose strands tucked behind the point of his ears and he leaned forward conspiratorially, saying something that had both women giggling.

"They've been here for two hours, but everyone seems to be

enjoying themselves," Sidney said, before grabbing the coffee pot and going to refill cups for two customers at the far end of the counter. Dom struggled for a moment, trying to think of something to do besides blush and stare. Why was it so much stranger to see Asterion in the diner than in Dom's own kitchen? And now that the shock was wearing off, why was Dom so pleased to see him? Flustered and confused, Dom ducked into the back, fetching new desserts to fill empty spots in the case.

He busied himself reorganizing the trays of cookies and pies and eclairs, trying very hard not to pay attention to whatever was happening at Asterion's table. But Asterion's laughter made the hair on the back of Dom's neck stand up anyway; he couldn't stop himself from looking over, and his stomach flipped when his eyes met Asterion's across the counter.

Oh, God.

When was the last time he had deep cleaned the fryer? That was a long, labor-intensive task that would keep him in the kitchen with his head down for a while. Dom stepped back to close the dessert case, and nearly jumped out of his skin when he realized Dierdre was across the counter from him.

"We love your new server." Dierdre smiled, handing Dom several bills folded inside her check.

"Which one?" Dom asked, as though he didn't already know.

"Sidney's a doll, but that one will have Maude bleaching and dying her hair within a week. He's a menace. Oh! Are those fresh eclairs? Go ahead and box up four for us." She began to tell Dom about an impending visit from her granddaughter, and Dom only half listened, making change as Asterion escorted Maude to the counter. She blushed as he whispered something in her ear, grinning all the while, a softness to him that had only been hinted at before. It was paired with a courtly gentility that had absolutely fallen out of fashion centuries ago, Asterion handling the woman's crepe-paper thin hand with elegant delicacy as he took Maude's fingers from his arm and placed them on Dierdre's.

"Miss Villante, Miss Buchanan," Asterion smiled. "I look forward to serving you again on Friday."

"You're a peach." Maude patted Asterion on the cheek. Dom handed Dierdre the eclairs and her change, and then he and Asterion watched as they hobbled toward the door. When the bell rang behind them it was like a spell had been broken. Dom cleared his throat and handed Asterion his tip from Dierdre across the counter.

"Oh, unnecessary," Asterion shook his head. "They were a delight. Also, Maude slipped me twice that back at the table."

"What were you talking about?"

"Mostly you," Asterion said casually, though his smile was mischievous. "Dierdre's been trying to get you to go on a date with her granddaughter for eight months."

"She doesn't live nearby," Dom said, though he could feel himself blushing again. Asterion snorted, an intimidating impersonation of the old woman.

"Is there someone else?"

"No." Dom said, too honest and definitely too quick. Asterion only hummed, and before Dom could ask what the hell *that* meant, Hector came out of the kitchen, tying an apron around his waist.

"Why are you here?" he said to Dom. Dom struggled to switch the gears in his brain, Asterion's vague hum buzzing in his ears.

"I'm on dinner shift tonight."

"No, you're not," Hector snorted. "I am. You had breakfast and lunch."

"No—"

"It's alright," Asterion interrupted with a grin. "I was here to help." Hector's eyes widened. He looked at Dom, who could only shrug.

"Well, you don't need to be here. Marley and Winslow are both coming in. And you're not on the schedule board."

"I was going to clean the fryer," Dom said.

"I can take care of it," Hector said, glancing around. "Not much else to do, at least not for a couple of hours. Why don't you go home? You've been here every day this week."

Dom knew Hector was trying to be nice. Was willfully pretending that Dom had anything else in his life besides the diner.

"Did you finish tuning up your motorcycle?" Asterion asked. Dom stammered, surprised that anything from that morning had registered to Asterion beyond coffee.

"It's a beautiful day for a ride. You ought to go up to Harlan's Crest," Hector said. "Take your new tenet with you."

"I've always wanted to try riding a motorbike." Asterion smiled at him. Whether he was teasing or not, Dom couldn't tell. And he hated it. Dom inhaled, desperate for his brain to supply him with any reason at all why this wasn't going to happen. Hector and Asterion were both looking at him expectantly, and Asterion cocked his head, grin widening, like he was enjoying watching Dom struggle. Teasing him.

Fine. Two could play at that game.

"Okay." Dom shrugged and tugged his apron off over his head. "Let's go."

17

"You've never ridden a motorcycle before?" Dom asked. They were the first words he'd spoken to Asterion since they'd left the diner, and Asterion could already see the street sign for the road they lived on. Asterion shrugged.

"No."

"And you actually want to?"

"I pride myself on being willing to try anything once," Asterion said. This much, at least, was true. Maybe he had never wanted to ride a motorcycle until he'd seen Dom Silva stretched out beneath one, but that seemed rather beside the point. "Where's Harlan's Crest?"

"Up on the cliffside. Past Elmmond House and the chapel. It's," Dom hesitated, his expression unreadable before he quickly looked back at the ground. "It's nice."

"You don't have to take me," Asterion said. He couldn't tell if Dom was uncomfortable or not. And he didn't want to make the kindest person he'd ever met uncomfortable. "And you don't have to go. But you should take a day off now and again."

"I take time off."

"Don't be ridiculous. You've worked dawn to dusk every day

this week. And when you're not working at the diner, you're still working."

"There's a lot going on," Dom protested.

"Not so much as all that, I'm sure. When was the last time you sat down and relaxed? Read a book?"

"I read every night. To fall asleep." Dom pushed open the front gate. Even as he nodded his thanks, Asterion continued to argue.

"That's not the same thing as reading for enjoyment."

"I enjoy what I read."

"So much that it puts you straight to sleep?"

"Is it a crime to keep busy?" Dom asked.

"It might be, the way you do it." Dom paused on the porch and looked at Asterion. His cheeks were rosy, eyes bright, and his mouth half-open like he was about to speak. There was a beat, a moment where Asterion was so captivated by Dom's liveliness, the gently assertive way he'd argued, that Asterion half-forgot what they were talking about.

Dom chuckled and shook his head, a wide hand coming to cover his handsome smile. The bottom dropped entirely out of Asterion's stomach. Dom Silva was gorgeous; Asterion had to bite his own lip to keep from saying something about it. And Dom was single, somehow. And none of that meant anything to Asterion, because Dom was his landlord and had shown absolutely no signs of being interested in anything other than being precisely that.

"When you went shopping, did you buy a jacket?" Dom asked.

"How did you know I went shopping?" Asterion asked, crossing his arms over his chest.

"I don't know." Dom's blush deepened. Beautiful, Gods. "I guess I just assumed they didn't have crewnecks in—wherever you're from."

"It's called Andurnei. And they don't. And I did buy a jacket, but it's really not that cold—"

"You should grab it," Dom said, turning to unlock his door. "And boots. Do you have boots?"

"I do."

"Those too. Put them on and meet me around back." Asterion did as he was told, anticipation making him grin as he unlocked his own door and made his way up the stairs.

WHEN ASTERION ARRIVED IN THE BACKYARD, DOM WAS WEARING more leather than Asterion thought was strictly appropriate in daylight hours, tight in all the places that Asterion was trying hard not to notice. Beside him was the motorcycle, black and gleaming in the bright afternoon sun.

"Have you ever ridden a bicycle?" Dom asked, as Asterion approached.

"I've ridden a horse," Asterion offered. Dom pursed his lips.

"I've got no idea if that's similar or not."

"Where do I sit?"

"Behind me," Dom said. "But helmets and goggles first."

The helmet was sure to flatten his hair, and the goggles made the world seem a little foggy, but thankfully Asterion could still see Dom's shirt strain across Dom's chest as he turned and patted the six inches of seat behind him.

"Hop on."

"You want me to sit there?" Asterion asked, not sure he could manage to make that sound like a sincere complaint. Dom shrugged.

"You're the one who wanted a ride." Boy, did he.

Asterion rolled his eyes, mostly at himself and approached, deciding that he could have all the filthy thoughts he wanted so long as he kept them to himself. He was lonely. And Dom was good looking and competent and kind. It would have been impossible not to have a crush on him. Likely, everyone in town did, Asterion decided, as he delicately mounted the motorcycle behind Dom.

"Slide forward a bit," Dom said. Asterion bit his tongue. His knees were already astride Dom's hips, and his tailbone was hanging off the seat.

"I don't think there's room."

"Here, hang on." Before Asterion knew what was happening, Dom's hand wrapped around the back of Asterion's knee and yanked him forward. Asterion's thighs spread wide, his front pressed against Dom's back.

"Good Lord! Buy a man dinner first!" Asterion squawked into the back of Dom's neck. Dom chuckled.

"I already did."

"Jonas paid for that."

"I'll cook something tonight then. Hold on to me," Dom said, and before Asterion could say that there were very few places left where they weren't already touching, the engine roared to life between their legs. Asterion almost slipped off the beastly machine and was far too scared to be embarrassed. He wrapped his arms around Dom's waist, holding on tight as they rumbled out of the backyard and into the alley.

IT HAD BEEN A FEW YEARS SINCE DOM HAD BOTHERED TO MAKE the drive to Harlan's Crest. He and Ares used to go up all the time as boys, but now it reminded him too much of then to really be enjoyable. He'd gotten in the habit of avoiding anything that made him think about Ares more than he already did. Like he'd said to Nina the night before, his life was what it was. He knew enough to know it wasn't a bad lot, even if it was a little lonely sometimes. And at the moment, it wasn't even that.

At the moment, a very pretty man had his arms wrapped around Dom's waist. Asterion had straightened up a little while ago, not clinging for dear life anymore. The sun was setting to the west, and he could feel that that was the direction Asterion was turned. It was a beautiful sight, made all the nicer by the fresh air, far from the ports, and the crisp red and orange of the leaves that blurred as they drove past the forest that bounded in the Elmmond property.

About two miles further down, Dom turned them to the east, onto a dirt road that ran through the sparse edges of the forest. Eventually, the road widened into what passed for a parking lot, barely big enough to hold more than four cars.

When Dom put the bike into park, it wasn't silent, but there was a moment when the rumble of the motorcycle died away, that everything was quieter. Wind rustled through the trees; waves crashed against the cliffs far below. Asterion's hand splayed above Dom's hip, digging in slightly with his fingernails, as Asterion braced himself to dismount. It wasn't an intimate touch, but it sent shivers down Dom's spine anyway.

Dom hopped off, tucking his helmet and goggles into the saddle bag. Asterion was turned away, toward the setting sun, and maybe it was just the golden light, or the way the breeze caught Asterion's hair—blue wisps that reminded Dom of the foam caps of waves— but for a moment, looking at Asterion, Dom forgot to breathe.

"I can take your helmet," Dom offered. Asterion turned, and his smile was broad enough that Dom couldn't help but smile in return.

"That was brilliant."

"Not too fast for you?" Dom asked. Asterion shook his head,

stepping closer. He smelled like warm vanilla and a summer breeze.

"Does it go faster?" Asterion asked. Dom grinned.

"Yes. But not on these dirt roads." Asterion hummed, a similar sound to the one he'd made at the diner when he'd asked if Dom was seeing anyone. It wasn't disapproving, Dom decided, but it wasn't approval either. Like Asterion was considering an opinion and not saying it out loud. Restraint, like softness, wasn't something that Dom had expected from Asterion. But he liked knowing it was there.

Before Dom could think of anything to say, Asterion started toward the cluster of trees and the worn stone path that led to the cliffs.

"This way, actually," Dom said, heading to the left, through leaves that covered the slowly dying grass.

"But the path's over here," Asterion protested, even as he turned to follow. Dom smiled.

"I know. Come on."

18

Asterion could barely catch his breath. Exhilarating was the first word that came to mind, and not just because he'd spent the journey pressed against the sturdy wall of muscle that was Dom Silva's back. It felt wonderful to move hard and fast away from Hindry. Away from Elmmond House and Jonas, and the whole world that knew him.

Asterion had never considered what it might be like to be anonymous. He'd pretended before: donning masks at masquerades, gallivanting through the human world where people didn't know him. But humans still knew he was special, even if they couldn't place why. On Dom's motorcycle, driving into the unknown, with someone who knew what they were doing to guide him, without magic, Asterion was free in a way he never had been before. It made it all the easier to follow Dom now, intoxicated by the sense that they'd landed somewhere entirely new. Asterion's world had never felt so big.

The light was brighter, as they walked out of the forest, the sound of the water fading as they strayed from the cliffs. Dom led them to a small copse, where a wide, wooden swing hung from the branches of the largest tree in the little outcropping.

"Have a seat," Dom said, gesturing to the swing as he slid his jacket off his arms.

"Are you going to push me?" Asterion winked, too giddy still to stop himself. Dom only smirked, dropping his jacket against the base of the trunk.

"I think you can manage on your own, can't you? Or did you never learn how?" Asterion rolled his eyes as he sat on the wooden plank, thick ropes rough beneath his palms. The balls of his feet brushed the ground and Asterion pushed off, as Dom Silva reached up and grabbed the base of a low branch.

Asterion had seen people climb trees before, but Dom hung for a moment, biceps bulging beneath the short sleeves of his white undershirt. A shirt which must have been a size too small, as it also untucked itself to reveal a soft stomach, a trail of dark hair that started just above Dom's belly button. Dom grunted as he swung his leg up, boot catching gracefully in the vee of a lower branch. Asterion tried to be grateful that Dom half-disappeared amongst the leaves; it at least gave him time to readjust himself on the swing, arousal so sharp and sudden as to be distinctly uncomfortable.

It was a shame Dom never flirted back. He wasn't seeing anyone, but then maybe he didn't ever see anyone. And even if he did, he wouldn't pick Asterion. Dom didn't trust magic, and though Asterion didn't have magic anymore, he was sure that Dom still thought of him that way.

Asterion found Dom in the branches above him as Asterion continued to swing. He was sitting toward the trunk, reaching for something higher.

"What are you doing?" Asterion asked.

"Picking apples," Dom said. Asterion squinted up, looking for red or green orbs, which were difficult to spot among the changing leaves. "This tree always holds onto them a little longer than the others."

"Will you be making a pie later?"

"I can," Dom said. "Do you like apple pie?" Asterion blushed for no reason.

"I've never met a pie I didn't like, and I'll have you know I have a voracious sweet tooth. The shoo-fly pie Sidney gave me this morning was particularly divine."

"I'm not sure if I believe you about the sweets. You're as thin as a rail."

Asterion looked down at his stomach. Everything about him had narrowed and shrunk with his magic gone. Perhaps Jonas knew something about how his nutrition needs had changed without all the supplements magic provided.

"Apple?" Dom asked, boots thudding against a branch as he hopped down from the one above.

Asterion reached for it, trying, sort of, not to look up Dom's shirt. Dom dropped a bright red apple into Asterion's hands before he settled himself against the trunk.

"I didn't used to be so skinny," Asterion said, watching as Dom took a bite from his own apple. Dom arched an eyebrow, his attention immediate and intense. Asterion swallowed, nervous for no reason. He wasn't trying to sleep with Dom. It wouldn't ruin anything to be honest with him. "Fae magic," Asterion started, kicking out his legs, trying to swing himself higher. "It's what they call a 'natural' magic—morphological, technically—is concerned with the body. Healing, but also physical alteration and some aspects of growth. I wanted broader shoulders, golden skin, a muscular physique, so I had those things. But I could change them at any time, of course, or to suit someone else—"

"To suit someone else?" Dom interrupted. Asterion shrugged.

"Sure. Dating someone who likes a strong jaw, have a strong

jaw. Someone prefers dark hair, you have dark hair. You've never changed yourself for a partner before?"

"I mean, I didn't think you were supposed to." Dom's nose took on an adorable and judgmental wrinkle that Asterion didn't appreciate.

"You're not supposed to please your partner?"

"I was under the impression that partners are supposed to like you for who you are," Dom said. Asterion snorted.

"Maybe when you look like you, they do. The rest of us are stuck making whatever modifications we can manage." Perhaps that was showing his hand a bit, but Asterion didn't really care. Dom looked appropriately abashed. Served him right.

"I wouldn't know, I guess." Dom said after a moment. "I've never had a partner before."

Asterion laughed, sure that Dom was joking, but he stopped all at once, when Dom's face shuttered and he turned away.

"You're serious?" Asterion asked, too stunned to think of how rude it sounded. Dom continued to look off toward the sunset.

"It's not that shocking. Lots of people don't."

"No, no. Of course!" Asterion tried to amend. "Lots of people don't like sex or aren't—"

"I didn't say I didn't like it." Dom huffed, turning his glare onto Asterion. "I'm just busy. I have a lot of responsibilities. I don't have time."

"It doesn't have to take that long," Asterion said.

"I meant for a relationship!"

"Oh, well, the point still stands. It doesn't have to be serious."

"I guess. But, honestly, I don't know if I know how to be casual," Dom sighed. "About anything."

"I can see that," Asterion teased, even though it was true. Dom wasn't the sort to do anything by halves. It was ridiculously charming. "Your integrity should be applauded."

"It probably makes me boring."

"I'm not sure living a life of deceit is more interesting. More complicated, maybe."

"People don't actually do that, though, do they?" Dom asked. "Maybe in books, where the drama is interesting and not just painful?" Asterion thought of Desdemona Briarthorne. Of himself. How they toyed with each other, cruelties for the sake of what, exactly? Not pleasure. Entertainment, perhaps? Power? Just because it was what they'd been told they ought to be doing. Asterion took a deep breath, the cold air rushing into his lungs. The sun was lower on the horizon, spikes of orange illuminating distant thunderheads.

"Maybe," Asterion admitted. "But sometimes having the upper hand is more useful than being honest. Or being liked."

"I like you," Dom said. Asterion blinked up at him, tightness in his chest returning sharp and sudden. "I mean, I like you as you are now. And I don't get the sense that you've been lying to me or trying to cause problems."

"I've got enough problems without trying to make more. And what's the point of lying to you?" Asterion tried to imbue his words with any amount of derision. "You've already seen me at my worst. I mean, Gods, look at me. I'm hopeless. When we get home, you're going to have to teach me how to use a coffee pot. A *coffee pot*." Dom's gaze had turned toward the sunset, but Asterion could see the corner of his mouth lift in a smile.

"I don't mind teaching you."

"That's because you're too nice for your own good," Asterion accused. Dom shook his head.

"When Ares disappeared, it was like I'd gone to bed in one life and woken up in a different one. If my Aunt and Uncle hadn't been there to help me, I don't know where I'd have ended up. I didn't know how to do any of the things he'd been doing."

"You took his place?" It explained some things about Dom's

life, Asterion supposed; a mystery he hadn't realized he wanted to solve.

"I didn't have a choice, exactly. It's not like there was anyone else around to pick up the pieces, take care of the diner. It was just us. And then it was just me."

"Well, you're very good at it," Asterion said. Dom snorted.

"Thanks." It was the first time Asterion had ever heard him sound less than sincere. Asterion cocked an eyebrow, sensing he'd unearthed something.

"What?"

"Nothing," Dom shook his head. "It took me a long time to get good at running the diner. I had a lot to learn. That's what I was trying to say. You're learning. You're trying. That goes a long way."

"I don't have a choice either, I suppose," Asterion said.

"You could have stayed with Jonas."

"Jonas can only tolerate me for so long. And besides, I don't like being helpless. And don't say that matters, because no one likes being helpless."

"No one likes being helpless, but you're trying to learn not to be. *That's* what matters."

And that shouldn't have meant anything to Asterion. But it felt good to know that Dom did like him, even if he was giving Asterion too much credit. Or perhaps Asterion wasn't giving himself enough credit. He'd never considered it before.

Dom hopped down out of the tree, landing with a grunt that allowed Asterion to ignore his self-esteem issues in favor of attempting to commit that particular sound to memory.

"Do you want to go over and see the water? We'll have to head back soon. I forgot how early it gets dark these days."

"Alright." Asterion drug his heels in the dirt, appreciating the stretch in his legs, the smile on Dom's face, and the sweet, crisp taste of apple, as he took his first bite.

19

It took less than ten minutes to explain the french press to Asterion, and then he was busy making coffee, so Dom decided to heat up some leftover soup from the icebox. They worked in tandem, quietly, pleasantly, even, as the darkness of night crept in around the edges of the apartment, the wind making the windows rattle as it gathered steam.

"Dom," Asterion groaned Dom's name, his mouth full of the first bite of creamy parsnip soup and day-old sourdough. Dom forced himself not to react to the sound. It was just a compliment. He needed to grow up. "It's so good. How is it so good?" Dom glanced over, only to be confronted with an expression of ecstasy on Asterion's face that made Dom blush and look back down at his own plate.

"Thanks. It's my mom's recipe."

"You've done her extremely proud," Asterion said. Dom tried not to let it go to his head, but he was pleased. He liked cooking for people, and it made him happy when a recipe got a positive reaction. That was why he was so warm. Dom leaned back and took a sip from his glass of water. "She taught you how to cook?"

"She did. She was a cook. And her mother was a baker,"

Dom said. "The diner was theirs first. And then when my mom passed, it sort of... My dad worked on the trawlers. And Ares was young, but by the time he was done with high school, our dad wasn't in good enough shape to take it on. Hector stepped in to help, but when Ares could take it over, he did."

"And then you did," Asterion said. He was pulling apart a piece of bread, but his golden eyes were watching Dom intently.

"I still cook her recipes. And some of my grandmother's too. Most of the pies are hers. My Aunt Ree always told us grandma had a sweet tooth too."

"A woman after my own heart," Asterion grinned. Dom smiled down at his soup. He was having a nice time. The thought struck him like a static shock, small but noticeable. How many days had he gone without enjoying himself before this one? He'd told himself that he didn't mind being lonely. He'd been saying it for so long that he'd thought he willed it into truth. But now that he had company, he didn't want Asterion to leave.

"You know," Dom said, apropos of nothing, because he could think of no obvious lead-in. "They'll replay *Nocturne Mystery Theatre* in half an hour, or," he glanced at the clock, "closer to twenty minutes. If you want to try and catch the end."

"You mean to find out if Cassandra gets out of that hole?" Asterion scrunched up his face, an obvious judgement on a weak plot point. Dom was obligated to defend the show, not because the writing was good, but because it was his favorite.

"It's not a hole. It's a cave."

"Oh, and you expect me to believe that makes some great difference?"

"It matters," Dom assured him. It did matter because there was an important key hidden in the cave, but Asterion didn't get to find that out, because once again he fell asleep half an hour into the show.

Dom smirked at him from the armchair opposite the couch. Asterion's wiry arms clutched a throw pillow to his chest, and his head rested on the arm of the sofa. By the looks of things, sharing a bed with Asterion meant you were liable to get snuggled to death. Not that Dom would have minded.

It was such a startlingly invasive thought that it woke Dom from his after-dinner stupor.

He needed to get up. Dom needed to clean up the dinner dishes and did not need to not think about sleeping next to Asterion. He should have woken Asterion, but the show was almost over, and it wasn't going to hurt anything to let him rest, if Dom could just keep himself under control.

But as he was cleaning, Asterion was where his thoughts strayed. Dom didn't know anything about magic, but it made sense to him that the loss of it would make Asterion tired. And he was so thin; the fact that his weight loss was noticeable over only the few days of their acquaintance, even if it was just the magic that had done it, seemed bad. Dom wanted to feed him and let him sleep. The couch was comfortable enough. Dom had spent more than a few nights on it himself.

He was just being a good host, that was all. Nothing more to it than that.

A bowl slipped out of Dom's hands and clattered loudly against the pot in the sink. Asterion jerked awake.

"What the—?!"

"Sorry," Dom said, lifting soapy hands in apology and explanation. "It slipped!"

"Oh. What? Oh." Asterion's brow furrowed but he laid his head back down, and Dom went back to cleaning. When he glanced up from the sink, Asterion was beside him, and he jumped.

"Why are you doing the washing up?" Asterion frowned. "You cooked."

"It's fine."

"Do you think I can't do the washing up?"

"You were asleep," Dom insisted. Asterion glared at him, but his hair was smushed to the side of his face and he was too out of sorts for Dom to take him seriously. "You're company."

"I live here," Asterion said. Dom hadn't quite considered it that way, but he couldn't argue the point. Didn't really want to.

"That's true. I mean," Dom considered. "You don't live here. You live," he pointed up at the ceiling. "And it seems like it might be your bedtime."

"I'm taking the french press."

"I brought it for you," Dom said. Asterion blinked at him, then he scowled.

"Thank you." Asterion padded over to the french press and scooped it up off the counter, holding it to his chest like a baby.

"Do you have coffee?" Dom asked, turning back to the pot in the sink.

"In the tea cabinet," he yawned. "I missed the end of the show again. Was it a cave or a hole?"

"It was a cave."

"Are you sure? Seems like a hole makes more sense."

"Go to bed, Asterion."

"Goodnight," Asterion said, turning and padding toward the door. "Thank you for dinner and for the drive. I had a lovely time."

Dom glanced up then, and maybe it was a mistake. Asterion was unavoidably lovely, all his edges softened by sleep, the corner of his mouth curled up in a smile as he caught Dom's eye.

"Goodnight," Dom said, and his voice sounded unfamiliar, steeped in something that made his chest ache. Something he was terrified to even think of a word for.

Asterion didn't seem to notice, just opened the back door that led to the stairs that ran between their apartments and left.

The sound of the door closing rattled something loose in Dom. Maybe loneliness was familiar, but it felt newly sharpened, as though having a nice evening with company had taken a whet stone to it. Dom had been alone for too long. He ought to have Nina and Casey over.

As he finished the dishes, he made a mental plan for a dinner party he wouldn't end up throwing because he didn't have the time. But thinking about it was a good way to close out the evening. It at least helped him stifle the strange longing that was still making his chest tight.

And if he was going to host a party, he'd have to invite Asterion. After all, the man did live just upstairs.

20

"Dom!" Ugh. It was too early in the morning for running, but from his perch in the front bay window, where he'd been enjoying his coffee, Asterion saw Dom leave. It was late enough that Asterion had been sure he'd already missed him. But there he was. Asterion hopped up and hurried down the stairs. "Dom!"

Dom turned; the collar of his black motorcycle jacket was tucked beneath his stubbled chin. Asterion realized how cold his feet were on the concrete. And how oddly warm his chest was.

"Something wrong with the french press?" Dom asked, a teasing smirk drawing up the corner of his handsome mouth. Asterion huffed.

"No. I'm practically an expert. Best coffee I've had in days. No. I was doing my breakfast dishes, and I heard a sound. I think the kitchen sink is leaking."

"Really leaking? Or just a little?" Asterion rolled his eyes and did a small series of stamps to try and warm his feet, tugging the cardigan he'd pulled on over his pajamas around himself.

"I genuinely, Dom, genuinely don't know what that means. Is

the floor covered in water? No. Is there water coming out of places it shouldn't be? Yes." Dom sighed and pulled his hands from his pockets.

"Alright, let me take a look."

Asterion had been trying to be a good tenant, that was all. He certainly didn't want to get blamed for damaging something that he hadn't damaged. He'd heard the slow trickle of water even after the faucet was off, and so he'd crouched down and squinted into the darkness below the sink and agreed with himself that yes, something down there was making a dripping sound. Sink repair basically accomplished.

Back in the apartment, Dom took off his jacket and got down on his knees, straining the fabric of his trousers across his back-side as he ducked his gorgeous head of hair below the counter. He moved things around, and then, without warning or cere-mony, he flipped over, laid on his back, and with a small noise of effort that made Asterion's hips jolt, pulled himself under the sink. His shirt rode up (did this man own no shirts of an appro-priate size?) and Asterion thought it might be for the best if he turned around and stared out the window, for everyone's decency. Before he could move, Dom huffed, and Asterion was captivated.

"Yeah." Dom bent his arm and reached beneath the sink, the bulge of his bicep nearly enough to bring Asterion to tears. "I think there's a toolbox in the coat closet on the top shelf. Do you mind?"

Asterion found the toolbox and brought it over. Dom grabbed a tool and then disappeared into the cabinet again. There was a squeak of metal and a small grunt from Dom that made Asterion instinctively swallow, and then Dom sat up, brushing several errant curls away from his face.

"Alright, try that," he said. Asterion tucked his cardigan around himself, grateful for its length, and stepped forward, turning on the faucet as Dom watched below the counter. "I think it's just the joint was loose, but I'll get some putty from the hardware store to be sure," he said. He grabbed the edge of the counter and pulled himself up to standing, so that he and Asterion were suddenly beside each other. Asterion turned off the water and took a half a step back. For decency's sake.

"Thank you," Asterion said. Dom shrugged.

"Thanks for letting me know," he grinned as he picked his coat up off the chair he'd tossed it over. "I have the lunch and dinner shifts tonight, so I won't be home to make you more soup. But if you come to the diner, I'll make sure you get a hot meal."

"Do you need any help? At the diner, I mean." Dom put the toolbox back up on the shelf, glancing at Asterion.

"Do you want to help?"

"I think we can both agree I don't do well in isolation. And I enjoyed myself yesterday." And if he wanted to make himself miserable by spending more than his fair share of time in Dom's presence, that was no one's business but his own.

"Alright." Dom said with a shrug. "I can put you to work." Asterion grinned.

"Free meals for staff, right?" Dom rolled his eyes, but he was chuckling as he started down the stairs.

"Be there by noon! Don't be late."

DOM STARTED HIS SHIFT IN THE KITCHEN. HE'D PROMISED THE local women's auxiliary a donation of three cakes for their holiday cake walk. Little tasks for folks in the community kept him busy in the lulls. Nina was preparing sandwich ingredients for the lunch rush, and Dom had the wide center station to himself, so he spread out, humming along with the radio as he worked.

"You're in good spirits," Nina said, looking up from her cutting board of sliced tomatoes with a smirk.

"So?"

"I'm not sure I've heard you hum in the last six years."

"Shut up," Dom chuckled. "Am I not allowed to be in a good mood?"

"You're allowed. I'm not sure I like it though."

"Wait until I have to ice these. The sour attitude will come back quick." Nina laughed, and Dom smiled to himself, thinking about last night. How much fun he'd had. When was the last time he'd felt this way? Lighter? Between the sudden potential for answers about Ares, and Asterion's company, he was just in a better mood. That was all. And if Asterion made it to work on time, they might even have enough staff to manage lunch.

Dom was two cakes deep, the third, just about ready to come out of the oven when he heard a commotion from outside the kitchen. He wiped his hands on his apron and pushed through the swinging door to find half a trawler crew settling themselves at two tables that Sidney and Hector were still in the process of pushing together. Asterion was there too. He must have come in the front, and was already dutifully laying down plates and cutlery, an apron tied around his waist.

He was in his most staid outfit yet, though it didn't make him any less attractive. The angles of his face and the soft blue of his hair only made him stand out. His light grey knit sweater tucked into dark grey wool trousers, tightly belted around his waist. The way his clothes hugged him showed off the almost inhuman grace with which he moved. Asterion seemed to have a magical (though it couldn't have been) way of fitting into small spaces, and then filling larger ones. Maybe it was the breadth of his smile, or the way he turned his shoulders. Maybe it was just that he was making more room for himself in Dom's mind than Dom had ever anticipated.

Asterion stepped back and pulled up his hair, quickly exposing the freckles that dotted his neck and ran behind his ear, where today, three silver teardrop earrings dragged Dom's gaze to the line of Asterion's throat. Warmth curled beneath the collar of Dom's shirt, and he rolled up his sleeves absently as he watched Asterion and Sidney take the fishermen's orders.

"We've got it covered out here," Hector said, appearing beside Dom so quietly that Dom nearly crashed into the coffee maker. Hector chuckled. "Sorry. I thought you saw me coming." But no, he'd been too busy watching Asterion lean down to take a fisherman's order. "Go help Nina with the griddle," Hector said, scooping up the coffee pot and heading back to the table.

Yes. That would be more helpful than noticing the way the man at the end of the table was saying something that made Asterion laugh. It was Anders, from two days ago, and if Dom had even considered for a second that Anders had been flirting with him then (he hadn't been) what he was doing with Asterion was practically obscene. Anders leaned in to point at something on the menu, asking a question Dom couldn't hear. Their shoulders brushed, Asterion lifted an eyebrow and Anders said something else that had Asterion laughing again. Then he leaned up to say something closer to Asterion's ear, and Asterion leaned down, and Dom's good mood vanished as he turned around and swung back into the kitchen.

Between orders and cakes, Dom was busy enough that he barely looked up when Asterion went out to smoke with Nina a couple of hours later. Sidney left and then Hector left, and the evening crew rolled in before Asterion cornered Dom by the sink. He was trapped, his hands covered in suds and half the cutlery still under water.

"You need to take a break."

"I'm fine," Dom said, wishing his cheeks weren't suddenly so hot. Why was he so hot?

"I made you a sandwich." Dom did glance up then, and Asterion grinned. "Don't look so horrified. Nina supervised. I told her I wanted to learn how to cook bacon."

"Oh."

"She told me I was pathetic. I told her she didn't have to try so hard to get me into bed." Dom nearly choked.

"And she punched you?"

"Some people find me amusing. Charming, even. Now, come on." Asterion reached forward into the water, yanking his hand back before he could find Dom's under the suds. "Gods above! That is so hot!"

"It has to be hot," Dom said, rinsing off before turning off the faucet with his wrist.

"Do you still have skin on your hands? Do you need a bowl of ice? Christ, Dom!"

"I know you don't have 'Christ' in Andurnei."

"Sidney taught me. It rolls so well off the tongue!" He turned and walked over to the small, wobbly table in the corner where some staff took breaks, and Hector left his old newspapers folded up, crosswords half done. Two plates sat opposite each other, each holding a bacon and tomato sandwich and a pile of french fries.

The bacon was perfectly done, crispy but not burnt. Dom devoured half his sandwich in two bites.

"Thanks," he said, after he'd swallowed. "I was hungrier than I thought."

"I could tell. You're not usually such a grouch." Dom knew he was blushing again and put a french fry into his mouth for something to do.

"Are you going to head home soon?" Dom asked.

"I don't think so. We don't close until ten, do we?" Asterion bit into his sandwich, mayonnaise smearing across the corner of his mouth. Dom looked around desperately for a napkin.

"You don't have to stay the whole time."

"What else am I going to do? Though, I did invite Sidney and Jonas over for breakfast tomorrow."

"Here?" Dom asked.

"At the house." Asterion said.

"Do you have breakfast food?"

"There's plenty of bacon in the walk-in." Asterion pointed to the walk-in. Dom lifted an eyebrow, and Asterion cocked his head to the side. "Or... that's not my bacon."

"No." Dom gave him a small smile. "It's not."

"No," Asterion agreed. Then he hummed. "I ought to go grocery shopping."

"Probably."

"But what do I get?" Asterion frowned. "I only know how to cook bacon."

"Do you have paper?" Dom asked, reaching for the stack of newspapers, where there'd at least be a pencil. Asterion produced a folded napkin from his pocket and grabbed the pencil as it tumbled from the pile of paper and clattered to the table between them. "I'll tell you what to get, and then I'll come up and help you tomorrow morning. I'm only on dinner shift, so I'll have time." Asterion flipped open a folded napkin.

"Have I told you lately that you are very kind and generous?" Dom kept his head down to hide his grin.

"You may have mentioned it."

"Well, you are. Exceedingly kind and generous. Alright," Asterion took a deep breath. "What do I need?"

"Let's see." Dom glanced at the napkin, and it took him a moment to realize that there was already writing on it. A name and address scrawled upside down on the thin paper. *Anders Casmir. 72 Bernes Street.*

All breakfast food vacated Dom's mind. He bit his bottom lip and tried to stifle the words that were bubbling up in his chest. It made sense that Asterion to be getting addresses. Making plans with people other than Dom. It was a good thing. Dammit.

"Maybe we should find you something else to write on. You don't want to accidentally lose that." Ugh. Crumpling up the napkin and throwing it across the room would have been more subtle. Thankfully, Asterion didn't seem to notice.

"Oh, I don't know." Asterion hesitated, his eyes skating over the name. "Do you know him?"

"He's been in a few times." Dom frowned. He should have been pleased that Asterion wasn't more excited. But instead, he liked the lack of enthusiasm even less. "Did he ask if he could give you that? Was he being too pushy?"

"Huh?" Asterion cocked his head to the side, and then after a moment he laughed. "Oh. No. It was fine, really."

"If anyone in here ever makes you uncomfortable, you don't have to serve them. Come get me. Or Hector. We'll take care of it."

"That's very sweet," Asterion was blushing, his golden gaze drifting over Dom's face as his smile widened. "I'm sure you get your fair share of passes from customers." Dom scoffed and shook his head.

"Most people around here know better."

"What does that mean?" Asterion asked.

"It means they know how busy I am. How I just—I'm just a fixture in this place. This diner, this town. It'd be like asking out the phone booth on the corner." Dom tried to smile, but Asterion was already shaking his head and rolling his eyes.

"You're delusional, Dom Silva."

"What?"

"Nothing." Asterion scratched through Anders' name and address before Dom could tell him not to. "What do I need to buy for breakfast?"

21

For the first time in his life, Asterion had set an alarm. Jonas and Sidney were coming at nine, and that meant Asterion had to get up because he had things to cook. Except, it was already seven thirty. The alarm clock had gone off half an hour ago and Asterion still lay in bed, staring at the ceiling. Rain pounded down on the roof outside so loudly that he could barely hear his own heartbeat. But it wasn't loud enough to drown out his thoughts.

The mirror mounted above the dresser across from his bed had greeted Asterion that morning with his own unfriendly reflection. His appearance was so appalling that he'd immediately lay back down and resolved not to get up again. The beginnings of a beard, the palest blue against his freckled skin looked like the first fuzz of mold. Like an algae bloom. Like his father.

Kyrian had been a handsome man by all accounts. His hair, in particular, stayed a seafoam teal well into that later centuries of his life. But vanity wasn't the problem. Or at least, it wasn't the entire problem. Asterion had always been a calculated disappointment to his father, and the last place he wanted to see the man was in his own bedroom mirror. And Asterion didn't know how to shave.

To anyone else it would have barely been an inconvenience, but it had sent Asterion spiraling. His father had been dead twenty years, after a long and very lauded lifetime of kingship, but Asterion couldn't bring himself to miss him. He didn't miss any of his family, really. He worried about his older sister, who was sure to take the brunt of their mother's bad behavior and their brother's assassination attempts as the new head of state. His older brother, Kephisto was their mother's favorite, despite the potential regicide. Asterion was the third son, only good for being amusing or disappointing, and more often the former than the latter. Neither of his parents had ever shy about telling him so.

Asterion put his hand on his chin, lost in thought, and stubble prickled against the pads of his fingers. He jerked his hand away. Dom was going to be so annoyed when he came upstairs and found Asterion still in bed. Dom, who looked so good with stubble, dark hair shadowing his jawbone, making it seem even sharper than it was. Asterion wished Dom was only good-looking. But he was kind, and funny. And Asterion was going to disappoint him. Just like he disappointed everyone else.

It was a thought he couldn't bear. It would be an indignity too far to let down his landlord, so with an audible whine and followed by an over-exaggerated groan, Asterion heaved himself out of bed. He began to dress, only getting as far as pulling on a pair of corduroy trousers until another accidental glance in the mirror made him scowl. He'd purchased a long black cashmere scarf on his shopping trip, and it was still sitting in the box on his dresser. Asterion tugged it out, wrapped it around the lower half of his face and stomped into the kitchen to make coffee.

∾

Dom's alarm clock rang, interrupting a dream which vanished the minute he opened his eyes. He fumbled for the brass clock on his nightstand, struggling against sheets twined around his shoulders, and the discomfort of an extremely stiff erection. Whatever he'd been dreaming about, it must have been pleasant.

He finally managed to silence the alarm with a well-placed slam of his palm and collapsed back into the sheets. Half an hour before he had to be upstairs. He needed to shower and dress. It would take longer to wait for his hard on to go away than it would to deal with it.

Jerking off was perfunctory to Dom. Being single for as long as he had been meant that he had a reliable rhythm when it came to self-pleasure, and rarely was there time to relax and enjoy it. He had a few stock fantasies that worked every time, each of them absolutely lifted wholesale from the small stash of erotic novels he'd collected over the years. There was only one bookstore within driving distance of Hindry, and the proprietor was an older woman who Dom already felt embarrassed ordering his favorite pulp novels from. Any erotica he'd gotten, he'd found in thrift stores and charity shops, stashed among the regular books, unnoticed by the overworked employees.

One of his favorites was *Desires of the Desperado*, a filthy book that primarily told the story of the kidnapping of a sheriff's deputy by a wicked desperado and the members of his gang. The bulk of the story was about the gang holding the deputy for ransom, using him for their pleasure in the meantime.

Dom thought about the scene where, after a day of being bound to the wall, smacked and teased and taunted and prodded, the gang abandoned the deputy, leaving him so they could all go off to do some vague villainy. The deputy tried to escape, when of course, down the stairs, came the desperado.

'Easy there, Deputy,' the desperado's dark eyes gleamed in the low lamp light.

Dom imagined the way he'd squirm as the desperado ran his black-leather-gloved fingers over the ridges of Dom's ribs, and then lower, over the edge of his hip bone before sliding down over his backside.

There were words exchanged then. Dom couldn't remember them exactly, and it didn't matter. One hand brushed lightly over a nipple before sliding over Dom's throat, into his hair, grasping, pulling his head back. Dom moaned at the thought, imagined the glove coming off, long slender pale fingertips sliding against his lips before Asterion pushed his middle and fore fingers into Dom's mouth and forced him to—

No.

Wait.

Dom was not about to start masturbating to thoughts of Asterion tying him up and forcing his fingers into Dom's mouth. Actually, Dom wasn't about to start masturbating to thoughts of Asterion doing anything. He took his hand off his cock and opened his eyes, staring at the blank wall beyond his bedside table, trying to get his thoughts under control.

Yes, Asterion was very good looking. Yes, he was clever and funny and many other things. He was also a prince, not a desperado. And an actual person, not someone for Dom to dress up like a cowboy and parade around in his dirty fantasies.

The desperado had dark eyes, dark hair, sunburned skin and wicked rasp to his voice. Dom forced himself to recast the role in his mind's eye: rougher, meaner, calloused fingers pressing down against Dom's tongue.

That was better. Dom closed his eyes again and thrust his hips up slowly, brushing his cock lightly along his palm. The desperado slid behind his hips, rubbing a still-clothed crotch against his ass.

'*My boys have been a little rough with you today, haven't they?*' Asterion murmured, his soft lips brushing against the shell of Dom's ear. '*Now it's my turn.*'

Dom released himself with a frustrated groan. He was so close he was aching, but he just couldn't. It wasn't right. How would he feel if Asterion was upstairs fantasizing about Dom while he masturbated? His slender body arching against the mattress, heels digging into the sheets as he moaned Dom's name.

Oh, God.

Dom's cock throbbed and he grit his teeth. Arousal had removed every scrap of decency and rationality from Dom's head. It was the desperado or nothing. Not Asterion. Certainly not Asterion upstairs, all alone in Dom's spare bed. His pillows. His sheets.

Dom bit his lip. He was going back to the desperado fantasy. He was going to come in three strokes, take a shower, get dressed, and go help Asterion cook breakfast.

His own hand was calloused, marred with a dozen small scars from cuts and burns in the kitchen, and he stroked himself roughly, quickly. In the story, the desperado teased the deputy cruelly, touching him, stroking him, then letting go right before the deputy's release, bringing him right up to the edge over and over again. Dom had managed that part at least.

He turned his head slightly, pushing his face into the blanket. The same blanket Asterion had slept under. It smelled like vanilla and a summer breeze, and it would have felt so good to have Asterion rocking against him, teasing him. Asterion and the desperado morphed into one person again, and Dom moaned, too close now to stop.

'*Look how desperate you are,*' Asterion's voice purred the lines from the book. Dom panted, knowing the next bit by heart, hating himself as his pleasure mounted. *'Come on, cowboy. Come for me.'*

He twisted against the sheets, moaning, cock pulsing, as he came harder than he had in years. Dom slowly became aware of the heat of his skin, and the way his heart was still pounding in his chest.

God, that was so...

Not good. Don't think 'good.'

It would never happen again. And if Dom felt embarrassed about it, which he did, he was going to have to get over that very quickly, because he had to look Asterion in the eye in approximately fifteen minutes.

Or he could just stay in bed and die of shame.

He wanted to, but he couldn't. Asterion needed his help. So, Dom got up and climbed into the shower, totally resolved to never in his whole life think about it ever again. He was going to have to get rid of *Desires of the Desperado* too, for his own sanity.

By the time he got out of the shower, he was almost late. He threw on jeans, an undershirt, a sweater, and slippers were going to have to do for shoes. He grabbed his good cast iron skillet off its hook beside the stove and hurried up the back stairs. Dom knocked twice on Asterion's door, and then took a deep breath and scrambled to remember what a regular, totally unashamed facial expression looked like.

Unfortunately, Dom failed at making a regular face, because when Asterion opened the door, his golden eyes were glinting at Dom from above a black scarf that was draped to cover his mouth and nose. Very much like a desperado might wear. Dom felt his own eyes go wide.

"What?" Asterion snapped.

"What are you wearing?"

"You're late."

"No, I'm not." Dom ducked his head and pushed in past

Asterion. Ingredients littered the kitchen counter. Not all of which were ingredients Dom had asked for, but that was alright. He was relieved to have a problem to solve that didn't involve looking at Asterion for any amount of time.

"I did what you told me to do," Asterion said. Dom nodded, as he began moving things around on the counter.

"You did. Mostly."

"Mostly?" Asterion huffed, and Dom couldn't help but smile.

"Take the fruit bowl and the toast to the table."

"Some of the pieces of toast are burnt." Asterion brushed Dom's arm accidentally as he came up beside him, and Dom glanced up at the same moment that Asterion's scarf slipped off his chin. The blue stubble on his cheek looked like a brush of icing sugar. Dom's brain shorted out as he tried to stifle the urge to lean in and lick the sharp line of Asterion's jaw. What was wrong with him?

Thankfully, breakfast prep involved a lot of Dom paying attention to cutting up potatoes and cracking eggs, and not watching Asterion flit around behind him, fussing with the table setting. It wasn't until the potatoes were sizzling happily in the cast iron, that Dom dared to look back at Asterion. Only once, and very quickly, over his shoulder.

"I like your beard." Asterion jerked to a stop, his whole body stiffening unnaturally. Dom frowned. "Asterion?"

"You like it?" Asterion's tone was absolutely void of emotion, as he pulled his scarf back over his chin. Dom had no idea what he'd done wrong, but he apologized anyway.

"Sorry, I—"

"It's not good manners to retract a compliment." Asterion's back and shoulders were rigid as he leaned forward to rotate an empty plate.

"Are you okay?"

"Fine," Asterion snipped. Dom blinked and tried again.

"Are you... not a fan of facial hair?"

"I hate it," Asterion replied without looking up. He shifted a spoon a centimeter to the left and then put it back.

"Well," Dom tried for levity as he brushed a hand against his own stubble. "I'll try not to take it personally."

"Not on others." Asterion looked at Dom and rolled his eyes pointedly, as though this was obvious. "Only on myself."

"Why don't you shave?"

"And take my own head off?"

"You've never shaved before?" Dom asked, incredulous.

"I've never had to," Asterion huffed, waggling his fingers at Dom. "Magic, remember?" Dom hadn't remembered, and he felt bad for forgetting.

"I can teach you how to shave. You just need a safety razor and some shaving cream, and you're more than welcome to borrow mine." Asterion stopped fussing with the place settings and looked over at Dom. Then he crossed his arms over his chest, like he didn't believe him.

"Are you sure?"

"Of course I'm sure," Dom said, even though he wasn't exactly. Getting into Asterion's personal space probably wasn't a great idea, considering the way his thoughts had been drifting all morning. But if it was upsetting Asterion so much to have a little stubble, well then Dom could put his own discomfort aside for ten minutes and teach Asterion how to shave.

"Alright," Asterion sighed, turning immediately toward the back stairs. "Let's go."

22

Dom took an extra moment to stir the potatoes in the oven, and Asterion sulked. He hated having to ask Dom for assistance. Again. And Dom had been strangely quiet all morning, very consumed with the chopping and mixing of ingredients, which was probably normal, but wasn't doing anything to settle Asterion's nerves. Why had he thought he could host a gathering? In the past, having people over for breakfast took no more effort from Asterion than rolling out of bed and into an outfit. But this was different. This was hard.

Asterion followed Dom downstairs, into Dom's apartment and down the hall toward the bedroom.

"Are you sure we have enough time?" Asterion asked. Dom nodded.

"It won't take long. There's barely anything to shave." Easy for him to say.

The bathroom in Dom's bedroom was identical to the one upstairs, but the walls were dark blue, and a panel of stained glass hung above the mirror. Dom's bedroom was a lovely shade of green, and the living room had a bright orange pattern on the walls.

"Who painted?" Asterion asked.

"Me." Dom gestured Asterion to the toilet, and then opened the medicine cabinet that hung on the narrow sliver of wall beside the door.

"It's so much more colorful than upstairs."

"Well," Dom cleared his throat, turning toward Asterion with a metal apparatus in his hand. "When I decided to rent the space, Hector convinced me that muted colors would be more appealing to people."

"It's bland," Asterion said, criticizing because he was in a bad mood. Dom chuckled all the same.

"I know. When it was Ares', it was full of plants. And he had these great wall hangings."

"What happened to them?" Dom shrugged, his smile fading.

"Storage."

"We could splash some paint on the walls if you want," Asterion offered. "I wouldn't say no to a bit of color. A little chartreuse, maybe."

"You've painted?" Dom asked, his tone teasing.

"I've pointed at walls and told people what color to paint them." Asterion shrugged. "I can do that for you too if you like. How are you at taking orders?"

Dom's cheeks flushed in exactly the same way they had on the stairs earlier. His gaze was down, as though he was expecting the floor to move beneath his feet. His chuckle sounded forced.

But when Dom looked up, he met Asterion's gaze with an appealing expression of determination. His brown eyes were wide and for the first time Asterion could see that his irises were flecked not just with grey, but with specks of shining silver. Before Asterion quite knew what was happening, Dom stepped forward and lifted his hand toward Asterion's scarf. He only hesitated when his fingertips brushed the black fabric.

Asterion pulled his scarf down and then off, saving Dom the trouble and attempting to stave off his own unbidden pang of desire. It was only then that Asterion realized he'd not finished dressing. He was still in his silk pajama shirt.

Dom reached back for a blue tube on the sink, avoiding Asterion's eye. Asterion couldn't decide what to make of it. He was pale and strangely angled, the handsome glow he projected over his skin fully gone. He had stubble, for Gods' sakes! It seemed highly unlikely that *this* version of himself was making Dom blush, when his earlier self, still transformed, still beautiful, definitely hadn't.

Dom opened the tube and squeezed a thick, lotion looking white substance into his palm.

"Shaving cream," Dom said, as he stepped forward, holding out his hand. His hand came within an inch of Asterion's chin. Then he hesitated again.

"I'm not sure we can manage this without you touching me," Asterion said, annoyed by Dom's sudden weird aversion to looking him in the eye. "If that's a problem—"

"No," Dom said quickly, his flush now broaching the tops of his ears. "It's fine. Tilt your chin up." Asterion did as he was told, turning his eyes up toward the ceiling as Dom pressed the white cream against his jawbone, spreading it with his fingertips toward the point of Asterion's chin.

Asterion exhaled slowly. The touch of another person, even as clinical as this was, soothed him. Or it just felt good. Or something. He could feel his shoulders relax, and what did it say about him that the simplest way to improve his mood was to be tended to? Babied and coddled.

No. He wasn't being babied. He was learning. Wasn't that what Dom had said before? Asterion forced himself to focus on the movement of Dom's hands, and the light soapy scent of the shaving cream. Dom's brow was furrowed in concentration as he slid his fingers around to the other side of Asterion's jaw. Dom turned away, rinsing his palm before he picked up the silver razor from the edge of the sink.

"I'm going to do one side, and you'll do the other," he said with the same easy tone of command that he took in the diner. Perfectly fine. Asterion was going to be attentive to this lesson, because that was what it was. He ignored the shiver of want that tingled up his spine as Dom tilted Asterion's chin up, two fingers pressing into his jaw. It wasn't like that. It wasn't.

The silence returned. Their knees kept bumping, but that was unavoidable, as Dom was practically straddling Asterion's thigh to get close to him. Which Asterion definitely wasn't thinking about or paying attention to.

"Alright. Up," Dom said before Asterion had managed to focus on shaving at all. Dom stepped back, and Asterion stood, moving forward to look in the mirror. The skin on the right side of his face was clean and clear of the offending fuzz, and he couldn't help but let out a sigh of relief. Dom handed Asterion the razor. "Now you know what it feels like, I think you can get the rest. Start at the top." Asterion placed the razor on his left cheek and Dom reached up, adjusting his hand. "There. Steady, short movements. You don't have to push."

Asterion looked at himself in the mirror and concentrated. It was easier than he'd expected, and didn't take much time at all. He made it to the last stroke of the blade without embarrassing himself, until, of course, his eyes drifted toward Dom's reflection in the mirror. Dom was leaning against the doorframe, muscular forearms folded over his chest, an appreciative smile turning up the corners of his lips. Asterion hissed as he nicked the skin beneath his chin.

"Here." Dom pushed off the wall and grabbed a tissue from the back of the toilet. He slid in front of Asterion, turning Asterion's head with his fingers to look at the cut under Asterion's chin, pressing the folded paper against the small spill of blood.

Dom was wedged between the sink and Asterion's hips, his teeth pressing into his bottom lip as he frowned at Asterion's injury. Asterion could feel his own pulse in his throat. His mouth was dry.

"Not bad for your first time," Dom said after a moment. Asterion rolled his eyes and snorted.

"Oh, please."

Dom chuckled and glanced up at Asterion. And even though Asterion was trying to be irritated, he couldn't help but smile back.

And that was when Dom leaned forward and kissed him.

Dom's rough, full lips brushed against Asterion's mouth and Asterion's knees got unaccountably wobbly. The spiced smell of Dom and the caress of his thumb against Asterion's chin almost made Asterion whimper, and when Dom pulled away, Asterion chased his mouth like he'd never been kissed before.

More. Gods. He needed more.

Asterion leaned forward as his eyes opened again, and he was surprised to see Dom's mouth hanging open in shock. As though someone had slapped him. Before Asterion could say anything (and what was he going to say?) Dom ducked around him with record speed, and was halfway out the bathroom door before Asterion could stop him. Dom swung around, his eyes wide as they met Asterion's.

"I am so sorry," he breathed. Asterion was frozen, afraid that by moving he might fracture the tenuous, strange thing that had sprung up between them.

"No. I—It's fine."

"I don't know—" Dom was red even beneath his collar, and Asterion wanted to kiss the flush off his skin. "That's not— I don't— I didn't mean to do that."

Oh.

Asterion's heart sank at the look of utter humiliation on Dom's face. Whatever Asterion had thought the kiss had been, how nice it had been, how much he wanted it again, he had clearly been mistaken.

Of course he was. How long had he been telling himself that Dom didn't want him? And Dom didn't. And that was fine. Asterion should have been used to it. He *was* used to it.

"Of course you didn't. It's fine. Doesn't mean anything. Happens to the best of us."

"I—" Dom began, but he fumbled his excuse. He shifted his weight to his back foot, leaning out into the hall as his gaze dropped to the floor. "I'm sorry."

"Trust me," Asterion laughed, shaking his head. This *was* funny, wasn't it? Just a silly misunderstanding. Asterion's fingers brushed against the cut below his chin and came away smeared with red; he swiped the blood off on the leg of his trousers. "It wouldn't be the first time. I look good injured, many people have said." A frown flickered across Dom's face, and Asterion shook his head. "Besides, I know better than to take any overture made in a bathroom seriously." He winked. Dom winced, swallowed and opened his mouth, but Gods, Asterion could not actually stomach any excuses. He'd spent all morning feeling vulnerable and precious and he was over it now. Or he would stuff those emotions far enough down that he could pretend to be.

Before either of them could speak, there was a knock at the front door. Dom didn't move to answer it, his umber eyes fixed so firmly on Asterion that Asterion wondered if Dom had even heard it.

"The door." Asterion prompted.

"But Asterion—" There was another knock.

"It's Sidney and Jonas, I'm sure." Asterion said. "Do you mind getting it? I need to run up and put on a shirt." Dom opened his mouth, but Asterion needed to be away from him. He slid out of the bathroom past Dom before he could say anything and started down the hall.

Asterion folded up his scarf and ran his hand over his newly clean cheek as he walked, ignoring the tingle of sensation in his lips. It would fade. That sort of thing always did.

23

"I suppose I should have guessed," Jonas teased, as Asterion brought a fresh stack of toast to the table. "When Sidney said you invited us over for breakfast, I almost believed it would be you making it." Dom sat across from Sidney, in Ares' old spot, trying not to clench his fingers around the sides of his chair. He couldn't stop thinking about what he'd done, and now he had to sit through breakfast beside Asterion. After he let Sidney and Jonas in, he'd tried to beg off, but Jonas said he had news about Ares, so that was the end of that.

"For your information," Asterion set the toast in front of Jonas haughtily, "I did all the shopping. And the toast, fruit and coffee."

"Which is delicious by the way," Sidney said, taking a sip from his mug.

"Thank you, Sidney." Asterion returned with the bowl of fruit and sat down without a glance in Dom's direction. "So, Jonas, how goes the unbinding?"

They talked for several minutes about 'the unbinding,' which Dom didn't understand even the slightest bit of, though he might have if he'd tried to pay attention. Unfortunately, Asterion's knee brushed Dom's beneath the table, and it sent Dom's tenuous focus to all the places their bodies had touched in the bathroom downstairs.

He hadn't meant to kiss Asterion. Except, now that he had, all he wanted was to do it again. But Asterion had dismissed him and now was ignoring him and it was all so stupid. And if Dom had been a better brother, he wouldn't be thinking about Asterion at all.

"You found something about Ares?" Dom blurted in the first brief break in the conversation. Jonas nodded as he chewed a piece of toast.

"I did. I don't know how useful it's going to be to us, but your brother is in Assembly records for two different wagers. Well, specifically, one wager and one deal."

"The Sorcerer's Assembly is a sort of magical governing body across the nine realms," Sidney inserted.

"The Assembly does a lot of the legwork of upholding the contracts made between species and across realms," Jonas continued.

"And it's primarily staffed by insufferable, power-hungry bureaucrats." Asterion smiled thinly at Jonas. Jonas conceded the point with a small nod.

"Speaking of. One of the people Ares dealt with was our very own Edmund Morrow," Jonas said.

"Charming," Asterion scoffed. "Like a bad penny, our Edmund. What did Ares deal with him for?" Jonas shrugged.

"I don't know. The terms of a deal or wager can only be accessed by either party of the wager, or by a blood relation of either party."

"I could do it," Dom said immediately. Asterion's pale cheeks pinked beneath his freckles, and he busied himself buttering his toast. It wasn't so absurd an idea, was it? Dom turned to Jonas. "Right? I'm blood related—"

"Humans can't cross into the Catacombs, or any supernatural realm without being marked," Jonas said.

"Sidney told me." Dom looked over at Sidney, as the details of that conversation came flooding back. Or the now significant lack of details. '*It can happen different ways, and I don't think all of them are pleasant... Some of them are, though.*' Dom avoided thinking about the implication of Sidney's statement. "So, can I get marked?"

Asterion cleared his throat and got up from the table, going for the coffee pot.

"There are a few ways to take a mark." Jonas said. "The first is that you can enter into a deal or a wager of your own with a creature. I suppose, in some perspectives, that would be the easiest route. Though depending on who you try to deal with, it may not be."

"You could do it," Dom said to Jonas. "Couldn't you?" Jonas shook his head, as Asterion returned to pour more coffee.

"Beyond a few basic cantrips, I can't do magic anymore. Any deal you make with me would have to contain a soul wager, which I do not recommend."

"Meaning you'd take part of my soul?" Dom clarified, his own throat suddenly dry.

"Correct."

"What would that do?"

"Hurt. A bit. Other demons might be able to offer you something less damaging, but I couldn't. I would need your soul, because my magic has been so significantly depleted. It's a matter of energy conversion—"

"How?" Dom asked, his brain tripping on the idea that it wasn't just Asterion who had lost his magic. "Sorry, I mean, how did your magic get depleted?"

"Edmund Morrow," Jonas said. Asterion muttered darkly

below his breath, his eyes narrowing and jaw tightening. If looks could kill, his would have. Dom frowned.

"The same man Ares made a deal with?"

"Yes," Jonas nodded. "And I certainly don't recommend him." Dom was curious about this man they apparently all hated, but he would come back to it. One thing at a time.

"Right. Okay. So, not a soul wager, but you said there were other ways to get marked."

"You could exchange component fluids with a creature," Jonas explained, a deep merlot color seeped across the red-orange skin of his cheeks, though his expression stayed neutral.

"What's a component fluid?"

"Most commonly blood or semen," Asterion said. Dom choked on his coffee.

"But some species have different component fluids," Sidney added, as though it might be helpful. "Mermaids, as an example." Mermaids? What?

"Okay, wait—"

"Mermaids are more likely to kill you than mark you," Asterion huffed.

"A vampire," Jonas offered. Dom thought of the Elmmond House party, of Indigo, the vampire he'd met on the stairs. He shook his head.

"I don't think—"

"I wouldn't bother with vampires," Asterion said with a blithe wave of his hand. "Terribly chilly and they tend to get a little carried away with the biting."

"How easy are they to find anyway? Vampires, I mean." Sidney asked. Jonas opened his mouth to answer, and Asterion held up a hand.

"Dom already said he didn't want one. And besides, we don't need to go so far as buying tickets for Transylvania. Jonas was able to mark you, was he not?" Asterion asked Sidney. Dom froze, coffee cup halfway to his mouth. Asterion could not be implying what it sounded like he was. Was he?

"Asterion—" Dom began, but Asterion cut him off, turning to Jonas.

"You marked Sidney, didn't you?"

"I did," Jonas admitted.

"Well, then," Asterion looked at Dom and gestured to Jonas. "There you go." Asterion *was* suggesting that Dom sleep with Jonas. Dom shook his head, dumbstruck.

"No."

"No? Do you have a better suggestion?"

"Why not you?" Dom snapped, irritated and embarrassed. Asterion rolled his eyes, and Dom found that he suddenly regretted everything he'd done the entire day, from the moment he'd woken up in the morning to the last words that had come out of his mouth. Especially the kiss.

"As flattering an offer as that is, I don't have the ability anymore. Magical removal has some very distinct limitations. The inability to mark among them."

"But Jonas marked Sidney, and he doesn't have magic."

"His magic was stolen," Asterion said. "And not perfectly. He can glamour. He can mark. Small cantrips, as he said. I can't."

"There is another option," Jonas interrupted.

"You're the nearest and most handsome option in a fifty-mile radius," Asterion smirked. "Give yourself a little credit."

"I'm not going to sleep with Jonas," Dom said firmly.

"Why not? Half the people at this table already have." Asterion winked at Sidney, as though this was all very funny. "He comes highly recommended."

"No! And even if I— Jonas has a boyfriend!" Dom stammered, gesturing toward Sidney, who was sipping his coffee and not saying a thing.

"Oh, for the love of Gods," Asterion huffed, throwing up his hands. "I obviously meant for you to include Sidney! There's nothing that says you can't." Dom's mouth was hanging open and yet he couldn't think of a single thing to say.

"There's the wager," Jonas pressed on. "Ares made a deal with Morrow, and we won't know what it was without marking Dom. That's all true. There's also Dantalion."

All the amusement flooded out of Asterion's face like a sieve, as he inhaled suddenly and sharply.

"Dantalion?" Asterion's brow furrowed, like it hurt to say the name aloud. "You're not serious."

"I am. Ares made a wager with Dantalion."

"Who's Dantalion?" Dom asked.

"He's a Duke of the Abyssal Plain," Jonas said.

"Colloquially, we call it 'Hell,'" Sidney said. Dom stammered.

"Ares made a deal with a Duke of Hell?"

"I used to be one," Jonas said with a shrug. "It's not really all that thrilling. There are loads of us. But I'm still on speaking terms with Dantalion. I can probably arrange a meeting with him, if you'd like."

"Will he tell me what Ares was looking for?" Dom asked.

"Probably. Though he might ask you for something in exchange. You'll certainly get further with him than you would with Edmund. And you don't have to get marked to do it."

Dom's stomach hurt. He was hot and uncomfortable, and his skin felt prickly all over. He wanted to get on his motorcycle and drive away from this house, this conversation, and especially Asterion. Asterion, who had gone suspiciously quiet. He was slouched back in his chair, his gaze fixed on the coffee cup in his hand like he might be trying to reheat it with his mind. Clearly he knew Dantalion, and Dom tried not to consider that in any depth, as it wasn't his business, except—

"What do you think, Asterion?" Dom asked. "I take it you

know Dantalion." Asterion laughed humorlessly and stayed silent. "Should I talk to him?" Dom prompted again, annoyed still. Of course, he was quiet now when Dom actually wanted to hear his opinion. Asterion stilled. After a moment, he met Dom's eye with a considered gaze.

"He's a bastard and he's capricious. If you talk to him, I wouldn't recommend doing it alone, and I doubt it will be a pleasant conversation. That being said, he might be willing to tell you something."

Dom let several digs about unpleasant conversational partners come and go. He looked back at Jonas.

"I'd like to speak to him."

"I'll set something up," Jonas said. Sidney nodded and leaned back, putting his napkin on his clean plate.

"I'm glad that's settled. Unfortunately, I have to go. I told Nina I'd meet her at the diner at ten. We're trying a new pineapple upside down cake recipe." He got to his feet. Then he fixed Dom with a pointed look and nodded toward the door. Dom recognized the out he was being given and got up so quickly that he almost knocked over his chair.

"I'll come with you," Dom said. He tried to come up with a reason why he was leaving and failed. It didn't seem to matter though. Sidney leaned over to kiss Jonas, and then straightened up and smirked at Asterion.

"Asterion, thank you for breakfast. Always a pleasure."

"Yes, yes," Asterion waved his hand in Sidney's direction, looking away toward the kitchen. "I'm sure I owe you an apology for something."

"Nonsense," Sidney smirked. "I love it when you recommend new sexual partners for Jonas and me. Especially when we're all having breakfast."

"I wasn't trying to—" Asterion scowled, his cheeks pinking,

as he glanced at Dom, and then quickly looked away. He cleared his throat. "I was just thinking of what might be—"

"It's quite alright. We all know that you were just thinking about protecting Dom." Sidney cocked his head to the side. "Isn't that right?" Asterion fully blushed, his gaze landing on his empty plate.

"Of course," Asterion muttered. He looked so cowed that, suddenly, Dom felt a little bad for him.

"Very kind of you." Sidney squeezed Jonas' shoulder. "See you after lunch," he said, and then started for the stairs, leaving Dom to follow behind.

24

"How did you do that?" Dom asked as he slid into his coat. He and Sidney were standing on the porch, and Dom could feel his face finally cooling off, as a frigid breeze blew in off the water.

"What do you mean?" Sidney asked, covering a yawn.

"With Asterion just now. You sort of... put him in his place."

"Well, he deserved it. Just because he's feeling vulnerable doesn't mean he needs to be a prick to the rest of us." Sidney started off the porch, pushing his hands into his pockets. Dom locked the front door and caught up with Sidney in two strides.

"What do you mean, feeling vulnerable?" Sidney looked over at him with an arched eyebrow. "Because his magic is gone?" Sidney huffed and then shook his head.

"Sure. Because his magic is gone." It made sense, but was it a good enough excuse?

"I'm sorry anyway," Dom said. "Asterion shouldn't have suggested that I—or we—" Dom was blushing again, but Sidney only shrugged.

"It genuinely doesn't bother me. The whole marking thing is

just meant to fuck with humans, as far as I can tell. It's not even about sex. It's just power and politics to them."

"Not all of them, though. Right? Power and politics. You and Jonas," Dom trailed off, fumbling for what he was trying to say. What was he trying to say? Sidney looked over at him.

"You really care, don't you?" He asked with a small smile. Dom stammered.

"Well, I mean, if he's— Or if you— I don't like the idea you're being taken advantage of," Dom finally managed.

"Jonas and I are fine. He's not like that."

"Even though he marked you?"

"It doesn't do anything if there's not an oath or a deal tied to it. It's just sort of there. At least, as far as we can tell. I promise you, I'm perfectly fine. And so is Jonas. The worst that's happened to us is that sometimes other creatures can sense when a mark's been placed. It's not a big deal, but it doesn't allow for much privacy." Marking had more layers to it than Dom had thought. And maybe Asterion really hadn't meant to offend any of them by suggesting it. Certainly, Dom would rather be tied to a former Duke of Hell he did know than a vampire he didn't. He still would have preferred to be marked by someone who wasn't happily in a relationship.

He would have preferred to be marked by Asterion.

And that was embarrassing. Because if Asterion's bad behavior at breakfast hadn't entirely turned Dom off, what did that mean? Had Asterion really been trying to protect Dom all along? Or was Dom deluding himself?

The best course of action he could come up with was to try and forget about the whole thing. Clearly their kiss hadn't had an impact on Asterion in the slightest, and Dom knew he should be grateful for that. And he was going to try to be.

∾

ASTERION MOVED HIS PLATE ON TOP OF DOM'S AND PUT HIS HEAD down, pressing his forehead onto the cool wood of the table.

"Impressive work, Asterion." Jonas' sarcasm was deeply unappreciated.

"Shut up," Asterion replied weakly.

"You're gone on him, aren't you?"

"No."

"Head over heels."

"Shut up."

"You know how I can tell?" Jonas asked.

"How?" Asterion mumbled, too wretched to deny it.

"When you like someone you always try to push them into bed with someone else."

"I do not."

"I thought I had a fighting chance with you when you offered to introduce me to Alberti Von Dietrich."

"You mean Alberti Von Big Dick? You should have thanked me for that." Asterion lifted his head up just enough so that he could see Jonas' smile. Asterion rested his chin on his hand. "Dom's not interested."

"How do you know that?"

"Because he just kissed me," Asterion said. Jonas blinked at him. Then he cleared his throat.

"Asterion, you are one of my oldest friends, so please believe this question comes from a place of love and respect, but are you stupid?"

"Shut up," Asterion groaned, laying his head back down.

"Think about all the words you just said to me. Really think about them."

"He kissed me and then he immediately apologized! Who does that? Not someone who's interested in more kissing." Asterion was quite sure he was right about this. "And maybe I shouldn't have suggested he sleep with you. But he doesn't need to be just going out finding someone to mark him for the sake of getting marked. You know how some creatures can be!"

"I do," Jonas said.

"I don't care who he sleeps with!" Asterion announced, just to try out the phrase in his mouth. It made his stomach clench. Or he'd had too much coffee. That was probably it.

"You're making a very convincing show of not caring about who Dom sleeps with." Asterion could hear the amusement in Jonas' voice and scowled.

"Oh, what the hell do you know?"

"I know that you should probably apologize to him. And maybe endeavor to ask if he'd like to kiss you again sometime. *If* he's willing to forgive you for being a massive prick." Asterion rolled his eyes and sat up.

"Tell me you won't let Dantalion try and fuck him," he said. Jonas shrugged, and Asterion threw a spoon at him. Jonas caught it and placed it gently back on the table.

"I'm not sure that's up to me. Also, I thought you didn't care who he sleeps with?"

"Jonas."

"Maybe *you* ought to talk to Dom about it," Jonas suggested, pushing back from the table and getting to his feet. "You've probably got a couple of days to get up the courage. I don't imagine I'll hear back from Dantalion before Saturday." Jonas began to gather dishes into his arms, and Asterion watched him for a minute, trying to decipher his own feelings.

He liked Dom. He hadn't quite realized how much. Or how the thought of Dom sleeping with someone else, anyone else, would turn Asterion into a raving lunatic. It wasn't any of his business who Dom slept with. One kiss, that Dom clearly regretted, didn't mean anything to either of them. Even if it did mean a little something to Asterion.

What Jonas was right about, however, was that Asterion

needed to apologize to Dom. And to tell him more about Dantalion. The best way to deal with the duke was to be prepared, and Asterion had experience on his side.

Asterion and Jonas cleaned up the breakfast dishes and shared another cup of coffee. When Jonas stood to go, he gave Asterion a pat on the shoulder and then seemed to think better of it halfway through and pulled him into a hug.

They'd talked about many topics over the past hour, so Asterion was a little surprised when Jonas ended their embrace by holding him at arm's length and looking him in the eye.

"Talk to Dom," Jonas said. Asterion bit his lip.

"It won't come to anything."

"Then what do you have to lose?"

25

D om was alone in the diner and finally able to breathe again. He had decided to stay late, still struggling to forget the events of the morning.

The memory of Asterion telling him to sleep with Jonas mixed weirdly with the phantom sensation of Asterion's mouth pressed, however briefly, against Dom's own. He'd been distracted and a little tetchy all day, and as a result, he hadn't gotten as much done as he needed to. He was only halfway through icing the cakes for the women's auxiliary, when there was a knock at the door.

He glanced at the clock. Nina had left about twenty minutes before, and Dom looked around as he went to answer it, trying to spot whatever she'd forgotten and come back for. But when he pulled the door open, it wasn't Nina standing on the dilapidated stoop. It was Asterion.

He flicked one of Nina's cigarettes to the ground. Smoke was still drifting out of his mouth, as he pushed loose strands of lavender blue hair out of his face. Asterion looked so good. His thick wool coat gave him more width, collar turned up against the wind and accentuating his cheekbones. Dom, in a dirty apron, covered with grease and icing, took a step back out of courtesy.

"Asterion? Is everything—"

"I came to apologize," Asterion said, glancing past Dom into the kitchen. "And to, uh, offer to walk you home. Can I come in? It's rather cold." Dom stepped back and let him in.

"How long have you been out there?" Dom asked, closing the door behind him.

"Well, I was talking to Hector for a little while."

"Hector?" Dom frowned. "Hector left an hour and a half ago." Asterion shrugged his arms out of his coat.

"I didn't know what time you got off. I just thought I'd wait."

Dom's heart thudded hard against his ribs.

He had spent the last twelve hours telling himself that what he felt for Asterion was not reciprocated. Asterion had emphatically and sincerely told Dom to sleep with another man that morning, with *two* other men, and did not want to be with Dom. Did not want anything to do with Dom, beyond their friendship. A friendship which was honestly, mostly predicated on the fact that Dom was helping Asterion get his footing in this strange new world. A prince didn't want Dom. No one wanted Dom. And that was fine, because Dom didn't want anyone either.

Except.

Except Dom wanted to make Asterion breakfast. He wanted to watch Asterion fuss with ancient, cracked dishware like it was fine china. He wanted to listen to Asterion talk about himself and magic and how Dom ought to paint his walls. He wanted to kiss Asterion again and see if Asterion would kiss him back.

And Asterion had waited outside for him. For nearly two hours.

Dom bit his tongue and walked to the counter. There were still cakes to ice. He needed to focus.

"I'll be a little bit." Dom picked up the piping bag from the counter and exhaled, trying to steady himself. "I need to finish the decorations on these and box them up for tomorrow."

"I don't mind waiting," Asterion walked around to the opposite side of the cakes. "As long as you don't mind the company."

"It's fine," Dom said. It was fine. It didn't mean anything that Asterion had waited and was willing to keep waiting.

"I am sorry about earlier. I wasn't trying to be inappropriate."

"I appreciate that," Dom said, relieved he had something to look at that wasn't Asterion. He blushed anyway. "In the future, if you could refrain from suggesting I sleep with our friends when we're with them."

"Of course."

"Or at all."

"I can do that," Asterion said. There was a pause, and then he cleared his throat. "But before we put a moratorium on talking about your sex life, let me just say, I would not recommend agreeing to sleep with Dantalion. If he offers, of course. When you meet him."

"Oh?" Dom asked, glancing up. Asterion's cheeks were flushed, probably from the cold, but his expression was deadly serious. Throughout Dom's day not thinking about Asterion, Dom had developed a theory about Asterion's connection to Dantalion. "You have, though? Slept with him, I mean." Asterion chuckled a little.

"If you'd like a list of all the people I've slept with that I also wouldn't recommend sleeping with, we're going to be here for quite some time. How many cakes do you have to decorate?" Dom smiled, even as his chest tightened. Even though it shouldn't have meant anything to Dom, this was dangerous territory. Asterion smirked and then continued. "I did sleep with him. Dantalion was a special case, though. My mother favored him as a suitor for me. And in an attempt to please her, I allowed for more...misbehavior than I should have." Dom frowned and straightened up, wiping a loose hair off his forehead, and was unsettled by Asterion's thin, unhappy, smile.

"Misbehavior? What do you mean?"

"Dantalion is a brute. And generally unpleasant to be around." Like that morning at breakfast, Asterion got quiet, and Dom hated it. His vagueness felt like it was speaking volumes. Before Dom could ask, Asterion lifted his hand and checked his nails. "We were never formally engaged. When he did ask, I refused him, and he took that as quite the offense. Broke several priceless heirlooms on his way out."

"Charming," Dom murmured. Asterion chuckled.

"All of which to say, you should be careful when you speak to him. He has a bit of a hair trigger. And he expects to get his way."

"I'm surprised Jonas still talks to him. He doesn't seem like the type to put up with that."

"Jonas doesn't know. I mean, he knows we were together. And he knows Dantalion can be a bit brash. He doesn't know about the rest of it. He wasn't around at the time. And I've never told him. He and Dan are friends from their days on the Abyssal Planes. Military men. I'd appreciate if you wouldn't say anything to him."

The thought of someone being cruel to Asterion and Asterion not even telling Jonas who, as far as Dom could tell, was Asterion's best friend, made Dom uneasy. And a little angry.

"I don't have to speak to Dantalion," Dom said. "I'm sure there's another way."

"Don't be absurd. If you want to find Ares, you don't have many other options. And I certainly wouldn't want you to waste the opportunity. Dantalion loves showing off when he knows things other people don't. He may try to make you feel like a fool, but he'll tell you what you want to know."

"He sounds like an asshole. Why did your mother like him so much?"

"She's always appreciated those who show a certain unbridled lust for power and a disregard for others' feelings. It's why she favors my brother Kephisto." Asterion hoisted himself up onto the counter, with a thoughtful smile, his gaze on the clock. "Kephisto's greatest tragedy in life is that he's the second child. He's been competing with my sister Cressida since the day he was born."

"And what about you?" Dom rotated the cake, barely sure where he'd left off in the decorating. Asterion lifted his hands in an exaggerated shrug, drawing Dom's attention again.

"I'm not much of a threat, I'm afraid."

"You don't want to be king?"

"Oh, Gods no!" Asterion laughed and leaned back, the long line of his body as tempting as his smile. Dom turned his attention to changing the nozzle on the piping bag. "I honestly haven't even thought about it since I was a boy. My father made it clear to me from quite a young age that I wasn't suited for it. And even if I had been, Kephisto's determination to have the crown for himself would have put me right off."

"I think you'd make a good king."

"That's kind of you. Though I think I lack an essential component of decent kingship."

"What's that?" Dom asked, looking up.

"Well," Asterion shrugged, his grin mischievous and infinitely handsome. "I don't want to be a king."

"That does complicate things, I suppose." Dom caught himself smiling.

Distracted again. Ice the cake, Dom.

Dom set down the piping bag and wiped his hands on his apron. There was no harm in taking a break.

"So, what do you want to do, if you're not going to make a play for the throne?"

"Ugh," Asterion groaned. "Now *you* sound like my mother. I don't know. I suppose I was hoping to be indolent and shiftless for the rest of my days."

"Several centuries of lying about?" Dom stretched. Lying about sounded nice, in theory anyway.

"Oh no. Without magic, I'll only have to endure for seven or eight decades at least. Most creatures have a lifespan much closer to humans once you take away their access to enchantments and the like."

"So, wait," Dom dropped his arms. "You're just like a human now?"

"Basically. Except the ears. And the hair."

"How old are you?" Dom asked. Asterion pursed his lips, his golden eyes casting up toward the ceiling in thought.

"I mean, I've been alive for almost three centuries, but there's not exactly a perfect ratio when it comes to human years. I suppose somewhere in my late twenties or early thirties, biologically speaking. And it's not as though I've been living a monastic existence. Indulging can age one, so I've been told."

"But if you hadn't lost your magic, you'd be immortal?"

"No," Asterion shook his head. "No, no. The average fae lifespan is only eight or nine hundred years. My father lived to be a thousand and nine, if you can believe it. But then, he never indulged in anything at all."

Dom swallowed. So, it wasn't just magic that Asterion had lost. It was centuries.

"It doesn't—that doesn't bother you?" Dom asked. Asterion hummed.

"I don't know. Jonas gave up on magic at least a decade ago, and he still looks as handsome as ever." Asterion grinned. Dom still couldn't manage to wrap his head around it. He came around to the other side of the counter.

"It *really* doesn't bother you?"

"I did get hideously drunk and behave abominably for a few days. You saw. You were there."

"I mean, if someone had told me then that you'd just lost six hundred years of possible existence, I might've understood a bit better."

"Pity is a lovely thing to have and a horrible thing to receive," Asterion said. "I neither need, want, nor deserve it." And what could Dom say to that? Asterion's eyes settled on Dom's frown, and he smiled kindly. "I promise, Dom, I'm not as pathetic as I seem. Magic being gone... It's a blow, for sure. Primarily because of how inconvenient it is not to have it. Dying isn't that big of a deal. It's not as though I have scads of friends I'll be leaving behind, and I would have done it eventually anyway. Everyone does. Leaving my home. My family. It's complicated. But family always is, isn't it?"

"I suppose," Dom said. "So, you're just going to, what? Make the best of it?"

"Well, not every day," Asterion's smirked, and the tension in Dom's chest eased a little. "I'll probably snivel and rage a bit more here and there. I'm sure I'll say some more horrible things, and you all will have to decide if they're forgivable or not."

"I think you're allowed."

"I think you're letting me get off easy," Asterion leaned forward, his golden eyes crinkled at the corners as his smile widened.

Dom wanted him.

Dom wanted to kiss him and be kind to him and he couldn't stop himself from stepping forward. He pressed his palms onto the cool counter on either side of Asterion's thighs and leaned forward. Asterion bent down, and their mouths met in the middle.

Asterion kissed him back.

Dom's mind fizzled, no thoughts in his head except desire like he'd never felt before. Asterion slid off the edge of the counter, his body perfectly flush with Dom's, as his feet touched the floor. The heat of him, the thin, firm lines of his body, long fingers gently resting on Dom's hips. Dom moved closer, deepened the kiss, his thoughts turning desperate and feral as Asterion opened his mouth and slid the tip of his tongue over Dom's lips. Dom put arm around Asterion's waist, partially to bring him closer, and partially to hold himself upright. Asterion whimpered, his fingers twisting in the fabric of Dom's sweater, and Dom felt the brush of Asterion's knuckles all the way down to the tips of his toes.

He forced himself to pull back. To breathe. Asterion's eyes were wide, his lips gorgeously flush, and a dozen beautiful, filthy thoughts rushed through Dom's mind. He leaned back on his heels.

"Sorry."

"Is that always what you say after you kiss someone?" Asterion's voice was breathy, his chest rising and falling heavily. Dom blushed.

"I just. I should have asked. I should have asked earlier. In the bathroom, and I—"

"I don't mind." Asterion was smiling. "I like it."

"You like being mauled?" Dom asked. Asterion laughed.

"If it's you doing it, then absolutely yes. By all means. You have my express permission."

"You've got icing sugar all over your sweater," Dom said, glancing down between them and then taking another step back. Asterion's black outfit was smeared with white. "Christ, Asterion, I'm—"

"I'll wash it," Asterion said. Then he stepped forward and slid his long narrow fingers into the back of Dom's hair. Dom shivered at the sensation, letting Asterion close the gap between their bodies, as they kissed again.

Asterion's fingers tangled in Dom's thick curls, pulling gently, making Dom's legs shake. He moaned. So embarrassing. But Asterion only kissed him harder, backing Dom up against the table where the cakes sat. There was a thud behind them, and they both jerked apart. Thankfully, only the piping bag had fallen to the floor.

"It's fine," Dom said, before Asterion could apologize.

"I should let you finish the cake," Asterion said, taking a step back. Oh, it could wait until tomorrow, couldn't it? Dom could get up early, and— "Maybe I can help?"

"It's fine. We can just—"

"It's little icing flowers," Asterion shrugged. "How hard can it be?"

26

L ittle icing flowers were a bitch. After twenty minutes of
watching Asterion flounder (by his own insistence,
because how was he ever going to learn otherwise?) Dom
nudged Asterion out of the way and finished the top of the cake
in five minutes. Asterion had never been turned on watching
someone ice a cake before, but then, he probably would have
gotten hard watching Dom read the dictionary. The situation
was dire.

Dom was such a good kisser. Thick, firm arms, strong hands,
and the way he wanted Asterion. It was so clear that Asterion
wondered if he'd accidentally blinded himself over the past
week. How had he not known? Why had he let so much time go
to waste?

As Asterion watched Dom put the last cake with its fellows
in the walk-in, he suddenly had a pang of worry. What was going
to happen? The warm, quiet of the kitchen felt sacred to him
now, a holy space, where there were many surfaces Dom could
have Asterion up against. Because that was what was going to
happen, wasn't it? Dom came out of the walk-in, pulling his
apron off over his head.

"Alright. Are you ready?" Ready? Yes. Very much so. But for what?

"Yes," Asterion agreed. Dom looked over at him, then arched an eyebrow.

"You don't even have your coat on. It's going to be freezing out there."

"Where are we going?" Asterion asked, moving obediently for his coat. Dom chuckled.

"Home?"

Ah. Yes. Home. That made sense, Asterion supposed. Or did it raise more questions than it answered? Home was where beds and couches and other soft surfaces were, so that was good. But technically home was two different apartments. Not together. Not more kissing. So maybe that was bad?

In Asterion's world, kissing the way Dom had kissed Asterion meant something. It was a precursor to physicality, mostly, and Asterion knew that physicality was the way he was most likely to please a partner. The thought of not pleasing Dom made Asterion's stomach hurt a little bit, and he wasn't going to think about why. Instead, he tugged on his coat and came to stand beside Dom, as Dom pulled open the kitchen door to reveal a steady rain.

"Shit," Dom frowned. Then he glanced up at Asterion. "Guess we'll have to make a run for it." Asterion balked.

"You're not serious."

"I'm not sleeping in the diner."

"I'll freeze to death out there!" Asterion gestured widely at the weather. Dom rolled his eyes, grinning.

"No, you won't. Come on." And he stepped out the door.

"You're trying to kill me," Asterion said. Dom grinned and took Asterion's hand gently, guiding him onto the stoop.

"After everything you've already been through, I think you can survive getting a little damp. Flip your collar up." Dom let go of Asterion's hand to lock the door, and Asterion barely stifled a pout as he shoved his hands into his pockets.

They were halfway home when it really started to downpour, and then they did run. Asterion couldn't remember the last time he'd run anywhere, and judging by the burning in his lungs and the aching in his legs, it was likely at least two hundred years ago. Soaking wet and out of breath, they careened onto the damp porch, sliding up the stairs and into the small, dry space, between their doormats.

Asterion felt like an old wet dog, but Dom's eyes were bright with amusement, his cheeks flushed, flyaway curls framing his beautiful face. When Dom kissed him, Asterion forgot, for a moment, every uncomfortable sensation. He melted against Dom's body, fingers curling in the damp fabric of Dom's coat, as all the ways he wanted Dom came rushing back.

Dom's hand slid over Asterion's jaw, the callouses on his thumb making Asterion arch his back. He was ready to feel those rough hands all over his body. He was so ready. And then Dom pulled away. The silver in his eyes shone, a small smile twitched at the corner of his mouth.

"I'll see you tomorrow?"

Tomorrow.

Tomorrow?

Asterion blinked. Then he closed his mouth which had been hanging open.

"You don't—" Asterion fumbled, bit his lip, and then started again. "Do you want to—?" Dom gaze dropped to the ground, then shifted to his door.

"Let's uh..." he stammered, and Asterion watched Dom's adam's apple bob as he swallowed. "I'll see you tomorrow."

Dom opened his door and closed it again, and suddenly, Asterion was alone on the porch. Disgustingly wet, aroused, rejected and all alone.

Asterion had done something wrong. He must have.

He trudged up the stairs to his apartment trying to figure out where he'd fucked up. He'd thought Dom was interested. He'd seemed like he was interested. Had Asterion been too forward? Some people didn't like that. But Dom had kissed *him*. And Asterion was a good kisser. Everyone said so.

Asterion hung his wet coat over the back of a chair and went into the bathroom to dry his hair. Nothing made sense anymore. He ran a towel over his head and shoulders, and then tugged off his sweater, soaked through at the collar. The reflection in the mirror above the sink looked particularly pathetic. No wonder Dom had declined.

Asterion had gotten used to his pale skin, his freckles, the washed-out color of his hair. It wasn't attractive, though. And if Dom didn't want to sleep with him, if he didn't want Asterion like this, did Dom really want him at all?

No one ever waited to sleep with Asterion. Desirable was the thing he knew how to be. It was what he was good at. People wanted him and they got him. And he never put anyone off. He'd learned a long time ago that if he asked someone to wait, they would leave with the next most handsome bachelor (usually Kephisto) and never come back.

So, maybe there was someone else. Someone Dom hadn't told him about. Asterion could find someone else too, he supposed. In fact, he did already know of someone in this wretched realm of existence who wanted to sleep with him. Who wouldn't kiss him and then leave him with nothing more than an: *'I'll see you tomorrow.'* What did that even mean? Somewhere in Asterion's apartment was the napkin he'd written his grocery list on— the list with Anders the fisherman's address written across the top.

Asterion went into his bedroom, scanning the top of his dresser as he started to strip. He didn't have anything particularly suggestive to wear, but Asterion could play at sexy long enough to bag a fucking fisherman, especially one who'd given Asterion his address when Asterion had been wearing an apron. Yes, Anders' judgment was obviously questionable, but that wasn't really Asterion's problem.

A white button down, sleeves rolled to the elbows and clean corduroy trousers made him look soft. Scholarly almost. Apparently, he was taking fashion cues from Sidney Quince, but whatever. Asterion was tired of being discarded, so he would go where he was wanted and pretend he wanted to be there as well. He'd had years of practice, and even without magic it couldn't be that hard.

But the napkin with the address wasn't on his dresser. Not in the pockets of his trousers from the day before. Perhaps his coat. Asterion slid back out to the kitchen in his socks, fumbling through the damp wool, until finally he found it. The napkin was folded in half, creased across the list. And even though he'd scratched it out, the address was still readable. *72 Bernes Street.* No idea where that was. But this town was small. How hard could it be to—

A knock at the door made Asterion jump. He swung toward the hallway, where the sound had come from, and stared at the closed and latched back door which led to Dom's apartment and the backyard. Which meant it could only be Dom knocking with another apology.

Asterion wasn't interested.

Dom knocked again, and Asterion almost missed it because of the way his heart was pounding in his chest. Maybe the house was on fire. That was probably it. There was some kind of emergency. Asterion could answer the door and then be on his way. Dom would probably be able to tell Asterion where Bernes Street was, which would save him some time mucking about in the rain. He should have bought an umbrella.

Asterion strode over to the door, napkin clenched in his fist. He unhooked the chain lock and the bolt, and pulled open the door.

Dom looked disheveled. His hair was loose, and it poured over his shoulders, pushed back from his forehead, like he'd been running his hands through it. He was in a thermal undershirt, snug over the muscles of his arms and shoulders, and jeans, smudged with grease. Socks on his feet. His brown eyes were wide, his gaze fixed on Asterion's face. Asterion opened his mouth to speak. Definitely to tell him to fuck off. Certainly not to beg him to come in.

And then Dom's hands were on Asterion's waist. Their bodies flush as Dom pushed Asterion back against the wall, door swinging closed behind them. Dom kissed Asterion, and Asterion moaned into Dom's mouth, fingers digging into Dom's shoulders, holding on for dear life. Yes. Please. Gods. Yes.

All the useless, nervous chatter in his mind vanished, replaced with the blissful rush of blood in his veins. One of Dom's hands was on Asterion's face again, and Asterion pressed his jaw against Dom's palm, eager, aching.

Dom pulled back, his eyes bright, mouth wet and gorgeous.

"I don't know what I'm doing," Dom's voice was ragged. Asterion tried to come up with something pithy to say, but the look of desperation on Dom's face left him speechless. He was certain no one had ever looked at him like that before.

Asterion kissed him, primarily to avoid the intensity of his gaze, but Dom kissed intensely too. His grip was firm, but his hands were gentle. He wasn't tearing, ravenous; it was better than that. Every twitch of his fingertips was lust barely contained. Hesitating, perhaps, but not for lack of wanting. The Asterion of two minutes ago had been a fool. Dom did want him, and he was making it perfectly clear. Asterion slid one hand into Dom's curls, fingernails brushing the nape of Dom's neck. Dom's hips pressed forward in response, and his desire was undeniable. And considerable. A small moan escaped the back of Asterion's throat.

Asterion let his hand trail down, sliding his fingertips beneath the collar of Dom's shirt. His skin was so warm and soft and Asterion wanted to touch it. He wanted Dom beneath him, and it made his heart beat hard in his chest. Asterion didn't usually want his partners. He tried not to, at least. Sex was easier when it was simply an avenue for giving and receiving pleasure. Desiring a person was much more dangerous than desiring a sensation.

Asterion's other hand found the hem of Dom's shirt, and he toyed with it, wanting to pull it off him, not sure if that would be showing his hand too much. Dom pulled back, one of his hands dropping to curl around Asterion's fingers. His cheeks were flushed, his eyes dark as he looked at Asterion.

"I've never done this before."

Asterion wasn't sure if he had either. There was a force, an intensity, to the whole thing that he was finding rather over-whelming, but in a good way, like—

"Wait," Asterion said, his brain finally reaching the conclusion that Dom might not have been speaking metaphorically. "What do you mean?"

"I mean," Dom's flush crept up his ears. "I've never done this before."

"What?" Asterion asked. Dom blinked slowly and exhaled a huff that could have been a chuckle or a sigh.

"Had sex. I've never had sex."

Oh.

Oh.

Now Asterion was blushing. He was also harder, somehow, which was embarrassing and deviant of him. The thought of being the only one who'd ever been with Dom: gorgeous, sweet, funny, kind, muscle-y Dom—

"How?" Asterion stammered. Dom opened his mouth to speak, but nothing came out. He shrugged in lieu of speech. Asterion shook his head. "Christ, Dom. If I looked like you, I'd be running a one-man brothel in the diner during off-hours."

Dom burst out laughing. He folded forward, resting his head on Asterion's shoulder, as he shook with amusement. Asterion couldn't help but grin.

"I'm not joking, you know," Asterion continued, pressing his advantage. "Think of the additional revenue you could make."

"Oh my God."

"Don't they say you should diversify your—" Dom turned his head and kissed Asterion's neck. Asterion lost his train of thought immediately, his whole body jerking forward to press against Dom in a wholly undignified manner. Dom's arms were around Asterion's waist again, and then one hand was untucking Asterion's shirt, sliding beneath the hem. The press of Dom's palm against the bare skin of Asterion's waist lit a fire in him.

Asterion leaned in, slipping off the wall, tugging Dom into his bedroom.

27

D om was breathless. He followed Asterion because his body wanted to and his mind, filled with a heady mix of desire and anxiety, had fully shut off.

Before, downstairs, when he'd closed the door on Asterion's offer to come up, panic had gotten the better of him. Dom wanted Asterion with a fervor that made it hard to breathe. He'd stood in his room, alone, like an idiot, practically vibrating with the way his hands wanted to be on Asterion's body. Dom wanted to be close to him, breathe his air, feel Asterion's voice against his skin. His desire far outweighed his fear, and when he'd realized that, half-dressed and still trying to catch his breath, he'd run upstairs, ready to beg for forgiveness.

He hadn't needed to, though. Or maybe he would need to, but later. They were in Asterion's bedroom. The bedside lamp was on, the nightstand cluttered with books and teacups and earrings. Dom knew the room, the white walls, the dark curtains closed over the large window at the front of the house and open above the bed, where rain-streaked glass reflected the rippled movement of their bodies.

Asterion kissed Dom. They hadn't stopped kissing, exactly,

and Dom had managed to fully untuck the button-down from Asterion's trousers. Asterion's waist was too small; Dom was certain he'd be able to count his ribs.

When their kisses slowed, Dom's anxiety melted away. Maybe it was the low light of the bedroom, maybe it was just that Asterion finally felt like he wasn't being pounced on, but they'd gone from frantic to fluid, and Dom's perception of the world narrowed to the small spaces between their bodies. Dom didn't know what he was doing, it was true. But he'd read enough books to have a sense of the rhythm of things. And an instinctual, desperate part of him knew exactly what it wanted.

Fingers shaking, he began unbuttoning Asterion's shirt. Asterion watched Dom's hands for a moment, and then leaned close, kissing his jaw lightly. It was barely a peck, but it made Dom gasp.

Asterion moved closer, lips trailing soft kisses beneath Dom's jaw, down his neck. Dom could hear his own labored breathing along with blood rushing in his ears as he slid his hands over Asterion's skin, reveling in the softness of him. The heat. When Dom ran his fingers over Asterion's ribs, Asterion twitched, pulling away, his cheeks pink as he stepped toward the foot of the bed.

"Don't tickle me."

Dom held up his hands, a wordless apology, and Asterion reached out and grabbed one, pulling Dom closer. Closer to Asterion. Closer to the bed.

Dom wasn't afraid of sex, so much as he was terrified of having waited all this time to find out that he was either bad at it, or he didn't like it. When Asterion had asked Dom if he wanted to come up, all Dom could hear in his head was a small, horrible voice, saying, 'you are going to disappoint him.' And the thought was creeping back in again.

"We don't have to fuck," Asterion said. Asterion was slowly

untucking Dom's undershirt from the top of his trousers and studiously not making eye-contact. Oh no. What did that mean? Dom watched his fingers pluck at the fabric, trying to figure out what to say.

"I want to." He did want to. But that wasn't all of it. Asterion finally looked up at him, gold eyes sparkling in the lamplight.

"I want to too," Asterion swallowed. "But I've just been thinking—"

"When?"

"Just now," Asterion said. Dom raised a skeptical eyebrow and Asterion smirked at him. "Some of us are capable of doing two things at once. Anyway, I was thinking. If you've really never," he paused and glanced at Dom who nodded in confirmation. "I, uhh... well, I've never *not*."

"You've never not...?" Dom was trying to figure out the nuance. "You've never not slept with someone?"

"I prefer rushing into things." Asterion's gaze was gone again: over Dom's shoulder, flush creeping down his neck as he looked at the wall. "It's so much more efficient. Over and done with." As though sex was a chore. To be gotten through, rather than enjoyed. Dom frowned.

"Okay."

"I don't usually like those people. I mean, I— I do. I like them. But it isn't quite the..." Asterion trailed off, glancing at Dom before quickly looking away. Asterion cleared his throat and straightened his spine. "But, as neighbors, and occasional coworkers, I wouldn't want there to be any awkwardness if things don't—"

"Asterion, I like you." Dom interrupted. Because he hadn't said it yet, and he should have. Asterion looked at him. Finally.

"I like you too."

"I want to keep spending time with you, whether we do anything more tonight or not." This, Dom knew for sure. Asterion opened and closed his mouth but didn't speak. Dom couldn't help but smile. "Do you believe me?"

"I don't know," Asterion said. And then Asterion kissed him. It was gentle. Almost a question. He could feel the hitch in Asterion's breath, and the way Asterion's fingers were knotting nervously in the front of Dom's shirt. Dom stepped back, tugged the shirt off over his head, and tossed it to the side. Asterion looked him over, eyes widening for a moment.

"Oh, for the love of the Gods!" Asterion groaned, throwing his hands up.

"Sorry?"

"Why do you look like that?"

"Like what?" Dom asked, genuinely. Asterion ignored him. He stepped closer and ran his fingers over the top curve of Dom's chest, dragging his fingernails through Dom's dark chest hair. Asterion bit his bottom lip and nudged at Dom's waistband with his fingertips, as the back of Dom's calves bumped against the foot of the mattress.

"Sit," Asterion said. Dom sat, mesmerized as Asterion stepped forward. Shirt hanging off his slender shoulders, he straddled Dom's thighs and climbed into Dom's lap.

Dom's skin prickled, his breathing heavier even though nothing had happened. When they were standing, they were nearly the same height, but Asterion was a bit taller than him now. He liked it, and it must have shown on his face. Embarrassing, but probably unavoidable.

"What?" Asterion asked, as he brushed long strands of Dom's hair back over his shoulders.

"I thought we weren't doing this."

"We're not," Asterion said quietly, bowing his head to look down at Dom. Dom blushed and Asterion arched an eyebrow. "What?"

"I like having you above me," Dom admitted. Asterion's smile widened.

"I see." Asterion leaned forward and ran his hands down Dom's back. Dom couldn't resist brushing his lips against Asterion's chest, shoulder, collar bone. Asterion eased back and coaxed Dom's chin up with long fingers, before sliding his tongue against Dom's lips. Dom opened for him. His hands found Asterion's waist, traced the nubs of Asterion's vertebrae until Asterion spread his legs wide and rocked forward. Dom's whole body shuddered with the perfect friction. He moaned, head tilting back, bearing his neck and chest to Asterion's mouth.

"Good?" Asterion murmured.

"So good," Dom panted, his skin tingling. "Please, Asterion." Asterion's hands were between them, unbuttoning the waistband of Dom's trousers. Oh, God, yes.

"Is this okay?" Asterion asked, sliding his fingers down Dom's stomach. Being touched was mesmerizing. His brain was having a hard time staying focused. Dom leaned back, bracing himself against the mattress as he watched Asterion's hand slide lower. "Dom?"

"Uh huh. Yes. So—" One of Asterion's fingers brushed the base of Dom's cock and Dom arched his back, desperate for more.

"Lay down," Asterion said. The commanding tone made Dom ache, and he bit back a whimper as he did what he'd been told, leaving himself propped up on one elbow. When he glanced at Asterion, Asterion was smirking, eyebrow arched.

"So obedient," Asterion commented off-handedly.

Dom's breath caught in his chest. He was embarrassed, not by the desire itself, but only having been caught at it. And then Asterion leaned forward and kissed him so thoroughly, that anything beyond the sensation of their bodies vanished from Dom's head.

Dom's trousers were open and Asterion's shirt had gone. They were both breathing hard. Asterion tumbled to the mattress beside Dom, leaving him nearly dizzy with arousal. Before he could roll over to follow Asterion, Asterion scooted close and murmured in Dom's ear.

"Shall I tell you what I want you to do next?" Dom shivered. A tickle of anxiety tried to derail him, but he was so turned-on, it was easy to ignore.

"Yes. Please."

"Unbutton my trousers for me," Asterion said. Gladly. Dom skated his hand down Asterion's pale stomach and flicked open the buttons on Asterion's waistband. His hand lingered on the skin of Asterion's hip as Asterion lay back and shimmied gracefully out of his trousers and shorts.

Dom didn't bother with the pretense of looking away. Asterion's cock was long and hard, the tip of it glistening with precum that Dom needed to taste. Asterion took himself in hand. He stroked himself once, his back arching as his eyes fluttered closed.

"Asterion," Dom prompted. Asterion hummed and opened his eyes.

"Oh. Did you want more instructions?" Dom wanted more than he had ever wanted in his life. He wanted everything. He wanted to flip Asterion over and fuck him into the mattress. He wanted to go down on Asterion, and for Asterion to pull his hair. He wanted to please Asterion in every way he'd ever read about in his dirty books. He wanted everything.

"Tell me," Dom grunted. Asterion bit his bottom lip.

"Take off your trousers and let me see you stroke yourself." It was a mild request, all things considered, but it felt plucked right from Dom's filthiest fantasies. He kicked off his trousers and wrapped a hand around himself, not bothering to pose. He was strong, but he wasn't as cut as some men. And he wasn't lithe and beautiful like Asterion. Posing wasn't going to do him any favors. He ran his hand over his cockhead tight and slow, the way that he liked, and was surprised when Asterion let out a small, choked sound.

Dom looked over at Asterion, who was more splayed out than he had been before. His eyes were bright, and his chest was getting a little blotchy with heat. He licked his lips, his gaze fixed on Dom's member.

"Slower," Asterion commanded. "Start at the base." Oh, yes. Dom began to stroke himself, shoulders shifting against the blankets as he found a new rhythm. The way Asterion liked. His skin felt hot, embarrassment fleeting as Asterion slid closer, his legs touching Dom's, his body shifting as he stroked himself in time with Dom's movements. "Yes, Dom," Asterion's voice was breathy. "Just like that. Keep going."

The encouragement made Dom's back tighten, one heel coming up to brace against the mattress. He needed more. He let his thumb slide over his slit, and Asterion moaned. Then Asterion leaned forward and pressed his lips against Dom's shoulder in a delicate kiss.

Dom's hips leapt, he groaned.

"Asterion."

"Getting close?" Asterion purred. Dom nodded, whimpered. "Oh, I can't wait to see you come." It was barely dirty talk, but Dom arched his back all the same. "Faster, Dom. Tighter." Dom tightened his grip and moaned Asterion's name. "Come for me."

Dom came hard, back arching, moaning, desperate. He felt like he was floating, even as his legs turned to mush and he collapsed back onto the mattress. Asterion was still stroking himself, his eyes skating over Dom's body, lingering on his cock.

"Can I?" Dom offered, reaching toward Asterion. Asterion's

eyes widened, and he lay back immediately, sliding his hand to his stomach. Dom rolled onto his hip, closed his hand around Asterion's cock and stroked him.

"Dom! Oh!" Hearing Asterion say his name so eagerly made Dom ache low in his stomach. He slowed his movements, wanting to draw this out, make it good. Take his time. Asterion's fist clenched between them in the blankets as he moaned.

"Like this?" Dom asked. Asterion whined, nodding frantic, pressing up into Dom's fist. Dom slid the fingers of his unoccupied hand into Asterion's hair, and then Dom leaned forward and kissed him.

Dom pressed his tongue into Asterion's mouth, and he could taste Asterion's groan of pleasure, feel Asterion spilling over his hand.

The moment Dom tried to let him go, Asterion grabbed Dom by the shoulder's, pulling them together, deepening the kiss. After a few seconds, Dom gave up trying to keep his sticky hand from grasping Asterion's hip, and Asterion sighed at his touch.

Having Asterion only made Dom want him more. Disheveled, chest heaving, Asterion pulled back and looked at Dom. He was beautiful all the time, but especially flushed and disassembled. More beautiful than Dom had thought it was possible for a person to be.

Asterion's gold eyes searched Dom's face, and Dom leaned forward and kissed him again. Asterion made a small huff of surprise, and then he sank against Dom's chest. Dom held him and tried to embed the feeling of it into his memory. Nothing had ever felt so good, so right. And maybe that was foolish. But it was also true.

28

Dom got up and went into the bathroom, pulling open the drawer below the sink where he kept spare washcloths. There were none.

"Where are the washcloths?"

"Oh, I moved them," Asterion called back. Then he yawned. Dom wished it wasn't all so endearing.

"To where?"

"They're in the long cabinet. They make more sense there."

"No, they don't," Dom said. But he found them easily enough.

Dom cleaned himself up, and then came back into the bedroom to find Asterion, stretched out, totally unabashed, one arm draped over his eyes. Dom snorted as he knelt beside him.

"Comfortable, your majesty?" Dom asked, sliding the wash-cloth over Asterion's hip. Asterion huffed and batted him away, propping himself before grabbing the washcloth from Dom's hand.

"I didn't ask you to," he grumbled. Dom chuckled, sitting beside Asterion. When Asterion glanced over at him, Dom leaned forward and kissed his shoulder. Asterion's eyes narrowed. "What are you doing?"

Dom stilled, surprised by his tone.

"Nothing." Asterion watched him warily for a moment. Was he doing something wrong? Even the smutty pulp novels he'd read had made it clear that cuddling was good. And he'd sort of thought... well, he'd wanted to stay. To keep Asterion in his arms a little bit longer. But maybe that wasn't what this was. "Should I go?" Dom asked, straightening up. Asterion blinked at him.

"You don't have to stay."

"I want to stay," Dom said, ignoring the heat that crawled up the back of his neck, because if he couldn't be honest with the first person he'd ever gotten into bed with then *really* what was he doing? "Unless you don't want me to say."

"I mean," Asterion bit his lip, then frowned as he turned toward Dom. "I don't have magic anymore, so I probably won't be able to fuck again right away, but—"

"Wait, what?" That was not what he'd been getting at. Asterion stared at Dom like he was an idiot.

"And, no offense, but I doubt your refractory period is particularly—"

"I wasn't trying to get off again," Dom said, because his mind was too soupy to make it sound better than that. "I just wanted to stay with you."

THE NUMBER OF PEOPLE WHO HAD EVER STAYED IN ASTERION'S BED for anything more than a quick cat nap, Asterion could have counted on one hand. And out of those few, the only one who hadn't been trying to get something from Asterion was Jonas. Asterion's chest felt tight. There was a knot in his throat.

Dom wasn't trying to get anything from him. Asterion was

sure of that because Asterion didn't have anything. Everything in his apartment, aside from his wardrobe, was already Dom's.

So, did Dom actually want to stay?

That was impossible.

"I really can't—" Asterion blushed, gesturing to his cock. "I mean, it'll take me a minute—" Even when he could use magic, erection spells weren't exactly the most comfortable way to have sex. The sensations were always weird, and—

"I don't want to have sex," Dom said.

And that was insulting, wasn't it? Yes. Probably yes. Asterion was insulted; he frowned. Dom pressed a hand to his own forehead.

"Asterion."

"You don't have to be rude about it."

"I want to have sex with you, but not—"

"I already told you, I can't. I don't know what you've heard about fae folk, but—"

"Literally nothing!"

"But without magic, I—" An exasperated sigh escaped Dom's kiss reddened lips.

"I want to just *lay* with you. I just want to—" he fumbled, cheeks, chest all gorgeously red. "I like holding you. And maybe that's something you don't like. Or want. And that's—" Dom turned, putting his feet firmly on the floor. "You can just say so."

Asterion appreciated that Dom tended to speak in plain language, and all the words he'd used were very simple. But somehow, Asterion's mind was tripping over the meaning. When was the last time he'd snuggled with anyone? He'd had a stuffed toy fox as a child. Whatever had happened to Little Red?

Dom was standing up.

Oh, shitting hell.

"No, wait—" Asterion reached in Dom's general direction, was caught momentarily off guard by the gorgeous curve of

Dom's ass, and then forced himself to focus. Dom was frowning. Because Asterion had just effectively kicked him out of bed. Like an idiot. "Please stay. I mean—If you want to stay. I don't... I can't promise I'm a decent bedfellow."

"I can go. It's fine." Dom's voice was toneless, empty. How had Asterion fucked this so badly? He'd never slept with someone nice before. That was the problem.

"I want you to stay," Asterion said. He felt hot and cold at the same time. He grabbed the blanket and pulled it across his hips, hoping that perhaps it would make him feel less exposed. It did nothing. Especially not with Dom's gorgeous physique standing over him. Big but not so big as to be intimidating. Not so well-sculpted as to make Asterion feel like he needed to lift weights. And for having never had sex before, Dom was awfully comfortable standing there naked. No decorum to speak of. Asterion pursed his lips. "Get back into bed," he tried. Dom's lips cracked into a smirk.

"I don't think that's how this works."

"Oh, you don't know the first thing about how it works, Dom Silva!" Asterion huffed to try and obfuscate the fact that he didn't know how it worked either.

Dom was too nice to call him out on it though. He watched Asterion, his gaze soft, considering. It made Asterion's stomach turn over; he hated being looked at when he was fumbling, but there was nothing he could do but meet Dom's eye. He was afraid if he opened his mouth Dom would leave, and now that he knew Dom staying was an option, he was doing his best not to put his foot in it.

Dom knelt on the edge of the bed slowly, muscles tensing in his thighs, and Asterion nearly jumped for joy. Or he would have, if he wasn't trying to be aloof and unbothered. Unfortunately, when Dom kissed him, all the tightness flooded out of Asterion's chest and a small, satisfied sound escaped the back of his throat. He could feel Dom smile, smug against his mouth, and Asterion truly, deeply didn't care. Until Dom backed off the bed again.

"No. Dom," Asterion whined. Dom smiled, bending over to pick up his trousers. Asterion pouted.

"I'm just going downstairs to get my pajamas."

"Oh." Good. Asterion's heart was beating hard in his chest. He pressed his hand against his sternum and watched as Dom shimmied into his pants.

He wanted Dom. That wasn't strange. Anyone with eyes would want Dom Silva warming their bed. The thought of laying next to him. Of having those strong arms wrapped around his waist again. Of being with someone without having to put on a show. It had been lovely.

Dom was halfway out the door, winding his hair into a knot at the back of his head as he spoke.

"Tea, Asterion?"

"Please," Asterion said, blinking in surprise.

"I'll put the kettle on," he said, and was gone.

Asterion's chest was tight again, and it took him several moments to realize that it wasn't the grip of anxiety he was so used to, terrified of having not performed his role to audience expectations. This was something else. Something like desire, but almost tangible. He'd never been brought tea in bed, by someone who wasn't paid to do so, or who wasn't trying to impress him. At least, he didn't think Dom was trying to impress him.

But Asterion was impressed. And he wanted to stay. And he tried not to think too hard about what that might mean, as he lay back against the blankets and waited for Dom to return.

29

Movement on the mattress beside him woke Asterion from the best sleep he'd had in months. Dom's chest brushed against his shoulder and before Asterion could open his eyes, Dom kissed his cheek.

Asterion snuggled into the bracket of Dom's arms, chasing Dom's lips with his own as he got himself situated. Dom was leaning over him, a position Asterion would happily endure for the rest of his life, if at all possible.

Maybe that was too bold. It *was* too bold. But waking up to kisses, and Dom's strong arms; he could get used to it.

Not that he would. Just that he could.

"I have to go to work," Dom said quietly as he pulled away again. Asterion pouted, opening his eyes to do so more effectively. Dom smiled. "No. I'm already running late as it is."

"Sidney can take care of it." Asterion waved his hand, as if he could shoo away Dom's responsibilities. And then he realized the buttons on Dom's shirt were easily within reach. He toyed with the top one with his thumb, watching as Dom's gaze slid down to Asterion's hand. Dom dragged his teeth over his bottom lip, consideration clear on his handsome face. Yes. Perfect. Asterion slid the top button out of its hole.

Before Asterion could come up with something suitably seductive to say, Dom kissed him again. It was a firm kiss, the heat and intensity of it pressing Asterion back into the pillows. For a moment he was so caught off guard that he forgot to breathe.

"Later," Dom mumbled against Asterion's lips, his stubble scratching Asterion's chin. Dom's attention made Asterion brainless; he could barely nod his agreement.

Asterion got up after Dom left, wandering into the kitchen to make coffee. He stretched as he waited for the brew and caught himself smiling at nothing. It was ridiculous how good he felt.

Initially, he chalked it up to the sex, which he'd really enjoyed. Dom's expressions, his eagerness and openness, were thrilling because they had been real, unguarded. Dom had been honest with Asterion. And Dom had stayed.

And maybe that was a stupid thing to be happy about. Asterion was living in the man's house, after all. It wasn't exactly like Dom had far to go to get into his own bed. But he hadn't gone. And it seemed like he was going to come back.

Inordinately pleased, Asterion took his coffee to the window seat. He read and lounged and eventually, a little after lunch, he showered and dressed and made his way to the diner.

He ran into Nina in the back parking lot, where she was unlocking her bike. She smirked at him; a knowing tilt to her eyebrow made Asterion blush. Dom didn't seem like the type to kiss and tell, but Asterion was going to have to be subtle until he knew for sure.

"Good afternoon," he said, as Nina stood, adjusting her rucksack on her shoulder.

"Are you working tonight?" she asked.

"I don't think so," he shrugged. "I suppose if he's short staffed."

"The opposite, I think." Nina's grin widened. "The schedule board is almost overfull. Dom mentioned he might head out before the dinner rush."

"Oh!" That was very good news. A night with Dom available and at home. Not tired from having pulled a double shift. Asterion almost shivered in anticipation of the bevy of enticing ways they might pass the time. Nina's eyebrows arched almost into her hair and Asterion scrambled to find a more innocuous facial expression than the one he'd been wearing.

"Do you know the last time Dom elected to go home early?" Nina asked, her smile turning sly.

"No," Asterion said, innocently.

"Never," Nina stated. "Never once." He could have guessed, he supposed.

"Perhaps he has plans."

"What are *you* doing this evening?" Nina asked. The first thing that came to Asterion's mind was gagging on Dom's cock. Gods. Horrible.

"Uh, nothing," he stammered, cheeks reddening. "Why?"

"My boyfriend Casey is playing tonight at a bar down on Garretts Avenue. I promised him I'd try to get some folks to come down."

"Is he any good?"

"Dom likes him."

"Is Dom going?" Asterion asked too quickly. Nina laughed and got on her bike.

"Ask him yourself." She nodded toward the kitchen door, which Dom was just stepping out of, buttoning up his coat. Dom waved as Nina rode out of the parking lot.

Dom's hair was tied back, thin gold glasses perched on the bridge of his nose, and Asterion caught himself staring. Which was silly and ridiculous. He was just a man. A very lovely man, who was smiling as he walked straight toward Asterion, taking off his glasses and tucking them in his pocket. Asterion could feel the heat emanating off his own skin.

"Did you tell her?" Asterion accused, widening his eyes for emphasis.

"Tell her what?" Asterion pointedly cleared his throat, and Dom chuckled as he put his hand on Asterion's elbow and turned him back toward the street. "Nina and I don't really talk about that sort of thing."

"Are you going to the show tonight?" Asterion asked.

"I don't think show is the right word."

"Performance?" Asterion adjusted with an eye roll. Dom snorted.

"Roosevelt's isn't exactly a performance space. It's a step up from a pit in the ground and a step down from a bar."

"Will there be dancing?" Asterion asked. He loved dancing, and he especially loved the idea of dancing with Dom. Their bodies pressed together. A few drinks. Sounded like the recipe for a perfect evening. When he glanced over, Dom was barely hiding a grimace in his coat collar. "Oh, don't tell me you don't like dancing?"

"I like dancing."

"But there won't be any?"

"I imagine there will be. Casey's a good fiddle player. And he usually has a bassist with him."

"But?" Asterion frowned. "What's the problem?"

"There's no problem. Do you want to go?" Dom asked.

"I'll do whatever you want to do," he said. And he would have. He would have worked the dinner shift, learned about motorcycles, jumped in the bay, if Dom had declared it was how he wanted to spend his evening. But now Dom was biting one corner of his bottom lip, his gaze out in front of them as they turned onto the street where they lived. Damn. The walk to and from the diner was far too short.

"If I was busy tonight, what would you do?" Dom asked. Asterion shrugged.

"You have the night off. Unless—"

The realization that Dom might not want to spend the evening with him came over Asterion like a wave, surprising and consuming. Of course, Dom didn't want to spend the evening out with Asterion. Why would he? Asterion was nothing to him. A tenant at best. There was no reason for Dom to want—

Dom caught Asterion's hand, and his touch derailed the train of disparagement that Asterion had been conducting in his own head.

"I want to be with you. Tonight, I mean. I—" Dom was blushing furiously as he walked on, nearly dragging Asterion alongside him, before Asterion remembered that he needed to move his feet. "I don't want you *not* to go to Roosevelt's just because I don't want to go to Roosevelt's."

"You don't want to go?" Asterion asked, trying to catch the thread of what was happening.

"It's not that," Dom sighed. "I do. I like Casey. It would mean a lot to Nina if I went. But I," he trailed off, his deep brown eyes searching Asterion's face desperately. "I don't go out."

"We don't have to," Asterion said quickly.

"But we should," Dom asserted. "And you want to, don't you?" Asterion considered lying. But he wasn't sure why he was considering lying. Habit, probably.

"Yes, but—"

"No," Dom shook his head. "Don't give me an out. It'll be fun. I'm just... I'll warn you, I'm not that great at socializing. And we should eat before we go because the food is horrible there."

"How are the drinks?"

"Also horrible," Dom said, as he led Asterion up the walk to their house. They were still holding hands, and Dom didn't let go until they stopped on the porch. "They'll get you drunk though." Asterion laughed, but he had no intention of getting drunk. Being with Dom made Asterion want to be present; he didn't want to miss anything. It was an urge he wasn't sure he'd experienced before.

Dom smiled gently.

"I want to go out with you. I want to do all kinds of things with you. For you." Dom hesitated, his eyes searching Asterion's face, and Asterion couldn't help but admire Dom's features in the soft light of the slowly setting sun. There was a freckle beneath his left eyebrow. A small scar by the corner of his earlobe.

"I don't want you to be uncomfortable."

"I won't be," Dom said firmly. "It might take me a minute to warm up. I'm out of practice." His sincerity was thrilling, in it's own bizarre way. Had Asterion ever met anyone so forthright in his life?

It made Asterion want to kiss him, so he did, gently. He was both relieved and amused when Dom grabbed Asterion's waist and hauled him closer. Dom smelled like fried food and burnt coffee and beneath that, the heat of a spice Asterion loved but didn't know the name of. Dom pulled back, his lips brushing the corner of Asterion's mouth, and Asterion was giddy. Like all the blood was rushing to his head. Or away from it.

"I should shower," Dom said. "Come in if you want. I have soup we can reheat for dinner."

"Alright," Asterion agreed, and followed him inside.

30

Dom left Asterion in the kitchen, watching the soup, and went to shower. He scrubbed off the diner stink and wondered what Asterion would do if he suggested that instead of going to Roosevelt's they stay home and crawl back into Dom's bed together.

Asterion was too willing, though, to agree to anything Dom suggested. Dom couldn't help but remember what Asterion had told him when they'd been at Harlan's Crest: that Asterion was used to changing himself for people. And Dom wasn't sure how he felt about that.

It made him uneasy, probably because it was something Dom was always coming up against himself. He'd given up so much of his life trying to fix everything after Ares, that the idea of changing himself any further: his long hair, his job, the way he spent his time, felt like it might be a sacrifice too far. Obligation and desire were always knotted together and pulling in opposite directions. Dropping out of college, coming home, he'd wanted to do those things. But he also wasn't sure he'd ever had a choice. Compromise was a nice word. He just wasn't sure he knew what it really looked like.

He stepped out of the shower and dried his hair, letting it hang, damp, over his shoulders as he wrapped a towel around his waist. Dom stepped into his bedroom in the same moment that Asterion closed the dresser drawer he'd apparently been rummaging through. A pair of black trousers Dom had forgotten he owned were tucked under Asterion's arm. Asterion looked surprised to see Dom, his eyes wide, mouth open, like he was trying to find the words to explain what he was doing. Dom chuckled.

"Did you need something?"

"No." Asterion put the trousers down on the top of the dresser and cleared his throat. "I was just wondering what you were going to wear, and I thought I would look and see what you had that wasn't work clothes."

"I think you might have the wrong idea about what kind of place Roosevelt's is."

"Well, what do you think I should wear?" Asterion asked, although his attention had seemed to stall out somewhere down Dom's chest. Dom's skin prickled.

"I'm sure what you're wearing now is fine," he said. Asterion stepped closer, his gaze snapping up to meet Dom's, a wicked smile drawing up the corner of his mouth.

"So, if I don't have to change, then, we've got a little extra time on our hands?"

"I suppose so," Dom said, arousal making his muscles tighten as Asterion came even closer.

"Thank Gods," Asterion murmured. He reached out and slid his fingertips down Dom's abdomen. Dom touched his hand, but Asterion stopped him with a sound.

"Ah! Wait." Asterion demanded. Dom blushed, desire rushing through him. Whatever this was, he wanted it. He could wait.

Asterion pressed against him, nudging Dom back against the

wall with the length of his body. Asterion took his time, dragging his fingers across Dom's chest, slipping across Dom's shoulders. The flood of sensation made his skin tingle, his cock heavy.

"You have no idea how good you look, do you?" Asterion asked. Dom let out a small huff of breath, as Asterion brushed his lips against the side of Dom's neck.

"Did you turn off the stove?" Dom asked. Asterion grinned against his skin.

"I'm not an idiot, Dominic." Asterion said, as he finally, gently kissed him. "And don't pretend you didn't hear my question."

Asterion's nimble fingers slipped over Dom's ribs, digging in just enough not to tickle, and Dom moaned against Asterion's mouth.

"I think you like how I look," he managed, breathing hard.

"I do." Asterion murmured, tucking fingertips beneath the edge of Dom's towel. "I really do. Do you want to touch me?"

"Yes." Dom said. Asterion smiled and dropped to his knees.

"Now you can," Asterion said, looking up at Dom coyly as he tugged Dom's towel off his hips.

Dom pushed a soft lock of blue hair off Asterion's cheek, as Asterion slid one hand down Dom's length, lifting it to his lips, leaving Dom breathless, his mind unhelpfully blank. Blue lashes half covered Asterion's deep golden eyes, and Dom had to flatten his palms against the wall to keep himself upright.

Asterion took Dom into his mouth and Dom groaned. He closed his eyes and then opened them again because, God, was he stupid enough to not watch? Asterion's grip shifted, and Dom shuddered, back muscles twitching. He tried not to thrust forward, and when Asterion's gold eyes flashed up at him again, Dom had to bite his tongue to stop himself from coming.

"Asterion! Oh. So—oh!" Asterion took him deeper, swallowed around him, and Dom scrambled for purchase against the wall. Asterion hair drifted down over his cheekbone, and Dom pushed it back, running his fingers into Asterion's hair, and Asterion moaned around Dom's cock.

Dom trembled. Everything he had ever thought about desire had been wrong. Pleasure in giving could be equal to pleasure in receiving. Something about compromise. He wanted both, and he was coming undone too quickly to untangle them from each other.

Dom leaned his hips back, sliding slowly down the wall. Asterion wore a smug smirk on his handsome face, wiping at his lower lip, and Dom had no control over the way he wanted Asterion. He pulled Asterion to his mouth, knowing the bitter taste on Asterion's tongue was likely his own. He didn't care. Asterion leaned against Dom, palms braced against Dom's chest, and Dom was undressing Asterion before either of them had caught their breath.

"THERE'S NO RUSH," ASTERION CHUCKLED, THOUGH HE TOOK ALL of Dom's kisses willingly, while Dom fumbled with the buttons on Asterion's shirt.

"I want you," Dom said.

"You were having me."

"I want to hear you make that sound again." Asterion got goosebumps. He'd told himself he was going to be happy with sucking Dom off, and he was, sincerely. It had been everything he'd hoped for and more, with those delicious noises and gasps and Dom's fingers in his hair. It was baffling that Dom didn't know how gorgeous he was. Asterion would've offered to pleasure him just for the joy of getting to touch him. There should have been people lining up around the block to get on their knees for Dom Silva.

And then, a naked Dom Silva was pushing Asterion's shirt off. Asterion was happy to let him; he wasn't a fool. Asterion braced himself against the fullness of Dom's biceps, as Dom leaned closer, his body arching over Asterion's, as Asterion fell back onto the floor.

It dawned on Asterion then, that he was about to be ravished. Which was interesting, because while his sexual history was long and varied, he'd never been taken like this before. Dom's desire was raw, potent. Embarrassingly real. He crawled over Asterion, unbuttoning Asterion's trousers with an intensity of concentration that made Asterion ache with arousal. Usually, sex was a performance and Asterion knew his part. He knew what he liked and how to get it, but there was something in the way Dom touched him. The way Dom was seeking Asterion's pleasure, as well as something for himself. Some kind of deeper satisfaction that Asterion hadn't known about before.

Dom's big brown eyes searched Asterion's face, and Asterion's stomach did a little flip of anticipation, as he braced himself with his spare hand against the floor. Asterion's trousers were low on his hips, and Dom did a push-up to slide his tongue against Asterion's hip crease.

Good Gods.

Asterion whimpered, cock leaking as Dom slid lower. Dom's hair skated over Asterion's skin, as Dom sucked a love bite into Asterion's thigh. Asterion twitched and moaned. Things were getting desperate.

"Dom," Asterion murmured. And then he couldn't think of anything else to say. Dom's name tumbled from his mouth, a plea interrupted by a hiss of pleasure, as Dom began to stroke him.

"Tell me what you like." Dom's voice was low and smooth, and it made Asterion throb.

"This. I— You—" Brainless. Guileless.

"Like this?" And then Dom leaned down and took Asterion into his mouth.

It was good before Dom found a rhythm, and then it was fantastic. He took Asterion deep and Asterion bit his lip, his back arching, hips thrusting unbidden. Dom pulled off, eyes watering.

"Sorry," Asterion panted. Dom went down on Asterion again without a word, leaving Asterion's toes curling in the thick pile of the rug. Gods, help him. "Dom," Asterion groaned, as Dom's grip tightened perfectly. Exactly. Fuck.

In minutes, Asterion was babbling nonsense, begging for release. Asterion tugged Dom's hair and Dom's shoulders drooped, his mouth dropping open just long enough to pant, before he stuck out his tongue and took Asterion to the base.

"Dom! Oh, Gods!" Asterion was being too loud, but Dom seemed to like it. It made him eager, made him go faster. Asterion was so close, and when Dom slid off him, Asterion whimpered, reaching toward Dom. He would give anything, everything, for just a little more. Dom looked like a god, kneeling between Asterion's thighs. His eyes were dark, lips flushed and full, thick chest rising and falling and Asterion was entirely at his mercy.

"Dom, please."

Dom bit his bottom lip and reached down with one hand. He grabbed Asterion beneath the knee, and hoisted Asterion's leg up over Dom's hip, pulling Asterion forward in one smooth, solid yank.

Asterion groaned at the manhandling. At the way Dom was looking at him like a starving man looking over a feast. Dom dropped to his hands, his cock heavy, sliding against Asterion's lower stomach, and oh, it was so good. Asterion slid a hand between them, wanting to touch him, wanting, just wanting. Dom pressed a sloppy kiss to Asterion's lips, and then moaned, as Asterion began to stroke them together.

Dom thrust into Asterion's fist, rutting against Asterion's cock. He bit his lower lip, hips jerking in a steady, furious rhythm and Asterion could have watched him like this for hours. Dom was in a haze of pleasure, dazzling and fuckable, dragging Asterion right along with him.

And then Dom ducked his head, his teeth grazing the soft skin at the base of Asterion's neck. Asterion's back tightened, the sharpness of his own arousal taking him by surprise. It was easy to find the counter-rhythm to Dom's. Everything with Dom was easy. Asterion's hips jolted, as Dom slid his hand down to cover Asterion's, his fingers interlacing with Asterion's around them.

It was too much. It was so good. Dom tightened his grip and Asterion pressed his head back against the ground, moaning because he was quickly losing the ability to speak coherently. "Come. Please, Dom. C—"

Dom came, and Asterion followed with a fevered groan. Never in his life. He was going to have rug burn on his back and he didn't care in the slightest.

Dom rolled off Asterion and onto the rug with a grunt. It was cold without him, so Asterion followed, curling into the warmth of Dom's chest. Asterion closed his eyes, and he was a little surprised when Dom leaned down and kissed him.

"I think you're going to have to shower again," Asterion mumbled against Dom's lips. Dom smiled.

"Whose fault is that?"

"No need to assign blame." Asterion scooted closer, resting his head on Dom's bicep. Dom's fingers slid slowly over Asterion's arm. His hand. His hip. Asterion could feel himself drifting off and protested in his head. On the floor! Covered in cum!

With the same person, twice in a row! Before, he would have stayed in bed long enough to have a cigarette and ascertain the whereabouts of his shoes. Now he was practically snuggling. What was happening to him?

Dom kissed Asterion's temple.

"Don't fall asleep. I thought we were going out. And *you* need to shower," Dom said, his touch soft, just above Asterion's belly button.

"What a rude thing to say to someone." Asterion yawned.

"You said it to me two minutes ago!"

"We could shower together."

"Not if we want to make Casey's show. And we still need to eat." Asterion pouted, opening his eyes again.

"Appalling. Now I see why you don't bother going out." Dom snorted, and then he kissed the corner of Asterion's mouth before nudging Asterion off his arm and onto the carpet. Asterion was about to whine about being abandoned on the floor like a pair of old socks, when Dom scooped him up.

Asterion yelped in surprise, and Dom chuckled.

"What are you doing?"

"Don't fuss."

Asterion was naked, being carried across a bedroom against the chest of the most gorgeous, pleasurable partner he'd ever had the great fortune to be with, and his stupid, foolish heart was trying to leap out of his chest. Fussing was the furthest thing from his mind.

Dom kissed Asterion before he set him down on the mattress. Then he turned and went into the bathroom, fully unaware of the fact that he'd left Asterion sitting in stunned, besotted silence.

31

Roosevelt's was exactly the way Dom remembered it. A dingy brass bar, creaky floors, a ceiling that sat half a foot too low, and more people than could responsibly be stuffed into one place.

The crowd was thicker at the back of the room than the front, where tables had been shoved to the side and some couples were already dancing to the jig that was sailing gracefully from the string duet on the makeshift stage in the corner. Casey was tall and broad shouldered, his head almost brushing the beams that held up the roof. Despite the shabbiness of the place, Asterion's eyes lit up when they stepped inside, his smile wide and beautiful, and Dom's heart melted.

It wasn't horrible. It was loud, and it would only get louder. There wasn't a doorman to turn anyone away, so there were sure to be even more patrons soon. But it was okay. Dom took a deep breath, and caught Nina's eye from across the room, her own widening in surprise as he waved at her. Asterion leaned against his side.

"What do you want to drink?" His chin rested on Dom's shoulder, and the press of his body made Dom feel steadier.

"Whatever you're having."

"Oh look! There's Nina!" Asterion waved and Nina waved back, still looking as though she'd seen pigs fly across the room. "She's really surprised to see us. Well, you." Dom rolled his eyes. Asterion squeezed Dom's butt with one hand. "I'll be right back." And then he pushed Dom in Nina's direction and disappeared into the throng surrounding the bar.

"What is happening right now?" Nina asked, as Dom settled his shoulders against the wall beside her. "Is the world ending out there? Did all your other cooks drop dead and you need me to come take a shift?"

"*You* invited *me*."

"How many things have I invited you to in the last ten years?"

"A couple?" Dom hedged. Nina snorted and smacked him on the arm. The song ended and the room burst into applause. People whistled and shouted and for a minute or two it was too loud to talk. It seemed like half the town had managed to squeeze into the building. "Is it always this crowded?" Dom asked when he thought she might be able to hear him again. Nina shrugged.

"Not when the weather's better. There are more girls here than usual too, but that's because both those big trawlers came back this week. Everyone from the fisheries is in here tonight."

The unease that Dom had managed to bury beneath the pleasure of being with Asterion returned with a vengeance. So many of his high school classmates ended up working at the fisheries. People who knew that Ares had vanished, and that Dom had dropped out of college to try and be a poor facsimile of his brother.

Logically, Dom knew that no one aside from him cared, but he couldn't help the shame. He wasn't like the other kids. He wasn't even like his brother: Ares had been defensive captain on the football team, a good kid, a young pillar of the community. The tragedy of their mother's disappearance and their father's death made all the matrons of the town misty-eyed whenever Ares had walked past, the weight of the world on his young shoulders. Dom was still trailing along in his wake.

"Here we go!" Asterion appeared, a drink in each hand, jerking Dom out of his downward spiral. Until Dom saw the man at Asterion's heels. Dom took his drink, as Asterion turned toward Anders the fisherman, pulling him forward into their small cluster. "This is Anders Casmir! He's new in town."

"Nice to meet you!" Nina said, tipping her beer bottle in his direction. Dom sipped his drink and made a sound that he thought could be reasonably interpreted as a greeting. Asterion opened his mouth to say something, when the fiddle came blaring to life on the stage.

"Oh, yes!" Asterion said, handing his drink to Dom. "Hold this. Come on. Ladies first." He grabbed Nina's free hand, and she let out a squawk of laughter as Asterion pulled her off the wall. Dom grinned, lifting his glass in her direction as Nina reached helplessly back toward him and Asterion tugged her onto the dance floor. Just as quickly, Asterion had an arm around her waist and was leading her through the open space. Dom laughed as he watched them go.

It took Dom a full minute to realize that Anders the fisherman was still standing in silence beside him, and when Dom glanced in his direction Anders' crystal blue eyes were studying Dom so intently that Dom jerked back in surprise.

"What are you?" Anders asked. No. That didn't make sense. Dom must have misheard him.

"What?" Dom leaned closer, and Anders moved in, his breath warm on the side of Dom's neck.

"What *are* you?" He repeated. Dom frowned. Anders sighed, exasperated. "Are you like him?" He nodded toward Asterion.

It took Dom several seconds of mentally shuffling adjectives to figure out what Anders was referring to. Beautiful? Queer? A prince?

"Fae?" Dom asked.

"You're not fae. But you are different, aren't you? Not human."

"No," Dom shook his head. Anders arched an eyebrow, skeptical. "I'm human. I work at the diner, remember? We met."

"I remember." Anders' expression had shifted to something closer to a smirk, his eyes skating over Dom's face like he was looking for a tell at a poker game. Then he glanced at Asterion, and Dom did the same. Asterion and Nina had found their rhythm, speeding up as the song reached its crescendo. "You and him?" Anders asked, without looking at Dom. Which was good, because Dom barely avoided spluttering into his drink.

"No. Well, not—I mean, we're not—"

"He has quite the reputation." Maybe it was just the strange accent (definitely not Scandinavian, like Hector had guessed) but Dom didn't appreciate how judgmental he sounded.

"What do you mean?"

"Nothing. Just considering the probability of magical transference between him and, well, anyone, I suppose." Dom blushed, which was annoying.

"Magical transference?" Dom repeated. "You mean, like, marking?" Anders shrugged.

"You wouldn't be the first to bed someone just to get a taste of their power."

"Excuse me?" Dom snapped. Anders' eyes flashed, the blue of his irises a strange quicksilver in the dim light of the bar.

"The Andurnei royal family. They're powerful magical stock."

"Asterion's not—" Not a piece of meat? Not magic? Dom fumbled, and Anders kept talking.

"I'm just wondering what you're trying to get out of it. His magic's gone. At least, for now." Dom's grip on his glass tightened.

'For now.'

Because if someone fell in love with Asterion, his magic would return. Which was certainly what Asterion wanted. And, as Asterion's friend, Dom should want that for him too. But where would that leave Dom? Would Dom love Asterion less if he became magic again? Because Dom was falling in love with Asterion, wasn't he?

No. Maybe. That wasn't— He didn't know yet, what it was between him and Asterion. Dom liked him. And that wouldn't change if somehow Asterion's magic returned. Standing on the wall at Rooselvelt's was a damn strange time to realize that.

"But then, he's one of the most eligible bachelors in the nine realms. It'll happen sooner or later. I suppose if you bide your time, he might—"

"How do you know so much about him?" Dom interrupted. "You're not a fisherman, are you?" Anders smirked.

"Of course, I am."

"What are *you*?"

"Oh my God!" Nina crashed between them as she and Asterion wheeled into the wall. She was laughing and Asterion was beaming, and suddenly Dom was breathless with rage. How dare Anders come over here and accuse Dom of... of what? Using Asterion? And then imply what about Asterion? That he was easy? That he was bound to fall in love with someone who wasn't Dom? Dom shifted his stance, blocking out Anders with his shoulder. Asterion was laughing, taking his drink out of Dom's hands. Their fingers brushed and Asterion met Dom's gaze with a bright, hopeful smile.

"Who's next?"

"Me." Dom drained his drink and handed his glass to Nina,

putting his arm around Asterion's waist. Asterion glanced up at Dom as Dom walked them out onto the dance floor with a confidence that was entirely buoyed by frustration with Anders.

The duo took up a slow song, and Dom's temper was cooled by a small wave of anxiety. Asterion stepped up in front of him and dropped his hand onto Dom's hip.

"Do you want to lead or shall I?"

"I can. Unless you prefer—"

"Go ahead." Dom put his hands on Asterion's waist, and they began to dance. Dom led them slowly around the edge of the floor, his heart pounding in his chest. Asterion smiled at him.

"Do you hate this?"

"No." Dom tried to smile back, but he ended up looking at the floor instead. Didn't want to step on Asterion's feet.

"Are you alright?"

"Do you know Anders?" Dom asked.

"Know him?"

"From before," Dom clarified. Asterion shook his head.

"Is he fae? From Andurnei?" Dom shook his head.

"He didn't say."

"What did he say?" Asterion's voice had gone a little hollow, his gaze fixed over Dom's shoulder. Dom wasn't trying to upset Asterion. But he also wasn't in the lying business. He sighed.

"He asked if we were together, and sort of implied that I was just trying to... I don't know. Get close to you for your magic." Asterion snorted.

"Well, joke's on him. I don't have any magic." He glanced at Dom, his cheeks pink. "Joke's on you too, I suppose. But you hate magic anyway."

"I don't hate magic." Even if he had only just realized it. Asterion arched an eyebrow. Dom swallowed. "I don't understand it. But I don't hate it."

"Okay." Asterion's tone was light, but it felt false. He looked down into the small space between their chests, and Dom tightened his grip on Asterion's waist. This wasn't right at all.

"Asterion—"

"Anders and I didn't know each other before last week. And I haven't slept with so many people that I wouldn't recognize their face if they were right in front of me." Asterion's defensiveness was startling; his cheeks were bright red, and his mouth was tight and narrow.

"Asterion, I don't think you slept with him. And even if you had, I don't care."

"I don't want you to think—!"

"I don't think anything," Dom said. Asterion sniffed and rolled his eyes. "I don't," Dom insisted. "And I don't care if you have magic or not."

"You're likely the only one. And you don't know," Asterion stammered, struggling. "I could be so much more."

"I don't need you to be any more. I'm sure you'd be wonderful with it, but you're wonderful without it. It doesn't matter to me. I want you to have what you want to have."

"I thought you said magic was dangerous," Asterion accused. Dom had said that, and he regretted it now. Asterion had taken it personally, and Dom should have known better.

"My stove is dangerous," Dom said slowly. Earnestly. "That doesn't mean I don't have one in my house." Asterion huffed and looked away, but a smile finally cracked the narrow line of his mouth.

"I never thought being compared to an appliance would feel romantic."

"I've never done this before," Dom said. It was true, and the truth was about all he had. After a moment, Asterion smiled.

"Me either."

Dom's neck warmed as Asterion slid his fingertips over Dom's vertebrae. So, Dom didn't know about magic. So what?

Dom knew how he felt about Asterion, and magic wouldn't change that in the slightest. And maybe he didn't know about the people from Asterion's past. But Dom did know that he was enjoying whatever was happening between the two of them. That he wanted more of it.

The song ended. Dancers hung onto each other for the last few notes, and Dom slid his hands to the front of Asterion's sweater and pulled him into a kiss. Not soft, not subtle. He hoped Anders could see them. Hell, he hoped Nina could see them. Asterion relaxed into Dom's embrace, one hand sliding down over Dom's shoulders. Maybe Dom didn't know exactly what he was doing with Asterion, but he knew what he felt. And he wasn't going to hide it anymore.

32

They kissed until someone hooted at them. A stranger slapped Dom on his shoulder in a jovial way and told them to go get a room. Nina looked more smug than Asterion knew it was possible for a person to look, and Dom was breathless and blushing.

"Can I get you another drink?" He stammered.

Whatever Anders had implied about Asterion, his habits, his past, his proclivities, Asterion was inclined to thank him for it. Dom's protectiveness had unlocked for Asterion an impressively powerful turn-on that he hadn't known about until just then. Remarkable in a man of his age, but then, he was learning a lot about himself these days.

"How about," he murmured, tugging Dom close, "you get me my coat?"

They didn't make it home. They didn't even make it that far. Halfway down the back alley, Asterion pounced on Dom, pressing him against the wall. Dom moaned when Asterion shoved his shoulders back, and yes, that was quite exactly what Asterion wanted to hear at the moment.

"We could go home, you know," Dom mumbled between kisses. Asterion slid his hands over Dom's chest and kissed him again.

What had happened in the bar that had tilted the whole axis of Asterion's world. He'd had his fair share of public kisses. Kisses where Asterion was the prize being won. Where being watched had been a part of being wanted in the first place. But Dom's kiss had felt committed, almost. Not that Dom was committed to him, or they were something to each other. Nothing like that. Because Asterion couldn't navigate that sort of thing. He just couldn't. But it felt good. It felt different.

Dom was different. No one wanted Asterion when he had magic. And he'd thought it would be impossible for anyone to want him without. But Dom had been, well, almost embarrassingly clear about what he wanted.

Dom grabbed Asterion by the waist and turned them, swapping places with Asterion, pressing him against the wall. Asterion sighed in pleasure as Dom began to nuzzle his way beneath the high collar of Asterion's coat. It was stupid, what they were doing. Two grown adults, necking like teenagers. But Asterion had never been desired like this, and he wasn't about to push Dom away.

Dom managed, somehow, to get his hands under Asterion's sweater, and Asterion hissed at the cold, and then at Dom's fingers tightening just so, as his tongue slid against the love bite he'd made on Asterion's throat.

"How are you still out here?" A deep voice asked. Dom jerked backward, and Asterion straightened his coat as he glanced over at the big fiddle player, Nina's boyfriend Casey. There was sweat on his face, and his forehead glistened in the light that was streaming out the back door. He smirked at Dom. "Go home, Silva."

Dom grinned, rubbing the back of his neck sheepishly, blush high on his cheeks. There had never been anyone who looked so handsome standing in this alleyway or any other, and Asterion was thrilled to know that they were going home together.

"You guys sounded great," Dom said. Casey rolled his eyes.

"Don't pretend you heard a single note."

"Well, I did," Asterion chimed in. "And you play wonderfully." Casey laughed and rolled his eyes.

"Thank you. Now do me a favor and take him home before Nina comes out here and yells at you both."

"Of course." Asterion slid his hand into the crook of Dom's arm. "Gladly."

"Good to see you," Dom waved, as Asterion pulled him around toward the entrance to the alley.

"Come over for dinner sometime. Bring your friend!"

"I will," Dom replied with no hesitation. Asterion knew his own smile was unflatteringly wide, but he couldn't stop himself. He was still grinning when they reached the spot where Dom's motorcycle was parked. Dom glanced over at him with a smirk. "What are you so happy about?"

"Nothing." Asterion plucked his helmet out of Dom's hands. "I'm having fun, that's all."

"Good." Dom said. Then he leaned forward and kissed Asterion. "Me too."

The ride back to the house was too fast and too slow. Asterion loved being pressed against Dom as they slid like wraiths through the darkness. He felt safe, relieved that Dom had control and aroused by how completely Dom had it. Like everything else Dom Silva decided to do, he had mastered driving and turned it into an art. Was that how he'd be in a relationship too? In love?

It wasn't really Asterion's business. No need to go making

mountains out of molehills. Dom and Asterion weren't together. They were just... whatever this was.

But what if they were together? Really together. Visions of domesticity filled Asterion's head: of sharing meals and a bed, going to the diner, coming home again. The life they could have together in Dom's small apartment.

It wasn't like that. The thing between them, whatever it was, was too new for Asterion to already be maudlin about it. He wasn't the sentimental sort anyway. They were just having fun. And so what if Asterion's stomach swooped when Dom took his hand to help him off the bike. And maybe Asterion's skin shouldn't have tingled when Dom helped Asterion out of his coat. But then Dom was kissing him again, and Asterion wasn't worried about those things. Or about anything else.

They fumbled down the hall, shedding clothes, and Asterion barely had the forethought to murmur a question against Dom's lips.

"Do you want to?" It would be Dom's first time if they—

"Yes," Dom said. He pulled Asterion close, their chests flush, skin against skin, and suddenly Asterion was blushing, his eyes drifting down, feeling shy. Dom smiled, brushing a strand of hair out of Asterion's face with a tenderness that made Asterion's knees buckle. Gods. What was wrong with him?

Asterion kissed Dom then, tried to turn it into a rough, impassioned thing. But Dom met his mouth with a smoothness that had Asterion aching in his unbuttoned trousers. Breathless. A little confused. What was this? And how did it feel so good?

Dom ducked his head, his nose brushing the side of Asterion's jaw, and Asterion lungs betrayed him; they weren't taking in enough air. Dom kissed him right over the rabbiting rhythm of Asterion's pulse, and Asterion gasped.

He needed to get this right. It became a sort of mantra as they undressed, and by the time the back of Asterion's legs touched the mattress, it was all he could hear in his head. Dom paused, his fingers curling around Asterion's palms.

"Do *you* want to?" He did want to. So much. But what if it wasn't everything Dom wanted it to be. What if it wasn't good enough? Asterion was far too flustered to lie properly.

"I want to please you," Asterion said. His stomach twisted in embarrassment, reviled by the vulnerability of it all.

"I'm very pleased," Dom said. Then raised Asterion's hand to his mouth and kissed Asterion's knuckles. Asterion stammered. "But we don't have to."

"I want to," Asterion insisted. He did. More than anything. But he couldn't remember how to have sex and have feelings at the same time. And it had been quite a while since he'd had to do something against a mattress that he wasn't familiar with.

"Do you trust me?" Dom asked.

"I think I'm supposed to be the one saying that," Asterion retorted. Dom smiled, and then he kissed Asterion, wrapping his arms around Asterion's waist as he lowered them both onto the bed.

Dom moved slowly, intentionally, and Asterion let himself sink into the sensations of Dom exploring his body with fingers and mouth and tongue. He caressed Asterion's hips, his ribs, fingertips pausing over Asterion's nipples, making Asterion cry out in pleasure. Dom rocked against Asterion, nipped at his earlobe, murmured against his skin.

"I want you."

"Dom," Asterion's limbs were weak as he reached for Dom, lost and loose in his own pleasure. Dom studied Asterion's face, as he dragged his fingers over Asterion's body. When he tucked a loose strand of hair behind Asterion's ear, his finger brushed against the sensitive tip and Asterion whimpered.

"There?" Dom sounded amused, and when Asterion opened

his eyes, he could see the small smile on Dom's face as he ran his calloused thumb around the long shell of Asterion's ear.

"Tease," Asterion accused in a sigh. Dom smirked, and then went to work, nipping, sucking, kissing, leaving Asterion writhing against the sheets.

Dom was methodical, almost agonizingly so, and eventually, in a daze, Asterion realized that *this* was how Dom learned something new. Studiously, with precision, Dom was learning how to have sex with Asterion. This was how he got so damn good at everything. Asterion tried and failed to hold back a snort of laughter. Dom looked up from the inside of Asterion's thigh with a small frown.

"What?"

"No, it's nothing." Dom considered this, lips pursed, and then bit him. Asterion yelped, twisting his hips, and then Dom was on him again, their bodies together, Asterion sighing, clawing at his shoulders as Dom rocked against him. Asterion was close, and Dom wasn't even inside him yet.

DOM COULD HAVE TOUCHED ASTERION FOR DAYS. HE LOVED THE way Asterion moved and looked and sounded beneath him, reacting to his touch. Even if Dom wasn't good at fucking, he at least knew he could please Asterion like this. And that was something.

Still, Dom was a little relieved when Asterion finally took charge, pushing Dom off him with a soft moan. Asterion reached up to the nightstand, and pulled open the drawer, shuffling blindly in it for mere moments before he produced the small bottle of oil that Dom sometimes used when he was on his own. Asterion tucked the bottle into Dom's palm, and then flipped onto his stomach, looking back over his shoulder at

Dom with a heavy-lidded gaze that was as arousing as any command he'd ever issued. Dom nearly fumbled the open bottle in his rush to give Asterion what he wanted.

He knew from explorations with his own body that this part might take time. That he should be careful, gentle. But Asterion's moans and whines as Dom fingered him, turned loud and desperate quickly. And Dom was practically vibrating with want.

But, no. He could wait. Dom was good at waiting—

"Please, Dom," Asterion begged. "Fuck me." Dom swallowed. He could. He wanted to. But there was something he'd wanted too.

"Would you—" He hesitated. "If it's comfortable—"

"Anything, Dom," Asterion panted. "Anything." Dom swallowed.

"Flip over," he said. "I want to see you."

For a moment there was silence. Asterion's head dropped down, and Dom could hear him chuckle.

"What?" Dom demanded. He wasn't going to let Asterion not answer this time, like he had before. Asterion turned over with a huff, his long torso stretched out before Dom, as he reached up for a pillow and shoved it beneath his lower back.

"You're too sweet for me," Asterion said, before he hitched his leg up over Dom's hip and yanked him close.

"What do you—" Dom began, but Asterion smirked and slid his hand between them, stroking Dom's aching cock. Dom bit his bottom lip and tried not to get distracted.

"It's alright." Asterion murmured. "It's nice. I have a terrible sweet tooth, remember?" Asterion tugged Dom down with his other arm and bit Dom on the shoulder. Dom pushed back, putting just enough space between their bodies that he could look Asterion in the eye.

"If you don't like—"

"I like it," Asterion said. His golden eyes were earnest, soft.

He clasped his hands behind Dom's neck and arched his back. "I really like it." Asterion pulled him down into a kiss, and then began to stroke Dom again, guiding him, shifting their hips until Dom was pressing into him.

At Dom's first real thrust, Asterion moaned loud enough to wake the neighbors, and Dom almost came.

"More," Asterion begged, as Dom slowed almost to a stop, trying not to end things as they were just beginning. "Dom. I want you." Asterion rolled his hips slowly, again and again, and then faster moving them into a rhythm that made Dom's heart race. Asterion's golden eyes fixed on Dom, his cheeks flushed in pleasure, and Dom only wanted to give him more.

"Oh, Gods, Dom!" Asterion's legs looped around Dom's back, urging him forward. "Faster, please. You're—Oh, so good!" Praise made Dom's skin prickle, feverish heat tearing through him, turning his measured thrusts erratic. He reached down and stroked Asterion. Asterion moaned Dom's name as he came, tipping Dom over the edge after him.

DOM SLID BACK SLOWLY, RUBBING GENTLE CIRCLES ON ASTERION'S thighs with his thumbs, watching Asterion's chest rise and fall. Asterion tossed the pillow that had been beneath him onto the floor, running his hand over Dom's hip. Dom collapsed next to him and then they were kissing, and Asterion wasn't sure who started it, but they couldn't seem to stop.

Asterion whimpered when Dom eventually pulled away.

"Need to clean up," he mumbled, and then Asterion must have passed out, only waking when Dom pressed a warm, damp washcloth against his skin.

It felt so good to be tended to, so much so that it made Asterion a little bit breathless. A little bit stupid. He just wanted Dom beside him all the time. Forever. Was that too much to ask?

When Dom slid into bed, Asterion wrapped himself around him like a snake.

"Never leave me again," Asterion murmured. He'd meant it to sound like a joke, even though it wasn't. Dom kissed his temple and said something so softly that Asterion couldn't make it out before he dropped off into a deep and dreamless sleep.

33

The next morning, Dom woke up slowly. The window above the bed was letting in a soft grey light that meant more rain, and before Dom opened his eyes, he took a long, deep breath. Asterion was snoring quietly into the pillow beside him, and Dom realized hadn't known how good it would feel to wake up beside someone. He stretched, lifting his arms over his head, and Asterion nestled closer, tucking his head onto Dom's chest.

When Dom finally opened his eyes, he was met with Asterion's soft blue hair, his warm touch. Asterion was the most beautiful being that Dom had ever seen. And Dom was pretty much a lost cause where Asterion was concerned.

He was crush. He had a smitten. He wanted Asterion's praise and pleasure and attention. And all of that was probably pretty stupid, because Asterion could have his pick of anyone in any of the nine realms, and the chance that he would choose Dom was really, very *very* low.

Dom knew that. Still, Asterion sighing, *'Never leave me again,'* would echo in Dom's ears for the rest of his life. He didn't think

Asterion had heard him say, *'I won't,'* like it was a real request. But that was probably for the best.

Definitely.

A dull thudding sound echoed through the house. Dom frowned and started to push himself up before he remembered that Asterion was lying on his chest.

"What's wrong?" Asterion mumbled.

"I think someone's—" A knock on the door. Dom glanced at the clock. He was late for work. "Shit!" He scrambled out of bed, snatching his trousers off the floor.

"What is happening?" Asterion grumbled, collapsing back onto the pillows.

"It's Hector. I was supposed to be at the diner half an hour ago." Dom grabbed a sweater out of the closet, tugging it on as he tripped toward the door. He'd been so relaxed that his knees still felt rubbery, and he willed them to hold his weight as he yanked open the door to face his uncle. But it wasn't Hector standing on Dom's porch.

Sidney wore a dark grey coat, speckled black with rain. A knit cap pressed his bangs flat against his pale forehead, his cheeks rosy with cold.

"Hey," Sidney said.

"Oh! Hi." Dom reached down and began to button his sweater, more quickly when he spotted the love bite below his right collarbone. "What's up?"

"I went to the diner, but Hector said you weren't in yet and were probably home, so I—" He stopped, his gaze sliding to the left of Dom's face. Dom glanced over to see Asterion padding toward the kitchen, wearing trousers and no shirt. Hickeys dotted his chest and really stood out against his pale skin. The heat from Dom's cheeks could have fried an egg.

"Morning," Asterion nodded to Sidney as he passed. As though him being there was the most natural thing in the world.

"Morning," Sidney replied, looking between Dom and Asterion, one eyebrow arching as he reached conclusions that Dom was in no position to deny. "I wanted to let you know," Sidney continued, his gaze finally settling on Dom, "Dantalion's here. Up at the cottage. He says he remembers your brother."

Ares.

Shame, sudden and overwhelming, made it hard for Dom to breathe. He'd been so preoccupied with Asterion, so, well, happy, that he'd almost forgotten.

"I should— I should go," Dom said. His hand had frozen around a button on his sweater, pushed halfway through its buttonhole.

"I would. He doesn't seem like he wants to stay long." Sidney shrugged. "It was quiet at the diner when I stopped in, and frankly, I'm not in any hurry to have more coffee with 'Dan.'" He threw his fingers up into air quotes before stuffing his hands back in his pockets. "I can stay with Hector for first shift, if you'd like."

"Are you sure?" Dom asked. Sidney smirked and nodded.

"Happy to do it. I'll see you back at the diner then."

"Thanks, Sidney."

"Good luck." Sidney left, waving over his shoulder as he started toward the red truck parked at the curb. Dom closed the door. His heart was racing. After ten years of waiting, he was finally about to get some answers, and he was terrified.

"Hey." Asterion was beside him, his palm pressed gently against the small of Dom's back. Dom hadn't even heard him walk up. Asterion's gold eyes drifted over Dom's face, and Dom tried and failed to smile. "Do you want me to come with you?"

"Oh. No, it's alright," Dom said. It wasn't true. He did want Asterion to come, but after what Asterion had told him about Dantalion, he couldn't possibly ask.

"Are you certain? I've had coffee with people I don't like

plenty of times before," Asterion said with an easy smile. Dom began to shake his head. He was an adult. He could handle this on his own. Asterion rolled his eyes. "Never mind. I'm coming."

"No, Asterion. If he's—" Asterion snorted.

"I'm not afraid of him," he said. Then he kissed Dom, and Dom couldn't help but lean toward him, his body slowly relaxing in all the places anxiety had tightened it. One of Asterion's hands drifted onto Dom's ass, and Dom smiled against his mouth.

"Sorry," Asterion murmured, though he didn't sound it.

"Are you sure you want to do this? I can go alone."

"Of course you could," Asterion said. "But you shouldn't have to." Asterion kissed him again, gently this time. "Come on. We should get dressed. Dantalion isn't known for his patience."

THEY TOOK THE MOTORCYCLE, DESPITE THE DRIZZLE. IT WAS faster than Hector's car, and the feeling of Asterion's arms looped around Dom's waist steadied him.

It was still hard to concentrate on the drive, though. Was he actually about to find out where Ares had gone? If Ares was still alive? And if he was still alive, what then? Dom tightened his grip on the handlebars as they came around the curve at the top of the hill. Elmmond House and Jonas Rookwood's cottage sat in front of them on the edge of the cliff, far above the bay.

Dom's stomach clenched. And not only was he terrified, but he'd also brought Asterion back to the place where Asterion had lost his magic, to sit down with his ex-suitor. He should have turned them around and driven Asterion back home, but instead Dom parked the bike outside the cottage and tried to exhale.

He turned to ask Asterion if he was really sure, again, that he wanted to do this, when Jonas stepped out onto the stoop. Asterion climbed off the bike to greet him, and Dom felt like he was going to throw up.

"Asterion," Jonas said. "I'm a little surprised you're here."

"I could hardly let Dom face Dantalion alone."

"I'm here."

"Oh, I doubt you'll be any help," Asterion's tone was too light, falsely breezy. Dom followed Asterion into the cottage, giving Jonas an apologetic shrug as he slid inside.

"He isn't that bad," Jonas lowered his voice as he followed Dom inside. "A bit of a know-it-all. But I suppose I would be too if I could read everyone's minds whenever I wanted."

"He can do what?" Dom hissed, nearly dropping his coat. Jonas took it from him and laid it over Asterion's on the end of the banister. Asterion was already pushing his way into the kitchen.

"It's fine," Jonas said. "He doesn't do it often."

"Dan!" Asterion's voice was transparently over-enthusiastic. Dom winced. Jonas sighed.

"Good Lord. Come on, before they kill each other."

34

Dantalion was thinner and taller than Jonas, who was the only other demon that Dom knew well enough to use as a comparison.

His skin was the dusty purple of a plum coated in wax bloom, and his hair was a light blonde, threaded with thin strands of gold. Dom hadn't considered that "Duke of Hell" might be a real title, but Dantalion was wearing a crisp white military jacket with a short collar trimmed in gold. Gold embroidery trailed across the left side of his chest, symbols fading in and out of Dom's perception in the thin lines of thread. Two long grey horns twisted upward from either side of his head.

"Dantalion." Jonas placed a hand on Dom's shoulder as they came through the kitchen door. "This is Dominic Silva. The human I was telling you about." Dantalion scanned Dom like an unwelcome piece of mail, his lilac eyes narrowing as he turned toward them.

"Mr. Silva." His voice was low in volume and soft in pitch, the kind of subdued that warned of aggression. "It's a pleasure."

"Thank you for meeting with me," Dom managed. Dantalion sniffed, reaching for the steaming mug of coffee in front of him.

Jonas offered Dom the seat at the head of the table, beside where Asterion was already pulling out a chair.

"Coffee?" Jonas asked.

"Please."

"For me as well, please," Asterion said. As Jonas stepped behind the short counter that separated the kitchen from the dining area, Dantalion watched him, one eyebrow arching as he lifted his own mug.

"This is really what you've been reduced to Rookwood? Playing innkeeper for a bunch of wayward creatures?" Dom stilled, and Asterion's shoulders stiffened. Jonas chuckled.

"And yet, I find I'm far happier than I ever was on the Abyssal Planes." Dantalion snorted and rolled his eyes, sipping from his mug. When he set the coffee down, he turned toward Dom with an abrupt jerk.

"Rookwood tells me you're looking for your brother."

Dom nodded, but before he could speak there was a sudden sensation of cold on his face, as though someone was pressing an ice cube to the center of Dom's forehead. It wasn't painful so much as surprising, but Dom shuddered all the same. Asterion huffed and leaned back in his chair, scooping up his coffee mug and muttering below his breath.

"I made a wager with your brother," Dantalion said slowly. "I remember it well." The cold sensation vanished, and Dom grabbed the mug Jonas had just delivered, clutching it to keep his hands from shaking.

"What was the wager?"

"That he could tell me something I didn't already know." Dantalion's smile thinned, two pointed eye-teeth gleaming over the edge of his bottom lip.

"Not a very good bet to make against someone who can read minds," Dom said.

"He offered the wager, not me."

"What did he want?" Dom asked.

"Oh, what they all want." Dantalion paused to sip from his drink. "Knowledge. The answer to some great riddle of their lives. Tedium, honestly."

"You agreed, though? To the bet?" Asterion asked. "Even though it was inherently unfair?"

"Oh? Oh no! The faerie prince of broken hearts thinks I was unkind to the silly little human?" Dantalion pouted, mocking. Dom's anxiety was so immediately replaced with anger that he didn't realize he wasn't nervous anymore. But Dantalion wasn't done, a cruel smile curling the corner of his mouth. "All the creatures you bed know exactly what they're getting into, do they? A little mark. A little yearning and pining. But that's not a nasty trick at all. Not like big, mean Dantalion's little game."

Asterion's cheeks were pink, but he didn't speak. He didn't even move. Dom opened his mouth, unsure what exactly was going to come out of it, but positive it would contain the phrase 'fuck you' when Jonas interrupted.

"What did Ares Silva want you to tell him, Dan? What did he want to know?"

"He wanted to know where his mother was." Dantalion set his mug down on the table with a thud that seemed to reverberate in Dom's head. All of a sudden, it was hard for him to think.

His mother was gone. She'd been gone longer than Ares. Their aunt and uncle, their father, eventually, had all told the brothers the same thing: she wasn't going to come back.

Dom had been too young to be anything but heartbroken and furious.

They'd all seemed so certain; he'd never thought to ask.

Everyone's eyes were on him, and Dom couldn't quite breathe. He tried to say something more worthwhile than what was already on the tip of his tongue and failed.

"She's gone," he said. Dantalion shook his head, looking smug. "She's—I mean, she's dead."

"No, she isn't," Dantalion replied. "She's at Leyland Hall, a large royal house in southwestern Andurnei." He nodded at Asterion. "Your brother's estate, I believe. Isn't it?"

"Leyland Hall is my brother's estate," Asterion said slowly. "Why is Mrs. Silva there?"

"I don't know." Dantalion's smile widened, showing his fangs. "I can find out for you, if you'd like to win a wager against me. Though you never were very good at that." Instead of speaking in his own defense, Asterion looked at Dom. Was he offering to make a deal with Dantalion on Dom's behalf? Dom bit his bottom lip and tried to think.

"Did you tell Ares?" Dom asked, after a moment. "You told him where she was?" Dantalion's smile dropped.

"Yes. He won the bet."

"He told you something you didn't know?" Jonas asked. "How?" Dom's stomach was trying to crawl up his throat, and he forced himself to swallow a burning mouthful of coffee, as Jonas pressed the other demon. "You've been conning people for years. You take wagers, read their minds and give them nothing. Not that it's ever been okay, but why didn't you do the same thing to Ares?"

"I couldn't." Dantalion's voice was low, his violet eyes twitching toward Dom. "I couldn't read Ares' mind. Just like I can't read his."

"Me?" Dom asked. Dantalion nodded curtly. "Why— I mean, why can't you?"

"My ability has few limitations." Dantalion leaned back in his chair again. The aggression, annoyance, that had lined his tone was palpable now, as though his dislike of this topic had taken a physical form and was making a place for itself at the table. "Humans are particularly simple to read. Fae, as well, likely because they're all so magic-addled and stupid. But there are certain creatures whose minds are closed to me. So, Mr. Silva, you're not human. At least, not entirely."

"That's not—"

"Possible? I promise you it is," Dantalion said. "Not only that, but it's true." Dantalion's smile turned distinctly unkind, one fang visible as he sneered. "I have to say, your brother didn't seem quite as shocked by this revelation as you do. If I had to make a guess, I'd say he knew it before he made his bet with me."

Dom tried to come up with something to say. It was stupid to argue with a being of boundless knowledge, but arguing was the only recourse he had. Before he could embarrass himself by saying anything at all, Dantalion chuckled.

"Every family has their secrets and their secret keepers Mr. Silva. I'm sorry you're just learning so now."

Dom and Ares weren't human?

And Ares had known somehow? But he'd never told Dom. And they told each other everything. Didn't they?

Air caught on the knot in Dom's throat, and his stomach was churning. He didn't want to throw up in front of Asterion, so he forced himself to stand. Asterion shifted in his chair, reaching toward Dom, and Jonas moved from behind the counter. Dom shook his head. He just needed a minute to himself. To catch his breath.

"Sorry. I just—I have to step outside."

"Dom," Asterion called, but Dom was already halfway down the hall, and he didn't stop until he stepped outside into the cold rain.

35

Asterion slumped back against his seat and stared down the now empty hall. Jonas was reprimanding Dantalion, but Asterion couldn't hear him. He couldn't hear anything over the effort it was taking him to not to pick up his coffee cup and throw its still steaming contents onto Dantalion's stupid face.

"That was particularly cruel, even for you," Asterion said, once Jonas had shut up.

"I don't make the truth, I just tell it." Asterion rolled his eyes and Dantalion chuckled. "I forgot how much you hated that."

"What do you think Dom is, then?" Jonas asked, ever focused on the task at hand, bless him.

"Could be a demon," Dantalion mused. "Demigod or Godspawn, I suppose, though that seems unlikely. Archfey, though there aren't so many of them around anymore. I imagine if one were siring errant humans we'd know about it."

"Where did Ares go?" Asterion asked, trying to follow Jonas' lead and point his attention toward something useful.

"Mr. Silva left after I told him where his mother was," Dan said. "I don't know where he went, but if I had to guess, I'd say it's likely he went to Leyland Hall."

"He'd have to take a mark to be granted access," Asterion said, thinking aloud. Dantalion scoffed.

"Oh, Asterion. It's a good thing you're pretty. Or at least, you used to be." Jonas began to chastise him again, but Dantalion continued. "If Mr. Silva's not human, then he doesn't need a mark to go through an open portal. I met him at the Ascension, so it seems to me that—"

"If he was going to try and go to Andurnei, he would have just asked someone which portal to take and gone through on his own," Jonas concluded.

"Precisely."

"I think I have a treatise about the taxonomy of interspecies offspring," Jonas considered. "Perhaps it would give us some traits to look for, or maybe things Dom's noticed about himself..." Jonas continued talking, as he walked into the library that was just off the kitchen. Asterion stayed firmly in his chair. Unfortunately, Dantalion did the same.

The wind had blown more rain clouds into the vicinity, the gentle sound of water droplets drumming against the eaves made Asterion straighten up. Certainly, Dom had had enough alone time by now; he'd be soaked. But before Asterion could get to his feet, Dantalion cleared his throat.

"It's not like you to worry about one of your conquests."

"Stay out of my head, Dantalion," Asterion growled, irritated at himself for not noticing the trickle of cold against the back of his neck before precisely that moment. This damn house was too drafty.

"I didn't have to go into your head. It's written all over your face. Also, you reek of his mark." Dom's mark? Dom had marked him?

Asterion usually hated being marked; the mercurial pull toward another person tended to make him nauseous. But he hadn't felt anything strange at all. And instead, the idea of taking

Dom's mark was making him a little warm beneath the collar of his sweater. All of which Dantalion could clearly read. Asterion scowled at the smug smirk on Dantalion's face.

"He's been kind to me."

"Indeed." Dan chuckled. "And clearly you've already repaid him for his kindness in your usual way."

"Fuck off." Asterion turned toward the door.

"It's a shame about your magic," Dantalion said. Asterion froze. How did he know about that? "Oh, everyone knows," Dantalion grinned, answering Asterion's unasked question. Asshole. "Word travels fast through the Assembly."

"Morrow made banners. Posted flyers?" Asterion wanted to gag. Dantalion only laughed.

"I thought you liked to be on the tip of everyone's tongue. Metaphorically speaking, of course."

"Bullying doesn't get me as hard as it used to, Dan."

"Pity," Dantalion sneered. "We could have had one off for old times' sake."

"It's hard to express how deeply uninterested I am in that offer."

"Are you sure? We could add another to make it more interesting. You could whine and be pitiful, while I fuck Silva for you. Show him what a good demon cock can—"

Asterion threw his coffee in Dan's face and slammed the mug down so hard onto the table that it shattered.

Dan laughed, his head thrown back as coffee dripped off his chin, staining the white of his uniform. Asterion stormed out of the kitchen before Jonas could emerge from the library and make one or both of them apologize, which Asterion would refuse to do or to accept.

Asterion grabbed his and Dom's helmets and his coat on his way out the door. The motorcycle was still parked on the side of the house, which was good, because it meant Dom hadn't left

Asterion at this infernal cottage and bad because he didn't know where Dom was.

He sat their helmets on the motorcycle seat and pulled his coat on as he walked through the side yard. The wind off the cliffs was merciless, flinging drops of rain like icy projectiles into his face. The sky was growing darker, and Asterion reflected on how much he hated this place, it's horrible cold and constant wet, and how much he would give to be back in Dom's bed, curled up in Dom's arms.

Dom was standing in the gazebo, shoulders hunched up to his ears. Asterion's foot on the first step made the wood creak loudly and Dom spun around, his mouth already open as if he was going to speak. His hands were shoved so deeply into his pockets that it took him a half-second too long to free them, tears sliding down his cheeks before he could wipe them away. Asterion's heart ached, even as he told himself that he'd never known what to do when anyone was crying. Dom sniffed loudly; his handsome face turned again toward the waves thundering against the cliffs below.

"It's cold out here," Dom said, as Asterion stepped up beside him. Asterion nodded, understanding the conversational diversion for precisely what it was: an observation which freed them both from the reality of what had just occurred. Nothing needed to be addressed that was more pressing than the weather, and that was fine.

"Let's go home," Asterion said. Dom nodded, but didn't move. Asterion waited. He could wait all day if he needed to. But after a few long moments, Dom looked over at him.

"I don't know how to get to Ares," he said, heartbreak clear in his gaze as he gestured toward the house. "I don't know what any of *that* really means, and I—"

"I do," Asterion said. He didn't. But he did have an idea, and if it was enough to grant Dom any comfort, then Asterion could pretend to have the whole mess fully in hand. "I know what we need to do next. And I know how we can start to find Ares. But neither of those things requires us to stand out here in the rain. Come on," he said, jerking his head back toward the front of the house, the motorcycle. He took Dom's hand and squeezed it. "Let's go home."

36

Raindrops stung the backs of Dom's hands as he drove them into town. Asterion had said he knew what to do, and maybe that should have made Dom feel better. Deep down, somewhere beneath all the roiling frustration and the sting of betrayal, it did settle something in him. There was a next step. There was something. And Asterion had offered to help.

But Asterion was more of a mystery to Dom now than he'd ever been. He knew Asterion hadn't settled for Dantalion, but how had he even considered him in the first place? The way he'd spoken to Asterion made Dom want to throw a punch. Not that fighting Dantalion would have gone well for Dom, even if he was magic. Which he wasn't.

Maybe Dantalion was all-knowing, but he was wrong about Dom and Ares.

He had to be.

They were halfway home when Dom realized that there was one other person he could ask, who might, when confronted, actually tell him the truth. Aunt Ree was his mother's sister, and there wasn't a more straightforward person in Dom's life. If anyone could shed a light on what Dantalion had said, it would be her.

"Where are we going?" Asterion called over the wind and the roar of the bike as Dom turned south, away from home.

"My Aunt and Uncle's," Dom replied. He doubted Asterion could hear him.

Ree and Hector's place was at the edge of town, nestled on a small spit of land that had improbably filled with houses and become the closest thing Hindry had to a real neighborhood. Their yellow clapboard house was at the very tip of the tiny peninsula, a smudge of brightness on an endlessly grey horizon. The driveway was empty, but light seeped out through the curtains, and smoke was wafting lazily out of the chimney.

Dom slowed, rolling down the dirt path, old scoldings about kicking up too much dust echoing in his ears. He parked and Asterion slid off the bike quickly. Dom's stomach clenched.

"It's my Aunt and Uncle's house," he explained, as he stood and pulled off his helmet.

"I heard you." Asterion already had his helmet in his hand, staring at the house as he smoothed down his hair.

Dom started toward the door, his boots crunching in the gravel. It wasn't until his hand was on the doorknob that he realized Asterion was lingering in the driveway in the rain.

"What are you doing?" Dom asked, irritable. "Come on."

"I can wait out here," Asterion said, apprehension plain on his face. Dom groaned. He didn't have the patience for this. If Asterion wanted to get soaked, that was on him.

"Fine. I'll just be a minute." Dom knocked and then opened the side door. It was always unlocked.

The kitchen was a mess of yellow gingham and rooster décor, just as it had always been. The yellow lace curtains that covered the window on the door swung out as Dom yanked the door closed behind him. Something was cooking, the kitchen warm with heat from the oven, and Dom stood on the ancient mat, leaning against the wall to unlace his boots. No matter what family emergency was going on, Ree would throw him out on his ass if he tracked dirt onto her floor.

"Ree!" Dom called, switching to lean on the other wall and nearly knocking down a framed needlepoint that depicted a proud rooster above the words 'Rise and Shine.'

"What on Earth?" Ree bustled into the kitchen, frilly white apron and house slippers at odds with the full face of makeup she always wore. "Dom Silva!" She grabbed him by the elbows and pulled him inside, shoving him toward the oven. "Get out of the way! I raised you better!" She pulled open the door and stuck her head out. "Young man! Young man—"

Asterion. She must have been watching from the front windows.

"Ree—" Dom tried to interrupt, but her attention was fully outside.

"Yes, you! Get in here right now! Standing outside in the rain, you'll catch your death." Dom dropped his head into his hands and pressed against his eyes with his fingertips until he saw spots.

"Ree, it's—" She glared at him over her shoulder.

"Never in my life! Shame on you!"

Somehow just existing in this house always managed to turn Dom back into a child.

Asterion stepped inside, and Ree was a flurry of movement around him, taking his coat, instructing him about the shoe policy. Dom wasn't sure having a new boyfriend meet his family could go worse than it was going. Thankfully he and Asterion weren't dating. Ree sent Dom down the hall to fetch a towel for their guest.

"You have a lovely home," Asterion said. Dom was glad his

back was to them. He barely had time to stifle the burst of laughter that tried to scramble out of his chest.

In the thirty seconds it took Dom to return with a towel, Asterion had been bundled into a seat at the circular table where Dom had spent his formative years eating breakfast and dinner and doing homework. Dom handed Asterion the towel, and Ree delivered a steaming mug of tea and a plate of molasses cookies to the table. Dom's favorite. He reached for one, and she swatted his fingers.

"Introductions," she prompted, looking up at him sternly. Dom sighed.

"Aunt Ree, this is," Dom stammered over potential titles and then settled on names only, "this is Asterion. He's been staying in Ares' old apartment. Asterion, this is my Aunt Ariadne."

"But everyone calls me Ree, dear. And I expect you to do the same."

"Yes, of course," Asterion nodded, as obedient and innocent as a well-trained puppy.

"Ree, can I talk to you about something, please?" Dom asked, desperate for this visit to get back on track so that he could go home and get drunk and go to bed.

"Go ahead," she sniffed. Dom glanced at Asterion, who blushed and turned his head toward the window, hiding the bottom of his face behind the mug of tea.

"Was mom—" Dom swallowed. He looked back at his aunt. "Are we magic?"

Ree's light brown skin flushed. Her mouth opened and closed. Asterion cleared his throat and started to get to his feet, mumbling something about going outside and privacy.

"No," Dom said, at the same moment that Ree said, "Sit." Asterion sat.

"You too, Dominic," she said after a moment. "Have a seat. I'll pour some more tea."

37

"We are demigods," Ree said. "Or at least, your mother and I are. Were. Which means that you and Ares are half demigod. One quarter. Tetartotheos would be the technical term, I think. But until the magic wanes more steadily in a generation or two, demigod would be the classification the Assembly would use." Dom was trying hard to listen over the sound of his heart pounding furiously in his ears.

Magic. Evil, dangerous. Avoid it at all costs.

He was magic.

"Why didn't you tell me?"

"Your mother didn't want us to tell you. Or your brother. It wasn't a life she wanted for you."

"But I can do magic?" Dom demanded. As though that mattered. Ree shrugged.

"We never suppressed it. I imagine if you tried, you could. Your mother was extremely powerful," she said with pride, a small smile returning to her mouth. Dom's chest ached.

"Where is she?"

"I don't know," Ree replied, frown reappearing as quickly as it had fled.

"Is she alive?"

"I don't know."

"You didn't look for her? After she disappeared?" Dom couldn't believe it. Didn't believe it, when Ree shook her head.

"She told us she likely wouldn't be able to come back. Whatever she was doing, it was to protect you and Ares, and she couldn't be talked out of it. Your father tried. Tirelessly. But she was always stubborn. It broke his heart, I think." Dom tried to decide how that made him feel, and realized he couldn't really feel anything at the moment.

"Did you try to help her, at least? Did you do anything?" Ree looked down at the table.

"If I could have taken her place, I would have. But my magic had been gone for years at that point. So, I took you boys. It was all I could do." Dom slumped back in his chair, and stared into the light above the table, trying to think of something to say, wishing he felt anything other than hollow. After a few minutes, Asterion leaned forward.

"Why don't you have magic?" Asterion asked quietly. His hair was curling up at the ends as it dried, and it made him look younger. Ree glanced over at him, wiping tears off her cheeks. Then she chuckled.

"When I was a young woman, I fell in love with a sailor. A fisherman, by trade. In our courtship, I had told him what I was. My sister begged me not to. It's the sort of information that can sometimes make humans act foolish. And he did. Act foolish, that is." Ree glanced at Dom. "He thought that to court me properly, being a goddess and all—or part goddess, at any rate—he would need gifts far beyond his meager means. So, he struck a deal with Nereus, the Old Man of the Sea. For pearls. One of perfect luster, one of perfect complexion and the third of perfect shape."

Dom's eyes dropped to Ree's hand, her pearl engagement

ring, in a simple gold setting, perfectly round, shining, creamy white.

"What did he have to give up?" Asterion asked.

"His soul, of course," Ree replied. "What else do humans have? The moment I said yes to the proposal, water leapt at Hector over the edge of the pier. The sunset turned dark, and the water grew limbs that dragged him down into the sea. I gave my magic to save him that day. To bring him back to me. And I've never regretted it."

Dom was dumbstruck. If he'd actually learned anything about magic over the past two weeks, it was that it always came with a cost. If someone wanted happiness, security, love, they were going to have to pay for it. And Dom hated that. His mother had gone to protect him. That was the cost. He blinked back tears. Beneath the table, Asterion's hand pressed lightly down onto the top of Dom's knee, and Dom scrambled for his fingers, holding him tightly.

"What do I do, Ree?" Dom stared down at the table, scratches he'd made as a restless boy, struggling with chemistry homework, staring up at him. He'd come here angry, and now as the rage seeped out of him, he was afraid. "Dantalion said that Mom's still alive. That Ares was looking for her."

"Your brother is as bull-headed as your mother was," See said, sliding the plate of molasses cookies toward Dom. "If he decided to track her down, then nothing any of us could have said would have stopped him. I did always assume it was something like that. The way he left on the Ascension. Perhaps I should have told you." She sniffed. "I guess it's selfish, but I just couldn't bear the thought of losing you too."

Dom couldn't blame her. He wanted to, badly. It would have been so much easier if there was someone to rage at. Ares was a better target. Their mother an even more deserving one. But Dom didn't have it in him. He was so tired.

"It's alright, Ree," Dom said. Because it was. It wasn't her fault. He pushed back from the table. "I'm sorry. We should go."

"Oh, Dom. Stay. It's pouring out there. And I've got a roast in the oven." Dom shook his head, though his stomach growled.

"I need to lie down."

"The guest room is all made up. Please."

Dom looked at Asterion. Why was he looking at Asterion? Asterion who had sat and listened to Ree's story without comment. Who had complimented the rooster décor. Who was still holding Dom's hand under the table.

"Whatever you want, Dom," Asterion said. Dom wasn't used to being coddled. He didn't like it. But he also sort of did.

"Do you mind if I—?" Dom gestured over his shoulder, down the hall, toward the guest room.

"Please," Ree said, nodding. "Do you want some of your uncle's pajamas?"

"I'll be fine." Dom got to his feet, surprised that his legs held him up. He pushed in his chair. Ree's hands were folded on the table in front of her, and her normally cheerful mouth was pinched and tight. Dom went to her side and leaned down to wrap an arm around her shoulders.

"I'm sorry for being so upset. I love you, Ree." He heard her sob and as she pressed her hand to his cheek.

"I love you too, my baby. And I'm so sorry."

"It's okay." He kissed the top of her head, her curls the same as his. "It's really okay." She sniffed and Dom straightened up. Asterion's gaze was out the window again, hand wrapped around a mug that had to be empty. "Asterion, would you come with me for a minute?" Asterion looked startled to be addressed but got up immediately and followed Dom down the hall.

38

Amidst all the drama and heartbreak, it was nice to have something garish to focus on. The rose patterned wall-paper in Ree and Hector's guest bedroom was an affront to every god that had ever existed and made Asterion's eyes cross if he looked at it for too long. Which he did as Dom stripped out of his coat and still damp sweater, down to his ever-tempting undershirt. Asterion probably wouldn't be able to get an erection in a room so ugly, but why risk it by looking at him? It wasn't the time for that sort of thing anyway. He let his eyes cross, and tried not to gag when he noticed the carpet beneath his socks was a pattern of gaudy green ferns.

"Are you okay?" Dom asked. Asterion nodded.

"Are *you* okay?"

"I'm sorry for being short with you before," Dom said. Asterion almost laughed.

"I think after the day you've had, you can be short with whoever you like." Dom shook his head. He took a step closer to Asterion and then hesitated.

"Why didn't you want to come inside?"

"I just assumed you'd want some privacy," Asterion said,

honestly. "And, well, I avoid introducing my partners to my family even under the most ideal of circumstances. I wasn't sure you wanted me here."

"It wasn't as though I gave you a choice. Sorry for that too. I should have explained before—"

"You don't owe me anything, Dom." Dom looked at Asterion, studying him, teeth digging into his bottom lip for a moment, like he was stopping himself from saying something. "You really don't." Dom sighed and looked away.

"Did Dantalion have anything else to say after I left?"

"Not especially. He speculated that Ares went to Leyland Hall, which I think we'd all pretty much guessed. But he does like stating the obvious." It also probably wasn't a good time to bring up the fact that Dom had marked Asterion. That Dantalion could smell it, and that now he knew it was there, Asterion could feel it. It wasn't strong or uncomfortable. Just that he could sense Dom's emotions rippling the air around them, and there was the slightest tug of something deep inside Asterion that wanted, badly, to be closer to Dom.

It didn't feel as foreign as marks he'd taken in the past, where the other creature's magic was a separate sensation, something he was fully able to compartmentalize. The pull toward Dom seemed to ebb and flow in and out of Asterion's perception, but that was probably because he didn't have his own magic anymore to act as a counterweight. He assumed. And anyway, it wasn't important right now.

"I'm sorry you had to see him," Dom said. Asterion huffed.

"You should endeavor to do something worth apologizing for eventually, so that I might be able to accept at least one of them." Dom snorted. Then he stepped forward and slid his arms around Asterion's waist. Dom nestled his nose into the side of Asterion's neck, and Asterion wrapped his arms firmly around Dom and held tight. Dom shuddered, snuggling close to him, breathing in Asterion's space. Asterion played gently with the tendril of Dom's hair that skated over the back of his hand and wondered if this was making Dom feel any better. It was making him feel better, at the very least. But that was quite beside the point.

"You should rest," Asterion murmured into Dom's ear. Dom nodded and pulled back. He bit his bottom lip again, but before Asterion could prompt him, Dom sighed.

"I know it's stupid, but will you stay with me? Just for a few— I mean, if I fall asleep, you can—"

"Of course," Asterion said. Because if Dom wanted Asterion beside him, then Asterion didn't want to be anywhere else.

The bed was small, but Asterion was too busy feeling exceedingly plain and a little embarrassed to be in just his own shorts and undershirt to notice. And then Dom slid up against the wall, and held the blankets back for Asterion to crawl in. The space beside him was narrow but welcoming. The mattress was lumpy, and the wallpaper made it hard to keep his eyes open, but Asterion had never been happier to be so uncomfortable.

ASTERION WOKE UP SOMETIME LATER WITH DOM'S ARMS threaded around his midsection and a puddle of his own drool beneath his cheek. What little light the day contained had faded while they slept. Dom was still unconscious, his curls a dark tangle on his pillow.

Asterion would have tried to reorganize their limbs and fallen back to sleep, but moving reminded him that he needed to pee. He got out of bed carefully, trying not to wake Dom, and slid his trousers and sweater back on before slipping into the bathroom, brushing his hair back into some semblance of order after he washed his hands. The smell of whatever Ree was cooking drew him out into the empty kitchen. Curious if the 'vibrant' design aesthetic was consistent throughout the house, Dom poked his head into the living room on his way back to the hall.

The room had thankfully not been wallpapered, but the glow of the fire rumbling away in the hearth clashed with the key-lime paint. A white sofa was occupied by Ree on one end. She held a bone-china teacup and saucer and was staring into the fire. Asterion cleared his throat, trying not to startle her, but she jumped anyway.

"I'm sorry," he said immediately.

"Oh, no. It's fine. Sit, please. Can I get you anything?"

"No. Thank you." Asterion sat in the white chair opposite her; it matched the sofa, but the cushion was worn in places that didn't suit him. He wanted to say something, but he didn't know what there was to say. While he might not agree with her design choices, he'd been moved by her story, her selflessness. Not just in raising her sister's children, though that certainly would have been enough on its own, but giving up her magic for love? Well, it was practically the greatest sacrifice he could imagine, and not one that he was sure he'd have been able to make.

"I know who you are," she said. "I mean, Hector told me. But even if he hadn't, I would have guessed."

"What gave me away?" he asked, trying to pretend like it was amusing and not irritating that he couldn't shake his old self off completely.

"Besides the ears? It's the hair. I can tell your roots are all natural," she said with a smile. Asterion snorted.

"I've been thinking of dying it."

"Oh, you shouldn't. It's a lovely shade."

"It makes me stick out. Life's hard enough as it is without magic. No need to add looking different on top of it."

"You did lose it, then? Your magic, I mean." Asterion nodded.

"Hector thought so." Ree said, nodding as well. They fell silent for a long moment. "You'll go back with Dom though, won't you? To Andurnei?"

"Of course. He can't go by himself." His own lack of hesitation surprised him. His mother had asked him not to return, and he knew he wouldn't be welcome, but he'd never once considered letting Dom go to Andurnei alone.

"Can I ask you something?" Ree turned her cup in its saucer, her gaze fixed on the shining edge of the china.

"Of course," Asterion nodded. He wanted to please her. He wasn't sure why.

"Not as any sort of deal or bargain—"

"I don't have any magic to bind you."

"I know, I just meant, as a favor. To me." Asterion nodded. Ree took a deep breath. "If he decides to stay, for whatever reason, could you make sure he lets us know. So we can say goodbye. I'll ask him too, but—Well, I just worry. That's all." Asterion found himself surprised into silence.

"I don't think he's planning on staying in Andurnei," he said, finding his words after a moment. "He wants to find Ares, but he wouldn't leave Hindry. This is his home."

"I'm not so sure," Ree's gaze fixed on Asterion, and his skin prickled, like he was being accused of something. "You'll make sure he lets me know, won't you?"

"Yes, I will." Asterion nodded. What else could he say? A bell went off in the kitchen, and Ree got to her feet.

"That's the roast," she chirped. "Do me a favor and wake Dom. Hector will be home soon, and we'll have dinner." And then she was gone, leaving Asterion trying to get his bearings in her wake.

39

"Dom." Cool, gentle fingers brushed against Dom's forehead. His chest felt open, shoulders looser, like something that had been holding them rigid was gone. The soft caress drifted down against his cheek. "Dom. Ree says it's time for dinner."

Dom opened his eyes slowly. Though his sleep had been dreamless, there was something about waking up to Asterion's touch that was sort of like shifting from one sort of rest to another. Asterion had stayed with him. Asterion was here now. It was hard not to feel like that meant something good. It had to. Didn't it?

Dom caught Asterion's hand against his cheek and held it there, appreciating the heat from his palm, and the way Asterion was watching him. All his hard angles looked softer, his mouth a pleasant smirk that Dom wanted to kiss.

"Come here," Dom grunted. And then without waiting, he tugged Asterion down into bed beside him. Asterion huffed but he didn't push away, curling over Dom's body. His hand slid behind Dom's back to steady them against the mattress.

"This is highly inappropriate behavior for a guest bedroom,"

Asterion chastised. Dom ignored him, tucking his nose against the side of Asterion's neck, kissing the sensitive skin there. Asterion hissed and pressed a firm hand to Dom's chest. "You heathen, your Aunt is in the kitchen less than a hundred feet away and your uncle should be home any minute." Dom glanced up at him with a small smile.

"You care about what they think."

"Of course I do!" Asterion pinched Dom's waist, and Dom drew his head back. Asterion was trying to look stern, but his cheeks were flush, and Dom adored him.

"Thank you for staying."

"Don't be absurd, Dominic," Asterion demurred, his blush deepening. "Where else was I going to go?" Dom kissed him then, and Asterion resisted for all of four seconds before sinking into Dom's embrace.

In the distance, the kitchen door opened. Hector and Ree's voices were muffled, and Dom had the strange sensation of being a teenager again, doing something forbidden in his bedroom, hoping not to get caught. He slid his tongue between Asterion's lips, and Asterion drew back, shaking his head.

"You're trying to get me in trouble."

"I like that you're worried about getting in trouble."

"Boys!" Ree's voice echoed down the hall. "Come set the table!"

Dinner was pleasant, even when talk eventually looped around to the reason for Dom and Asterion's visit, and their impending departure to another world. They didn't talk about going to Andurnei in so many words, but Dom appreciated that everyone seemed to recognize that it was happening. And that no one tried to stop him. Hector offered to watch the diner before Dom could ask him to, and Dom promised to be home before the holidays. It made Ree's eyes go a bit damp, and Dom had to take a sip of water to loosen the knot in his throat.

After dinner, as Dom and Asterion were working on the dishes in the sink, Ree came up and tucked her hand into the crook of Dom's elbow.

"Come with me a minute," she said. Dom followed her, his place at the sink quickly taken by Hector, as Ree led him into the living room.

She tucked him at the far end of the sofa near the fireplace, and then sat beside him, her hands clasping in her lap. When he looked at her, he noticed her cheeks were pink. She'd probably had too much wine.

"What's up?" he asked. "Everything okay?" Ree pursed her lips. Then she sighed and folded her hands in her lap.

"Has someone talked to you about marking?"

Once again, Dom was fifteen and dying of embarrassment. He tilted his head back and stared at the ceiling, cheeks almost painfully hot.

"Yes. It's been covered."

"Because, as a demigod—"

"I know." Dom said, forcing himself to straighten up and hear what she was saying. They were both adults, after all. And even if he hadn't considered until that moment that he could perhaps be a creature who marked—

"It works differently for us than it does for some other magic users," Ree said. "Demons and fae, they want to sap the soul or essence. But not us. Demigod marks are tied to devotion. In the old days it was to keep people worshipping, you see. And depending on your own feelings about a person, your magic might attempt to—"

"Is it going to hurt him?" Dom asked. It was the thing he cared most about, and that he'd wondered when Sidney had first introduced the concept as a branding. It wasn't until he glanced at Ree with her arched her eyebrows that Dom realized what he'd said. *Him.* Obviously Asterion. Doom took a deep breath. He wasn't embarrassed, just out of the habit of having a personal life to share details about. Besides, his aunt was a perceptive woman, and they hadn't exactly been subtle.

"No, it won't hurt him," she said. "Just be sure you're being careful."

"I will," Dom said. He stood up and she looked up at him. "Is that it?" She chuckled and shook her head.

"I suppose so. An Aunt's work is never done." She reached out a hand and he helped her to her feet.

"Thank you, Ree," he said, and meant it. She smiled up at him and patted him on the cheek.

"I think I need a cocktail."

Back in the kitchen, Asterion and Hector were finished with the dishes, so Dom and Asterion got their shoes and coats, and then said their goodbyes. Asterion shook Hector's hand. Ree was on her tiptoes, arms flung around Dom's neck.

When she hugged Asterion, Dom bit his lip to stop himself from grinning at the look of surprise on Asterion's face. Asterion's expression settled quickly into a satisfied smile as he squeezed her back, and Dom felt something warm and soothing bloom in his chest.

IT LASTED UNTIL THEY WALKED BACK INTO DOM'S APARTMENT, where his mind almost immediately began to spin. When should they leave? Where would they go and how would they get there? Before they'd left Jonas' cottage, Asterion had said he had a plan. Now he was in the kitchen, getting the cocktail shaker out of the cabinet. Dom looked over at him.

"What do we do now?"

"Well, I suppose we pack. In the morning, we'll go back to Jonas' and see if there are any portals left to Andurnei. If not, we'll have to make our own."

"Can we do that?"

"You're a demigod," Asterion said, his attention on the bottle of vermouth he'd just pulled out of his cabinet. "You can basically do whatever you want, as far as magic is concerned. Most branches are open to you, though depending on what deity is in your lineage, you may have more strength in one magic type than others."

Dom looked down at his hands, as though they were about to shoot sparks or start a whirlwind. He'd marked Asterion, and he hadn't even known it. They still hadn't talked about it, and Dom wasn't sure how to bring it up.

"Can you show me? How to do magic?" Asterion looked over his shoulder at Dom, and Dom immediately regretted his wording. "I mean, I know you can't show me, but I just... I don't feel it? I don't know how I would even start." Asterion pursed his lips. Then he put down the vermouth and walked into the living room, gesturing for Dom to follow. They sat on the sofa and Asterion turned toward Dom. He scooped up Dom's hands, holding them, palms toward the ceiling, in his own. Anticipation gave Dom goosebumps.

"Magic is different depending on lots of things," Asterion began, "but something that's true for everyone is that magic always follows intention. So, think of what you want to do."

"What do I want to do?" Dom asked. Asterion snorted.

"Never mind. Close your eyes." Dom did, but he could still hear Asterion's small huff of laughter. "Has anyone ever told you you're very trusting?"

"Now what?"

"Well," Asterion exhaled. "For me at least, magic always felt like heat. A warmth beneath my blood. Closer to bone than muscle. See if you can find a thread of that somewhere." Asterion's thumbs traced the sides of Dom's hand slowly, and beneath that touch was the first place that Dom could feel the tickle of heat. Was it magic? Or was it just the way he always felt when Asterion touched him?

Dom concentrated. He could feel Asterion's fingertips press against the back of his hands, and imagined those same fingers, sliding up his forearms, leaving a trail of sparks in their wake.

Fire curled in Dom's chest, seeping down his stomach. He chased it with his mind, ignoring the way it all seemed to swirl around Asterion, the thought of him, and all the places where they could have been touching. Arousal came on suddenly. Or perhaps Dom was just becoming aware of it all over again. Flexing something that was part of him now.

Asterion trembled, a full body shiver. Dom swallowed down the urge to reach forward and pull Asterion against his chest.

"Open your eyes," Asterion said softly.

At first, Dom thought the shimmer of warmth in the air was a trick of the light from the kitchen, or something at the edges of his vision. It rippled, the gentle tremor of a summer breeze. Asterion's hair fluttered against his forehead.

"You made heat," Asterion said. "Well done." He did look pleased, his golden gaze drifting up, following the light. "Do you want to try something else?" His eyes were bright when he looked back at Dom, his cheeks a line of pink. Dom shook out his hands, wondering if it would shake the heat out of the air.

"Are you sure you're not cold?"

"Cold?" Asterion lifted an eyebrow.

"I felt you shiver."

"Oh." Asterion's smile turned small and crooked. His blush deepened. "I wasn't cold."

"You like that I can do this," Dom guessed. Asterion shrugged.

"Let's just say, I'm glad that you don't hate it. And I'm sure once you get a little practice under your belt, you'll be as good at casting as you are at everything else."

Even though the heat was starting to dissipate, the praise made Dom's skin warm. He leaned in, feeling the charge in the air between them as he kissed Asterion eagerly. Asterion grabbed Dom by the lapels and pulled him forward. Their legs tangled, hips shifting against the squashy cushions of the old couch.

Dom threaded his fingers into Asterion's hair, and wrapped his other arm around Asterion's narrow waist, holding him close. After everything that had happened, this thing he had with Asterion, this strange, lovely thing, was still intact. Maybe Dom didn't know what to call it, but magic hadn't managed to change it, and that was a relief. After his conversation with Anders in the bar, Dom had wondered if he was in some sort of trap, where Asterion's magic would return, and then they would just break apart. As though it wasn't possible for both he and magic to exist in Asterion's world at the same time.

But they were now. And it was fine. Better than fine. Asterion shifted, dragging his fingers up over the small of Dom's back as they finally broke apart.

"*Nocturne Mystery Theatre* should be on soon," he murmured. Dom pulled back and stared at him, unable to stifle his laughter. Asterion huffed, indignant. "What?"

"How do you know that?"

"Because you talk about it all the time. And I remembered the ads from the other night. It's a new episode. The thrilling conclusion of the case of the something something."

"Twisted Bough."

"'Thrilling conclusion' seems like a bold claim to make, considering I can't stay awake through the episode before it," Asterion said smugly. Dom laughed and kissed him.

"Do you want to listen to it?" Dom asked. Asterion rolled his eyes. And then he nodded and pushed himself up to his elbows.

"Yes. But I want to be comfortable first."

40

When Asterion returned to the living room in his pajamas, he was pleased to find that Dom was waiting on the couch in his pajama pants and an undershirt. It was, Asterion decided, his favorite outfit of Dom's. There were two drinks on the coffee table, and a small bowl of nuts. Dom was folded up on one end of the sofa, and the radio was on, the chimes that came before the news break ringing out into the quiet living room.

Asterion took his seat and sipped his drink. He groaned.

"Delicious."

"I thought you might like it. It's good gin."

"And vermouth. My two favorites."

"I know," Dom smirked. Asterion rolled his eyes, trying not to feel too pleased. It was nice to be known, that was all. And he definitely wasn't going to be charmed by the fact that Dom had noticed what Asterion liked. And if he slid closer to Dom on the couch, before he got settled, so what. It had been a long day. And there were probably going to be several longer ones ahead. They deserved to relax.

The news reporter droned on, and Dom slid his arm around Asterion's shoulders.

"Should we be making a plan for tomorrow?" Dom asked quietly. Asterion sighed and sipped his drink.

"Maybe," he admitted. He didn't want to, though. Going back to Andurnei was sure to be unpleasant. No one wanted him there, and to be perfectly honest, Asterion didn't really want to be there either. But the trip wasn't about him.

"Tomorrow." Dom's fingers brushed the nape of Asterion's neck, and Asterion leaned into the touch. "We'll do what you said. Check at Elmmond House, and then, if not—"

"We can go tonight," Asterion offered, trying to be helpful.

"No. And I know that's awful. We might have found Ares, and I know I should be... I want to find him. I do. But after ten years, I just wonder, you know? What if he doesn't want to be found? What if he could have come back but didn't?"

"No one in their right mind would leave you like that. And Hector and Ree." Asterion was as sure of this as he was of blue skies and green trees. Gods, if he'd been blessed with a family like the Silvas, it would have taken a lot more than a little magic to keep him from going home again.

"But then why?" Dom frowned at his drink before he took a sip and sighed. "I thought I knew everything about Ares, and I'm afraid I'm going to find out that I never knew him at all. And then, mom..."

It wasn't often that Asterion dealt in truths quite so raw and unvarnished. It was beautiful, in a way. And it made him want to be honest with Dom.

"If Ares lied to you about who he was, that says more about him than it does about you. You trusted him, and you can't fault yourself for believing the things someone tells you. Take it from a consummate liar." He tried to smirk, but the shame that was bubbling up in his chest didn't let it land right. "He wouldn't have told you, even if you'd managed to ask him in all the right words. When you want to deceive, that becomes your entire objective. All the time."

"You haven't lied to me." Dom said it with such confidence that Asterion's chest swelled with affection. He knew he hadn't lied to Dom, but it was nice that Dom knew it too. At first it was because he'd felt like there was no need. But then, he hadn't wanted to. Dom's trust mattered to him. He wasn't exactly sure why.

"I haven't," Asterion agreed.

"You told me that at Harlan's Crest."

"It's still true."

"Do you really like the drink?" Dom grinned. Asterion lifted his eyebrows significantly and took a long sip. Dom chuckled, shaking his head, and when Asterion lowered his glass, Dom kissed him.

Asterion slid closer, draping his legs over one of Dom's thighs, nearly sitting on his lap. Dom leaned into him, his kisses gentle, stubble scratching lightly against Asterion's chin. The tenderness was making him unaccountably warm. Or maybe the drink was just strong.

The theme music for *Nocturne Mystery Theatre* started up, and Asterion leaned back, pleased when Dom moved toward him, granting him one more gorgeous, long kiss. And then Dom didn't pull away. Instead, he curled around Asterion, letting Asterion rest his head on Dom's shoulder, and Asterion barely made it past the introduction, before he dropped off to sleep.

When he woke up, he was in Dom's arms. The bedroom was warm and dark, and Dom was setting Asterion gently onto the mattress. Asterion's eyes adjusted, and he watched as Dom tugged off his undershirt, tied up his hair, and crawled into bed.

Asterion rolled toward him with a soft sigh.

"Was the conclusion really as thrilling as all that?"

"It was," Dom murmured, and Asterion could feel Dom's smile press against his temple, before Dom turned it into a soft kiss. "Go back to sleep."

"I'm sorry I can't seem to stay awake for your show," Asterion said with a yawn. Dom chuckled.

"I guess we'll just have to keep trying." And maybe it was just that Asterion was already half in dreams, but that sounded incredibly like an invitation. He grinned into the darkness. "There are other radio shows out there."

"Maybe something funnier," Asterion said, sliding one of his legs between Dom's. Dom dropped his arm over Asterion's waist, and Asterion scooted closer beneath the blankets. "Or more romantic."

"This one had a great romance," Dom protested.

"I wouldn't know," Asterion said with an innocent shrug. Dom huffed, and Asterion kissed him.

"How can a man so perfect have such terrible taste in radio?"

Asterion snorted, mock offended, and tried to roll away, but Dom held him fast, keeping Asterion's back flush with his chest. Asterion's body was so at ease in Dom's arms, that he couldn't stop a soft sigh from escaping his chest. Dom kissed the back of his neck.

"We can ask Nina for recommendations. I think she and Casey have a couple of comedies they like."

"Maybe when we go there for dinner," Asterion mused.

"Good idea," Dom yawned. Asterion could feel Dom's nose against his spine. After a few minutes, Dom's breathing slowed, and Asterion could feel himself sliding back into sleep, wrapped in the arms of a man who wanted Asterion just as he was. Someone who might actually want him to stay.

41

Once again, the day began with an interminable knocking on the door.

"If we ignore it, they'll leave," Asterion muttered into his pillow. Dom chuckled, fingers trailing across the small of Asterion's back. He leaned down and kissed Asterion's shoulder before getting out of bed.

Blearily, Asterion decided he hated any person or persons who pulled Dom away from him. Everything between Dom and Asterion had turned irrevocably, inconceivably romantic, and Asterion was desperate to hold onto it. It was wonderful being kissed and caressed and cared for. Asterion understood now more than ever why people deluded themselves into thinking they were in love.

Dom came back into the bedroom, knotting his hair at the base of his neck.

"Jonas and Sidney are here." Asterion groaned and pushed himself up, squinting over at Dom as Dom began to dress.

"Why?"

"Well, Jonas said he wanted to speak to you about throwing coffee on people."

"Oh," Asterion collapsed back down against his pillow.

"Who did you throw coffee on?"

"Dantalion. He deserved it. He deserved worse, actually."

"Jonas also said that he came with some portal runes. If we want to go through."

Oh.

Not that it was a surprise. Or anything different than what Asterion and Dom had planned to do anyway. Asterion pushed himself up to sit. Dom was pulling on a sweater over an undershirt, trousers belted at his waist. He was so handsome. And everything between them was so perfect, so easy here. Andurnei would be different. Nothing was ever easy there for Asterion. Which was why he spent so much time away. And now, without his magic, it was only going to be harder.

It didn't matter. Just because all the niceness was fast fleeting didn't mean Asterion couldn't enjoy what he had left. He sighed dramatically and then threw back the blankets, arching his back with a loud moan, morning erection proudly tenting his pajama pants.

"I think I'll take a quick shower," he said, glancing over his shoulder at Dom to make sure he was looking. Gratifyingly, he was. Dom smirked, and there was something wolfish in his eyes that sent a small shiver down Asterion's spine. "Care to join me?"

"We have company," Dom said. That wasn't a no. Asterion shrugged and got up, tugging his pajama shirt off over his head and sliding off his pants before sauntering naked into the bathroom.

Four minutes later, Asterion's chest was pressed against the cool shower tiles. He bit his wrist to stifle the moan of pleasure as Dom slid into him. Dom's hands were hard and eager, one on Asterion's hip, the other on his cock. Hot water pooled in the places where their bodies stayed joined and Asterion was delirious with desire. Dom rocked into him hard and fast, and Asterion whimpered, begging, breathless.

"Dom! Dom, harder."

Dom grunted, timing his thrusts and his strokes. Perfect. So perfect. Asterion was close. And then Dom's teeth grazed Asterion's throat.

"God. I want you, Asterion." It was too much. Asterion came with a barely stifled moan, as Dom pumped into him, groaning as his own orgasm followed quickly behind.

Being wanted was intoxicating. It was making Asterion stupid. He slumped against the shower wall and let Dom kiss his neck and shoulders, murmuring praise against his skin. Every time Asterion thought he was in control of the way he wanted Dom, it ended up like this, with Asterion overwhelmed by the strength of his own desire. Marked as Dom's. Not that he minded. He likely should have minded. But Dom was kissing him, and Asterion had forgotten already that it didn't really mean anything. That it was all about to change again.

Dom got out of the shower first, and by the time Asterion emerged, dressed and perfectly put together, Jonas and Dom were seated at the table poring over a notebook. Sidney was at the counter, pouring a fresh mug of coffee.

"You've ruined our experiment," Sidney said, as Asterion joined him in the kitchen.

"Good. It's too early to be experimenting." Asterion fetched another mug out of the cabinet and held it out to Sidney, who filled the cup almost to the brim, bless him. Asterion raised the cup to his lips gingerly and took a sip, following Sidney's gaze to where Jonas was pointing at something emphatically on the page between him and Dom. "And what experiment have I so handily destroyed?"

"We weren't sure you'd be able to portal to Andurnei with a suppressed magical signature. Fae blood might not have been enough to allow you passage. Jonas and I spent the better part of yesterday trying to think of ways around it so that Dom wouldn't have to travel to Andurnei alone."

"Oh." Asterion frowned. He hadn't thought of any of that when he'd agreed to go through with Dom. "And what have you determined?"

"Well, what we were going to propose doesn't matter," Sidney mused. "Seeing as you've taken a mark from a demigod as recently as," he checked his watch for effect, "twenty minutes ago, you portaling through to Andurnei shouldn't be a problem at all."

"Oh," Asterion said again, ignoring the fact that he was blushing and appreciating Sidney's delightful bitchiness. "I suppose you ought to congratulate me for being so clever and forward-thinking."

"I might, if I thought cleverness played any factor in your decision-making whatsoever."

"Of course it did," Asterion lied. "Why else would I have taken a mark?"

"Why, indeed?" Sidney's tone dripped with sarcasm, and Asterion grinned.

"You enjoy me, don't you?"

"You have your moments," Sidney admitted with a small smile.

"Asterion," Jonas called from the table. "Come have a look at these runes." Asterion sighed and pushed himself up off the counter, winking at Sidney as he walked away.

42

E ight runes were all it took to build your own portal. And blood. And intent.

Once Asterion confirmed that the runes Jonas had written would lead to his home, Paravel Palace, they had everything they needed. Dom just had to work up the nerve.

Leyland Hall, where they suspected Ares had gone and where Dom's mother apparently was, was about a day's ride from Asterion's palace. By horse, which was apparently the primary mode of transportation in Andurnei.

"Imagine an amalgam of Medieval, Arthurian and mid-Nineteenth century aesthetics all rolled into one," Jonas explained as he traced runes above the doorway to the back stairs. "Whatever will entice human nostalgia and allow for overdramatic flair. With the fae, the appearance of fantasy is more consequential than practicality. It is quite literally like a fairy tale. And that's on purpose." Asterion had gone upstairs to pack, otherwise Dom imagined he'd be hearing an irritated rebuttal right about now.

"But it's not real, is what you're saying?" Dom asked. Jonas shrugged.

"Reality is a bit different in Andurnei. Fae are generally a capricious people. Used to changing the world to suit their whims. It can make reality a bit... fuzzy." He stepped back from the doorway and glanced at Dom. "For some of them anyway. Truth is more malleable than we might be used to."

And maybe that was why Asterion was so explicit about it all the time, separating truths and lies. Honesty and dishonesty.

But Dom didn't really have any doubts when it came to Asterion and his truth-telling. Maybe that was stupid. Clearly his own instincts weren't that reliable where trust was concerned; he'd been wrong about his own brother, after all. His family had been keeping secrets from him for years.

"What about Asterion?" Dom asked, curious if Jonas would agree that Asterion was as trustworthy as Dom thought he was. Of course, it was only after he asked that Dom remembered about the nature of Asterion and Jonas' relationship. He winced at the weirdness of the unintended implications and tried to backtrack. "Never mind. I—"

"Asterion can mislead with the best of them," Jonas said. "He'll misdirect and obfuscate. But once you've learned who he is, it usually comes across as a little bit obvious. Don't tell him I said that."

"I trust him," Dom said. Jonas nodded and clapped him on the shoulder, his hand hard and heavy.

"And you're right to. But you may still have to keep him out of trouble." Dom arched eyebrow his eyebrow and Jonas smirked. "All I can do is wish you good luck. Now, come on. It's time for the blood."

A small cut on his palm, and eight smudges of blood later, Dom's once normal hallway was looking rather sinister. Until Asterion huffed in from the other side, dragging one of Dom's old suitcases. He dropped it at his feet and turned to examine

Jonas and Dom's handiwork like he was looking at art on a gallery wall.

"You've got the tail too long on this one," he said, pointing to a rune at the top corner. Jonas rolled his eyes and Dom grinned, as Asterion set about criticizing and adjusting things. Dom left Jonas to handle it and dipped into his bedroom to grab his rucksack. When he came back, Asterion and Jonas were leaning against the wall chatting.

"Ready?" Jonas pushed himself up.

"As I'll ever be. Thanks for your help," Dom added. Jonas nodded and turned to Asterion, pulling him into a hug before Asterion could get away.

"Don't get into any trouble."

"Leave me alone, you brute." Asterion leaned up and kissed Jonas' cheek, and Jonas released him with a smile.

"At least call me when you do get into trouble."

"I always do."

"Enjoy Andurnei, Dom. It's beautiful this time of year. Now, one hand goes here." Jonas touched the center of the rune on the left side of the door jamb. Dom pressed his palm to the mark, and then his other hand to the rune opposite, where Jonas pointed. "That's it."

"That's it?" Dom asked. Jonas nodded.

"Close your eyes and imagine a door opening beneath your hands. Just a push is all it takes." Dom closed his eyes and nodded, trying not to feel like an idiot. It would be worse if it didn't work, he decided, as he got around to imagining himself opening a door. The door at the diner, from the kitchen to the space behind the counter. A gentle push.

"There we go." Asterion's voice was even, but Dom imagined he heard a tinge of pride in it. He opened his eyes, and before he could look back at Asterion, he was distracted by what was in front of him.

The door, which had led to Dom's back steps, now opened into a room where nearly everything was gold. Shimmering wallpaper lined the far wall, where a second door was manned by armed guards. Cream-colored carpet set off the cream-colored ceiling adorned with gilded molding. Opposite from where they stood was a white marble fireplace, also veined with gold, above which hung a massive mirror, where Dom could see his awe-struck expression reflected back at him.

"Excuse me," Asterion sighed, slipping past Dom to intercept the guard that was walking toward them.

"THAT," ASTERION SAID, THREE MINUTES LATER, ONCE THE GUARDS had recognized him and rifled through Dom's bag, "was ridiculous." They stepped from the portal room into a parlor, where there were couches, small side tables, and a drink cart well-stocked for guests. It was too ornate. Gold lined every wall panel and gilded every piece of furniture. "I've been gone for two weeks, they act like they don't know who I am. Mind, it's been forty-five seconds, so, the whole of the security staff will know you're here by now. And in five minutes, so will everyone else. The problem with employing gossips is that they gossip." Asterion moved to the drink cart, and Dom took a moment to catch his breath.

"This place is—"

"Hideous. I know," Asterion sighed. Dom almost laughed out loud; Asterion continued pouring drinks.

"I mean—"

"You wouldn't say it like that because you're far too nice. But, believe me, I know what I inherited."

"Inherited?" Dom asked, taking the drink Asterion offered him.

"When my father died, he left Paravel to me. And I don't

think I opened the doors until about five years after that. Not that I was overcome by the loss or anything. We weren't on good terms. I was just doing a bit of travelling." Asterion sipped his drink, his golden eyes casting around the fixtures, looking anywhere but at Dom. Still, his eyes were the brightest, most lovely things in the room. "I have made some renovations. But I've been taking my time with it. I doubt it's even a third of the way done. And anyway, people like this sort of thing."

"What sort of thing?" Dom asked, really wondering if he'd ever heard Asterion ramble so much before.

"All the gold and the royal sort of, flourishes, I suppose." He gestured loosely with his free hand, his nose wrinkling in disgust as he looked around again.

"Who cares what they like? It's your house now," Dom said. Asterion finally looked at him. For a moment Dom was sure he'd said the wrong thing, until a grin flashed wide across Asterion's face. He shook his head, gaze drifting up, but Dom was relieved to see that his handsome smile remained.

"I could show you some of the rooms I've renovated," Asterion offered. Before Dom could agree, Asterion stopped, a blush coloring his cheekbones as he frowned again. "But no. We should go. Leyland Hall is a day away still."

Dom glanced toward the window. An orange sky lit up the rolling hills covered in pristine, sparkling snow.

"It's dawn?" He asked. Asterion followed his gaze, then after a moment, shook his head.

"Dusk. The lake is just beyond those hills. West."

"How—? We just woke up."

"Portaling isn't quite like traveling overseas. It's not uncommon to lose or gain a day here or there in the transit. Which is why most magic users aren't doing it to get from home to, say, the corner shops. You run the risk of being late for dinner. Or unfashionably early."

"I see," Dom said. "So, did we lose time? Or is this last night?"

"I don't know," Asterion shrugged. "We could find someone and ask. But I really think we should prepare to leave either way."

Dom ran his tongue along the back of his teeth, as he considered. He wanted to find Ares. He wanted answers from his brother. But ten years worth of doubts were catching up with him. They had started the night before, and Dom still felt mired in them.

"We have gained twelve hours, though," Dom hesitated. Asterion lifted an eyebrow, but didn't speak. "We might have a little bit of time. We could wait until morning."

"Isn't that what you said last night?" Asterion asked evenly. Dom winced.

"Maybe. But what if Ares isn't even there?"

"Then you're in exactly the same place you were when you started. And as much as it pains me to admit it, Dantalion isn't usually wrong. If Ares isn't at Leyland Hall now, it's likely he'd have at least gone there at some point. It's the best place to start." Dom took a deep breath.

"I know you're right," he said.

"Music to my ears." Asterion's mouth turned up at one corner, a slanted smile that Dom wanted to kiss.

"Is it safe to travel overnight? If we stay here, we could leave early—"

"This is your journey, Dom," Asterion said gently, giving a small shrug. "We can do whatever you like."

"I know it's cowardly—"

"I wouldn't go that far." Asterion said, and Dom chuckled.

"You're being too nice to me."

"I think you deserve a little niceness," Asterion said, and the sincerity in his voice pulled Dom to him.

They'd been standing apart since they came through the portal. Since they'd gotten out of the shower that morning. Like Andurnei and this trip was a barrier between them. When Dom put his hand on Asterion's waist, Asterion leaned into him, his eyes dropping down to the single place where they were touching. When he looked up again, his gaze was intense, and Dom closed the distance to kiss him.

It took a moment for Asterion's mouth to soften, but when they pulled apart, it was barely, and Asterion's attention stayed on Dom's lips.

"Maybe we could both use a few extra hours to get our bearings," Dom suggested.

"Maybe," Asterion murmured. Before Dom could respond, the outer door to the room opened, and a woman with moss green hair, tawny skin and pointed ears burst in. The sleeves of her blouse billowed out around her arms as she stopped abruptly, the many layers of her indigo skirt rustling even as she stood stock-still.

"What are you doing here?" She demanded. Asterion grinned and nudged Dom in the ribs.

"That's how she talks to me. When her salary comes straight from my coffers."

"I told you I was going to come back," she snapped. Asterion shrugged, his grin charming and needling at the same time.

"I got tired of waiting."

"Of course you did," she sighed, her gaze finally drifting over to Dom. "Introductions," she chided. Just like Ree. Dom caught himself before he laughed. Asterion rolled his eyes.

"Oh, of course. Forgive me. Dom, this is Ellery Van Ahlberg. She runs everything. Ellery, this is Dominic Silva." Ellery didn't respond, just put her hands on her hips, sizing Dom up.

"It's a pleasure to meet you," Ellery said, though it didn't sound like she meant it.

"We're going to be staying here tonight. We're leaving in the morning for Leyland Hall." Ellery's eyebrow's shot up to her hairline.

"Why?"

"Dom has some family business there," Asterion said. "I offered to take him." Ellery's full lips thinned to a ruby slash of disapproval. "I promise, it'll be perfectly fine. Now, could you do me a favor and have some food sent up to my room, please? We haven't had breakfast yet."

"We're going to have a conversation, you and I," Ellery said sternly, as she glared at Asterion, apparently entirely immune to his charms. Which was both impressive and scary. "But, yes. I will. Also, it's supper time."

"Thank you," Asterion said. Ellery sniffed, then turned on her heel and swept from the room.

"Are we in trouble?" Dom asked. Asterion laughed, linking arms with Dom.

"I always am with Ellery. Come on. I'll show you around."

43

As Jonas had warned, the castle was exactly, absurdly, something out of a fairytale. Wide, high-ceilinged halls were lined with rows of frosted multi-paned windows that must have made the heating cost astronomical. The floors were marble, the wallpapers were silk, and Dom was beginning to wonder how Asterion had gone from this massive, magical place to a shoebox-sized apartment with a leaky sink, without feeling like a caged animal.

"You're being awfully quiet," Asterion said, as they turned a corner, strolling past a grand staircase that could have held the entirety of The Silver Platter between its bannisters.

"Just taking it all in," Dom said mildly. Asterion snorted, and Dom cracked a smile. "You really don't like it?"

"It's fine," Asterion shrugged. Then he shook his head. "It's too much. Most things here are. All fae magic is about beauty to excess. It enchants people. It's easy to lose track of yourself when everything around you seems perfect."

"*Seems* perfect?"

"After a while, you start to see the cracks. Maybe not in the scenery," he admitted as they passed a window, where the sunset had shifted to a glorious glittering pink. "Other places, though. It's not as seamless as it looks." They turned another corner, and the hallway shrank to a much more realistic proportion. Trimmed with wood beams and lined with glass sconces, it almost felt cozy.

Asterion stopped in front of a large wooden door on the right side of the hall. For a moment, he hesitated, and then, before Dom could ask why, Asterion pushed open the door.

IT WAS STUPID TO BE PROUD OF A ROOM. BUT ASTERION WAS proud all the same. The walls were dark blue, inlaid with mahogany panels, and the tall ceilings were tamed by careful layers of matching crown molding. It was still regal, and probably still over-decorated. But it wasn't big and garish and gleaming. And it was his.

Asterion pulled back the curtains, letting in the last of the sunlight. The trees that surrounded the palace, and became, in the distance, a proper forest, were all long black shadows. Asterion stared into them for a moment, worried about what Dom's face would be doing when he turned back around. But when he got up the courage to look, Dom was studying the painting above the mantle with a small, perhaps appreciative, smile.

"I'll have someone light a fire. Forgot how chilly it can get in here," Asterion said quickly. He started through the narrow archway that led to his bedroom. "Are you hungry? Do you want a drink?" Gods, he was nattering. And he hated feeling so self-conscious. He'd brought plenty of lovers to Paravel before, and they'd all loved it. Not that he'd brought them to these rooms, of course. The wing for guests was on the other side of the palace. But he couldn't imagine keeping Dom all the way over there.

Asterion smoothed his hand over the thick grey fur blanket at the foot of his bed and took a breath. His bedroom was small, dominated by his bed, and the fireplace across from it. On the wall opposite was his wardrobe and two doors: one to the ensuite, the other to his study. But he wasn't going to show off his bathroom. And he certainly wasn't going to show Dom his study.

Was he?

"The paintings are beautiful."

Dom leaned in the doorway, his attention on the art above the fireplace. The painting in the bedroom was the sister to the one in the sitting room, but instead of the fluted orange blossoms, wide white water lilies were bracketed in by sloping leaves and curling vines. Both were more patterns than true paintings, but that didn't make the compliment any less pleasing.

"Thank you." Asterion said. Then, he found, he couldn't help himself. "I have more."

"I'd love to see them," Dom said. There were a dozen little bells of warning chiming in Asterion's head, telling him that it had to be a trick, there was certainly an ulterior motive for this kindness, warning him that he was letting Dom get too close to something real.

But Asterion believed him.

And perhaps that was why Asterion walked across the room and pushed open the door to his study, as though he'd always planned to.

The room was exactly as he'd left it. A bit colder, perhaps, but that was because he'd put in too many windows when he'd renovated and refused to regret it. Otherwise, the drafting table was still a mess, spilling over with designs and inks. In the far corner, a months abandoned easel was boxed in by a stack of paintings leaning against it. And large pieces of draft paper were tacked up around the one sofa in the room. He'd been working on the redesign for the ballroom before he'd left.

"Asterion, what is all this?" Dom's eyes were wide. Possibly in appreciation, though more likely in horror. It looked like the work of a madman.

"It's a mess." Asterion waved his hand, as if he could shoo the disaster away. "The paintings are over here if you can make it without killing yourself. Sorry it's so cold."

"Wait, the paintings are yours? You painted them?"

"I did. Not really as paintings," Asterion paused by the easel, examining it so he wouldn't have to look at Dom. "I know they're large, but I was thinking of them as wallpaper or etching patterns. Something to do in relief, maybe, but I—"

"You didn't tell me you were an artist." Dom arrived next to him, his expression something that was either offended or amused. Asterion straightened up, ready defend himself.

"I am not an artist. Nor would I claim to be. I don't have the skill."

"I disagree," Dom said. Asterion huffed and rolled his eyes.

"There's really no call for flattery. I'm already sleeping with you." Dom burst out laughing, a beautiful sound that echoed up the stonework and made Asterion cringe. Dom shook his head and wrapped his arms around Asterion's waist. "I don't appreciate mockery," Asterion scolded. Dom's expression softened as he looked Asterion in the eye.

"If you believe nothing else I ever say to you, believe this: I'm not mocking you. I am extremely impressed by you. Even more than I was before. Which was already an awful lot." And then Dom kissed him. Asterion's cheeks were hot, and the warmth of praise coupled weirdly with the sensation of being thoroughly exposed. He wanted to be less affected by it than he was.

Dom broke away from him and went to the paintings, gingerly flipping through the oversized square canvases, as Asterion haltingly stammered out explanations between Dom's compliments.

"The back few I designed to be stained glass. Never got around to making them, but maybe someday."

"They're gorgeous," Dom said. He looked back at Asterion, his gaze all sincere and terribly lovely. "I thought you told me you were—what was it? Indolent and shiftless?" Damn. Asterion was blushing again.

"Well, a prince should be well-rounded, so I had to come up with a few hobbies."

"I feel terrible for having put you up in the blandest apartment on Earth."

"Believe me, bland is better than garish. And *your* apartment is nice, anyway. Your bedroom, especially. I like the dark green."

"And to think, the wall color was what you liked most about my bedroom," Dom teased.

"The curtains were nice," Asterion considered. Dom rolled his eyes and slid his arm around Asterion's waist again. "Though if we're being painfully honest, they don't quite match the bedding."

"Now who's mocking who?"

"Whatever do you mean?" Dom chuckled, and the ball of nerves that had been thudding around in Asterion's stomach finally began to loosen. Maybe returning to Andurnei wasn't the worst thing they could have done after all.

Dom kissed him, and Asterion relaxed a little. It was a strange relief to be seen, and not taken to task for what was there. It made something beneath his skin buzz, like the first moments of a casting a spell.

A door opened in the distance, a clatter of noise going up from the sitting area.

"That'll be supper."

"I could have cooked something," Dom said. Asterion snorted.

"Undoubtedly. But the kitchen staff don't like any intrusion."

"But I'm—" Dom protested.

"Believe me, Dom, a late-night snack is akin to an incursion in enemy territory. You're better off asking to be served, I promise. Come on. Let's see what they've brought up."

44

Coming to Andurnei on an empty stomach might've been the right move. Endless plates of charcuterie, dried fruits and vegetables, dips and honeys crowded the table in the sitting room. For a little while, Dom was trapped, shuttled into an armchair to keep him out of the way of the endless parade of staff who were lighting fires and pouring wine. At least a dozen people came and went within a quarter of an hour. Blankets, robes, fresh linens, and other things no one had asked for arrived anyway.

Asterion knew everyone by name, walked with them, chatted as they worked. He didn't seem to notice the way every person who entered the room gawked at Dom when they spotted him in the corner. It didn't feel judgmental; more that they were surprised to find him there, like he was a zebra that had wandered in somehow. Hadn't Asterion had plenty of lovers? Wouldn't the staff just assume that he was one more?

Asterion ushered out the final footman with a pleasant farewell. He was a short, young-looking man with long pointed ears, peachy skin and a halo of dark brown curls. His jaw had dropped open at the sight of Dom when he'd walked in, and even as he was leaving, he glanced at Dom curiously before Asterion closed the door after him.

"Sorry." Asterion collapsed on the couch with a sigh. "Unannounced visitors always send the house into a frenzy. It's my fault really. I should have called ahead." He picked up a glass of wine and glanced over at Dom with a frown. "I hope this is—I mean, I know it's too much. Have you tried the sugared dates?"

"Not yet. And it is too much food, but everything looks delicious." Dom picked up a dish. He hesitated, not sure if he really wanted to know the answer to the question he was about to ask. "Maybe this is stupid, but was everyone staring at me?"

"Ah," Asterion focused on moving a tray of crackers, as a light blush high on his cheeks. "Probably."

"Because I'm... human?"

"No. Andurnei has a decently sized human population. It's not all that unusual. There are actually a few humans who work in the—"

"Then why?" Dom pressed. Asterion cleared his throat, and then took a sip of wine. "Is it because I'm with you?"

"It's because you're in *here*," Asterion said. He leaned back on the sofa, setting his plate down on the cushion, a small, nervous smile trying to tug up the corner of his mouth. He shook his head. "It's silly. Don't take it personally."

"I shouldn't be in your room?" Dom struggled to understand. "Is it a propriety thing? I don't want to offend anyone."

"No," Asterion laughed. "It's not offensive. I just don't have guests in this wing. Ever." His golden eyes flicked toward Dom, like he was afraid of Dom's reaction, but before Dom could say anything, Asterion kept talking. "I think I mentioned before that people expect certain behavior from a—well, from me. And I find it's easier to meet those expectations in other areas of the palace. Less personal. Grander." He gestured around. "These rooms are small. Quiet. Far from the ballroom and the salon. The view is better on the other side of the palace."

It didn't sit well with Dom, the way Asterion hid in his own house. Privacy was one thing, something Dom understood and appreciated. But this wasn't that.

"You designed these rooms, though."

"Yes," Asterion nodded, picking up a cracker, and studying it like it was a complex math problem. "It's my wing, I suppose. There's a library on the other side of the hall, and a small receiving room. Not that it's ever been used. Just in case I needed it." He trailed off, dropping the cracker onto the plate and straightening up. "I should have offered you a room in the guest wing. It's drab in here. Dark—"

"Stop," Dom said firmly. "I like these rooms. They're warm and comfortable."

They feel like home.

He couldn't say that. It was too honest. Too forward. And besides, Asterion wouldn't believe it.

"Look, if you want me to go somewhere else, I will. But only if *you* want me to. I like it here. Really."

Asterion was still, stiff and straight, and Dom thought, for a moment, that Asterion was actually about to send him to another wing of the palace. But instead, Asterion set his wine glass on the corner of the table, leaned over and grabbed Dom by the front of his sweater, pulling him into a kiss. It was firm and passionate, and then Asterion tugged, and Dom was scrambling onto the couch, on top of him.

There was a plate of crackers somewhere between their shins, but Asterion was sliding his fingers up the hem of Dom's shirt. His hands were on Dom's waist, pressing into his skin, and they could eat later. Dom wasn't hungry anyway.

Asterion pushed up on Dom's shirt, and Dom got to his knees, tugging his sweater and his undershirt off over his head.

Asterion kissed the center of Dom's chest, fingers dropping to the button on Dom's trousers, when the door swung open.

Ellery Van Ahlberg made a choked sound in the back of her throat. Dom froze, not quite embarrassed, even though he probably should have been. Asterion twisted himself around to look at her.

"Ellery," he said, managing to disentangle his legs from Dom's just as Ellery backed out, pulling the door closed.

"No," she said from the hall. "It can wait."

"It's—" Asterion stood. Then he leaned over and kissed Dom soundly, before going to join Ellery in the hallway.

"Do not come out here," Ellery hissed. Asterion's hand was wrapped around the door jamb, so she couldn't close it on him. "You're clearly in the middle of something."

"You said you wanted to talk to me." Ellery huffed loudly enough that Asterion was sure Dom could hear her.

"You are losing your mind! He's the most handsome thing you've ever had between your sheets and you're out here with me? Are you ill or something?"

"Most handsome?" Asterion arched an eyebrow. She was right, of course, but, "I thought you liked what's his name. Colonel Fairweather. Smaller fellows."

"We're not doing this right now! Get back in there!"

"This is not like you, Ellery," Asterion chastised, putting one hand on his hip. "Usually, you can't wait to interrupt my—"

"If you think that everyone isn't talking about you and him and the way he looks at you, and the way you brought him *to your rooms* then you're dumber than I thought. And that's saying something."

"Unkind, Ellery!"

"We can talk later. Goodbye." And with that, she turned Asterion around by his shoulders, shoved him back into the sitting room and closed the door firmly behind her.

Dom was sitting on the couch, undershirt back on, glass of wine in his hand. He did not have the good grace to look anything less than extremely amused.

"How much of that did you hear?"

"Nearly all of it. Who's Colonel Fairweather?"

"A sprite from about fifty years ago, give or take." Asterion sat back down and grabbed his wine.

"A sprite?" Dom asked. Asterion nodded and handed him a sugared date.

"There are at least a dozen fae races. Likely more, honestly. It's all a bit of a mishmash. Ears, wings and height are the only real physical tells, and you can't even trust those, because plenty of folks will just magic themselves to a different appearance whenever it suits them."

"But Ellery likes short fellows?" Dom smirked. Asterion laughed.

"Ellery likes anyone who will try and argue with her."

"Which isn't you," Dom said. Asterion grinned.

"Certainly not."

45

Asterion woke to a softly crackling fire in his fireplace and Dom Silva curled around him, still asleep. Morning light filtered in through the seams in the curtains and Asterion raised himself up on one elbow, pleased to see a breakfast tray sitting just inside the doorway. Coffee, pastries, tea and donuts. They wouldn't be as good as Dom's, but they'd be close.

Before Asterion could get up, Dom shifted next to him, curling toward Asterion's chest. His lips pressed against the silk fabric of Asterion's pajama shirt, Dom's own chest gorgeously bare. Then, Dom's hand slid over the front of Asterion's pajama pants and Asterion hummed his approval.

"Good morning," Asterion murmured. Dom stroked him again. Breakfast could wait. After Ellery's interruption the evening before, they'd stayed up late talking and drinking and making an impressive dent in the charcuterie. They'd crawled into bed full and drunk, even though they'd only crawled out of it a few hours prior. But there was certainly no time like the present to continue what they'd started.

Dom stroked Asterion a few more times before wordlessly rolling onto his stomach, shimmying out of his pajama pants, beneath the blankets. Asterion smirked down at him, pressing a kiss to the back of his neck.

"Are you awake?" Asterion asked. "Or is sleep-stripping a bad habit of yours I'm just learning about?" He curled his hand over Dom's hip and Dom shifted into the touch.

"I was dreaming about you," Dom said into the pillow, arching his back as Asterion slid his hand down, curling his fingers around Dom's rigid length. Dom groaned, and Asterion bit his bottom lip, surprised by the sudden strength of his own arousal. He loved the way Dom wanted him. He loved that Dom was asking for him like this.

"Was it a good dream?"

"Very good."

"Tell me about it."

"Oh," Dom exhaled, shifting his hips. "Well, you were fucking me." Asterion's mind temporarily blanked, and it took him a moment to find words again.

"Lucky me." Dom chuckled, and then, when Asterion tightened his grip, let out a soft choked sound.

"You had me pinned down—"

"I see." Asterion took his hand away so that he could undress more quickly. "Shall we try to recreate this dream of yours?"

"Yes, please."

Asterion would have torn open his pajama shirt if it wasn't already in a crumpled heap on the ground. He accidentally pulled the blankets away from Dom in his hurry to get his own pants off. Dom rolled onto his hip, smiling up at Asterion.

"Ah, no. Roll over," Asterion ordered. Dom chuckled but did as he was told. The long expanse of his smooth light brown skin, taut over the bulges of the muscles in his shoulders, over his gorgeous ass. It would have brought Asterion to tears, if he weren't already so ridiculously turned-on. He ran his hands over Dom's back, as he settled himself on his knees between Dom's thighs. He stretched, naked, over Dom's body, ostensibly reaching for the nightstand, but really just enjoying the feeling of Dom beneath him. When Dom lifted his hips, Asterion bit back a groan.

"Comfortable up there?" Dom murmured.

"Extremely," Asterion replied, finally finding the small bottle of oil he kept in the corner of the nightstand drawer. He eased back, but not too much. "Was there anything else of note in this dream that I should endeavor to accomplish?"

"How do you feel about tying my wrists together?" Dom asked, his voice muffled by the pillow, though Asterion could still see that his ears were turning pink.

"Was I fucking you while you were tied up?" Asterion asked, mock affronted, and trying desperately to remember where he'd stashed the silk ropes he had. "What sort of a deviant do you take me for?"

"We could always save that for next time," Dom suggested, lifting his hips just enough to rock back against Asterion's cock. Asterion ran his hand over Dom's ass and grabbed his hips, keeping them lifted so that he could slide himself against Dom. Dom moaned and arched into him, eager and making Asterion shiver with lust.

"Gods, but the things I would do to you tied up."

"Like what?" Dom already sounded breathless, desperate. Asterion was already aching for him.

Before he could answer, the door opened in the sitting room.

They both heard it: Dom lowered his hips, and Asterion scrambled for the blanket, as they looked toward the doorway. No one was used to Asterion keeping company in his private rooms. He was going to have to send around a reminder about knocking.

"Come back later," he called out.

"Asterion?" A female voice, followed by footsteps, had Asterion's arousal chilling in record time. He rolled off Dom just as his sister poked her head into his bedroom.

Cressida was shorter than Asterion, but they had similar features. The same pointed chins, high cheekbones and thin, wide mouths, so Asterion knew that the look of shock on her face was almost certainly mirrored on his own. She covered the round 'O' of her mouth with her hand and unhelpfully, didn't leave.

"What are you doing here?" she asked.

"In my room? In my house?" He snapped. She dropped her hand and rolled her eyes.

"Oh, honestly."

"Would you mind terribly giving us just a moment?" Asterion asked. Cressida's gaze dropped to Dom, one thin eyebrow arching appreciatively.

"I'm not leaving until I get an explanation from you," she leaned in and scooped up a cup, saucer and the entire teapot off the tray near the door. "So do hurry up." And then she vanished into the sitting room.

Asterion exhaled through his teeth. Damn, he hated being home.

Dom rolled over, eyes wide, question clear on his face.

"My sister. Cressida," Asterion said quietly. Not quietly enough, though.

"Queen Cressida of Andurnei," came Cress's lilting voice from the sitting room. Asterion scowled.

"I should probably get dressed," Dom said as he sat up, blankets draped temptingly around his hips. Asterion wasn't sure if he wanted to curse or cry. Dom kissed him.

"Later," Dom murmured. The outer door opened again, and Dom pulled away, as another voice echoed into the room.

"Ah, there you are my lady! I thought we were starting in the east wing."

"Our conversation will have to wait a moment, Remus. Asterion's here and he has company."

ASTERION GOT UP WITH A GROAN AND FETCHED HIS HEAVIEST dressing gown from his wardrobe. He pulled out a spare for Dom, and left it on the foot of the bed, striding out to try and intercept his sister and any more of her attendants before they turned his sitting room into a circus.

Cressida was seated on the armchair by the fire, cup and saucer held delicately in one extremely pale hand. Her skin was as fair as she'd ever made it, and her hair was in a loose twist at the back of her neck, the vibrant orange of autumn leaves. For some reason, she was wearing a powder blue robe volante that nearly engulfed the chair and the side table and ballooned out dangerously close to the fire.

Remus, Cressida's long-time stylist, was a brownie with silver grey skin and a twist of lilac hair that clashed horribly with his lime green suit. He hovered beside the fireplace, notebook clutched in his expertly manicured nails, eyes wide as Asterion walked into the room. Cressida's coral lips pursed, as she held out her arms to receive him. Asterion wrapped his arms around her shoulders, and her large, surprisingly firm stomach bumped against his. He took a step back, examining her at arm's length.

"You're pregnant?" Cressida gave him a small, possibly even genuine, smile.

"You've been gone for a while."

"Not as long as all that. Good gods." Cressida pulled back the corner of her robe, revealing a silver underdress strained over her round belly.

"You've been gone a year," she said.

"That's not that unusual for me," he said, his voice strained with frustration, surprise. When he went to Earth, he was almost always gone a year. Barely a blink of an eye for them. "You could have told me."

"I didn't know how to reach you!" Oh, bullshit.

"Cress. Really?"

"After we heard what happened with your magic—"

"I may not know so much about the burdens of childbearing, but this certainly looks like more than the work of two weeks." Cressida sat with a huff, rolling her eyes, as though he was the one being ridiculous. The fact that she was prevaricating meant there was more to the story than she wanted to reveal to him. And honestly, he wasn't sure how much information he wanted about it just now. Before he could ask her anything else, Dom walked into the room, and Cressida immediately turned on him, a cat swiveling toward a mouse.

"And who is this?"

"Dominic Silva. A friend," Asterion said, ignoring that Cressida had walked in on them in a more than friendly embrace. Cressida didn't so much as bat an eye, dipping her head mockingly in Dom's direction. Asterion's shoulders stiffened, as Dom bowed at the waist. Too formal, but then, Asterion hadn't given him any pointers on royal address because he had assumed, perhaps foolishly, that they wouldn't encounter his family while they were here.

"A pleasure to meet you," Dom said, still bent in half.

"You haven't met me yet, because my brother is a boor with no manners."

"Redundant," Asterion said, as he circled back around the couch, grabbing Dom's hand and pulling him upright. "All boors have no manners. Dom, this is Cressida, Queen of Andurnei and my bothersome older sister."

"Bothersome," Cressida muttered. "That's rich."

"Why is Remus here?" Asterion asked, as he led Dom around to the couch, so they could sit. "Hello Remus, by the way," he said, nodding to Remus, as he nudged Dom onto the sofa, hoping that would dispense with the uncomfortable formalities.

"Well, Asterion," Cressida looked down, shifting the skirt of her robe volante like a sail, "we didn't know whether or not you'd be returning, or what condition you'd be in when you did. Magically speaking, of course. We would never presume to know what *condition* you'll arrive back from Earth in," she added with a chuckle. Asterion tried not to wince. "I was looking for someplace outside the capitol to convalesce after I have the baby, and mother suggested Paravel."

"I see." Asterion said, though what he saw made his stomach hurt. If his mother was giving away his residence, then it was no longer his residence, and they both knew it. Cressida's stiff shoulders softened in pity.

"Obviously, if you're going to be here, there's no room for me and my staff." Her giving in to him so easily was far worse than her trying to redecorate.

"Nonsense. We serve at the pleasure of the queen," Asterion said. Cressida snorted.

"Oh, do shut up," she sighed. "We can talk about it tonight over dinner."

"We won't be there, unfortunately—"

"Of course you will. Mother is coming. And Felix."

"Felix?"

"Lord Di Rilke," she said. Asterion sifted through his admittedly slightly hazy mental directory of the members of realm peerage and landed on Lord Felix Di Rilke. Handsome, dark hair, luminous, usually beige skin. A jaw that could crack a walnut. Dumb as a sack of rocks.

"Lord Di Rilke?"

"Yes," Cressida sighed.

"Why?" Asterion asked. Cressida blinked at him, and

finally, Asterion realized what she meant. He could feel his eyes grow wide. "Oh," he finally managed. Di Rilke was a moron. Cress could have done leagues better. Cressida's lips thinned to a straight line, and she crossed her arms over her chest.

"I don't need your opinions, Asterion."

"No," Asterion snorted. "Certainly not. What's done is very clearly done," he added with a pointed look at her stomach.

"He has many fine qualities."

"Certainly," he allowed a very generous nod. She smacked him hard on the wrist, like he'd spoken out of turn in class.

"Don't be an ass!" Cressida reprimanded. "If you were anyone else, I'd have you publicly flogged for saying such things. Of course, knowing you, you'd probably enjoy it." Asterion bit back a retort, irritated at the embarrassment that flooded his cheeks. He could feel Dom watching them and couldn't meet his eye. Cressida didn't seem to have the same problem. She smiled patronizingly at Dom. "I apologize," Cressida huffed. "Though I'm sure if you've been my brother's acquaintance for long, you'll understand the occasional overwhelming urge to do him bodily harm."

"Not so long as that, ma'am," Dom said, and Asterion did look at him then, surprised by the clear look of disgust on Dom's face. "That being said, I do have a brother, and I know how grating siblings can be." Cressida watched him curiously for a moment, not quite smiling, but not frowning either.

"Then hopefully you'll excuse my misbehavior," she said. "And his." Before Dom could speak, she looked to Asterion again. "You'll have to see him properly dressed for the night. Mother can barely abide humans at the table as it is."

"He's not hu—" Asterion caught himself just before he'd revealed Dom's heritage to Cressida. Out of any of the members of his family, she was probably least likely to try and use it to her own advantage. Still. "We're not coming to dinner." Cressida rolled her eyes and turned toward Remus.

"Send up Amina with one of her books." Remus nodded and bowed, looking relieved to be allowed to leave the room. Asterion was extremely envious. Cressida took a deep breath. "You have to come tonight."

"We don't. We have plans." Cressida pouted. Asterion only blinked at her, and she huffed.

"If you come tonight, I'll tell mother I don't want to stay at Paravel," she said, finally. "I'll let you keep it." That was playing dirty. Asterion's stomach tightened. Cress's approval was the only conceivable way he'd be allowed to have his palace. If he even still wanted it. Which he did. And didn't. The thought of losing it had stung more than he'd thought it would, but at the same time—

"We'll be there," Dom said.

"Wonderful," Cressida smiled and got to her feet. "Dinner is at a quarter past six," she said. "Don't be late." Then she stood up and swept from the room.

46

"So. That's Cressida." Asterion busied himself with pouring a cup of coffee, studiously not looking in Dom's direction.

Dom couldn't stop watching Asterion, though. He'd seen the shame on Asterion's face, and how Asterion hadn't stuck up for himself. It was like Dantalion all over again, but this felt worse. Cressida was Asterion's sister. His family. Dom and Ares might have had their spats over the years, but neither of them would have been so cruel to each other. Asterion cleared his throat.

"She has a lot on her plate. Coronation was eighteen years ago, and I still don't think she's quite gotten the handle on ruling. But don't tell anyone I said that, because it's treason," Asterion added quickly. Dom snorted.

"Who would I tell?"

"I don't know."

"She wasn't very nice to you," Dom said. Asterion hummed noncommittally and got up.

"She doesn't have to be nice to me," Asterion said, dipping into the bedroom and returning with the breakfast tray. "She's the queen. And honestly, her offering to leave me Paravel was more generous than she had any reason to be."

"You're her brother." Asterion put the tray on the table, and sat on Dom's other side, as though the chair where Cressida sat had been tainted.

"If I disappeared for ten years, I promise, neither of my siblings would notice. And if they did happen to notice, they certainly wouldn't care. My being here is an inconvenience. And if my mother wasn't coming to dinner, Cress probably would have shown us the way out herself."

"Why does your mother being here matter?" Dom asked, accepting a cup of coffee from Asterion. Asterion snorted.

"Have you ever heard of the term 'whipping boy?' I promise it's not quite as salacious as it sounds." Dom frowned, and Asterion shook his head with a small chuckle. "Oh, and now my jokes aren't funny?"

"Asterion."

"Don't feel bad for me. I've been the family disappointment my entire life. I can handle one dinner with my mother. I'm sure Cress just wants a break from her nagging." Asterion sipped from his own teacup, his eyes drifting over Dom's face. "You didn't have to say we'd attend. It'll put off our trip another day."

Dom knew that. But he hadn't been giving in to cowardice this time.

"I don't want you to lose all this," he gestured around with his coffee. "Not over dinner. That's ridiculous."

"It's just a house."

"It's *your* house," Dom insisted. "And even if you hate the rest of it, these rooms are your home." Dom's apartment, the diner, those were the places that anchored him. They'd kept him sane and sheltered on his worst days. And he could feel the way these rooms were a part of Asterion. Places he'd carved out for himself in an unforgiving family. Ares had been gone for ten years; another day wasn't going to change anything for Dom. But it might for Asterion.

Asterion looked over at the breakfast tray and seemed for a moment to be lost in thought.

"It feels more like a home right now more than it ever has before," Asterion said, almost to himself. He glanced at Dom. "Thank you."

"I'm happy to do it."

"You say that now," Asterion sighed. There was a knock on the door, and Asterion huffed. "At least they're knocking. Come in!"

The first person in the room was Ellery Van Ahlberg. Today she wore tortoise shell glasses that were large for her face, a black tunic over narrow striped trousers, and flat leather slippers. She assessed both Dom and Asterion with intense scrutiny over a professionally short number of seconds.

"You're a traitor, Ellery," Asterion said with a smirk and no heat. "Letting Cressida move in? My bed wasn't even cold yet."

"I know whose coffers hold my wages," she said, though she didn't sound pleased about it. Asterion smirked at Dom.

"Ellery is properly mercenary. You could take lessons from her," he said. "I suppose that's what you wanted to talk to me about last night." Ellery nodded.

"But, since I didn't get to you in time, Remus says you'll be staying for dinner. So, I brought reinforcements." Ellery stepped aside, and two others came in. Asterion got to his feet, shaking hands, and then making introductions. Amina, the tailor, was petite with olive skin, long black braids and sharply pointed ears. Two slashes of gold eyeliner that set off striking ruby eyes that seemed to measure Dom in every direction as she greeted him, holding a thick notebook against her chest.

Orion, the valet, was next. A man with soft features and a round stomach, Dom thought at first that he might have been the palest person Dom had ever seen, and then realized his skin had an iridescent shine to it, like it was made from mother of pearl. His hair was an ethereally shimmering rose gold, and he carried an immensely plain brown satchel in one hand. When he looked at Asterion, he tsked his tongue.

"I know," Asterion said, apologetically, running a hand over his chin where the barest hint of stubble was beginning to appear. "I'm lost without you."

"You're not in as bad of shape as I thought you'd be," Orion replied with a thick accent that Dom had definitely never heard before.

"Dom has done his best," Asterion said.

"Bless you for making an attempt." He winked at Dom and then strode into the bedroom. "I'll be waiting for you in the washroom, my lord."

"Flirt," Asterion called after him.

"Go on," Ellery said to Asterion. "We'll look after Mr. Silva."

"Yes, that's what I'm afraid of," Asterion said, his glittering eyes meeting Dom's. Dom smiled, and maybe it was his imagination, but he thought Asterion's shoulders softened slightly.

"If he's managed you for a couple of weeks, he'll surely have no trouble fending us off."

"Managed?" Asterion snorted.

"Go," Ellery said, joining Dom on the sofa. Amina set her book down on the table with a thud.

"Spare no expense, Ellery," Asterion said as he started toward the bathroom. "Fine silks. Gorgeous leathers. Whatever he wants."

"Thank you for your input," Ellery replied dryly.

"Don't let them bully you, Dom," Asterion called from the other room. A door closed, and Amina let out a quiet chuckle. Dom looked between Ellery and Amina. Ellery's eyebrow arched.

"Well, Mr. Silva," she said after a moment. "Where would you like to start?"

47

Amina and Ellery were efficient and thorough. Amina made notes as Dom flipped through her book, pointing out colors he liked, or fashions he thought he'd be comfortable in. There were a considerable number of bared chests and sheer fabrics. Things that looked structured and formal at first glance, that upon examination were cut low or tight.

"For centuries everything was long and flowing, diaphanous fabrics and... oh I don't know, everything draped in something sheer," Amina said with a scowl.

"Not your preference?" Dom asked. Amina shook her head.

"It's just boring," Amina replied. "I like the structure of your realm's fashion. More interesting lines and construction." Fashion wasn't something that Dom thought about beyond if it could be cleaned easily when he splattered food on it in the kitchen, and he said as much to Amina and Ellery, who ignored him. Before he knew what was happening, Amina was gone, and Ellery stood, looking at Dom with a raised eyebrow.

"Well, Mr. Silva, is there anything else you need at the moment?" Dom swallowed. He had about a hundred questions; there were probably centuries of things he should have known about before he met Asterion's mother. But there wasn't any simple way to ask for that without sounding like a total idiot. Still, it would probably be dumber not to ask at all.

"Is there anything I should know before I dine with the family?" It sounded embarrassingly shallow, like he was looking for gossip. Ellery's eyebrow flattened, her mouth flicking briefly into a frown before she took a step back.

"Come with me," she said and strode out so quickly that he almost tripped in his rush to keep up with her.

"Shouldn't I get dressed first?" He asked uselessly, as he was already following her across the hall in his pajamas and Asterion's robe. Ellery shrugged.

"You're a human. No one expects you to dress well. And even if you did, no one comes up here anyway. No one who matters, at least." She pushed open a door at the far end of the hall and ushered Dom inside, before he could decide whether or not he was insulted.

Even if he hadn't known that Asterion had designed this room, Dom would have been able to guess. The library was gorgeous, another round room, but this one infinitely warmer, insulated by rows and columns of neatly shelved books. A balcony ringed the second floor, crowned with a wide window bracketed in by dark green curtains. Wallpaper, green-silver ivy climbing endlessly up a deep blue background, filled the spaces between the shelves. Words Dom never used, like: 'plush' and 'sumptuous' drifted to mind as he eyed the velvet upholstered sitting area.

Ellery slid in past him and was off in a corner, scanning titles with a finger.

"Asterion doesn't keep much in the way of non-fiction," she said. "Much to his mother's chagrin. He's always preferred novels. But he does have some histories of the region stashed over here somewhere." She crouched down, sliding out a couple of tomes that looked heavier than Dom's weekly meat order. He went to help her, and she heaved the books up into his arms.

"How long do I have until dinner?" Dom grunted. Ellery snorted as she got to her feet.

"If you have any questions in particular, I'm happy to answer them." The black leather-bound book in Dom's hand shone up at him. There was no title, but it was ornately embossed, a coat of arms in the center, four small flowers on the center of each side of the cover. Dom ran his thumb over what he thought was an ivy vine, curled into a small circle around itself.

"Asterion's mother. The Queen—"

"Queen Dowager," Ellery corrected. "Cressida is the queen."

"Is she," Dom took a breath, willing himself not to sound so childish when he finally choked out the rest of his sentence. "Is the Queen Dowager... What's she like?"

"As a queen?"

"As a mother."

"That's a question you're better off asking Asterion," Ellery said, but her tone was flat, and her body had gone stiffly professional, the way Dom's did when dealing with unpleasant customers.

"When she found out about his magic, what did she do?"

"I wouldn't want to presume to know the thoughts of the Dowager," Ellery said slowly. "She was disappointed to learn what had happened with the Assembly. She made that clear."

"But did she try to help him? I'm sure she has some sway—"

"Appealing to the Assembly is unpleasant even in the most clear-cut of circumstances."

"She's his mother."

"Asterion is a third son, and the Dowager is a firm believer in allowing natural consequences to occur as they will." First Cressida, now this? It was no wonder Asterion spent so much time on Earth. Dom must have been grimacing, because Ellery shook her head. "I wouldn't overly concern yourself, Mr. Silva. Asterion has become adept over the years at brushing off his family's disinterest in his affairs. In fact, I believe he prefers it."

"That doesn't make it okay," Dom said. Ellery shrugged.

"That's a matter of opinion."

"Still," he pressed. She laughed then, her round cheeks crinkling her eyes at the corners.

"I can see why Asterion likes you," she said. "And yes. Though my opinion certainly doesn't matter to anyone, I do agree with you. Asterion's family doesn't care about him, right up until he's made a fool of himself at which point he's trotted out as the great disappointment. It's unpleasant to watch, but speaking up about it is liable to put you in a worse position, so be aware of that."

"In a worse position than what?" Dom said indignantly. "I don't care if they don't like me."

"No," Ellery said. "But Asterion will."

Asterion wanted them to like him. Which was why Asterion never defended himself. It was all beginning to make sense, in a horrible, ugly sort of way.

Despite all of Dom's family's flaws, all their troubles and trials, their affection had never once felt conditional. And Dom wondered, suddenly, if Asterion had ever known a love that wasn't.

"If that's all, Mr. Silva, I have a few things I need to see to." Dom's mind was still whirring in distress, and he couldn't think of anything to say. Ellery gave him a small smile. "Someone will find you when Amina needs you for a fitting." Dom put the books down on the coffee table. He didn't feel like reading anymore.

"Could you show me the kitchen?"

∼

"So." ORION'S TONE BECAME SING-SONG, AS HE RAN HIS FINGERS through Asterion's newly trimmed hair, catching Asterion's eye in the mirror. "Who's the human?"

Orion had been Asterion's valet for at least a century, and Asterion had been the one who'd broken the formality of their arrangement by gossiping openly about his lovers. It was definitely uncouth of him to do so, but he'd been lonely, and it made him feel like he had a friend. Over the years, Orion had proved that he was reasonably discrete, but somehow, Asterion still hesitated.

Dom probably wouldn't have cared. And absolutely, Asterion had nothing critical to say about Dom's performance. But the whole thing felt tender still. Fragile. He smiled.

"Mr. Silva? A friend. From the earthly realms."

"A handsome friend." Orion pushed some pomade into Asterion's hair, sweeping it back into a soft pompadour. Asterion could tell that Orion wasn't happy with the length of it, though Asterion couldn't sense if it was too long or too short for the valet's liking. On the other hand, he had sort of grown fond of his new appearance. And his hair looked fine styled this way.

"Is he handsome? I hadn't noticed."

"That's because you have too many mirrors about. You get distracted with your own appearance. But if he's no one to you, I'll tell Roger and the other footmen that he's fair game. Everyone's been asking." Asterion snorted. It was just a joke, of course. But then, why was it making him grind his teeth?

Asterion didn't get jealous, as a rule. It was hypocritical for a man with as many partners as he'd had; a man who refused, actively avoided, commitments to anyone. Why, he himself, had suggested that Dom have a threesome with Jonas and Sidney less than a week ago! It made his stomach sour, now, to think about. Orion had taken a step back and was watching Asterion with a single arched eyebrow.

"What?" Asterion demanded, more sharply than he'd meant. Orion smiled, a wide, friendly grin as he shook his head.

"Nothing," he said, and went back to work.

A couple of hours later, Asterion had been cleansed and soaked and shaved and styled to within an inch of his life. It was certainly past lunchtime by the time Orion left, and when Asterion walked into the bedroom, Ellery was there with a tray of sandwiches and three outfits laid out across his bed.

"Where's Dom?"

"I've got no idea. Though I heard a rumor he was chased out of the kitchen about an hour and a half ago."

"Has he eaten?" Asterion asked, picking up a sandwich of his own and taking a bite.

"Well, he is a guest of yours, and we do normally feed them." Asterion rolled his eyes.

"It's so hard to get good help these days."

"I've been saying that for years," Ellery smirked. "Di Rilke and your mother have arrived, by the way." Asterion barely managed to grunt, as his stomach sank further, appetite vanishing. "Di Rilke's traveling with a coterie. Eight additional guests."

"It'll fill up the dinner table, at least." Asterion set the rest of his sandwich aside. Time to get dressed.

"Do you want a drink?" Ellery asked.

"No." Asterion was trying to preoccupy himself with the outfits. One a burgundy tailcoat, another an elaborately beaded tuxedo, and the third a blue velvet number. They each had their good bits, but none was what he wanted. He glanced over at Ellery to ask her opinion, but she was staring at him rather pointedly. He blinked at her. "What?"

"Usually I can't stop you from reaching for the decanter once your mother arrives."

"Oh."

There was a reason he wasn't drinking, though admittedly, it hadn't exactly been a conscious decision. He just felt, ever since Cressida's appearance, a little like he needed to protect Dom. His family could be brutal. And as much as he might want to be drunk out of his mind when they began picking at him, he couldn't stand up for Dom if he couldn't think straight. Or speak straight.

And maybe Dom didn't need Asterion's protection. Certainly, he'd handled Cress's little jibes well enough. But Asterion was better able to provide a defense this way, should one be required.

A knock on the outer door filled the silence that Asterion had let go on for too long. Ellery went to answer it, and Asterion turned back to the outfits laid out on the bed. He wanted something more like armor—the best option with his mother in attendance.

"Ellery said she'll come back later."

Dom stood in the doorway holding a plate of cherry turnovers in one hand and a mug in the other. Someone had dressed him in a simple white shirt and black high waisted trousers that double buttoned in the front like breeches. His hair was in a knot at the back of his head, and dark brown stubble covered his jaw and the line of his throat. Asterion's stomach growled.

"You haven't eaten?" Dom asked. Asterion shook his head, trying not to feel anything about the sweet look of concern on Dom's face. He met Dom at the foot of the bed and plucked a pastry off the plate.

"I'm amazed they let you in the kitchen."

"I needed to do something with my hands. They took pity on me." Asterion looked down at the delicate triangle of dough, golden brown and dusted with sugar.

"How are you feeling?" Asterion asked. Dom smirked. "Nervous?"

"A little. Amina was nice though," he gestured down at himself and then took a sip from the mug of coffee. "She gave me this after my fitting. Said I couldn't go around in my pajamas all day."

"You can do whatever you like." Asterion took a bite of the turnover, and his appetite came roaring back. He let out a small groan of pleasure, and Dom smiled. "You need to teach the pastry chef how to make these. *Exactly* the way you do." Dom chuckled, then he shrugged.

"Can't. Secret family recipe."

"Liar," Asterion laughed. Dom shook his head, still grinning.

"No, it is!"

"I'll ask Ree. She'll tell me."

"Not if I tell her not to."

"Then she'll *definitely* tell me." Asterion took the coffee from Dom's hand and sipped it, grateful for the sharp, smooth bitterness that sliced through the sweetness of the cherries. It felt fortifying. What had he been worried about before? He slid his arm around Dom's waist, relieved when Dom leaned into his side. "What should I wear tonight?" He gestured to the outfits. Dom looked at him sideways.

"I own one pair of nice trousers. You know this."

"Well, what do you think?"

"I think you look good in anything."

"Sweet," Asterion kissed Dom on the cheek. "But unhelpful." Somewhere a clock chimed, and Dom glanced around.

"Is it really that late?" he asked. Asterion shrugged.

"Probably."

"Amina told me to be back downstairs for a shave at two."

Ugh. How had Asterion lived like this before? Constantly being shuttled between minders and dinners. Dressed by staff and undressed by strangers. And why was it so much less enjoyable than it had been before? All he wanted to do now was keep talking with Dom, standing in his bedroom, eating turnovers.

"You'd better go," Asterion sighed. Dom put the plate of turnovers on the bed and kissed Asterion firmly, his mouth sweet, hands deliciously tight on Asterion's waist, and for just that moment, Asterion couldn't feel worried about what that evening would bring. It was all fine. With Dom here, everything was going to be fine.

"I think my suit is green," Dom said, when he took a step back. "If that helps at all. Eat another turnover," he added, as he slid out the door.

Dom's presence and then his absence made Asterion's knees tremble slightly. It was almost embarrassing to be so affected by another person. And strange. But maybe not as unpleasant as Asterion had assumed it would be.

48

The shave had been fine, but by the time Ellery arrived to fetch him, Dom was sweating. The two valets tending to him had valiantly argued with Dom for more than half an hour about the length and style of his hair. One had wanted to cut it, the other coiffe it. Then it was to be braided, then shaved at the sides, then worn long, and all the while Dom kept reminding them that he could not, like everyone else in this realm, grow it back with a snap of his fingers if he didn't like it.

He wasn't sure if that was true, actually. But he wasn't willing to test out whether or not he had hair growing magic right before dinner with Asterion's mother.

"Are you ready?" Ellery asked, her hands on her hips. "Cocktail hour started fifteen minutes ago."

"What?" Dom panicked, trying to stand, when four hands pushed him back down into his seat.

"We're almost finished, Ellery!" said the shorter of the two valets. A pin dug into Dom's scalp, and he winced. They'd settled on one thick, possibly french braid at the top of his head, into a complicated twist of hair at the nape of his neck which seemed to require no less than two dozen hairpins.

"You are finished. He looks handsome. Very chic." Then Ellery was in front of him, taking his hand, pulling him out of the chair. "Come on," she said, dragging him along behind her. "You definitely need to get a drink in before dinner."

Dom could see through the long windows in the hall that it had gotten dark outside. High above in regular intervals along the wall, lamps emitted a soft golden glow, the way he imagined the gas lamps they were always describing in *Nocturne Mystery Theatre*. Ellery swung them around a corner, through a doorway, and into a narrow hall. The lights were brighter here and there was a hum of activity as staff moved in and out of rooms, carrying glassware and buckets of firewood, folded towels, and a formal dinner jacket that still steaming from being pressed.

Ellery shouldered her way into Amina's studio, where the fabricator was moving around a dress form with identical measurements to Dom.

Though he truly had never had an eye for fashion, Dom knew that the garments she was making were beautiful. A bottle green dinner jacket had been ironed to stiffness, black snakes intertwined with ivy vines along the collar and placket. Silver buttons closed the front at the waist. A silver shirt, sheer in most places except the lapel, followed the line of the jacket. Ivy-shaped cufflinks were quickly applied by Ellery, as Amina wrapped the silk around him, showing him the two buttons that kept it closed above his right hip.

His trousers were tapered, black, and high waisted, cinching him in and removing the need for a waistcoat. Finally, he was given black leather boots with dark green piping and silver buttons that hugged his calves like gloves.

Ellery paused in front of him, three boxes stacked in her hands. She held them out to Dom and he opened the one on top. A necklace, so elaborate and brilliant that it was hard to look at, nearly blinded him.

"I don't really wear jewelry," Dom stammered.

"You do tonight." Ellery turned and set the three boxes on a small table behind her. "Besides, they're only necklaces. I would have done earrings too, but I wasn't sure you'd agree to having your ears pierced on such short notice." Before he could think of a response, Ellery had opened all the boxes and turned to him with the cases balanced in her arms.

Every piece was dripping with diamonds and green stones that might have been emeralds. It was hard for Dom to think of them as anything other than paste, like his aunt wore when she went out with her friends, because if these were real stones, that meant that any necklace he chose would have bought the diner three times over. Dom swallowed, suddenly very nervous.

"Which one do you like best?" Ellery prompted.

"They're ivy?" He'd finally found the connecting thread in the pieces: they were all sculpted and angled to take on the appearance of leaves and vines of ivy. Like his cufflinks.

"When children in the royal family come of age, they choose a plant to represent them in the house. On the crest. The family motifs. Everywhere. Asterion chose ivy."

"Isn't it invasive?" Dom asked, his eyes fixed on the center necklace. It was the least ornate option by far, a plain chain, silver vines molded into a two-inch crescent, tiny diamonds among the silver. At the base, a mossy colored gem only a half an inch wide was nestled, veins of dark green shining inside the cut stone.

"Ivy can be invasive," Ellery said. "It's also incredibly resilient and can grow with almost no cultivation. Though, I think it's more beautiful when it's well tended." Dom pointed at the center necklace.

"That one."

"Excellent choice." Ellery closed all three boxes, handing Dom the one he'd picked before flitting away. Amina slid behind him, taking the necklace and latching it around his neck, and then nudging him over in front of the mirror.

Dom had never thought of himself as handsome. He cleaned up okay, and he could look good if he put the effort in. Maybe it was the necklace or Amina's tailoring, but tonight he looked like something out of a fairy tale himself. Like maybe he could belong here. Or with someone as beautiful as Asterion.

Ellery turned toward him holding a much larger piece of silver filigree in her hands attached to some sort of choker, and Dom balked.

"What's that?"

"This," Ellery said, pressing the lattice of silver to his chest, "is a heartrender."

"What's a heartrender?"

"Not that one," Amina said, coming around to see what Ellery was doing. "I don't like that one. The smaller one, with the hooks at the back."

"You don't think—"

"I do," Amina said, her fingers flitting up to prod at the thick braid of hair on the top of Dom's head. Ellery sighed and went back to the counter, fetching a much smaller, though still ornate piece of jewelry.

"What's a heartrender?" Dom asked again.

"It's a piece of formal jewelry that accentuates another piece," Amina said. "They're traditional." Ellery held the heartrender up to the base of his throat. He could feel Amina's fingers against the nape of his neck, fiddling with a clasp. "When you're wearing someone's colors, or their sigil," she explained, clasping the collar and then tucking it beneath the fabric of his shirt, "a heartrender is supposed to set off that piece. Draw attention to the fact that you're wearing it." Ellery's hands slid across his chest, tucking the heartrender beneath the jacket and over the edge of the silk, and then she stepped back, finally allowing him access to the mirror again.

There was a large open circle in the center of the heartrender, and in that gap, the necklace he'd picked was framed against his skin. It was too much. Probably. He bit his lip, but before he could ask if there was another, smaller, heartrender available, Ellery spoke.

"Eyeliner," Ellery said.

"What?"

"Just a little. Please don't be a baby about it. It'll detract from the circles under your eyes."

"Circles?" Dom began to protest, but Ellery was already coming at him with a very sharp looking black pencil.

"Close your eyes," she demanded. He did, and she slid the pencil against his eyelids. "And if you haven't been getting your beauty rest before now, that's not my fault."

"Here," Amina said, rubbing a gloss over his lips with her finger, muffling his protests because he couldn't open his mouth. "The lights in the dining room might be low, Mr. Silva, but you will be under scrutiny."

"Believe me," Ellery sighed, stepping back and looking at him. "It's the least we can do." She pursed her lips as she looked him over and then shook her head. "It'll have to do. You're forty-five minutes late as it is."

49

Asterion was beginning to worry. They were halfway through cocktail hour, and even though it generally lasted two hours rather than one, neither Dom nor Asterion's mother had arrived.

Asterion was having nausea-inducing visions of his mother cornering Dom somewhere, pinning him to a wall with cruel questions, preparing to drag him in and display him like a dead butterfly. *Here is the only man foolish enough to attend one of our family dinners.* Asterion never brought his lovers to dinner with his mother or his siblings. If ever they asked why, though they rarely did, Asterion was quick to point out that he generally liked the people he took to bed, and he wouldn't want them to suffer needlessly. The food would be good, sure, but little could make up for his mother and Cressida at the same table.

There were three men, two ladies and three people of indeterminate gender in Lord Di Rilke's coterie. Asterion likely had known them once but had been granted the occasion to forget. He took no pleasure in their reintroductions now, straightening his cuffs nervously after each handshake.

He'd decided to wear a dark teal waistcoat and tapered

trousers. The suit jacket was cut high and had satin lapels that matched his shoes. The shirt beneath his waistcoat was white silk and open to just below his collar bones, showing off his freckles. He hadn't cared for them much before, but he'd caught Dom eyeing them twice now, and he had no magic to cover them, so framing them seemed like the next best thing.

Cressida, in a red gown with gold satin spilling out over her ample stomach, sauntered over. Di Rilke was on her arm like a trophy. He was very pretty, Asterion would give her that much. Easily six feet tall, broad shoulders and a trim waist, with a weirdly bright golden sheen to his skin. Maybe he was trying to match Cressida's dress.

Asterion had forgotten that Di Rilke also had four crystalline dragonfly wings that extended from his back. The veins were sparkling black and the membrane between was like a thin shaving of diamonds. Di Rilke's perfection was the sort that made Asterion's eyes glaze over. At first glance, of course, it was compelling; the line of his jaw, the straightness of his nose, the brilliant blue of his eyes. It was also boring. A precisely symmetrical face, with less than an ounce of brain behind his unwrinkled forehead.

"Where's your Mr. Silva, Asterion?" Cressida cooed, smirking. "I hope I didn't scare him off."

"He's with Amina," Asterion said, raising his gin to his lips and taking a measured sip. Cressida hummed.

"Well, I suppose you can't rush an artist." Before Asterion could roll his eyes, Di Rilke clapped him on the shoulder as though they were friends.

"Cress told me all about your magic, old chap. Bit of a rum do, that, isn't it?"

"I suppose so," Asterion admitted, amused by the lightness of the phrasing. Cressida snorted and shook her head.

"Any chance you'll be able to sort it out with the Assembly, then?" Di Rilke asked, his eyes wide and startlingly sincere.

"I doubt it," Asterion said. Di Rilke sighed and shook his head, looking as though someone had just run over his dog. Even his wings seemed to slump.

"Oh, Felix, really," Cressida huffed.

"Well, it's a terrible thing, darling," Di Rilke chastised Cress gently and her eyebrows arched against her hairline. Maybe Asterion did like him after all. At least, he certainly liked how irritated Cressida was. Before he could try to egg Di Rilke into saying something else, the side door of the parlor opened, and Dom stepped into the room.

Dom's hair was tied up and back, revealing his sharp jaw, and the shade of his long lashes as he looked around the room. His shoulders, already perfectly adequate, looked even broader and stronger in the tailored suit jacket. His trousers conformed beautifully to the shape of his ass. He looked stunning.

A waiter waylaid him, so it was another moment before Dom turned toward them, and when he did, Asterion's jaw went slack.

On Dom's beautiful, broad chest was a heartrender, and in the center was Asterion's favorite ivy necklace.

Asterion was rapidly losing his faculties. His heart was beating rather furiously in both his stomach and his throat. He couldn't breathe. He couldn't hear. Why was the parlor so warm? Someone needed to open a window.

Dom had Asterion's sigil around his neck. Over his heart. Dom was marking himself as Asterion's. That's what everyone else would see. It was an extremely foolish thing to do. Asterion was going to kill Ellery.

And then he was going to give her a raise.

And then he was going to banish her somewhere gorgeous.

A heartrender. Around his ivy. Against Dom's chest.

Asterion knew it was more than he'd ever hoped for because

it hadn't occurred to him to hope for it. It was unbelievable even though it was happening right before his eyes. Dom marking himself as Asterion's. Wanting to be his. Asterion could have been felled by a feather.

"Sorry, I'm late," Dom's voice was quiet, as though perhaps he could go unnoticed. As though he hadn't taken all the air out of the room and Asterion's lungs. Dom put his hand on the small of Asterion's back, and Asterion grabbed him by the waist and kissed him.

Dom's hand tightened on Asterion's hip, body bending to go flush with Asterion's. Somewhere behind them Cressida was making a sound of affront and Asterion knew he would be breathing hard when he pulled back, but it was kiss Dom like this or take him upstairs immediately, and one of those things would likely be far more acceptable to Cressida than the other.

Asterion stepped back, sliding his arm more firmly around Dom's waist as he tried to catch his breath. For the briefest of seconds, he admired the flush high on Dom's cheeks and then turned toward Cressida and Di Rilke.

"Lord Di Rilke," Asterion began the introduction as he would have any other. "This is Dominic Silva."

"Pleasure, sir!" Di Rilke was, blessedly, entirely unfazed. Dom moved to bow, but Di Rilke held out his hand, and when Dom met the gesture, Di Rilke shook his arm vehemently. "So nice to meet a friend of his majesty!"

"Thank you, sir."

"Tell me, Mr. Silva, do you ride?" If Asterion was lucky. Asterion snorted into his drink, insane with lust. Dom jabbed his thumb sharply into Asterion's side.

"No, sir. I've never had the opportunity. I do have a motorcycle—"

"Oh!" Di Rilke's mouth dropped into a perfect circle of delight. "A motorbike?! Absolutely cracking! I've always wanted to ride one! I imagine it's quite like a horse. My fellows and I are going out for a trot tomorrow morning. Just around the grounds. What's say you come with us, and I can show you the reins, so to speak, and then you and I can—"

"A motorcycle, Felix?" Cressida interrupted, putting her hand on Di Rilke's arm. "Really?"

"Oh, they're brilliant, Cress! You've got to see one! What do you say, Mr. Silva?" Cressida detached from Di Rilke, glaring daggers at Asterion.

"You've done it now," she grumbled as she swanned past him and the waiter, who'd returned with Dom's drink. Asterion took it for him, as Dom's arm was being shaken vigorously again by Di Rilke before he hurried off after Cressida.

Asterion handed Dom his drink, and Dom kissed him. It was a simple press of lips, soft and brief, but it felt like someone had pulled a string in Asterion's chest and drawn it tight. Tighter at the warmth of Dom's gaze.

"How do you like the outfit?" Dom asked, a small smirk lifting the corner of his mouth.

Before Asterion could respond, the doors to the dining room opened, and the Queen Dowager stepped into the room. Two translucent wings, the shape of a monarch butterfly and the color of amethyst, opened slowly behind her, to admittedly impressive effect. Her auburn hair was more streaked in silver than it had been the last time he'd seen her, and her skin was paler and a bit over-powdered, but then Cress had only gotten her out of those ghastly tall wigs a few decades ago.

As though she could hear his mental critique, the Queen Dowager's onyx eyes found him from across the room. Asterion's chest deflated. Her smile did not meet her gaze. It never did.

"Please, everyone," she said, clasping her hands in front of her sparkling lavender gown. "Come in for dinner."

50

H is mother's reign of terror began with the name cards. She'd had to do it, though, otherwise Cressida would have been at the head of the table, where the Queen Dowager was now preparing to take her seat.

"It's only a family dinner, dear," he heard his mother coo to Cressida as their chairs were pulled out for them. Asterion supposed he should have appreciated that Dom was only to Cressida's right and not down at the other end of the table with Di Rilke's entourage. Cressida was given the secondary rank on their mother's right, Asterion on her left. Beside Asterion was Di Rilke, already straightening his back, aligning his wings with the carved gap in the low-backed dining chair.

Asterion glanced across the giant plates of food that were stacked amidst the greenery and gilt of the table and caught Dom's eye. Dom's eyebrows lifted, a small smile playing over his lips, likely amused by the amount of food as well as the shine and pomp surrounding it. It was all absurd. He'd rather have been in Dom's kitchen eating leftovers from the diner, listening to commercials on the radio.

Cressida and the Queen Dowager sat. Everyone else sat. Attendants came around to pour wine, and finally Asterion's mother turned to him.

"You look wan," she said. Then she moved on, her eyes scanning the rest of the table, her fingers smoothing the foot of her wine glass as though it were cloth.

"It's good to see you too," Asterion said. His mother sniffed.

"I knew you'd think it beastly of me to ask if you were well, so I thought we'd skip ahead a bit, conversationally." She lifted her wine goblet to her mouth and then lowered it, leaving Asterion to wonder if even a drop of the liquid had made it past her lips. "Tell me about your friend."

"He's a friend," Asterion said, narrowing his eyes. "It's not like you to take an interest."

"It's not like you to bring a paramour to our dining table."

"His family are at Leyland Hall. I offered to accompany him."

"Servants?" she asked.

"Well, not the lords of the house at any rate," Asterion replied. "Speaking of which, where is Kephisto? Since this *is* a family dinner."

"He's occupied by work at the moment," his mother sighed, her head tilting to the side as though Kephisto's absence was deeply felt.

"Oh, no! Someone else will have to flip the table. Or throw a bottle of wine at the waitstaff. Cress? Are you up for it?" Cressida snorted into her cup. Asterion's mother rolled her eyes, but she didn't bother to deny it. No one could ruin a family dinner like Kephisto.

"Don't be ghastly, Asterion. Kephisto takes the running of the estates very seriously." Asterion knew that Kephisto only took an interest in things that yielded great profits or great power. Running the estates was not likely to do either.

"Has he re-instated the rents?" Asterion asked. His mother huffed as silver bowls of soup were placed in front of them.

"Nothing so loathed as rents. Your sister would never allow it," she said, picking up her soup spoon. Asterion turned his attention to the soup as his mother chatted idly about some sort of mercantilism Kephisto had gotten involved in.

"So, tell me," the Queen Dowager finally returned her gaze to Asterion as their soup bowls were lifted away, "what will you do after you take Mr. Silva to Leyland Hall?" Asterion drained the rest of his wine and looked around for an attendant to take his glass away so he wouldn't be able to have another.

"Petitioning the assembly, I'd thought," Cressida said before he could make up an answer. She was holding her filled goblet aloft like it was a trophy.

"Should you be drinking?" Asterion asked, delighted by the opportunity to change the subject.

"It's a specially formulated vitamin elixir," Cressida said with an air of haughtiness that was undercut by her sticking her tongue out at him. "Kephisto had his private alchemist turn it up for me, and I can't tell you how absolutely revitalizing it is!"

"Bold of you to drink anything Kephisto has prepared."

"Asterion!" his mother chided.

"I'm not an idiot," Cressida grumbled. "I had it tested, obviously."

"Obviously," Asterion muttered.

"Anyway, weren't you friends with that Assembly Sorcerer?" This again? Great shitting hells. "What was his name? Edward—"

"Edmund Morrow," Asterion said. "Viceroy of the Assembly."

"That's the fellow," his mother agreed, ignoring the heaping plate of venison placed in front of her. Asterion ignored it too, his stomach curdling at Morrow's name. "Couldn't you speak to him?"

"Unfortunately, I cannot," Asterion said with an air of finality that was entirely disregarded by his mother and sister, who spent the remainder of the course talking all about the Sorcerer's Assembly. For lack of any way to deafen himself, Asterion turned to Di Rilke and began to tell him all about the ride he'd taken on Dom's motorcycle. Di Rilke was very vocally enthused, so much so that Asterion could barely hear his sister continue to sing the praises of Viceroy Morrow.

Though they were across the table and half-obscured by a spray of flowers, Asterion managed to work Dom into a conversation with Di Rilke about motorcycles and bicycles and other modes of wheeled transportation that involved moving too quickly and slightly dangerously. Di Rilke was growing on Asterion, only because his boundless enthusiasm made him an easy conversational companion. If anything about this could be easy, Asterion would welcome it.

It wasn't until they were finishing up dessert that the Queen Dowager placed her hand on Asterion's arm. He turned his attention away from the discussion Dom and Di Rilke were having about riding pants and met her narrowed gaze.

"Are you going to tell me anything else about your Mr. Silva?"

"I'm not sure I've told you anything at all," Asterion said. "Though you seem to know something about him already."

"Not as much as I'd like." She pursed her lips thoughtfully as she scanned Asterion's face. "I suppose that's enough to be getting on with, though."

"What is?"

"Nothing." She raised a flute of ice wine to her mouth and finally took a full sip. This was nearly as unnerving as the statement itself; the hair on the back of Asterion's neck prickled. "You know, Asterion." She paused, her eyes on the golden liquid sparkling inside her glass. "I've always worried that I'd not done right by you, raising you as I did." Gods. Perhaps she'd been drinking more than he'd thought.

"Nonsense," Asterion said perfunctorily. She'd been a terrible mother, of course, but he wasn't about to say that now. Or ever. She gave him an unfathomable look, something between affection and exasperation, and then she pushed back from the table and stood.

"Let's go through to the parlor, shall we?" Her smile was small and prim. Everyone stood, since the question had not really been a question at all. Asterion got to his feet, steadier than he'd ever been at the end of a family dinner. Or he was, until his mother spoke again. "Mr. Silva, I request a private audience, please. For just a few moments."

"Mother—" Asterion began to protest. She took him by the arm and stepped to the side, out of the way of Di Rilke, who was moving to escort Cressida through.

"We always knew you weren't going to come to much," she said quietly, smoothing non-existent wrinkles from Asterion's lapels. "You don't have the proper ambition, Asterion. You never have. So, any meddling you feel as though we've done, it's always been about keeping you from making a bad match. Your father was terrified you'd force us to bestow a title on whatever milkmaid or stableboy caught your eye." She chuckled thinly, adjusting his collar with her thin fingers.

Asterion's mouth was hanging open. Usually her cruelty was adorned in pointed metaphor; she'd never insulted him so plainly before. As he tried to think of something to say in his own defense, she hummed, straightening his chin, closing his jaw with her knuckles.

"Now I'm not sure what to do with you. No magic and no *real* desire to have it back," she shook her head. "Worthless, in all but name. What are you going to do?"

Asterion could barely swallow for the knot in his throat. He'd known it was what she thought of him. What they all thought. He'd known it for so long. So why did it hurt so much?

Without waiting for him to speak, his mother turned away, leaving Asterion to watch through the amethyst veil of her wings as she took Dom's arm and led him out of the dining room.

51

The Queen Dowager led Dom through the foyer and down a long, high-ceilinged hall where the heat floated up and away, and a chill seeped in quickly through Dom's silk shirt. Or perhaps that was just the chill brought on by the horrified expression Asterion had worn, as his mother straightened his jacket, examining his face like the parent of a toddler after a messy meal. Dom hadn't heard what she'd said. He couldn't even begin to guess what terrible thing she'd said to make Asterion make that face, and he wasn't sure he wanted to.

Outside, it was snowing. The flakes were bright against the blue-black sky, and the windows threw distorted reflections of Dom back at himself, as he tried to keep his breathing measured. For Asterion.

The Dowager Queen didn't speak to him until they entered a small nicely furnished study. The ceiling was finished in deep wine-colored panels and the walls were primarily windows. Not just windows. Stained glass of hundreds of crimson and green hues, a scene of tall ruby amaryllis, under exquisitely molded arches. Clearly Asterion's work. Dom took a step toward them, in awe all over again.

"Beautiful, aren't they?" Dom tore his gaze away as the Queen Dowager settled behind him on a green chaise.

"Yes. Very."

"Whatever one may say about my youngest son, no one can question his aesthetics. He was a prolific artist in his boyhood. Mostly working in sketch. I believe the window was a design of his. He has an exceptional eye."

"I imagine a list of all Asterion's exceptional qualities would be very long."

"Indeed." Her tone was flat. She looked him over, then patted the empty cushion beside her. Dom sat, feeling the wine and the heaviness of dinner in his stomach as he pressed his palms against his knees. She was scanning his face with an intensity that Dom couldn't match.

"Is there something I can do for you, ma'am?"

"What *are* you, Mr. Silva?" she said with a small sigh, her back rounding slightly in defeat. "I can't seem to put my finger on it."

"A demigod," he said. She narrowed her eyes, leaning forward.

"Demigod," she nodded. "Yes. I suppose that explains the silver in your eyes. You must have wondered about it before?"

"Not really." Ares had the same silver flecks in his irises. Good genes, Dom had always assumed.

"So many men never take the time to appreciate their own natural beauty. Though you do come from a world that values it less. Still, likely not a son of Aphrodite," she added with a considered cock of her head. "Have you any natural proclivities?" Dom blinked at her, and she rolled her eyes. "Not Apollo either. What are you good at? Do you fight or excel at sports? Are you particularly wealthy?"

"I'm a cook, ma'am," Dom said. "I own a diner, and I cook."

"A diner?" Her tone made the word sound small. "I see." She

pursed her lips. "Well, even though you may not be using them, you likely have some considerable gifts. Which still leaves me with the question I brought you here to ask. What are your intentions with my son?"

Oh.

Dom's skin warmed under the thick collar of his coat; he flattened his palms against his thighs and stood, opening his mouth without knowing exactly what was going to come out of it.

"Asterion is very important to me," he said as he turned to face her. It was true, and as good a place as any to start. The Queen Dowager interrupted with a shake of her head.

"Asterion is considerably lessened. Without his magic, even a lower demigod of mixed birth could marry someone with greater standing. He won't inherit anything more than he already has," she gestured around at the palace as though it was trivial. "And, in fact, less now than he would have before."

"I don't care about his inheritance," Dom said. He'd truly never thought about it before. The Queen Dowager didn't seem to hear him.

"My elder son Kephisto, or even Cressida, if your tastes are flexible— Now, that would be a pretty match."

"Cressida?" Dom stammered. He'd misunderstood her, surely. "She's pregnant."

"Please," Asterion's mother snorted. "If you've set your cap toward Asterion, you won't convince me maidenhood is important to you. The child can be given to Di Rilke and cared for by his family. Marriage to a demigod would be a considerable boon to her status. The citizens of Andurnei are dedicated to the traditions of their forefathers. As far as magical beings are concerned there are none greater than the descendants of gods, excepting of course, the gods themselves."

"I have no interest in marrying Cressida," Dom managed.

"Kephisto, then," the Queen Dowager offered. Like a butcher trying to upsell Dom on a cut of meat.

"I don't think you understand why I'm here."

"You think you're in love with my son. He's a kind boy, but Asterion is soft. He has no real interest in power, so little, in fact, that he's lost what small claim he had to it. He won't be useful to you."

"Useful?"

"Certainly, he got you this far. Commendable, of course. But no one would blame you for trading up. Kephisto is well established. Leyland Hall is a proud house."

"I didn't come to Andurnei to find a spouse," Dom said. "And even if I had, I—I—Asterion is—"

The words caught in his throat, but she had said them for him. He was in love with Asterion. He was. In his mind, in his imagined future, Asterion was in the diner with him, covered in flour and laughing. He was in the kitchen at their house making tea. Curled up with Dom in their bed, listening to the rain. Dom wanted Asterion, and whether or not Asterion would ever want the same thing wasn't the point. Dom loved him, and that was all that mattered.

"Asterion is inconstant," she snapped. The smile had dropped off the Queen Dowager's face, her lips straight and stern. "He doesn't mean to be, but his affections are whims only. He tries, but you will find yourself disappointed. His devotion to his family, to his duties, has always been less than satisfactory."

"And why should he be devoted to people who are terrible to him?" Dom demanded, furious now. How could she talk this way about her own son?

"I have given him so much, and he's chosen to throw it all away. Money, prestige, power! Nothing is good enough for him."

"Did it ever occur to you that he might want something more than that? Something real?"

"What else could we possibly give him? What could be a more revered gift?" These people were insane. Dom was speechless and when he didn't respond, the Queen Dowager assumed the conversational victory. Her wings flattened against her back, and when she spoke again her voice was low and threatening. "And so, I see that you are well suited for each other, as I have offered you the same boons, and you've turned your nose up at all of them."

"Your other children, you mean." Dom said. "Not as people. As objects. With some calculable worth." The Queen Dowager's lips became a thin line.

"That is the very nature of the world, Mr. Silva. Whether you like it or not. You can use it to prosper, or you can waste your energy on fleeting affections."

"My feelings for your son are not fleeting."

"We'll see about that," she said. Then she gestured toward the door. "This conversation is over. One of the servants will see you back to the parlor."

52

D om was so furious that he didn't realize he'd reached the parlor until a footman was already ushering him in. Cressida and some of the others were playing a game of cards at a small table in the corner; Di Rilke was the only one who turned his head when Dom entered. Asterion was nowhere to be seen.

Dom was flushed, and he wanted his fists to uncurl but that didn't seem likely to happen anytime soon. He needed to punch down some thick bread dough. He needed to find Asterion. He also needed a drink. Dom went to the gold and glass drinks cart in the corner, only to find that his hands were still shaking with anger.

"Ah, here we go, old chap." Di Rilke appeared out of nowhere, grabbing a bottle and a glass. "Allow me."

"Thank you." Dom took a breath, flattening his palms to his sides. Di Rilke glanced at him as he began to pour.

"A bit of a battle axe, isn't she?"

"Yes." A massive understatement. Di Rilke nodded, stoppering one bottle and scooping up another. When he spoke again, his voice was quieter.

316 | EMILIA LEE

"I've always been surprised they ended up as well-adjusted as they are, all things considered. Amazing they're not feral wolfhounds, gnawing at each other in a pen." He handed Dom a gold rimmed glass, the amber liquid inside still spinning. Dom looked down at it, and then up at Di Rilke. His blue eyes were crinkled in the corners, drawn up by a sad sort of smile.

"You and Cressida—?" Dom began and then stopped. It would have been rude, invasive. Even though he hadn't asked, he felt the need to apologize. "Sorry."

"It's fine." Di Rilke patted Dom warmly on the shoulder. "I understand. Cress cares for me in her own way," Di Rilke said, his gaze drifting over to the back of Cressida's head, her ginger tresses finally freeing themselves to float around the nape of her neck. "I know she does. And she knows how I feel about her. Going toe-to-toe with the old bird makes it seem hopeless, but it's not as bad as all that. I imagine even Kephisto has a heart, at the end of the day. Even if he does keep trying to kill his sister." Dom snorted and took a sip of his drink.

"This is a strange place," he said. Di Rilke shrugged.

"No stranger than any other. You ought to go find Asterion. He went out onto the terrace twenty minutes ago and he hasn't come back in yet."

"The terrace?" Dom asked, glancing around. Di Rilke nodded to a closed curtain on their left, and Dom reached out and pulled back one corner of heavy damask to reveal a pair of glass doors and long windows. Outside was an empty terrace, covered in snow, marked by footprints. Dom pulled the curtain aside and opened the door.

"Take a cloak!" Di Rilke called after him, but Dom was already walking away.

The snow was still falling. It crackled quietly as flakes landed on top of each other and piled slowly onto leaves and bannisters. It was easy to follow Asterion's footprints, except in some small patches where high hedges blocked the snow and threw the path into shadow.

After a few minutes, Dom found himself walking up to a stone folly. The columns that supported the roof were wrapped in thick blankets of ivy, and a thin line of smoke floated up from the darkness beneath.

When Dom came around to the entrance, he saw him. Asterion's head was tipped up toward the ceiling as he leaned back against the stone, half wrapped in a thick cape. The tip of a cigarette glowed red in his fingers, and the snow clung to his hair.

Asterion was so beautiful that Dom momentarily lost track of the anger that hadn't chilled on his walk. It was dim under the shadow of the stone, but still, Asterion's gold eyes flashed, widening for just a moment, as Dom walked up the steps. Asterion straightened, his limbs stiff.

"You must be freezing," Asterion said, his free hand moving to the clasp on his cloak.

"No," Dom said. "I'm alright. I needed to cool off." Asterion chuckled at that, but it was a dry, unhappy sound. He lifted the cigarette to his lips and inhaled, moving it away from his mouth with a frown. He glanced up at Dom and shrugged, holding the cigarette out to him.

"It seemed better than drinking. In case I needed to try and explain myself."

"Explain yourself?" Dom leaned back against the stone, his shoulder brushing Asterion's. "You don't have to explain anything to me."

"Perhaps an apology would be a better place to start." The sides of their thighs touched as Asterion settled beside him. "I'm sorry for whatever my mother said to you. She's... I don't know. I'd like to say she's not herself, but that wouldn't be true."

"*I'm* sorry," Dom said. Asterion's chuckle was hollow.

"You don't have to apologize."

"Someone should. For how she treats you."

"I'm used to it."

"That doesn't make it right," Dom insisted. Asterion flicked his cigarette to the ground and pressed it into the stone with the toe of his shoe.

"Look, I'm sure she's told you what sort of a person I am, by now. Enumerated my many failings, and if you—"

Dom couldn't stand it. This was the dejected, depressed Asterion of days ago. The one who'd sat at Jonas' table, being unkind on purpose, except now it was all turned inward. Maybe it always had been.

Dom pivoted to face Asterion and tugged him into a kiss. Asterion's body sagged into him, as Dom slid his arms around Asterion's waist, wool cloak warm against the back of Dom's knuckles.

"She's wrong about you," Dom said quietly, pulling back, trying to look him in the eye. "Asterion, she has no idea how good you are."

"Why are you being so kind, Dom? What do you want from me?" Asterion's voice was barely a whisper, and it broke Dom's heart.

"Nothing, Asterion." Asterion looked up at him, frowning in disbelief. Maybe there was no easy way to make Asterion understand, but Dom knew he would gladly spend the rest of his life trying. "The only thing I want is for you to think as highly of yourself as I do."

Asterion moved his lips, but no sound came out. He shook his head, his gaze down, lost in the small space between them again. Before Dom could figure out what to say, how to reassure him, Asterion slid his fingers through the center of the heartrender, pressing the silver circle back against Dom's chest.

"Did Ellery tell you what this is?" he asked. Dom nodded.

"She did."

"My sigil. Under a heartrender," Asterion's fingers dragged against the ivy. His eyes flicked up to meet Dom's, full of questions.

Dom was ready. He knew how he felt, and it was on the tip of his tongue. But before he could say it, Asterion tugged him close, kissed him deep, long and slow. Their mouths and bodies twisted together. Asterion smoothed his palms up Dom's back, like cold hands widening toward the heat of a fire.

In a lifetime of wanting, Dom had never wanted something as badly as this thing with Asterion. This relationship, because that's what it was. He wanted to be the person that would finally love Asterion in all the ways he deserved to be loved.

Dom ran his palm over Asterion's jaw, deepening the kiss, speaking with his body what he hadn't been quick enough to say. Asterion leaned into him, and he had to know. Dom couldn't have said it more plainly, even if he'd put words to it.

When Asterion pulled away, his cheeks were flush, and his eyes were bright. He ran his thumb over the nape of Dom's neck, catching against the small latches of the heartrender.

"We should go in," Asterion said.

"Alright," Dom agreed. As though he had the power to do anything other than exactly what Asterion asked of him. Asterion smiled; he kissed Dom lightly and then straightened up and linked his arm with Dom's, shaking his head as he guided Dom out of the folly.

"I still can't believe you're out here without a cloak."

53

Happiness twisted between Asterion's ribs, foxlike and particularly smug, as though it had gotten its fill in the henhouse. Dom was with him, still, somehow. And even though Asterion truly hadn't done anything, he felt like he'd gotten away with it.

As they got closer to his rooms though, satisfaction began to drip away into anxiety. How was it that Dom hadn't been scared off by Asterion's mother? Or Cressida with her snide comments. Even sweet, good Jonas had always been made uncomfortable by the Dowager Queen, and had seemed standoffish, after their few, limited conversations.

But whatever Asterion's mother had said to Dom, Dom was still here. Still trying to protect Asterion. And Asterion ought to be doing *something*. He'd missed a piece, stepped over his own line in the play. This wasn't how things usually went.

Before he'd sorted it out, they were in the bedroom, getting ready for bed. Asterion turned from hanging his jacket in his wardrobe to see Dom taking his hair down, pin by pin. The thick muscles of his shoulders rippled under the shimmering, sheer silver fabric of his shirt as he worked, and a few minutes later

Dom groaned, running his hand through his hair as he tossed the last pin onto the dresser. That was when Asterion realized what he should have been doing: he was supposed to be seducing Dom.

That was the order of things. He ought to have been making up for the whole mess by bringing Dom to some sort of earth-shattering orgasm. The man had practically been accosted by Asterion's mother, and the least Asterion could do to apologize was... well, whatever Dom wanted. Wasn't it?

"Can you help me with this?" Dom had pulled his hair over one shoulder, and his fingers fumbled over the clasps of the heartrender behind his neck. Asterion kicked his shoes off, and then stepped behind Dom. The latches on the heartrender were delicate. Purposefully intricate, like if someone had gone through the trouble of wearing one there should be some seduction or foreplay involved in its removal. A clasp slipped from beneath Asterion's thumb, and he scowled.

"I think I'd do better with wire cutters."

"I won't tell Ellery, if you don't," Dom chuckled and Asterion felt that tightening in his chest again, his heart swerving into locations unknown.

"We'll tell her I yanked it off you in a fit of passion." Finally, the clasp gave.

"I'm not sure she'd believe us."

"Of course, she will. Tales of my exploits are legendary," Asterion said. It sounded hollow. Obvious. Dom didn't respond. Asterion's fingers lost the second clasp. He ran his tongue over his bottom lip, shaking his head in a weak attempt to clear it. He hadn't lied to Dom yet, and this seemed like it would be an irresponsible time to start. He cleared his throat. "I'm supposed to be seducing you, I think."

"What?" Dom cocked his head to the side. "Right now?"

"Yes. Obviously. You look gorgeous. We're here, in my

bedroom. We survived dinner. You're wearing my necklace. You, the stuttering virgin. Me, the royal libertine."

"We had sex yesterday," Dom interrupted in a skeptical tone. "And I know I didn't stutter." The second clasp on the heartrender finally opened, and it dropped heavily off Dom's neck. He caught it in his hands and turned to face Asterion.

"Fine," Asterion conceded, "but the fact remains, this is the part where I ravish you. Tie you to the bedposts and—" Dom was smirking. Asterion scowled at him. "What?"

"How many of my smut novels did you read?"

"I know how this goes, Dom!" Asterion insisted. Because he did know. He hadn't had to read about it, he had lived his whole damned life this way.

"Do you want to have sex?" Dom asked. Asterion rolled his eyes.

"Why on Earth would that matter?" Dom pursed his lips and looked at Asterion with a pointed stare. Asterion threw up his hands. "You know what I mean! That's not—"

"The way this goes," Dom gestured between them, "is the way we want it to go. Both of us. Together. I'm not going anywhere, Asterion, whether you seduce me tonight or not."

And what was Asterion supposed to say to that?

"I have no idea how you can exist in such a constant state of sincerity," Asterion declared, exasperated and painfully fond. Dom laughed and turned his attention to the button on his trousers.

"Practice. Foolishness. Take your pick."

"You're standing here being sweet, when you should be riding as far away as you can, as fast as you can. You've seen what it's like here. What we're all like."

"You're not like them." Dom said abruptly, and with such absolute conviction, that Asterion almost believed it.

"You can't know that."

"I do know that." A sharp knot had appeared in Asterion's throat. Gods. He was not going to cry right now.

"I might be a horror."

"We're all horrors sometimes."

"Me more than most," Asterion said. Dom rolled his eyes and grabbed Asterion by the hand, tugging him close enough to kiss him. It felt like he'd been thrown a rope while he was drowning.

"Asterion." Dom's voice was gentle as his hands drifted up Asterion's forearms, stroking them lightly. "You're fine. I promise. Let's go to bed."

Asterion was still waiting for the moment that it would all fall apart. Or that he would say or do something that would reveal the depths of how fucked up he was, and it would be too much for Dom. But then he was throwing back the covers, crawling between soft sheets. Dom tied up his hair, settling back against the pillows, looking like everything Asterion hadn't known he really wanted: a partner, a friend, someone who thought the best of him even when he couldn't think it of himself.

Dom rolled toward Asterion on the pillows, and Asterion turned off his bedside light. Firelight threw them into shadow. Dom's eyes were closed, and Asterion knew he should just let the man sleep, if that was what he wanted. But he couldn't stop himself.

"I'm not sure I understand you," Asterion said quietly. "You could have anything, you know? And I would give you— I mean, if you—"

Dom opened his eyes, silver flecks in his irises catching the firelight. His hand curled around Asterion's beneath the blankets.

"Do you trust me?" Asterion did trust him. Like a fool. Like an idiot.

"Yes," Asterion sighed, dejected. Dom smirked and squeezed Asterion's hand.

"Asterion, when I'm with you, I have everything that I want. I don't need anything else."

Asterion kissed him then. What else was he supposed to do? Who said things like that and really meant them? Gods, it was so romantic, it made Asterion's chest ache.

They slid closer beneath the blankets, their bodies pressed against each other as they kissed, and Asterion could feel that Dom wanted him. He was getting hard, and Asterion was both relieved and eager for a physical way to expend all the emotion that had built up over the last half hour. Asterion rolled onto his back, wondering if he had, in fact, just been seduced by Dom. And he didn't care, because he doubted very sincerely that Dom had intended to seduce him at all.

"Get on top of me," Asterion breathed, glancing at Dom, whose smirk was almost a genuine small smile.

"I thought we said—"

"You said we could be the ones to decide what we wanted." He reached down and stroked Dom through his pajamas. Dom bit his lip as he kept eye contact with Asterion. "I want you. And I think," he slid his hand up Dom's length more slowly, "you want me too."

"It sort of diminishes the point I was trying to make," Dom murmured, his eyes fluttering closed as Asterion moved his hand again.

"Nonsense. This is further proof that you're right. We should be in agreement about our activities, and—" Dom chuckled, kissing Asterion as he crawled on top of him, his knees between Asterion's thighs.

They were still kissing as Asterion slipped Dom's pajama pants down, over his backside, getting a wonderful handful of Dom's ass while Dom shucked his own pants the rest of the way.

His fingers fumbled with the buttons of Asterion's silk shirt, as his mouth moved down Asterion's jaw, onto his neck.

Dom's stubble prickled Asterion's breastbone as Dom kissed his chest, his fingers digging in against Asterion's hips. It was an overwhelming sort of foreplay, his kissing and nipping and touching, that quickly severed the tether between Asterion and his logical, performative brain. The one that stopped him from panting and moaning and saying embarrassing things. Asking for what he actually wanted.

"Mark me, Dom. Please."

It was out of his mouth before he could stop himself, and he stared down his own body in shock, afraid of what Dom's reaction would be.

He'd been too honest. But Asterion wanted to be wanted. He wanted to know that Dom had chosen him, to feel it beneath his skin. And that was too much to say out loud, too vulnerable to admit. But the way Dom stood up for Asterion, took his time with Asterion, taught him things, was kind to him, made Asterion want to be Dom's. For now. Forever.

Embarrassing, but there it was.

Dom looked up at Asterion from beside a fresh love bite on Asterion's ribs. And he didn't look horrified.

He was biting his bottom lip like he was just trying to keep himself under control, his eyes wide and dark. Dom raised himself up slowly, biceps bulging, and Asterion gasped as Dom practically pounced on him. His kisses were deep, passionate, and his hands were frantic, stripping Asterion out of his clothes. Asterion undressed more quickly than he ever had in his life, and when he flopped back onto the mattress naked, he was met with Dom's hungry gaze.

"So, we both want...?" Asterion said quietly. Dom nodded, breathing hard.

"Oh, yes. Very much." Dom slid his hand beneath Asterion's

knee, tugging Asterion down the mattress. Asterion bit his lip, eyes widening as Dom leaned over to kiss the soft, pale skin on the side of Asterion's knee. It was so tender, it sent shivers down his spine. And then Dom hooked Asterion's leg over Dom's hip and leaned forward, and Asterion praised honesty as he lost himself to pleasure.

DOM SLID HIS HANDS OVER ASTERION'S HIPS, KISSING THE freckles on Asterion's chest again, indulgent and aching. Asterion was laid out before him, twisting against the mattress; he whimpered when Dom kissed his throat and Dom wanted him desperately. He tasted the sweat on Asterion's neck and felt Asterion's hand fist in the sheets.

He hadn't known he wanted to mark Asterion, but Asterion asking for it was electrifying. Something deep in Dom lit up at the request, eager, willing. Magical.

Dom wasn't lost to it, but he could feel it egging him on, marrying his own desire with something raw and fundamental. Something that told Dom he would never be the same if he marked Asterion like this. Asterion's desire was etching itself into Dom's heart.

Asterion moaned as Dom slid his fingers against him. Into him.

"More, Dom," Asterion gasped. So Dom went deeper, slower, steadier, stroking Asterion with his other hand. Asterion thrust, trembling, golden eyes going wide. "Fuck! Dominic."

Oh.

Dom hadn't known he wanted to hear his name said like that. It sent a shiver down his spine.

"Asterion. I want you." Asterion nodded, whimpering when Dom took his fingers away and sighing in pleasure as Dom shifted forward, his cock brushing against Asterion's entrance. Dom held Asterion's wrists against the mattress over his head, pinning Asterion down as he pressed into him.

Asterion arched his back and cried Dom's name so loudly that anyone in that wing of the palace would have heard him. He leaned up, kissing Dom, wrapping one leg and then the other around Dom's ribs. "I *need* you inside me," he gasped against Dom's lips. "Mark me." Dom's magic sparked, the heat of it curling up his spine.

Their bodies moved together, a perfect rhythm. Asterion clung to Dom's hands, moaning, digging into Dom's back with his heels as Dom thrust into him. Dom's muscles tightened, his body yearning for more, just a little bit— Dom kissed Asterion's neck, panting softly, digging in gently with his teeth and Asterion came with a shout, grinding down, taking Dom deeper.

"Mark me," Asterion begged. "Please, Dom. Please. I want it." And, oh, Dom wanted it too. Asterion gasped Dom's name, his voice ragged with pleasure, and Dom's orgasm shorted out his brain. He understood rapture and bliss and ecstasy a little bit better. Nothing was different, but everything had changed.

And something *was* different.

It took Dom a minute to realize it, as he floated back down to his body. Asterion's head rested between Dom's forearms, slowly turning back and forth, like he was watching an impossible game of tennis.

"What is *that*?"

Around Dom's wrists was a bloom of glowing golden filigree. It was brighter in the thin skin above his veins, but snaking steadily up toward his elbows, like a quickly crawling vine.

"I... don't know," Dom said. Asterion loosed his fingers from Dom's and reached for Dom's wrist, sliding the pad of his thumb over the raised lines. Dom shifted carefully back, and then lay beside Asterion on the mattress. He ran his own hand across his forearm, where the magic seemed to be slowing, stalling at the top of his forearms; it was warm to the touch.

"Does it hurt?" Asterion asked, grabbing Dom's hand and studying the lines again. Dom shook his head. It didn't hurt. It was almost like the sensation of cracking a knuckle. Something stretched that he'd not known he should have been stretching.

"A demigod thing? To do with marking? Ree warned me that it was different." He should have let her say what she had been trying to say. All that he remembered was that it might affect Asterion. Dom turned, scanning Asterion's arms, his body. "Are you okay?"

"Goodness," Asterion chuckled, shaking his head. "That's a ridiculous question."

"Ree said marking might—"

"You told her we were sleeping together?"

"Asterion," Dom said sternly. "Focus."

"I'm fine. Truly." He leaned forward and kissed Dom. And then he kissed him again, deeper. "I mean, I've never been better. So long as you're okay." Asterion ran his palm over Dom's arm. Whatever magic it was, it seemed to be ending. The light faded away, but the lines were still there, like little golden etchings just beneath his skin.

"I think I'm okay."

"Perhaps you've managed to please your patron deity somehow."

"Who's my patron deity?" Dom asked.

"I don't know. I didn't think to ask your aunt last time I chatted to her about our sex life." Asterion paused, arching his eyebrows significantly as he stretched his arms above his head. Dom snorted. "Your patron must be someone who approves of vigorous lovemaking, I suppose," Asterion said, as he rolled out of bed, and Dom tried not to be thrilled by the fact that Asterion had said the word 'lovemaking' as opposed to, well, anything else.

Nothing was different. Everything was different. Just like he'd known it would be.

Asterion came back with a washcloth. Dom distracted him by kissing him, and eventually Asterion deemed them clean enough and collapsed on Dom's chest in a heap.

Dom gave in to the way his limbs all wanted to be limp. Asterion pressed a kiss over Dom's heart, his fingers toying gently with the ivy circle that Dom was still wearing around his neck.

54

Dom woke to the quiet clatter of cutlery in the sitting room. He turned his head, squinting at the brass alarm clock on the bedside table. Too early. He could've gotten up. Started to gather his clothes and gotten ready to leave. But it had been ten years and several days since he'd seen Ares. Another hour or two wouldn't hurt anything. And with that Dom fell immediately, soundly back to sleep.

The scent of hot coffee and pastry eventually permeated his dreams. Slowly, Dom rolled out of bed. Asterion gave a little whimper of protest at the loss of Dom's warmth, before turning onto his other side and wrapping his arms around his pillow. Dom quietly tied Asterion's robe around himself and stumbled into the sitting room.

As he ate a cinnamon roll the size of his head and sipped coffee, Dom came to the realization that he was relieved that they'd be leaving for Leyland Hall soon. The possibility of finding Ares didn't make him as nervous as it had, which was nice. He wasn't going to think too hard about why that was, even though he knew it had something to do with having Asterion in his corner, ready to pick him back up in case it all fell apart.

And it would be good for Asterion too. After Leyland Hall, they could go back home, get Asterion back to Earth, away from his wretched family. Dom didn't want to think of Asterion alone and lonely, even as he'd gone from party to party, lover to lover, the funhouse mirror version of the man Dom knew he was. Dom had taught himself how to be alone with years of concentrated isolation, though, it had never gotten any easier. Neither of them had been right, in the end.

And what was Dom going to do about it? Last night, he hadn't told Asterion how he felt. It hadn't seemed like the time, and he was afraid Asterion wouldn't have believed him. He would have thought Dom was just trying to soothe him or manipulate him. But once they were on the road, on the way to Leyland Hall, and Asterion could breathe again, then Dom would say it. And then they could decide what they were going to do next. Together.

A knock on the outer door almost startled Dom into dropping his coffee. He didn't want anyone to wake Asterion, so he hopped up, tightening the robe around his waist, as he walked across the room and opened the door.

Lord Felix Di Rilke stood in the hall in an obscenely tight, red riding outfit, complete with helmet and crop.

"Are you still coming on our ride, Mr. Silva?" Di Rilke asked. Dom distinctly remembered not agreeing to join Di Rilke when he mentioned the ride at dinner the night before.

"Ah." Dom shifted awkwardly, glancing down at his robe. "No, I'm afraid I'll have to skip this one. Besides, I wouldn't want to hold anyone up."

"We don't mind waiting," Di Rilke replied jovially. Dom smiled and shook his head.

"Next time. Really."

"Oh well," Di Rilke deflated grandly, like an aristocratic

balloon, his arms flopping to his sides. "Cressida said that you and his majesty would be leaving today."

"Yes," Dom said. "Soon, I imagine."

"Well," Di Rilke looked Dom over slowly, pursing his lips. "Perhaps I ought to show you something before you go."

"What is it?" Dom asked. Di Rilke considered him for another moment, and then he turned on his heel.

"Come with me," Di Rilke said as he strode away down the hall. Dom grit his teeth and followed, annoyed that no one in Andurnei seemed to care if Dom was parading around a castle in pajamas or a robe or even nothing at all. He caught up with Di Rilke as they turned the corner into the long, high-ceilinged hall that Dom and Asterion had first walked through when they arrived at the palace.

"Di Rilke," Dom said, slightly out of breath, and holding his robe closed across his chest, "what's going on? What are you showing me?"

"You'll see," he said. Dom slowed. Something strange was going on. Di Rilke noticed that Dom wasn't keeping pace and glanced back at him.

"What is this? What's going on?" Dom repeated. Di Rilke paused. Then he sighed.

"It has to do with Asterion. With his future."

Shit.

If it had been the Queen Dowager talking, Dom would have gone straight back to the bedroom. But Di Rilke had been kind to Dom after his run-in with Asterion's mother. He'd helped them.

"It won't take much time, I promise," Di Rilke said. Dom nodded, and so, they continued, turning down the next narrow hall. Di Rilke finally slowed, putting his hand on Dom's shoulder as they reached a door that was standing ajar.

"Just through here, Mr. Silva. If you'd be so kind," he said and steered Dom inside.

They were in the same receiving parlor that Dom and Asterion had walked through two days ago. If Dom hadn't been so preoccupied with Di Rilke's odd behavior, he might have recognized the second hall. And then he realized they weren't alone.

The Queen Dowager stood with her hands primly folded and her wings flat against her back. Dom was reminded, absurdly, of something Ares had said years ago, about how if Dom ever came across a bear, he should try to make himself look bigger to scare it away. Dom swallowed down a nervous grin, his shoulder stiffening under Di Rilke's grip.

"What is this?" He said, glancing back at Di Rilke, who shrugged.

"Sorry, old boy. Nothing personal."

"Your time at Paravel Palace has come to a close." The Dowager's voice was icy, her chin lifted, so that it was clear she was looking down her nose at him. Dom tried to take a step back, but he bumped into Di Rilke's firm chest. "It's time for you to leave, Mr. Silva."

"I'm not leaving without Asterion," he said. Her eyes narrowed.

"It was not a question. And you are in no position to refuse. We have given you what you came here for, and so you will take it graciously. And you will leave."

"What I came here for?" Dom tried to breathe, tried to think. He was doing too many calculations at once: what was she talking about, and how could he get back to Asterion, and did he reasonably think he could break Di Rilke's perfect nose as a distraction? Ares had taught him, once, how to throw a punch, but that had been a long time ago, and he'd never had occasion to practice.

The door behind the Queen Dowager opened, and Dom

recognized the woman who stepped through. She had bright pink skin, snow white freckles across her nose and cheeks, glistening, iridescent white horns. The demon who had entered into a wager with Asterion and stolen his magic.

Desdemona Briarthorne looked at Dom, her head slowly cocking to one side. An alarmingly wide smile revealed white fangs, long and sharp.

"Oh!" She grinned and clapped her hands, laughing merrily. "Oh ho! It's *you*? Now, that *is* funny!"

"What—?"

"Madame Briarthorne," the Queen Dowager prompted.

"Oh, yes. It's all done." She wiped her palms together, beaming at Dom, a cat with a mouse beneath her paw.

"Very good." The Queen Dowager stepped to the side, and Di Rilke pushed Dom forward, toward the door Desdemona Briarthorne had just come through. On the other side was the glow of a portal.

They were sending him somewhere. Away.

"No," he protested. "Wait—" he tried to sidestep, but Di Rilke grabbed him, shoving him hard. Dom turned and coldcocked Di Rilke. The satisfying crunch of bone and Di Rilke's yelp of pain was almost enough to make up for the throbbing ache in Dom's knuckles. Ares would be so proud.

Dom swerved around Di Rilke, trying to get to the door. Desdemona scooted out of his way, laughing and clapping like a toddler at the circus. He didn't know why, until he'd almost reached the exit and was tackled with such force that for a moment he couldn't breathe. Always keep your head up in a fight, Ares' voice echoed in Dom's head. Little late for that. The guards from the portal room were on him, and they were stronger than they looked. The hard crack of a fist against his jaw had Dom tasting blood and seeing stars.

Before he could shake off the hit, they had hoisted him up,

one on each arm, dragging his legs across the carpet. His robe was in grave danger of sliding all the way open.

"Asterion!" Dom screamed as loudly as he could. "Asterion!" And then, without ceremony, Dom was thrown through the portal.

He landed hard on the ground and scrambled to his feet. The portal was already shrinking, the Queen Dowager staring in at him with a miniscule grin on her face, before the magic sealed, and Dom was alone in the dark.

55

Asterion sank deeper into the tub, holding his breath and submerging himself under the lukewarm water. When he'd finally woken up, Dom was gone, probably to the kitchens. Asterion hadn't meant to sleep so late, but since Dom wasn't back yet (how long did it take to make turnovers?) he thought a bath was in order. He lost track of time as he soaked, enjoying the way all his muscles relaxed and loosened, how good it felt to be properly in love with someone.

And he thought he probably was in love. It was a hard thing to admit to himself. And it didn't do anything to help him get his magic back, but it was there all the same, undeniable and warm in his chest. He hadn't sorted out if he was going to do anything about it. Say anything. For the time being, until he and Dom were alone, and probably back home where they could talk, he was just going to enjoy it.

He spent another quarter of an hour in the tub, lounging in bliss, and got out just in time to receive a knock on the bathroom door.

"Come in," Asterion said, assuming it was Dom.

"It's me," Ellery replied. Asterion grabbed for a towel, wrapping it around his waist as she pushed the door open.

"Gods, Ellery! A moment!"

"No. Something is happening."

"What do you mean?" Asterion knotted the towel over his hips, straightening up. She was biting her bottom lip. Frowning. "What is it?"

"Desdemona Briarthorne is here." Ugh. Annoying, assuredly. But easy enough to handle.

"Tell her to fuck off."

"Your mother is already in with her."

Great shitting hell. Not an ideal combination of people, to say the least. Ellery stepped to the side as Asterion strode into his room, looking for clothes.

"Is Dom in the kitchen still?" The last thing he needed was Desdemona seeing Dom. She was nearly the most predatory being he'd ever met, and if she got even a whiff of Asterion's feelings for Dom, she'd undoubtedly try to ensnare him for herself out of spite.

"In the kitchen? Not that I know of." Asterion paused, his stomach dropping. That wasn't right.

"No, I'm sure he's there."

"I don't know," Ellery shrugged. Asterion frowned. He hadn't ever thought of himself as a particularly intuitive person, but Desdemona's reappearance and Dom not coming back to bed yet. It was off. Judging by the pinched look on Ellery's face, she thought so too. "I'll go look for Mr. Silva," she said slowly. "You dress and head to the parlor. Desdemona says she's here to speak with you."

"Can't we swap?" he asked. Ellery gave him a small smile.

"No." She patted him on the shoulder and then walked out the bedroom door.

It was probably fine. Dom in the kitchen making a nuisance

of himself and hopefully cherry turnovers, and Asterion could dismiss Desdemona, and they could continue to Leyland Hall without any further interruption. Asterion would be happy for them to get on their way before anyone else unpleasant showed up.

Ignoring the dread trying to creep into his chest, Asterion dressed in a simple, dark red suit, practically staid by his standards, and made his way downstairs to the receiving room, trying to take deep breaths. A quick conversation and it would be all over.

He pushed open the door to the parlor and stepped in as though there was nothing at all jarring about seeing his mother and Desdemona Briarthorne sharing the space.

Desdemona, with her cherry blossom hair and ivory horns was curled on the end of a chaise as if she was born to sit there. Her waist was cinched tightly in a white lace corset, embroidered with blue petals that drifted down the bodice onto a full skirt that ballooned away from her in absurd proportion to the rest of her body. Her lips were glossed to an almost blinding shine, and she was in almost all ways the exact opposite of the austere, high necked silver gown his mother wore. The Dowager's back was straight, and her smile was curiously wide.

"Asterion," the Queen Dowager said. Asterion's whole body tensed. He found he had a new and poignant appreciation for a rabbit being circled by hawks. "Lady Briarthorne has been waiting for you."

"My apologies," Asterion said. Desdemona looked up at him from beneath her lashes, her lips a demure smile. "I wasn't expecting company."

"She's just been telling me the good news," the Queen Dowager said.

"Oh?" His stomach curdled at the thought of what Desdemona and his mother might agree upon as good news. He looked between the two of them, and neither spoke. "Please, don't keep me in suspense."

"You haven't received your mail?" Desdemona asked, her voice lilting and girlish. Asterion thought back to the veritable mountain of correspondence he'd ignored in his study.

"I've been entertaining," he said. "I haven't had the time."

"It only came through last night. I'd have thought you'd be waiting by the door for it." She smirked. Asterion could have growled; he tried to shift his bared teeth into an approximation of a smile.

"What are you talking about, Desdemona?"

"Your letter from the Assembly, of course." She shrugged. "The terms of the wager have been fulfilled. Your magic can be restored."

56

"What?" Asterion had meant to demand an answer, but his voice was barely more than a whisper.

"Love is in the air," Desdemona cooed, her eyes crinkling at the corners. "Congratulations." Asterion could hardly breathe for the knot in his throat.

"We got notice last night?" Asterion managed. Desdemona nodded, producing a sheet of thick parchment from the cavern between her breasts.

"'*Upon fulfillment of the terms of the agreement, at approximately eight o'clock in the evening, we do so hereby decree,*' etc. etc. '*You can go to the Assembly to retrieve the forfeited items,*' and so on. I really thought you would have already done that, but then it says, if not to expect the Bailiffs at ten o'clock sharp. Not more than a quarter of an hour from now."

"I'll have a tea brought up," his mother said, getting to her feet. Asterion was entirely unmoored, and barely moved as she walked past him, pressing her hand to his cheek, before brushing out of the room.

"You don't seem pleased," Desdemona smirked. "I thought a man in love would be a little bit more—"

"Last night, the letter arrived?"

"The Bailiffs are nothing, if not prompt," Desdemona said, getting delicately to her feet. She held the paper out to him, and Asterion skimmed the elegant looping script, looking for the date and time that the wager had been fulfilled. Eight o'clock in the evening. Asterion swallowed, as Desdemona took his arm. "Thrilling, isn't it? I already planned a little do to celebrate. With your mother and Cressida decamping, I thought we'd host it here. You don't mind, do you?"

"A party?" Asterion asked, still trying to work out where they'd all been at eight last night. Dom was with the Queen Dowager at eight thirty. Or had that been later? But, no, that wouldn't make sense. "I'm not really sure—"

"Nonsense," Desdemona said, striding to the drinks cart. "Everyone's been dying to see you, of course. Dinner parties haven't been nearly as much fun." Asterion swallowed. Her nattering was making his head hurt. "Tell me, darling. Who is the poor sap?"

Gods. Asterion was going to throw up.

He loved Dom.

But did Dom love him?

How could he? Last night had been so complicated. A mix of good and bad and not anything worth falling in love over. The sex, perhaps? But that had been more Dom's doing than Asterion's. He hadn't earned Dom's love, had he? If Dom was in love with Asterion, why hadn't he said anything?

But then, why hadn't Asterion said anything either?

"So. Who was it? Do I know them, at least? I'd like to send flowers."

"No," Asterion said, sinking into her vacated spot on the chaise. "You don't know them." There was a knock on the door. Just one, and entirely perfunctory, as the door swung open and the same bailiffs from the Ascension party at Elmmond House, still bald and stern, stepped in. No sign of Dom. Or Ellery. Asterion swallowed.

"Your highness," said the female bailiff with a nod. "Congratulations on the conclusion of your accord," she said, producing one of the golden cuffs from her belt. The other bailiff stepped forward, the gold amulet that held Asterion's magic, pulsing gently in his hand. "Are you ready?"

Asterion remembered with a sudden wince what removing his magic had entailed, and how unpleasant getting it back was likely to be. He moved to stand, and the Bailiff shook her head.

"Why don't you stay seated this time?"

DOM SWUNG AROUND AS A DOOR OPENED INTO THE PITCH-BLACK room where he'd landed. He yanked his robe closed, as a young man with a mop of curly hair looked in at him with a curious expression.

"Where am I?" Dom asked.

"Leyland Hall. Are you the visitor from the Queen Dowager?"

"I—" Well, fuck. He guessed he probably was.

Which meant she'd let them know he'd be arriving. She had planned the entire thing. And Asterion was alone at the palace. With that demon woman who'd taken his magic. Dom needed to get back. He needed—

"Sir, are you alright?"

"This is Leyland Hall?" Dom was finally managing to put together all the information he had into something that could pass for understanding. The man nodded.

"It is, sir."

"Is Ares Silva here?" The man cocked his head to the side.

"The groundskeeper?" *Groundskeeper?* "Yes, he's here. Just got back from a trip. Shall I take you to him?"

"Please," Dom said. The man stepped back, gesturing that Dom should follow him out of the room.

Dom was terrified. He was furious. If the Queen Dowager thought that she could get rid of him just by handing Dom his brother, then she was going to be disappointed. He'd come back for Asterion, and he'd have Ares' help.

Dom followed the young man across a wide foyer and into narrow service halls, trying to balance his nerves at seeing Ares again, and the immense relief he felt at having someone to help him exactly when he needed it most. Ares had lived in this world for ten years. He would know what to do.

They rounded a corner and went down a close set of stairs that opened into a small mudroom. Cloaks were on hooks, and through a window in the back door, Dom was surprised to see that there was still daylight. Hopefully he hadn't lost much time in his unexpected portal trip. Snow was falling thickly all around, and heavy grey clouds blocked out all but the smallest patches of sky.

"You'll excuse me if I don't accompany you myself, your lordship." Dom was about to protest the title, but the man cut him off, sweeping a long wool cloak up over Dom's shoulders, ignoring the fact that Dom was wearing little more than a fancy bathrobe. He came around to fasten the clasp at Dom's throat, and nudged a pair of rain boots out from under a bench in Dom's direction. "It's only that Master Morrow is still here, and without a valet. He'll need tending once he wakes."

"I—" Dom stammered through about a dozen corrections and apologies, before he shook his head. "It's fine."

"The path's a little snowy, but you can see the light from the cottage just there." He pointed through the window toward a small stone cottage, a couple hundred yards from the house.

The path was fully obscured by the snow but was marked out by a well-manicured line of trees on one side and a fence on the other. "Let me fetch you a hat"

"No, really," Dom held up his hands. "I'll be fine." The man gave Dom a level expression, which Dom interpreted to mean that the man thought he was being stupid. But he nodded anyway.

"Very good, sir," he said, and pushed open the door.

The cold was biting, and almost painfully damp, moisture in the air sharp enough to taste. The snow was thick, and Dom felt like he was wading in it. His jaw, where he'd been punched, was starting to throb.

But, even snow covered, Dom could see that the Queen Dowager hadn't been exaggerating when she'd complimented Leyland Hall. Dom glanced behind him at the high stone walls of the façade, his neck craning to take in the three, or possibly four-story edifice. And Ares was the groundskeeper.

Ares' cottage shimmered, golden light tucked behind its curtains as Dom drew close, and his doubts burned brighter. Maybe Ares had never tried to come back. Maybe he wouldn't be pleased to see Dom. Maybe inside this cottage was a family, a life built up over ten years that Dom had not ever been a part of. And maybe Ares wanted it that way.

Maybe he wouldn't help.

Dom reached the fence that surrounded the house. Found the gate.

What if this was all a mistake?

But even if it was, Dom still had to try. He still had to know. His fingers, numbing on the metal latch, moved. With a deep breath, he pushed the gate open and stepped through.

57

Dom slipped almost immediately. A slick spot beneath the snow took his feet out from under him and he landed hard on his ass. A door opened, someone exclaimed and there was the deep woofing of a dog, as a mountain of black fur bounded toward him through the snow.

The dog was bigger than Dom, and collided with him with such force, that Dom was pushed flat onto his back. He barely managed to hold his robe closed.

"Dammit, Matilda! Get off, you ridiculous creature. Get!" It wasn't Ares' voice, but it was oddly familiar. Unfortunately, Dom couldn't see who it was, as Matilda the dog was frantically licking his face.

And then she was pulled off.

"Christ, I am so sorry." A man. A shorter, square shouldered man, with light skin, a mess of brown curls and a previously broken nose, hoisted Dom to his feet with an impressive yank. "Oh, God. She didn't give you that bruise, did she? She's not usually like this with strangers, I don't—"

He paused and cocked his head to the side.

"Dom Silva?" The man asked.

"Yes. How do I know you?"

"Leo Quince. We met at the Ascension Party. And at your diner—" The man who had been dressed as The Spectre. Who had been with Asterion and the others that night at Elmmond House.

"Sidney's brother." Dom said. Leo and Sidney sounded almost identical, though nothing else about them seemed to be.

"Yes! That's right. I—" Matilda barked at them from where she was standing on the front stoop, clearly waiting for them. Leo shook his head. "Fine. Alright." He turned back to Dom. "You'd better come in. It's freezing out here. Are you wearing a robe?"

The cloak had taken the worst of his fall into the snow, but Dom's legs were soaked and there was slush dripping into his borrowed boots. The moment Dom stepped over the threshold, Matilda was sniffing all around him, tail wagging and thumping him in the stomach, her head as high as his waist. Her fur was warm and soft, and he couldn't help but laugh at the sight of her.

"She's gigantic."

"She's a menace," Leo said fondly. "Here let me take your cloak, at least. Do you need ice for that jaw? It looks like you took a mean right hook."

"Where's Ares?" Dom asked. He fumbled with the clasp of the cloak with one hand, petting an insistent Matilda with the other as he looked around, trying to take it all in. The house was warm and bright, with red tile floors and carefully carved dark wood beams. Plants hung from the ceiling, flourishing, and Dom could smell rosemary and garlic in the air.

"Ares is checking on the pasture. We only just got back—" Leo stammered, and then shook his head. "We've been out. It's a long story. But Ares is determined to get stuck in a snowdrift all for the sake of a few errant sheep." Leo sounded affectionate. Which was interesting.

"How do you know my brother?" Dom asked. It seemed impossible that they'd met before. But as Leo began to answer, a door in another part of the house opened.

"Well, no damage to the hothouse," Ares called. "The wind's died down again. I imagine we'll make it through the night without—" The floor creaked as he walked closer. He sounded the same. Ares stepped into the hall and Dom stopped breathing.

He looked the same, somehow. Ares' shoulders were broad and rounded, nearly filling the wide doorway behind him. His face was softly curved, a thick layer of stubble, almost a beard, coating his chin. His hair still had the same short cut, just long enough to curl at the edges, especially now where it hung, damp over his forehead. His work pants were covered in snow, a thick wool sweater turning his girth teddy-bearish, even beneath the thick black suspenders. Ares' skin had always been a shade or two paler than Dom's and Dom didn't know if this flush in his brother's cheeks was from the cold or from seeing Dom standing in his foyer. Ares inhaled, his voice suddenly quiet.

"Dom?"

There he was. Dom had found him. After ten years of grief and frustration. Ares.

"Yes," Leo said too brightly, as Dom and Ares stared at each other in stunned silence. "Dom's here. I was just coming out to help, but then Dom arrived, and I thought it best to keep Matilda from mauling him." Leo spoke quickly, the tension in the room a burning fuse he was trying to outrun.

"Are you alright?" Ares' eyebrows were bundled together in concern. Dom was trembling and couldn't stop. Couldn't speak either; he nodded.

"Good," Leo said with something like finality. "Good. So, I'll go check on supper and Dom needs clothes. Ares' room is—"

Leo pointed at the stairs, his cheeks turning rosy as he hurriedly slid past Ares to get out of the hall.

Leo's absence made the room strangely quiet. Water dripped off Dom's hair and onto the rug. And then Ares strode forward and pulled Dom into his arms.

"What in Christ's name are you doing here?" Ares breathed as Dom collapsed into his brother's chest and buried his face in Ares' shoulder. Dom didn't bother hiding his sob of relief. He'd missed him. God. His brother was alive. And here. And Dom could breathe again.

Ares held him for several minutes, letting Dom cry, and when Ares stepped back to look Dom over at arm's length, his eyes were wet too.

"How did you get here?"

"It's a long story," Dom exhaled shakily.

"Upstairs," Ares nodded toward the steps. "Let's get you changed. Why are you wearing a dressing gown? Dinner should be ready soon. What happened to your face?"

"I'm fine," Dom said. Ares huffed, and Dom interrupted the incoming lecture. "It smells good in here. I guess you still know how to cook?" Ares snorted and nudged Dom toward the steps.

The upper floor of the cottage was small and only held Ares' bedroom and a bathroom. Ares shuffled through a wardrobe, pulling out a sweater for Dom, shaking his head as he moved for the dresser drawers.

"Leo's trousers will likely fit you better. Give me a minute," he said, and before Dom could protest, Ares had scooped up Dom's wet boots and was gone, his footfalls audible on the stairs. Dom glanced around, but not too hard. He felt like he'd been transported back to when he was ten and Ares was sixteen, and Ares had forbidden Dom from coming into his room. For lack of anything better to do, Dom looked at himself in Ares' mirror.

The bruise on his jaw wasn't so bad. It didn't take his breath away like the sight of the silver necklace hanging from his neck.

Asterion's necklace. Dom closed his fist around it. Some of the elation he'd felt at finding Ares melted away. He needed to go back. And soon.

Dom scooped up the undershirt Ares had left on the bed, the cotton soft and worn. Ares returned with a pair of plain black trousers.

"Here. Try these." He turned around so Dom could change. The pants were snug and a little short, but with Ares' sweater over the top, no one would notice. "You're alright?" Ares asked, still facing the door. His sleeves were rolled up, and Dom could see the faint lines of filigree raised on Ares' forearms. Curved golden scars.

"You can turn around," Dom said. "And what's on your arms?"

"Oh—" Ares stammered, and Dom held out his arm and yanked up the sleeve. The marks from last night were still there. Ares blinked at him.

"Did someone tell you what we are? Or did you figure it out on your own?" Dom hesitated.

"A little of both."

"They're called extolations. When you make an offering to a deity, and they're pleased by it. Or if you cast something that they like, you might get them. Some people call them Atlasions. Marks that show you bear the weight of the gods."

"So, we are, then?"

"Great, great grandsons of Demeter. Yes." Dom rubbed at his chin, trying to decide if he had the mental wherewithal to process that now. He touched his bruise by accident and winced.

"I'm sorry about Matilda. She's usually better behaved."

"Oh, that's fine. She didn't give me this." Dom glanced up,

breaking into a grin as Ares began to grumble. "How long have you had her?"

"Since she was a pup. About five years or so." Five years. Dom swallowed.

"Have you been here the whole time? At Leyland Hall, I mean." Ares pursed his lips. Then he nodded.

"Pretty much. C'mon. Supper's almost ready." Before Dom could say anything else, Ares turned and walked out the door.

Dom followed him down the stairs, through the hall, into the living room, then around the corner. The kitchen was warm and bright. Yellow tiles set off the large black stove and the black granite sink. Shelves lined the walls, full of jars and tins of herbs and spices, crockery and plates. A window over the sink looked out into what might have been the beginning of evening, snow drifting lazily out of the sky.

"Sit," Ares said, nodding to the kitchen table. "Coffee? Tea? Beer?"

"Anything," Dom said, finding his place at the small round table, tucked into a nook. "Whatever you're having." Ares snorted as he went toward the icebox.

"This is the part," Ares said, as he stepped back with a large brown growler in his hand. "Where you tell me how you got here."

"I will if you will," Dom said.

"You first."

So, Dom did. He traced the wood grain of the table with his fingernails, drank his beer, and told Ares the whole story. Of Elmmond House and Jonas and Asterion, the diner, the apartment, and his and Ares' own demigod-ness. At some point Ares brought him ice wrapped in a kitchen towel for his chin, but mostly Ares cooked, fussing with potatoes on the stove as he hummed along in agreement, or snorted in disgust.

It was strange how easy it was, but then this was how they'd always talked. Dom's first crush, when he was deciding what college to go to, when it was clear that Ares was going to have to take over the diner. One of them was at the stove, the other seated at the table.

Dom left some parts out. Mostly things about Asterion; intimacies that it didn't seem right to share. He'd explained how awful the Queen Dowager was, in loose terms. How she forced Dom to leave. Even if he hadn't given Ares all the details, having the story out of him made it feel like Dom could breathe again. He was sure that in a minute, Ares would sit down beside him tell Dom what they were going to do.

"Let me take a plate to Leo," Ares said. "But you start. Don't wait for me."

"He's not joining us?" Dom asked, grabbing for his fork. He didn't have to be told twice to eat. The cinnamon roll he'd had for breakfast felt like a lifetime ago.

"He said he'll eat in his room. Trying to give us some privacy, I think."

"Oh," Dom said. "How long has he—?"

"Eat, Dom," Ares said, grabbing a plate off the counter and going back through the living room. "I'll explain what I can in a minute."

Ares' explanation didn't start properly until Dom was on his second helping. Ares sat back in his chair, plate cleared in front of him, glass of golden beer in his hand.

"I've been here... for a while," Ares said. "Leo's only been here about two weeks. I have a supplier I use who goes back and forth between Andurnei and the human realm about once a month, and I was going to send Leo with her, but I'll feel better having him go back through with you." The piece of chicken Dom had just placed on his tongue practically fell out of his mouth.

"Wait, what?"

"Leo," Ares said simply. "He can't stay here. Once you figure out the runes you need to get back, you can take him with you."

"Wait," Dom frowned, shaking his head. Ares must have been more distracted by the potatoes than Dom had thought. "What do you mean? What about you? And mom?" Ares' face fell suddenly, his gaze shuttering as he glanced toward the window. Dom's throat knotted uncomfortably. "Is she...?"

"She's not here anymore."

"Not alive?"

"Not like she was. It's hard to explain."

"Try."

"Don't worry about it," Ares said firmly. Dom snorted, arching an eyebrow. Ares sighed. "Dom—"

"If you have a way back, why didn't you come home? This supplier. Why couldn't you come with her? Is it because of Mom?"

"I don't want to talk about this," Ares said, setting his beer down on the table hard. Something else that had not changed about Ares, apparently, was that he was still as stubborn as a mule.

"Well, Ares, I came a hell of a long way to talk about it." Ares scoffed and looked away.

"It doesn't concern you." Wow. Dom nearly choked on his beer.

"It doesn't concern me? Ares. You *disappeared*. For *ten years*."

"I did what I—"

"You left me!"

"I was protecting you," Ares snapped, as he glared at Dom.

"From what?"

"From all of this!" Ares gestured around at them. "This world is not—"

"Trust me, Ares. I know what this place is."

"Whatever you think you know isn't even half of it," Ares

replied, crossing his arms over his chest like he knew best. Smug bastard.

"I know enough," Dom insisted. He did. He knew what this world was like. He'd seen how Asterion's family treated him and how cruel Dantalion had been. Everyone was jockeying for power and position. People had some and wanted more. Would sell their own children for it. Dom may not have known *exactly* what Ares was talking about, but he did have an idea. Ares rolled his eyes like Dom was embarrassing himself.

"Dom, I'm not getting into this with you. I've got it handled, and you need to go home."

"And take Leo with me?"

"Ideally, yes."

"You're being an ass," Dom pushed back from the table. "And I'm not going home. I'm going back to Paravel Palace."

"And that's how I know that you don't know how dangerous this is. You'd have to be a fool to willingly get tangled up with these people." That was a bridge too far. Dom got to his feet.

"I need to help Asterion."

"You have no idea what you're talking about. He's a prince. He'll be just fine."

"You're being an asshole."

"Believe me, Dom. I know what I'm talking about."

"How can I believe you when you won't even tell me what's going on. Why didn't you come home?"

"Because I'm doing what's best. For all of us."

"You don't get to decide that!" Dom threw up his hands. "I'm not a kid anymore, Ares. You don't get to tell me what to do."

"You're acting like a kid."

"Oh my god," Dom leaned his head back and stared up at the ceiling. He tried to exhale and failed. "I need a cigarette," he said. Not because he did. Just because he knew it would annoy Ares.

"You're smoking again?" Ares demanded, as though he had any right to talk, since Ares was the one who'd taught Dom how to smoke in the first place.

Dom stormed out of the kitchen. He could hear the scrape of Ares' chair against the tiles and picked up his pace, knowing from experience that Ares was not above chasing him. There was a pair of dry gardening boots by the front door that Dom slid into, ignoring Ares' scolding, and Ares, as both followed him into the foyer. Dom pulled a coat off the hook and swung out of the front door before Ares could grab him by the collar and haul him back into the kitchen.

58

Asterion woke in his bed, body stiff, arms aching. He could hear murmurs in the next room, and he strained to make them out. It was Dom talking to Ellery. Wasn't it? And everything else had been a very strange dream. Or a very mild nightmare.

He shifted his fingers beneath the sheets, afraid he could feel the gentle pulse of magic beneath his bones.

Afraid.

Of magic.

Without a second thought, he cast a warming spell. The same kind Dom had cast on Asterion back in their apartment. Warmth bloomed against his skin, pulsing out against his thigh, his hip, in a rush. And why did he feel like crying? They were tears of relief, surely.

"Dom?" Asterion called out, pushing himself up onto his elbows. The talking in the other room ceased. Asterion's mother walked in and his stomach sank.

"Oh good!" Her smile was paper thin. "I was afraid we'd have to leave before you woke up."

"Where's Dom?" Asterion asked. She frowned and came over to his bedside, pushing his hair off his forehead.

"Dearheart, you still need rest."

"Mother—"

"Thank goodness you have your casting back. I truly can't stand to see you looking so unlike yourself. You should put a little flush back in your cheeks, dear."

"Where is he?" Asterion demanded. The Queen Dowager grimaced.

"He left."

"No." Asterion didn't believe it. Not for a moment.

"Yes, darling. He was quite insistent. I asked him to linger, but he said he couldn't be bothered. Whatever awaits him at Leyland Hall must be very dear to him indeed."

Asterion's chest rose and fell, but he wasn't breathing. Dom had gone to Leyland Hall. That was fine, he supposed. It stung a bit. But, well, he couldn't really expect Dom to wait around for Asterion to wake up, could he?

"How long have I been asleep?"

"Nearly the entire day. It's past dinner. Your friends are all here waiting to celebrate with you." His friends. What friends? Aside from Ellery, Jonas, Sidney and Dom, he had none. And Dom was gone. But he would be back. Of course, he would. Asterion hoped he'd found Ares. "Cressida is here. She wants to say goodbye before we go. She couldn't possibly stay in her condition. You understand."

"Of course," Asterion said, though he didn't care at all. The Queen Dowager patted him lightly on the shoulder, and then swept from the room.

Asterion had barely had time to sit up before Cressida strode in. Her face looked pinched, like she'd just smelled something unpleasant. She stopped at the foot of his bed and looked up at him.

"Congratulations," she said, emotionless.

"Thank you."

"I'd recommend attending to your complexion first."

"Fuck off, Cress," Asterion sighed, collapsing back against his pillows. The door in the outer room closed, and Cressida leaned over the foot of the bed and smacked the lump of blankets that was Asterion's feet. "Ow!" He pushed himself back up to glower at her. "Son of a—"

"Are you paying attention?" She snapped.

"Just because you're too pregnant to attend one of Desdemona's parties—"

"It doesn't strike you as a little bit strange that mother let Lady Desdemona Briarthorne into this house? After Desdemona made you a laughingstock?"

"Mother doesn't care that I'm a laughingstock."

"She's trying to distract you."

"Distract me from what?" Asterion frowned. His mind was too muddled for this. His body was in too much pain. "What are you talking about, Cress?"

"Lord Di Rilke and I are getting married."

"Congratulations?" Asterion said with a shrug.

"Mother has been dead set against him. For months. More than a year, in fact. Before this," she gestured to her stomach. "So, why is she finally relenting?"

"Aren't you queen? Can't you marry whomever you like?" Asterion asked. Cressida threw up her hands.

"Think, Asterion! This isn't strange to you?"

"What are you talking about?" He asked. It was all strange. Their mother had always behaved in ways that defied comprehension. Cressida practically growled in frustration, shaking her head.

"Never mind. Good luck, Asterion. I fear you'll need it," she said and then she walked out of the room.

"Can you send Ellery up?" Asterion called after her. In response, Cressida slammed the door.

~

WHAT A FUCKING NIGHTMARE. DOM TUGGED THE COAT ON AS HE walked down the path, more cautious with his footing this time. It was properly evening now, and still snowing, his footprints from earlier already filled in. His chin still throbbed, but less so, and his stomach was full, and he was a little drunk. If he hadn't been so angry with Ares, it might have even been pleasant.

Probably someone at the big house would know the runes that would get him back to Paravel. He didn't relish the idea of going alone, but Ares was only going to dig his heels in if Dom asked for help again. Leo might be willing. But would he leave Ares? Dom didn't quite have the measure of whatever was going on between them. But good for Leo for refusing to leave when Ares had told him to. Give Ares a taste of his own pig-headed medicine. Dom and Asterion could come back for both of them.

Or, maybe, if Dom could get the runes for Paravel, he'd go talk to Leo first, before going back. Maybe together they could guilt Ares into being useful. That might work. It was worth a try, at least.

Dom had wandered up to the hall and saw that the back door that he had come out of was open ajar. Dom stepped into the warmth of the small mud room, taking a deep breath. But, raised voices brought him up short.

"Why didn't you bring this to my attention before?!" They were furious, their voice high-pitched and nasal. It made the hair on the back of Dom's neck stand on end.

"I'm sorry, sir!" That was the servant from earlier, who had helped Dom. A hard thud, followed by a soft whimper. "He's just the groundskeeper, sir!" Then a hit, a hard one, and a gasp of breath. Dom took the stairs two at a time.

He turned down the hall, a yelp of pain telling him where to go. Dom strode into the kitchen, a wide, warm room, lit by several large fires. It would have been cozy if not for the violence that was occurring in the center of the room.

The aggressor was largely unremarkable, except for a ridiculous moustache above his upper lip paired with a goatee that only made him look like a cartoon villain. His dark hair was disheveled in anger, eyes narrowed and beady.

"Easy, Edmund." There was another man standing a few steps back, on the other side of the altercation. His perfectly smooth skin, as flawless as if it had been painted on, was cast gold by the firelight. His hair was a shine of bright seafoam blue, and there was a blush on the high line of his cheekbone. There was no one he could be except Asterion's brother, Kephisto, the lord of Leyland Hall. And he was enjoying this.

The man called Edmund pressed the servant hard against the wall. Dom could see a thin line of blood trickling out from beneath the man's hair.

"Stop," Dom said. Everyone looked at him. The servant whimpered and gave a small shake of his head.

"*Who* are you?" Kephisto's mouth curled up at one corner in an unpleasant smile. Edmund released the front of the servant's shirt, but the man didn't move. Silently, the servant mouthed one word at Dom:

'Run.'

Dom stiffened.

"Isn't it obvious who this is?" Edmund sneered. "It's the gardener's brother."

"And wearing *my* brother's sigil." Kephisto arched an eyebrow. Dom didn't dare look away, but he lifted his hand to his chest, tucking the necklace beneath the collar of his sweater.

"He probably stole it," Edmund said. He took a step toward Dom. Dom took a step back. "Your mother said he was making trouble, didn't she? He's a thief."

"Well, then there's your cause to arrest him, surely, Viceroy." Kephisto's tone was teasing, amused.

Viceroy? The Viceroy Morrow who Cressida and the Queen Dowager had talked about at dinner? Who was the same Edmund Morrow who'd hurt Asterion. Who Ares had made a contract with. Maybe Dom should have run, but he was starting to feel like fighting.

But, before Dom could do anything, a bright, hot bolt erupted from Morrow's hand and hit Dom like a bowling ball to the chest. He was on his back, legs and arms unresponsive, head throbbing where it had hit the floor. He tried to move, but nothing budged.

"See, Edmund," Kephisto laughed. "All your problems solved! There's no reason to get uppity." Morrow walked over to stand above Dom. He looked down at him with a thin smile, and then crouched beside Dom, pausing for a moment to look at the faint extolations on his forearms.

"I'll have to do a suppression on him too, before this is all over."

"Nonsense. He'll fall into line."

"Well," Morrow looked down at Dom and smiled. "I suppose he doesn't have much choice." Dom tried to jerk away, but his muscles barely moved. Morrow smiled.

"Before you send him away, Eddie, could you get me that necklace?" Kephisto cooed. "Asterion will want it back. It's his favorite." Morrow made a sour face that Kephisto couldn't see, before grabbing the ivy necklace and yanking hard. The chain snapped behind Dom's neck, and Dom wanted more than anything to scream. To fight back.

And then, Dom could move his fingers.

Sensation eked back into his hand, as his skin began to glow. Dom heaved his arm up and grabbed for Morrow's throat, missing by inches, his fingers clenching in the fabric of Morrow's shirt.

For the briefest of moments, the shock on Morrow's face gave way to fear. And then he clasped a golden cuff around Dom's wrist, and Leyland Hall was gone.

59

D om was on his back on a stone floor. His head still throbbed, but he could move again. He lifted his arms and looked at the cuff on his wrist. It reminded Dom of the cuff that Asterion had been made to wear before they took his magic. No visible latches or hinges. Too small to try and work off over his hand. A shrill bell rang, almost painfully loud, and Dom sat up with a groan.

The room was small. The walls were stone and bare, except for a door on one wall, and a window on the opposite. Dom made his way up slowly, hips stiff, limbs aching. He went to the window first and looked out to see that the entire landscape was white with snow. On a distant shore, pine trees stretched like long black fingers out of the ground. There was nothing below the window, except a sixty or seventy foot plunge into the dark, icy-looking water below. He thought about kids he'd known that jumped off the lower cliffs at Harlan's Crest into the bay in the summertime. How he'd never been brave enough to join them.

The bell began to ring again. Dom looked over his shoulder, and spotted it mounted above the door to his room, shaped like a little metal bird. Against the wall was a small bed covered in a wool blanket, a thin pillow at the top. That was all there it. A bed and a bell. Nothing else.

Dom turned back to the window, pushing up on the bottom of the iron window frame. It barely budged. He tried again, glass slipping up a centimeter. The door to the room burst open.

"Did you not hear the bird?!" The creature standing in the doorway was tall and broad-shouldered, with a gaunt white face and a mess of long, thick black hair. Their features were strange, almost too pronounced, with wide wet eyes like a porcelain doll, and a long angular nose. A boney finger pointed upward at the bird-bell in question. "Well, come on then!" They said, then turned on their heel and stormed out. Dom followed, entirely at a loss for what else to do. "No use jumping out of windows in the winter," the being said the moment Dom caught up with them. "Die on the rocks, most likely. Or break your legs and drown. What's your name?"

"Dom. What's yours?"

"Enid," Enid said. "Need medical attention?"

"Uh. I need to get out of here?"

"Hah!" It wasn't a laugh exactly. More like a shout of mirth. "No chance of that, boyo. Mr. Morrow got a cuff on you, then you'll be here for the duration." Enid paused in a doorway and tapped a finger with an extra joint on the metal around Dom's wrist. Dom's eyes widened in spite of himself. "What? Never seen a wight before?"

"No," Dom said. Enid scoffed.

"A sort of fae, some folks say. Something more akin to a spirit though. Something in between."

"Is Morrow keeping you here?" Dom asked. Enid laughed again.

"Wights are protectors. This is my home. We came to an agreement, of sorts, Mr. Morrow and I." Enid's smile widened and contained too many teeth. Dom took a step back, his shoulder bumping into the wall. "Don't worry. You've got nothing to fear from me. My job is the running of this place. Mr. Morrow sends me help, from time to time. That'd be you."

"I don't want to be here," Dom said. Enid shrugged and walked through the doorway, leading Dom into a massive kitchen.

"I don't much care where you want to be. That cuff is anchored to this land, and Mr. Morrow owns nearly all of it. The minute you step over the property boundary, they'll bring you right back here. Take a run for it if you don't believe me." Enid gestured to a door in the corner. "But go quick. We've got work to do."

Dom hesitated. Then he started for the door. He'd just pulled it open, when the wight spoke again.

"Head over the pasture. About a half a mile northeast, past the sheep. That'll be the quickest."

What the fuck was going on?

Still, Dom left, pulling the door closed behind him. He started across the pasture, wondering where in the hell he was now. He was getting tired of being portaled to places he didn't want to be. He needed to get back to Asterion.

What did Asterion think had happened to him? What had the Queen Dowager told him? Dom began to pick up his pace, anger driving him up the snowy hillside. Asterion had to know by now that something was wrong. He had to know that Dom wouldn't have just abandoned him.

But Dom remembered with sickening clarity all the doubt in Asterion's face when they'd met in the garden folly. Asterion had been so sure that his mother had turned Dom against him, apologizing for faults that were entirely made up. He'd expected Dom to leave him.

Dom had to get back. To explain what happened. And hopefully Asterion knew that Dom would never have left him there alone by choice. Dom loved him.

He should have said it when he'd had the chance.

Breathing heavily, Dom crested the hill. A wide, pine forest stretched out in front of him. It certainly seemed like the wrong way to go for help. But, then, if Enid was right, it wouldn't matter. Dom was stuck.

Dom jogged down the slope toward the trees, waiting for anything to happen, trying to just focus on Asterion. If he could get back to Asterion, he could fix everything. Asterion could help him with Ares. Asterion would know what to do.

Dom ducked under the first of the pine branches, and then crashed directly into the wall at the foot of the bed. He landed hard on the stone floor and stared around at his little cell.

He couldn't leave.

He was trapped.

Dom tried to breathe. He folded himself forward onto his knees, and reached up for the place where his necklace, Asterion's necklace, had rested against his chest an hour ago, and he screamed in frustration.

The bird-bell rang, and Dom clenched his fists against his legs.

"Come on out, boyo," came Enid's chipper tone. "I've got some errands for you."

60

E llery didn't come.

Eventually, after an hour of trying to ignore his stomach rumbling, Asterion dragged himself out of bed and dressed. He would find Ellery himself, and see if she'd located Dom.

Would Dom really go to Leyland Hall without him? Asterion struggled to believe it. There was no note. No message. And someone would have had to give Dom the runes. It just didn't make sense. Cressida had been trying to tell him something in her stupid oblique way. Something about Di Rilke and her wedding?

Asterion needed an espresso. And food. And a plan. He wished for Jonas as he walked into the hall. Jonas for the plan, and Sidney for the espresso. And Dom for everything else.

He could hear Desdemona's party before he made it to the wide staircase that led to the first floor. Music blared, shrieks of laughter, a veritable explosion of sound as a door somewhere opened and closed again. Asterion jerked to a halt on the stairs as a couple ran naked through the foyer toward some other part of the house. Nudity was the hallmark of a Desdemona Briarthorne party.

For the first time in his life, Asterion felt no pull toward the pounding swell of music, the bright peals of laughter. He needed to find Ellery. She surely would have located Dom by now, and if Dom had gone to Leyland Hall, then Ellery would certainly know that too.

And perhaps it was wishful thinking, but Asterion went to the kitchen first to look for Ellery. Or for Dom, as though he might've decided to spend all day there. Three chefs stood at the far end of the long room. Two were leaning back against the counter, the other gesturing with a spatula in a way that reminded Asterion immediately of Nina. It took him a moment to realize that the chefs had stilled. Were all looking at him.

"Have you seen Ellery?" he asked. They looked at each other.

"Not since this afternoon," said the one with the spatula. "Sir," he added quickly. Ugh.

"Thank you," Asterion said, and retreated into the hall, where a crowd was parading by.

Fae, demons, and other creatures of all different shapes, sizes and colors were carousing through his palace. A demon with crimson skin and violet horns was holding a tray of coupe glasses, all of which were sloshing over with champagne. Asterion was slapped on the back, kissed on the cheek, a bottle of something that smelled strongly of poisoned grenadine was shoved into his hands, and he was swept along with them. He didn't want to be touched, precisely. The fullness of his magic left his skin feeling taut and over-sensitive. Still, hands seemed to reach out to him from every angle, brushing against him. He didn't recognize a soul, until he was deposited, along with everyone else, in the ballroom.

They'd brought in couches and tables and there were easily fifty, sixty, eighty people, cavorting around, drinking, dancing, indiscriminately fornicating. The ceiling was bedecked with twinkling lights, drifting clouds, and nearly nude acrobats, who dropped down from silk sashes before winding themselves back up into the mist.

Desdemona shrieked when she saw Asterion, waving him over. In her corner of the ballroom, he did recognize some people. Special friends of Desdemona's, other royals and aristocrats, already drunk and gawking. Desdemona leaned back against a large man's hairy chest. One of her hands held a coupe of pink champagne, her other rested between the thighs of a small, lavender-skinned woman who was curled against Desdemona's side.

"Asterion," Desdemona said, handing the woman her glass. "I was beginning to worry you'd sleep through your own party!"

"It seems like you've been managing fine without me so far." The man behind Desdemona caught Asterion's eye and dragged his teeth across his bottom lip. Asterion looked back at Desdemona. "Have you seen Ellery?"

"Oh, she doesn't usually partake, does she?"

"No, but—"

"I do have someone who wanted to see you. Give me a moment." She straightened up, and held out her hands to him, which he took, intending to hoist her up. With a jerk she spun him into the place where she'd been standing and then pushed him down onto the settee. "Wait here. I'll be back."

Before Asterion could sit up, the woman who had been against Desdemona was leaning on him, one hand snaking around his hips. The man reached forward to catch the champagne coupe drooping from her hand before it spilled. His thigh slid alongside Asterion's, and his body came flush with Asterion's back.

"Careful, kitten," the man cooed, his breath hot on Asterion's neck. Asterion's shoulders stiffened. The woman straightened up, her eyes wide and glassy, as she blinked at Asterion.

"Have you tried the champagne?" Her lips were full and wet from drinking, her cheeks bright from whatever Desdemona had been doing beneath her skirts.

"No," he said. "I'm fine actually." Rough lips grazed his neck, as the man behind him shifted forward again, holding the coupe out in front of Asterion.

"It's good. Imbued, I think. You know how Desdemona likes it." Asterion did know exactly how Desdemona liked her champagne, strong and potent, magically imbued to create a sense of euphoria, release inhibitions. Clearly these two had had plenty. The woman's fingers were toying with the buttons on the front of his shirt, and Asterion could feel something long and stiff pressed against his lower back. "You seem tense."

"I just woke up," Asterion said, trying desperately to scoot forward off the chaise without knocking the drunk woman onto the floor.

"Bad dreams?" The man asked. The woman's head came even with Asterion's sternum and her lips found his chest. Asterion jerked backward, and the man behind him chuckled against the nape of Asterion's neck. "We could give you some better ones."

Two weeks ago, Asterion might have let it happen. He could have turned his mind off and let his own pleasure and theirs carry him through the rest of the encounter. But as the woman slid her hand between his thighs, Asterion was almost startled by the absence of his arousal. There was only one person he wanted to touch him. Just one.

Asterion pressed himself off the couch, staggering forward out of the grips of those on the settee and nearly tumbling headlong into Desdemona, who was standing in front of him with Kephisto on her arm.

61

K ephisto's smile widened and Asterion tried not to visibly recoil. He couldn't remember the last time he'd seen his brother, which made encountering him now feel all the stranger.

"Well, well," Kephisto reached out and clasped Asterion's shoulder with an uncomfortably firm grip. "Congratulations are in order, I'm sure."

"Thank you," Asterion managed, scanning the crowd behind them for the nearest tray of drinks, before he'd remembered that they were imbued and he didn't want any. "We missed you at dinner last night."

"I'm certain you did." Kephisto grinned, his hand slipping down to hold Asterion's bicep. "How was mother?"

"In fine form." Asterion tried to take a step back, but Kephisto yanked him forward. "I actually can't, I—Wait. Did you come from Leyland Hall?"

"I did."

"I'll leave you to it!" Desdemona trilled, flitting away to drape herself over the shoulder of a woman with mercury colored hair and skin. Asterion watched her go, before turning back to his brother.

"Did you by chance receive a visitor this—"

"Come along," Kephisto interrupted, linking his arm with Asterion's and steering them over toward the far corner of the room. It made Asterion feel like a child, and under better circumstances, he would have balked. Dom's disappearance had put him on his back foot, so he followed alongside his brother without protest, waiting for them to land somewhere before he pressed Kephisto for answers.

The door to an adjacent parlor was open wide, and the party had spilled in accordingly. A drinks cart, vacant of any of Desdemona's pink champagne, was crowded, but a cleared throat from Kephisto, coupled with his most degrading sneer, dispersed the partygoers in a swath.

Asterion watched as Kephisto held a decanter of amber liquid to the light, checking for the sheen of any enchantments. Kephisto had been convinced someone would make an attempt on his life for years. This time, at least, Asterion was glad for his caution.

"So," Kephisto said, handing Asterion a tumbler, once he'd mixed their drinks. "What do you intend to do now that your magic has been restored?"

Ah. That made more sense. Kephisto didn't actually have any interest in him. He just wanted to make sure Asterion wasn't getting ideas above his station.

"No plans," Asterion said easily. "Nothing different than what I was doing before. Which was also nothing." It wasn't entirely true, but Kephisto wasn't likely to believe that what Asterion planned to do was move to the human realm and run a diner with a demigod.

Oh.

That was what he was planning, wasn't it?

Asterion flushed and took a sip of his drink to steady himself. He was in far over his head.

"Did you receive a visitor at Leyland earlier today?" Asterion tried again. Kephisto sipped his drink primly. "A man, a human —" Kephisto didn't need to know Dom's personal details. "My height. Dark hair. Olive skin. Curls. He would have been asking for Ares Silva."

"Yes," Kephisto said. "I met him."

"Oh." Asterion was surprised and not quite sure why. He'd expected his mother had lied to him, he supposed. But then, Dom going to Leyland Hall was the only explanation for his absence that made sense.

"He asked me to give you something." Kephisto tucked a hand inside the jacket of his suit.

Thank Gods. It had to be a note. Dom would explain everything, and Asterion could finally relax.

But Kephisto's hand emerged from the inside pocket of his coat without a note. Instead, tangled in between his fingers was Asterion's ivy necklace. The one Dom had worn beneath the heartrender.

"He sends it back with his regards. He said he didn't need it anymore."

"Didn't need it anymore?" Asterion drew a shallow breath. When he tried to take a deeper one, his chest was too tight. "What do you mean?"

"I suppose, having located his errant brother, he's got no use for you. Polite of him to return the necklace. A lesser man would have pawned it. I suppose he might have been planning to, but no harm done."

No. That didn't make any sense. There had to be a mistake. Dom loved Asterion. Didn't he?

"I certainly hope *he* wasn't the person you fell in love with." Kephisto's smile returned, a small, mean thing. He dropped the necklace into Asterion's hand.

A message. But not the kind Asterion had been hoping for.

Dom had gotten what he wanted. He didn't need Asterion anymore. But that didn't make sense. Unless the wager cared about Asterion's feelings too. He *was* in love; he'd admitted it to himself just that morning.

He didn't know. He hadn't considered that it might work both ways. That his feelings weren't reciprocated.

Asterion's neck was flush with embarrassment. He closed his fist around the necklace and shoved it into his pocket.

"I offered to bring him back here with me tonight," Kephisto continued, "but he said he had no interest. He and his brother are returning earthside presently."

Asterion downed the drink Kephisto had made for him in two swallows, and then grabbed the neck of the crystal decanter with a shaking hand and held on tight.

"So," Kephisto's grin widened. "Who is your happy new partner? I look forward to making their acquaintance." He glanced over Asterion's head, as though there was some person there waiting to be introduced.

"Excuse me," Asterion said, turning away from his brother and fleeing into the crowd.

ASTERION DRANK AS MUCH AS HE COULD, AS QUICKLY AS HE COULD, before any errant feelings could set in. The weight of the decanter was comfortable against his chest. He waded through the dancers, the press of bodies and the pulse of music, both pleasantly numbing. He almost couldn't feel the weight of the necklace against his thigh anymore.

Almost.

Asterion's chest ached. Why would Dom give the necklace to Kephisto? After everything they'd been through, why would he —how could he go without at least saying goodbye?

Asterion took a swig from the decanter, crystal clacking painfully against his front teeth. He lowered the bottle with a grimace and found himself face to face with a beautiful creature. Some kind of naiad, if he had to guess, based on the gills. A webbed hand slid against the narrowest part of Asterion's waist.

Fine.

He took a more careful sip from the decanter, before stepping forward. The naiad's body went flush with Asterion's at the hips, against the chest. When they kissed, Asterion could taste pink champagne on her lips, and felt nothing.

Not entirely true. He was nauseous with heartbreak. Feeling nothing couldn't come fast enough, and Asterion was going to do everything he could to speed it along.

62

The town below the castle was the picturesque version of a miserable medieval village. About four streets branched off the main thoroughfare, which was crowded with carts and horses and Dom spent plenty of time exploring each of the narrow side streets, primarily out of spite. Enid had sent him with a laundry list of supplies that were needed for dinner and for the castle; Dom would do the chores, but only because he wanted to avoid any consequences that might make it even harder to escape. Escaping was all he could think about.

Could he compel someone to send a letter for him? To Asterion? But then, if Asterion's mother intercepted it, it wouldn't do any good. To Ares? That might work. Provided Morrow wasn't looking through his mail.

It took him an embarrassingly long time to realize that, based on the amount of horseshit he'd had to avoid stepping in, the town probably had some kind of smithy. Someone was making horseshoes. And that perhaps, if someone was doing metalworking, he might not need to send a letter at all. Enchanted cuffs were still made of something, after all.

It was easy enough to find the smithy, but there were enough people there that Dom had to wait in the back of the room for an opening to approach the counter. A short, ruddy-skinned shopkeeper tended to most of the customers, but orders were being taken by a soot-smudged woman with dark skin, whose forearms were the size of Dom's head. Her hair was twisted into a long, thick braid down her back, and she glanced up from a pad of paper as Dom approached. He'd barely placed his hands on the counter when she heaved a heavy sigh and shook her head.

"New in town?" she asked. Dom nodded, his stomach plummeting at the resignation in her tone. "I wondered how long it'd be until we saw another one of you."

"What do you mean?" Dom asked.

"What can I help you with?"

"I—" His hand drifted nervously to the cuff on his opposite wrist, and she shook her head.

"No," she said. Then she tucked her pad of paper under her arm and walked away.

"Wait." Dom followed her along the counter. "I need help. Please!" She huffed and glanced around, fists tightening at her side. Dom could feel eyes on him, and for the first time since he was a teenager, it made him nervous. He shut his mouth.

"Sir." The other shopkeeper was at his elbow, and Dom whipped toward him as the man put a hand on Dom's shoulder. "I think it's time for you to go."

"No. No, I—" Dom could feel his chances slipping away. "I have an order from Viceroy Morrow. It's—I—It's very specialized." He held up the shopping list he'd crumpled in his coat pocket as he'd stalked through town. It was a massive bluff. But if he could just get the blacksmith alone, maybe he could convince her—

The door to the back of the shop slammed shut. She was gone.

The shopkeeper kept his hand on Dom, steering him toward the door and gave him an unnecessary shove over the threshold.

"Into the alley and then take a left," he said quietly. "Wait for me."

"What?" Dom asked, but the man had already disappeared back inside.

The alley was short, and a split rail fence separated the wide space behind the shop from the narrow line of paving stones that ran alongside it.

Dom could see the foundry in the yard. A well of fire emitted a constant stream of smoke, partially obscuring a rack and three large anvils. Under any other circumstances, Dom would have been interested to watch the blacksmith work. But at the moment, his heart was pounding in his chest. He needed an ally. Badly.

The shopkeeper appeared a few moments later, shaking his head as he gestured for Dom to join him. Dom hopped the fence and jogged to meet him at the workbench.

"Let me tell you this," the shopkeeper said, his voice low and serious. "You don't want to cause any kind of scene in this town. That cuff marks you out. Everyone here knows what you are."

"I was kidnapped."

"That's not for me to say," the shopkeeper shrugged, his gaze fixed on Dom's wrist.

"If I could just explain to the blacksmith—"

"You can't." He said, holding up his hand. "She won't be able to help you, and you can't ask her again. You cause a scene like that, and people will talk. And if it gets back to him, then..." He shook his head. "I just wanted to give you a piece of advice." Dom stammered, anger tying his tongue. He needed advice like he needed a hole in his head. He needed actual help. "Viceroy Morrow owns this town. Half the village is on his payroll, and the other half would like to be. No one here is going to help you escape. We've all seen what happens when you cross him. You're better off keeping your head down and doing as you're told."

"That's it?" Dom snapped.

"That's it. Once you've been here for a little while, you'll see. You might even thank me one day." Dom's stomach ached with rage; his lips pursed thin to stop himself from shouting. The man held up his hand, as though he was telling Dom to wait. Then he lifted his other arm and Dom saw that the shopkeeper was missing his left hand. And a half inch scar, the same size as Dom's cuff, circled his wrist. "You should go," the shopkeeper said, his voice hollow. "You don't want to keep Enid waiting."

63

"Oh, Christ."

That was a funny voice. That was a funny thing to say. Asterion laughed. Then he slumped back against the wall. His legs were tired from dancing. His mouth was sore from kissing? Other mouth activities perhaps? He didn't know. The rest of the decanter and a bottle of champagne had made the last few hours a blur. Asterion had moved in the way he'd been pulled. He was breathless and weightless. He should have cast a sobriety spell, but he didn't want to be sober. And he couldn't lift his arm.

"He needs some water," the naiad said. Asterion laughed again.

"Fuck water," he said. Might be a rude thing to say in front of a naiad. She lifted an eyebrow, unimpressed, as someone who Asterion hadn't realized was next to him disappeared into the crowd. "Having fun?" he asked her. She smirked at him.

"Are you?"

"No," he laughed again. "Gods. No. Is this the first time we've spoken?"

"We've been talking all night," she said.

"Oh. I imagine that was interesting."

"Not especially."

"Serena!" A group of fae were hanging back, looking at them. One waved the naiad over. The crowd had thinned a bit. The room stank of sex. Asterion hadn't noticed. His head pulsed painfully. He watched one of the women in the group scowl at him.

"Grumpy," he observed.

"She doesn't like you."

"I'm very likable," he argued.

"She asked if she could get you off and you laughed at her."

"Oh," Asterion frowned. "Well, if it helps at all, it wasn't personal."

"You said the only people allowed to touch your cock are people who know how to make cherry turnovers so delicious you see Gods when you eat them." Asterion winced.

"A long-held rule, I'm afraid."

"And then you threw up."

"That sounds right."

"Gods," Sidney appeared, holding a tall, thin pitcher of water and looking irritated. "You would think an orgy would at least have a central refreshments table. Took forever to find this." He shoved the pitcher into Asterion's hands. "Drink," he said.

"What the fuck are you doing here?" Asterion demanded.

"Rehydrating you." He turned toward the naiad. "Thank you."

"It's fine," she shrugged. "Tending to him gave us a good excuse not to participate in any," she gestured vaguely around, "things. We just came for the dancing, really."

"Well, thanks all the same."

"Look out for that Briarthorne woman. She kept plying him with champagne. It's definitely laced with something. I think he threw up most of it, but—" Sidney was nodding and talking, and Asterion's attention was beginning to fade. The cold water was nice. It was spilling down his chest a bit. And that was nice. He thought he might be hungry. Or he was going to throw up again.

"Asterion?" Sidney was looking at him closely as Ellery led the naiad away.

"They should get together," Asterion said, watching them go. Pretty women. A little mean. They'd make a good couple.

"Come on." Sidney pulled Asterion forward, off the wall. Asterion whined as loudly as he could, but Sidney didn't care.

"You're a bastard. How did you get here?"

"Ellery came to get Jonas and me. Well, she came back to Hindry looking for Dom. And when she couldn't find Dom, she came to get Jonas and me." Of course she couldn't find Dom. Asterion knew where Dom was.

"Where's Jonas?"

"Looking for you. This party is quite... expansive. We had to split up."

They stepped into the hallway, where Asterion could see heavy snow falling against the pitch-black sky. After the noise of the ballroom, it was eerily quiet.

"Is it late? Or early?"

"Both." Sidney wrapped an arm around Asterion's waist. "After four, I'd guess." Sidney did his best to guide Asterion down the hall, but when they reached the staircase, grand, mountainous almost, Asterion had to stop. He sank down against the bottom step, sloshing water all over his front. Sidney looked down at him for a moment. Then he sat down beside him.

"What happened?" Sidney asked quietly. Asterion laughed. Then he choked down a sob, dropping his head into his hands.

"I got my magic back," he said eventually.

"Ellery said." Asterion wanted to sink into the staircase. He wished he was more drunk. The ability to have coherent thoughts was not what it was cracked up to be. "Was it Dom?"

"Of course it was."

"Of course it was," Sidney said. He sounded pleased, and Asterion had enough self-respect to turn his head and glare at Sidney.

"Shut up."

"It just doesn't surprise me, is all—"

"I said, SHUT UP!" Asterion screamed so loud that it echoed in the foyer. Tears welled up in Asterion's eyes. He slouched forward into a nest of his own arms and began to cry. It hurt. And he hated how much it hurt. He had thought that Dom wouldn't abandon him. That Dom had seen something more in him. Had liked him for who he was, or maybe even despite who he was.

But Dom was gone. And Asterion was alone again. More alone than he had been before because he'd learned what it was like not to be.

"There you are! Gods." Jonas' voice was low, full of worry, but then he didn't say anything else. The silence dragged on a bit too long, and Asterion knew Sidney and Jonas were having a wordless conversation above his head. He didn't care. Eventually, Jonas sighed, and then picked Asterion up off the step. Asterion curled, pathetic, toward his chest.

"Do I want to know why you're soaking wet?" Jonas asked gently. Asterion snorted, and then the next thing Asterion knew, Jonas was laying Asterion down in bed. "Take your shirt off."

"Jonas!" Asterion slurred, wiping his fingers beneath his still damp lashes. "What will Sidney say?"

"Take your shirt off," Sidney replied dryly from somewhere on the other side of the room. Asterion laughed, almost immediately getting tangled in sodden clothes. He stank. His body ached. He collapsed back against the blankets and inhaled the scent of Dom off Dom's pillow. Gods, he loved him still. So much. He was so distracted by his heartache that Asterion almost missed the sound of footsteps.

"Wait!" He pushed himself up on one arm, head spinning. He opened his eyes for the first time since they'd come into his room. Jonas was still in the doorway. "Don't leave, Jonas. Please."

"Sidney and I will be in the sitting room," Jonas said. "We won't leave. I promise." Asterion nodded, accepting a hundred disparaging thoughts about what a stupid, embarrassing child he was being, and then tumbled into blissful unconsciousness, wrapped around Dom's pillow.

64

D om slept horribly. Every dream turned into a nightmare, and Asterion was in all of them, always just outside of Dom's reach.

He woke early to find that Enid had left a pile of warmer clothes outside his door: a rough knit sweater and boots that actually fit. Dom dressed slowly, limbs heavy as he slid Ares' coat on top of his new outfit, just to keep it with him. He didn't know if he was going to be able to escape, or even if he was going to go anywhere, but he couldn't bring himself to take it off.

In the kitchen, burnt coffee sat in a rusted kettle on the hob. Dom drank it anyway, trying to suppress a headache that only grew stronger as he squinted at the list of errands sitting near the hob, Dom's name at the top. He'd left his glasses back home in the apartment.

He thought about the blacksmith. It had been hard to think about anything else, really. How had Enid or Morrow, or perhaps both of them, taken the man's hand? What sort of infraction would warrant that punishment?

Dom walked to town, stomach furious from the rancid coffee

and no breakfast. He didn't feel like eating. He wanted to finish Enid's shopping and go back to bed.

It must have been some kind of market day. Ships were in port, and the docks were full of stalls that hadn't been there the day before. The sky was a lighter grey, almost blindingly white in some places. Dom kept his head down and shopped in near silence, barely managing a 'Thank you,' when an elderly vendor practically shoved an extra apple into his hand and demanded he eat.

Following orders was easier than fighting, and the apple was bright and brilliantly sweet against his tongue. It reminded him of sitting in the tree at Harlan's Crest, watching Asterion swing below him. The first time they'd really talked.

For a moment, Dom missed Asterion so much that he didn't think he could breathe. Apple sat on his tongue as Dom staggered down the docks, and landed heavily on a small, rickety bench that bowed dangerously under his weight. That day on the motorcycle everything had been so bright and brilliant. Dom had told Asterion he liked him, without knowing what it meant. To either of them.

Dom sagged, his head dropping into his hands. He needed to sleep. If he was going to try to escape, he'd need energy. Asterion had to be looking for him by now. He had to be. And Dom had to find a way to reach out. Let Asterion know, at least, where he was.

The cuff couldn't come off. Alright. Maybe he needed to think smaller. It didn't seem likely that anyone would post a letter for him, but maybe if he pretended it was for Morrow. But then, would Asterion even read it? Or would he just throw it away?

A boat sailing into the harbor on frost-tipped waves drew Dom's attention. It was what he would have thought of as a historical ship, a great wooden thing with huge masts. Two smaller wooden trawlers were anchored in, tossing down their daily catch to fellow fishermen on the docks. If Paravel had been closer to water, he might have considered bribing a sailor to take a message for him. Not that he had any money. And if they knew about the cuff, he might not even get that far. Dom stopped, watching the waves lap against the ships, wondering how far he could swim out before his cuff catapulted him back to the castle.

Being sleep deprived and hungry was making it hard for him to focus. Dom finished his apple and got to his feet, ignoring the wobble in his knees, when someone called out to him.

"Mr. Silva. Fancy meeting you here!" Dom spun toward his name, and nearly toppled into the water. Luckily, Anders was quick enough to catch him by the forearm.

"Anders?" Dom blinked. He was dreaming. He had to be. "What are you doing here?"

"I told you." The man grinned. "I'm a fisherman." Dom's heart lodged in his throat. He barely dared to hope, and desperation must have shown on his face, because Anders' smile faltered. "What's wrong? Is everything alright?"

"No," Dom shook his head. "No, I need help. I—" Dom felt suddenly as though he was making too much noise, like he'd drawn attention to himself again somehow. "Is there somewhere we could talk?"

"My ship is right over there," Anders pointed toward the end of the pier. Far out in the water. Dom shook his head. Anders was a lifeline, and he couldn't risk losing him by stepping out of bounds.

"Come with me," Dom said. "Please." Anders nodded, concern knitting his brow, and Dom started back through town, leading him up the hill toward the castle, as fast as he could go.

They were surrounded by sheep when Dom finally felt like he could speak freely. He told Anders everything, and it seemed like Anders was listening closely enough, but when Dom got to the part of his tale where he encountered Edmund Morrow at Leyland Hall, Anders' blue eyes went wide for the first time. Anders patted a sheep absently, as Dom explained about the golden cuff, how it worked, and then drew up his sleeve to show him. Anders gave a low whistle, cradling the back of Dom's hand as he lifted Dom's wrist up to the light.

"It's a pretty piece of magic, I'll grant him that."

"Fine. But how do I get it off?"

"I don't suspect you do. It's probably dampening your own power, so you wont be able to do anything yourself. If you had a strong caster, you might be able to overload the containment spell, but I can't promise that would work. And if it did, that caster might lose a portion of their power. Maybe all of it. It'd be dangerous."

"Are you a strong caster?" Dom asked. Anders blinked at him, then looked back at the cuff.

"I'm a fisherman," he said. Dom groaned.

"You aren't! You know how to be here and in Hindry, and I need your help! I need to get back to Asterion."

"He *is* a strong caster," Anders considered, still studying the cuffs, and ignoring Dom's begging. Dom was going to lose his mind.

"Asterion doesn't have magic, but that's not—"

"Yes, he does."

"No, he doesn't," Dom said. Growled. God. He didn't have time for this. "Asterion made a deal—"

"And the terms of the deal were fulfilled. His magic has been returned. The party to celebrate began last night. I imagine it'll last for at least a week. It's been in all the papers."

"What?" Why could Dom never understand what Anders was saying to him?

"People are saying it's the biggest orgy Andurnei's ever seen,"

Anders continued. Dom's headache was returning with a vengeance.

"Anders, what are you talking about?"

"The party, to celebrate Asterion's magic returning. It's a big, well," he hesitated. "I mean, sex parties are sort of—" Dom could feel that his own face was doing something ghastly. Anders paused and cleared his throat. "It's probably not the *biggest* orgy they've ever seen."

"But... No. Because, how?"

But Dom knew how.

Dom was in love with Asterion. And so Asterion had gotten his magic back. And had promptly thrown an orgy.

Because, of course. That was the sort of thing Prince Asterion of Andurnei would do. He was just being himself. And Dom wasn't anything to Asterion. Not really. They were different men from different worlds. Why had he thought that he had mattered to Asterion? Why did he feel like he was drowning?

"Do you want to sit down?" Anders asked.

"No," Dom said. His legs were shaking.

"He might still be willing to help you," Anders said. "You two seemed friendly."

Friendly.

Dom sank to his knees.

Asterion still might be willing to help him. And that pathetic thought sat tightly behind the knot in Dom's chest. The biggest orgy Andurnei had ever seen. And Dom, stupidly, had thought Asterion would be searching for him. Worried about him. But Dom's disappearance had gone entirely unnoticed.

"I could try and speak to him for you."

"No," Dom said immediately. Which was stupid. He needed help. No matter where it came from. "Could you," Dom blinked back tears and pressed his palms against his eyes. Focus. "Could you go to Jonas Rookwood back in Hindry? Tell him what happened. Where I am. Ask him for help." One of the sheep tried to nose into Dom's shopping bag. Dom jerked it away just in time.

"Are you sure you're okay?"

"Where am I, anyway?" Dom asked. Anders' frown deepened, and Dom shook his head. "No, I just... what is this place?"

"Kinclere. One of Andurnei's northernmost provinces. I'll speak to Duke Rookwood for you. And when I come back with his answer, you'll have to do a favor for me."

"Fine," Dom agreed. As though he was in a position to refuse anything to anyone.

"Get me into Morrow's castle." Anders said. Dom nodded. "Consider it done, then," Anders said. Then he took Dom by the arms and hauled him to his feet. "Get back inside."

"Sure."

"Go on, Mr. Silva. Try to rest." Anders nudged Dom toward the castle, before starting down the hill. "I'll be back in a couple of hours."

"Hours?" Dom asked. That couldn't be right. But Anders was already gone, and snow was starting to fall.

A COUPLE OF HOURS CAME AND WENT, AND ANDERS DIDN'T return. So, he'd been delayed. That was alright. It wasn't as though anyone was waiting for Dom. No one knew to be worried about his absence. People who went through portals didn't come back. Ares had only known that Dom had stormed off, and Asterion...

Asterion didn't bear thinking about. He was free to be himself again. Dom wasn't his problem anymore. And Dom needed to come to terms with the idea that he couldn't lose something he'd never had. He went about his work and ignored the growing panic in his chest as morning crept into afternoon, and Anders still didn't come back.

Dom didn't attempt a nap, because he didn't want to be asleep when Anders arrived, but he forced himself to eat. As he was finishing his lunch, Enid returned and deposited a substantial portion of vegetables on the wide center counter of the kitchen. Dom had at least two hours of chopping and dicing ahead of him because Morrow was coming. He was expected that very evening. Fantastic.

Enid went to prepare rooms, and Dom tried to focus on chopping carrots and not on the possibility that Anders hadn't been able to find Jonas. Or that Jonas didn't care about helping Dom. Maybe Dom should have asked Anders to go to Aunt Ree instead. Not that he wanted to involve her in any of this. He just wanted to go home.

Another hour passed. Dom sat on a stool by the stove, peeling a mountain of potatoes. His hands were just beginning to blister, when Edmund Morrow swanned in.

"It seems like you're settling in nicely!"

Rage blossomed, hot, in Dom's chest at the sight of the man, his stupid moustache, cape fluttering out behind him. Dom gripped the knife handle tightly and continued to work.

"Enid says you've been a help, which is good. I was worried you'd give us some trouble. Gods know your brother did, at first." Dom clenched his teeth, and didn't respond. Morrow came around into Dom's line of sight, standing with his back against the wall as he bit into a shining red apple. After a minute or two of silence, he smirked. "You know, I have a special sort of appreciation for obedient men."

Dom focused on the potato in his hand: turn, peel, into the pot.

"Most of my servants greet me when I walk into a room. My

proper title is Viceroy. In case you were wondering." Dom bit his tongue to keep himself quiet. Morrow chuckled. "Strong. Silent. Brooding. It has a certain appeal, I'll grant." He stepped forward, getting closer to Dom's face, peering at him like he was some kind of caged animal. "Mr. Silva, have you considered what you might be able to offer in exchange for some partial freedoms?"

"I'm not interested in offering you anything," Dom said. Morrow arched an eyebrow and leaned back, taking a loud, wet bite out of his apple.

"I'm not a monster, Mr. Silva," he said with his mouth full. "I understand that you might not want to be here. But I think you'd do well to contemplate what might make your stay more pleasant." He finally swallowed. "More fulfilling." Dom thought of the shopkeeper with the missing hand.

"If I chop off my hand with the meat cleaver and remove the cuff, will that break the enchantment?"

Morrow blinked at him. Then he smirked again.

"I don't know. But I'd certainly be curious to find out."

"Why are you keeping me here?" Dom demanded.

"A man of your stature has many possible uses," Morrow shrugged. Then he chuckled and pushed himself off the wall. He walked past Dom and turned, suddenly pressing his front against Dom's back.

Maybe Dom was stupid, but the thought that Morrow might find him attractive, might want to sleep with him, hadn't crossed Dom's mind. It made him want to throw up.

Before Dom could push him off, Morrow's palm was pressed against Dom's ribcage. An electrical pulse tightened all of Dom's muscles at once; he was frozen to the spot, the knife handle biting into his own skin.

"Remember that I'm the one who will decide how you'll be most useful. So, a little respect would not go amiss."

When Morrow let go, Dom collapsed off the stool, knife clattering to the floor beside his hand. His heart was racing, but he stayed still until he heard Morrow go back up the stairs.

Slowly, with effort, Dom got to his feet. It wasn't until he was standing that he could feel the searing heat against his wrist. He looked down to see the golden cuff pulsing with a bright, magical glow.

65

Asterion felt beastly when he woke. He was cold, his body ached, and the only small comfort he had was that at least he could push a sobriety spell into his skull.

The magic made his sinuses throb and pulse like someone had smashed into his forehead with a cold hammer. He needed coffee and something greasy from Nina's griddle. Bacon. Eggs.

Asterion staggered to his feet, stumbled into the bathroom to wash his face and brush his teeth. He dressed in old casting clothes, listening to Sidney and Jonas murmur to each other in the sitting room. Asterion could smell fresh coffee, and he almost wept in relief. He may have been a wrung-out miserable husk, but at least there was coffee.

Jonas and Sidney both had the absolute discourtesy to stare at him as he walked into the room. He ignored them as best he could, collapsing onto the sofa beside Sidney and reaching for the coffee pot. He kept his gaze down, focused on the pour, and immediately spilled into his saucer when he noticed the ivy necklace curled up on the corner of the coffee table between Jonas and Sidney.

"Could someone do me the biggest favor and put that somewhere where I don't have to see it?" Asterion said, gesturing to the necklace with the back of his hand as he sopped coffee off his saucer with a napkin. Jonas scooped it up into his palm.

"We wanted to ask you about it, actually. Found it on the floor last night."

"I don't want to talk about it." Asterion leaned back into the couch cushions and sipped his coffee. The necklace had almost certainly fallen out of his pocket when Jonas carried him to bed.

"Humor me," Jonas said. Asterion blinked at him. "What's it doing here?"

"What does that mean? It's mine. Where else should it be?" Sidney arched an eyebrow, obviously taking issue with Asterion's tone. What snippy barb was he going to lob in Asterion's direction in retaliation? Asterion was looking forward to it, but Jonas interrupted with a practical answer instead.

"Ellery said that the last time she saw this necklace, Dom had it."

"He wore it to Leyland Hall, apparently by mistake, and he gave it to Kephisto to return to me. He went on his own. And I don't believe he has any interest in coming back. He found his brother, so... mystery solved, I suppose."

"The necklace is broken," Sidney said. Damn. It had been his favorite. Asterion scowled.

"Probably when it fell out of my pocket."

"No," Jonas frowned. "The latch is snapped."

Asterion sipped his coffee again and tried to decide if that was meaningful information or not.

"I think we should go to Leyland Hall," Sidney said. "Dom is probably still there. He wasn't back at home or at the diner. We checked before Ellery brought us through the portal."

Yes, they could go to Leyland Hall.

But wasn't this easier? To let the whole thing fizzle out without having to put words to it. It hurt enough without knowing *exactly* what he'd done to push Dom away. Dom might've loved him, but he still left. It was over. Surely that was all that mattered.

"You're welcome to go," Asterion said. "But I think it's probably for the best if I don't join you."

"You don't really intend to stay at Paravel, do you?" Jonas asked.

"What am I supposed to do? Move into a caravan with you and Sidney?" Asterion arched an eyebrow pointedly. Jonas pursed his lips, rolling his bright copper eyes. "I don't need looking after, Jonas. I'm not a child." Jonas scoffed. Asterion pressed on. "Last night notwithstanding. I think I'm allowed to have an indiscretion occasionally. Isn't that what one does when one finds themselves heartbroken? Sidney, you were recently heartbroken, I think?"

"Yes. All thanks to you, of course," Sidney replied with a small smile. Gods, Asterion so appreciated his willingness to be a bitch.

"I think we should all consider ourselves very lucky that I was just getting drunk with a bunch of naiads and not being drained of all my blood and soul on a massive stone altar like some people." He looked pointedly at Sidney, who only laughed.

"That one girl looked like she might have cut you open on an altar if you'd given her a chance."

"Oh, Sidney. Never on a first date."

"Her friend said you threw up on her."

"To know him is to love him," Jonas muttered, still turning the necklace over between his fingers.

"Give me that," Asterion said, holding out his hands. Jonas tossed him the necklace.

Asterion examined the clasp on the chain. Part of the hook had been ripped completely off, leaving only a sharp shard of metal in its place. It couldn't have been an accident. And Dom really wasn't the sort to go tearing things apart. Fits of pique were much more Asterion's style. He bit his lip. Something wasn't sitting right about this.

Before he could decide what it all meant, there was a knock on the door.

"Come in," Asterion said. Ellery opened the door and stuck her head in.

"Duke Rookwood has a visitor." Asterion and Sidney looked at Jonas. Jonas straightened up in his chair and glanced at Asterion, who shrugged.

"I suppose, show them in. Please, Ellery?" Jonas fumbled. Asterion smirked, loving the way formality no longer sat well in Jonas' mouth. Ellery stepped aside, holding the door open for a man with blonde hair and bright blue eyes.

Anders Casmir was dressed as he apparently always was: as though he'd just stepped off a fishing trawler. He hadn't even bothered to take off his knit cap. What a curious guest.

Ellery hesitated in the doorway, and Asterion made a low gesture for her to stay and close the door behind her.

The sound of the door latching seemed to jolt Anders into action. He tugged off his hat.

"Mr. Rookwood. I'm here on behalf of Dom Silva—" Asterion spilled his coffee. Great shitting hell.

"Ah. Yes? Is Mr. Silva well?" Jonas asked

"Uh, no. I should say not. He's been kidnapped, and he looked about half dead when I left him."

Sidney leaned over quickly and plucked Asterion's cup and saucer out of his hands before he could drop them.

Asterion's head was pounding. His heart was pounding. He might throw up again.

"Where's Dom?" Jonas asked. "Who kidnapped him?"

"He's in Kinclere—"

"Kinclere Manor?" Asterion almost shouted. Anders nodded, and Asterion leapt to his feet.

Goddamn Edmund Morrow.

"Is my shitheel brother still here?" Asterion demanded, looking at Ellery. She shook her head, eyes wide.

"No. He left hours ago."

"Desdemona?" Ellery shook her head again. "Goddammit!" Asterion stormed into his bedroom.

"Asterion," Jonas called.

"I hope you brought your coats," Asterion snapped as he threw open his armoire. "We're going to Kinclere!"

66

"Are you sure this is the fastest way?" Asterion demanded for about the fortieth time as they trooped through the woods toward the narrow river that ran along the far edge of the Paravel property.

"It is for me," Anders said.

"Yes," Jonas agreed. "Only you haven't exactly told us why that is. A portal would be quicker."

"If you know the runes," Anders said. He glanced over his shoulder at Jonas. "Do you know the runes?" It was just impudent enough that Asterion felt his own eyes go wide. Sidney looked like he was going to throw a snowball at the back of Anders' head. Jonas shrugged and didn't seem bothered in the least.

It was about a half hour walk to the river, and they spent the bulk of that time in silence. Asterion was trying to focus on anything he knew for certain, which wasn't much. A magically imbued cuff, like the kind the Assembly used for contract fulfillment bound Dom to Morrow's Kinclere property. He might be able to leave the manor, but he wouldn't be able to leave the town. Anders theorized that they could overload the enchantments on the cuffs, but he had no idea what that would do to the caster. Or to Dom.

Jonas and Sidney would look when they got there. But if they couldn't find a way to open the cuff... Then things were either going to get decidedly more violent or more litigious. And Asterion knew which of those options he was more inclined toward.

Fantasies of tearing Edmund Morrow apart in exceedingly painful ways were interrupted by their arrival at what was essentially a narrow looking canal boat. Asterion didn't know boats from anything else; he hated them, unless they were in crystal clear tropical waters and had enough room for him to sun himself on the deck for several hours. This met none of his requirements, and it didn't even look like it could go very fast.

"Are you joking?" Asterion asked, as Anders gestured that they should step aboard.

"Trust me, your majesty."

"Jonas," Asterion demanded. Jonas sighed and looked back at him.

"I don't know the runes."

"This is a river cruiser. Kinclere is a thousand miles from here!" Asterion was beginning to feel frantic. Magic had dulled his hangover to a low throb, but it was threatening to return to full strength. He clenched his fists, and Anders gave him a stern frown.

"Please, your majesty—"

"Stop calling me that!"

"I have a vested interest in this working out," Anders said. Asterion could have screamed, and then Sidney was looping his arm around Asterion's and guiding him forward.

"Come on. Let's give it a chance."

"This is ludicrous," Asterion grumbled, as Sidney ushered him onto the deck.

Asterion only grew more assured that this was madness, as they settled themselves below deck. There was only one cabin, a long room with a sitting area, bookshelves, a small kitchenette and, at the far end, a bed as wide as the space itself. Asterion threw himself onto the burgundy sofa, irritated at the way Jonas was looking around appreciatively, even though he had to keep his head ducked beneath the low ceiling. Sidney settled himself on an adjacent armchair, and as the engine roared to life, Asterion deeply resented Jonas' small smile.

"I might go and see the wheelhouse," Jonas said. Asterion rolled his eyes.

"For Gods' sakes, Jonas. Have a little decorum."

"Don't be rude just because you've fallen in love," Jonas smirked. Asterion growled.

"What we need to be doing is talking about is how we're going to—" The boat jerked hard to the left, and Asterion had to grip the arm of the couch to stay upright. "What the hell?" The boat jerked again, and Jonas worked his way over to one of the windows, a hand braced against the ceiling as he yanked back the curtain.

The banks of the river were moving by far too quickly. But what was more alarming was the water tapping against the bottom of the window frame.

They were sinking.

Jonas ran for the door and tried to push against it, but the pressure on the other side was already too great. They'd left Anders on deck, and Jonas pounded his massive fists against the door, shouting for him. Sidney vaulted over the back of the loveseat and tried a window, and all Asterion could do was sit and stare, shock rendering him utterly useless.

The boat submerged, and for a moment, there was silence.

No water came rushing into the cabin.

Asterion's ears popped as he got to his feet. The trawler should have smashed against the river bottom by now.

"It's not that deep," he said. Jonas and Sidney both swung to look at him, and Asterion nodded out the window where the muddy water of the river in winter had turned blue-black. Bubbles, thin, floated up around them, and the whole boat shuddered, as it began to rise toward the surface.

"What sort of magic is this?" Sidney asked, looking between Jonas and Asterion, eyes wide. Asterion bit his lip, ears popping again as they continued their ascent.

"Elemental," Asterion said. Jonas frowned. "Most likely. I mean, think about it. He's traveling across realms through the water. Portaling like that must expend so much magic. He was in Hindry. Now he's here? With an entire vessel?" It would take more magic than Asterion had ever dreamed of. Elementals were closer to Gods than even most demigods could ever hope to be. But then—

"If he is," Jonas said slowly, "then why is he here? Why is he helping us?" The roar of rushing water interrupted Asterion's train of thought. The boat surfaced with enough force to knock all three of them on their asses, and they were still struggling to stand when Anders, out of breath, but grinning, pushed his way through the door.

"Gentlemen. Welcome to Kinclere."

67

"This place ought to be spotless before you turn in," Enid said as they carried the third and final tray of food out of the kitchen. Dom tried to feel grateful that he hadn't been forced to serve Morrow his meal too, as he started to move pots and pans to the sink.

'A couple of hours,' had become the entire day. Anders never came back, and over the course of the evening, fatigue had numbed all but the very worst of Dom's feelings. He was heartbroken, and everything he touched, everything he did, reminded him of Asterion. The hot water in the sink reminded him of being in the kitchen with Asterion in the diner. Scrubbing out the coffee pot, of course, the way Asterion liked his coffee. The tea, the tea they'd drunk in Dom's bed.

But it was exhaustion, not heartbreak, that brought Dom to tears over the sink. At least, that was what he was going to tell himself. Washing dishes was the perfect time to cry. It was efficient, if nothing else. Tears went in the sink. The heat from the water was the perfect excuse for flushed cheeks. No one could hear him sob over the sounds of running water and scouring pads against pans. Over his years of working in the diner, after losing his mother and Ares, it almost felt like the right thing to do. Like he might as well cry, if he was going to scrub out a roast pan. Routine, his eternal savior.

By the time he was finished, his hands were raw and aching, and his chest was empty. He'd be too tired to dream tonight. And that could only be a good thing.

Dom was wiping down the counters, his final step, just like it was back at home, when someone knocked on the kitchen door. Dom threw the rag over his shoulder, too tired to even hope it was Anders. Who was the worst person it could be? Would Morrow walk around the outside of his own palace in the snow just to torture Dom? Probably. Dom pulled open the door and froze as Anders frowned in at him.

"I told you to get some rest," Anders scolded. White snowflakes clung to his knit hat and beard. Dom wavered on his feet. "Can I come in?" Anders asked. Dom nodded and stepped aside. Anders huffed. "You have to say it."

"Come in," Dom said. He took another step back, and Anders came into the kitchen, looking around with a grin.

"Did he get any shipments today?"

"Shipments?" Dom asked. He was feeling woozy. "I don't think so."

"Oh, Gods," Anders murmured, and caught Dom around the waist, pressing his palm to Dom's cheek. "You stupid, stubborn, fool." Anders' hand pulsed against Dom's skin, and Dom felt a strange surge of relief. Like he'd been given a glass of ice water on an oppressively hot day. He was still tired, but his head was clearer. Ander's palm pulsed again, and Dom could almost feel the sudden sharpness of water in his nose and against the back of his throat. He spluttered and pushed Anders off.

"Okay. Okay!" But Anders' eyes were down, looking at the soft blue ripple of light that reverberated off the cuff on Dom's wrist.

"I don't like that." Anders glanced at Dom. "Are you well enough to make it to the docks?"

"The docks? I think so. Why? Were you able to find Jonas? What did he say?"

"Go to the docks," Anders said. "And be quick. If I get caught here, we won't have a lot of time. And I *will* leave whether or not they've managed to free you. Do you understand?"

"Wait, Jonas is here?"

"At the docks. On my boat. I anchored her much closer. But you need to hurry. And so do I."

"What are *you* doing?" Dom asked. Anders smirked.

"Get to the docks, Mr. Silva. *Quickly.*"

The snow was just deep enough that running was difficult. The muscles in his legs ached and the cold air burned his lungs. He'd been in such a rush that he hadn't even bothered to go back to his room for Ares' coat.

The snow kept people inside, and Dom was relieved by the silence of the town as he focused on putting one foot in front of the other. The glow of streetlamps illuminated the snowflakes that muffled his footfall as he hobbled for the docks. He tried to remember the general shape of Anders' ship; the one Anders had pointed out to him that very morning.

Dom scraped his memory for the small details. The color of the varnish, the number of sails. Were there sails? He nearly slipped on the damp wood planks of the pier skidding to a halt in front of what could only be Anders' boat. It looked familiar, and it was the only one with lanterns lit and a gangway down. Dom's steps echoed as he climbed aboard the empty deck. He wanted to call out for Jonas, but that probably wouldn't be wise in case there was anyone listening. The town had seemed empty, but the warning from the blacksmith's shopkeeper had stuck.

The first door Dom tried on deck was locked.

The second one opened.

A narrow set of stairs with a low ceiling led down. Dom ducked and took two steps before—

"Dom?"

Dom looked up, startled by the sound of the voice he'd been imagining all day.

Asterion.

Asterion's golden eyes were wide, his beautiful mouth open, chest rising and falling in a gasp that was the only thing Dom could hear.

And then Asterion was on him. Dom's head hit the ceiling as their bodies crashed together. Asterion's arms wrapped around his waist, Dom's shoulders pressed against the wall. Less than an hour ago, Dom didn't know if he'd ever see Asterion again and now they were kissing. And Dom was so relieved, so ridiculously, giddily happy, that he started laughing.

ASTERION PULLED AWAY, AS DOM'S PRESSED HIS HAND AGAINST the back of his head. If anyone could make exhausted look good, it was Dom Silva. But Gods, he looked bad. A bruise purpled his jaw, there were bags under his eyes, and Dom was limping, slumped against Asterion as Asterion helped him down the last few steps and onto the couch.

Sidney was at his other side, and Jonas was kneeling in front of him. Dom was talking, mumbling, holding up his wrist, and all Asterion could think was that he wanted to heal him. He had his magic back, and for the first time in his entire life it could actually truly be useful.

"Here, come here." Asterion interrupted Dom mid-sentence and turned Dom's face toward him with both hands, gently. Dom's expression relaxed into a smile. He opened his mouth to speak, and Asterion wasn't ready for that quite yet. "Can I heal him?" Asterion asked Jonas. Jonas frowned.

"You can try, but as he just said—"

"He wasn't listening," Dom chuckled, his gaze on Asterion so impossibly soft that it made every imperious wall Asterion had ever built inside himself melt all at once.

"I was busy planning vengeance on whomever did this to your face," he said, brushing his thumb across the bruise. Dom smiled.

"I think I broke Di Rilke's nose."

"Di Rilke?"

"Later, Asterion," Jonas chastised. "Anders said we didn't have much time. You can try and heal him, but the cuffs have been absorbing some of everything that's been cast on him."

"Who's been casting on you?" Asterion demanded.

"Anders tried to heal me, I think," Dom said, taking Asterion's hands from his cheeks, and holding them. "Before he sent me here." Dom paused, a hesitation that Asterion hated.

"Who else?"

"Morrow," Dom said. Asterion found he was breathless with anger. Dom squeezed his fingertips. "But, any casting, the cuffs glow. They absorb some of it. I'm not sure—I mean, Anders' healing helped a little."

Gods, Asterion was going to kill Edmund Morrow. Sidney took one of Dom's hands away from Asterion, and Asterion almost snarled at him as Sidney spun the cuff, examining it.

"It's leaving a mark."

"It heats up quickly," Dom said.

"It's burning you?" Asterion demanded, leaning in to look at the red, angry looking skin of Dom's wrist. Dom squeezed Asterion's fingers again.

"Not badly. But it gets hot."

"Well, it's a magical suppressant pulling from a strong

source," Jonas said, gesturing to Dom. "Sapping Dom's magic and any other casting that comes his way. I suppose the good news is that if the metal is heating constantly, it's also weakening. Anders is right. We might be able to overload it with a strong cast."

"But if it's absorbing power," Dom said. Swallowed. "If someone casts into it, isn't that going to deplete their magic?"

"Magic is regenerative, up to a point," Jonas said. "It might not be permanent. Depending how much it takes."

"But if it is permanent," Dom started. Asterion groaned.

"Dominic, be reasonable. If we don't get it off, then we can't get you out of here. We have to try."

Dom ran his tongue over chapped lips. His brown eyes searched Asterion's face for a long moment, and Asterion's chest tightened. He couldn't leave Dom here. He wouldn't. Sidney cleared his throat.

"We're going to go on deck. To keep an eye out for Anders," Sidney said, getting to his feet.

"No, wait—" Jonas protested, as Sidney grabbed him by the arm and hauled him toward the door. Blessed Sidney.

Dom took a deep breath, as their footsteps faded on the stairs. His eyes searched Asterion's face, and slowly he shook his head.

"I don't think you should do this," Dom said.

"Oh, my gods," Asterion groaned.

"You just got your magic back. There's no need to risk it. Now that you know where I am, you can, you know... we can figure something out. I'm sure there's someone else. Ares, maybe. I found him. He—"

"Dom, if you think for a single moment that I'm leaving this place without you—"

"It's not safe here, Asterion. This whole town is under Morrow's control."

"Then why in the realms do you think I would leave you here?" Asterion demanded.

"Because you don't have a choice. We don't have a choice."

"I can put all my magic into that stupid bracelet until it breaks or melts or—"

"But you might not get it back. And you," Dom fumbled for the first time, his eyes darting away, and then back. He huffed. "I understand what it means to you now. I can't ask you to do that."

"I'm offering."

"Asterion," Dom shook his head. "You can't. It's your life. It's centuries. And we're—I mean. This isn't—" He gestured weakly between them, and doubt tried to unfurl itself in Asterion's stomach. But he couldn't stop himself.

"I love you," Asterion said.

Dom's jaw went slack, and he shook his head slowly.

"You don't have to say that." Asterion scoffed to keep from bursting into tears.

"I do. I love you."

"But Anders said you'd thrown a—" Dom shook his head. "And I mean, look, Asterion, it's fine. You don't have to pretend."

"Dom—"

"Your magic is back because *I* love *you*. But that doesn't mean—"

"I knew I loved you before I knew my magic was back," Asterion said. "I should have said something, but I was afraid it wasn't the right time, or that you didn't feel the same way. And I know that might not amount to much now, but you told me that we're the ones who get to decide what this means. And I know what it means to me." Dom's teeth dug nervously against his lower lip. "Do you trust me?" Asterion asked, trying not to be terrified of what Dom's answer might be.

"You haven't lied to me yet," Dom said quietly.

"And I'm not going to start now. I promise."

Dom kissed him.

Asterion leaned into it, letting their fingers tangle together, relishing in the heat of Dom's body, the soft sounds Dom made against his mouth. Asterion felt satisfaction for the first time in his life, a rightness that settled comfortably against his skin.

But there wasn't time to relax just yet. Asterion knew Dom. He knew how Dom would try to be selfless, and give up his own happiness, his health, his well-being at the expense of Asterion's. There were plenty of things Asterion didn't know. But he knew he loved Dom Silva. And he knew that he would give up everything that he had to keep Dom safe.

So, he did.

Asterion threaded his fingertips into the narrow space between Dom's skin and the metal cuff and kissed him long enough, hard enough to distract him. And then Asterion began to cast.

It was easy to let the magic go. Far easier than it had been the first time. Dom faltered; he must have felt it, and Asterion held tight to the cuff as Dom pushed back. Asterion focused, ignoring the searing pain in his fingertips.

"Asterion!"

Asterion grit his teeth. He could feel the magic of the cuff tightening around his own. Straining. Pulling. He gave everything he had, reaching for the shade of emptiness behind the last of his casting, as his magic faded into a thin thing. Dom tried to pry his fingers away. There was shouting. And then, there was silence.

68

The cuff snapped as though it hadn't just been glowing red hot. Burns blistered Asterion's fingertips and Dom's wrist, but Dom's magic was already sparking forth to fix the damage. His own damage, at any rate.

"Asterion! Goddammit!" Asterion was sliding off the couch, his eyes closing. Blood trickled down from Asterion's nose over his kiss-reddened lips, as Dom grabbed him around the waist.

Sidney thundered halfway down the stairs.

"Anders is here. He was followed, and we're going now. Right now! Are you—?"

"The cuff is off!" Dom called, still trying to get a good hold on Asterion's limp body. The door slammed above his head, and Dom heaved Asterion up onto the couch.

Asterion's head lolled to the side.

"Asterion. Asterion!" Dom tried to breathe through his panic. Asterion's chest rose slowly, and Dom tried to get a grasp on the tether of his own magic. Intention and desire were all he knew, but he had to try. Dom pressed his hand over Asterion's fluttering pulse and tried to cast. *Heal him*, he thought. *Heal him. Heal him, heal him. Please.*

Warmth pooled in the center of Dom's hand, soft like freshly tilled soil in the spring. It didn't flow out of him the way Anders' had. Dom's magic felt solid, like something that had to be absorbed, pressed into Asterion's neck. The filigree extolations lit up his arm, and then after a few minutes, the light faded along with the sensation of magic from his hand. It was gone. He tried to conjure up more, tried to focus, but his hands were shaking. He couldn't catch his breath.

The ship rocked violently, and Dom tightened his grip on Asterion's narrow waist. Dark circles bloomed beneath Asterion's eyes, his skin ghostly pale.

He'd given everything.

And he'd done it to rescue Dom.

"Asterion," Dom murmured, pressing his lips to Asterion's temple. "Please."

The sound of rushing water filled the silence.

Dom closed his eyes tightly and held Asterion close, trying to think. Asterion loved him. He couldn't lose him. He just couldn't.

Dom stared down at the golden glow of the extolation, still fading beneath his skin. Ree had said that Dom's mark was different. Tied to devotion. Maybe that was the answer. Asterion had proved he was devoted. More than Dom had ever deserved. Maybe Dom could do the same; show the Gods, somehow, that he was devoted too.

Dom turned Asterion toward him. He was so tired of seeing Asterion unconscious. Bloody. A storybook prince mixed up in some kind of horrible pulp fairytale.

Dom kissed Asterion gently, briefly. But when their lips brushed, Dom felt something. It was small, but familiar: the warmth of his own magic, beneath Asterion's skin.

He kissed Asterion harder, willing his magic to sink in, to heal him.

Wake him up.
Make him better. Please.
I can't lose anyone else.
I love him.

When Dom had marked Asterion, the magic beneath his veins had been eager, bright and hungry. But when Dom found it this time, it was a solid, languid thing, moving like a lava flow. Dom urged it forward, pushed on it, pleaded with it, and then Asterion's fingers tightened against Dom's arms. Dom pulled back, and Asterion's golden eyes were blinking open.

"Dom?"

Asterion smiled up at him and wiped away a tear that was sliding down Dom's cheek.

69

D om dozed against Asterion's shoulder, as Anders' boat (a different shape again) navigated the choppy waters of Bittergate Bay, delivering them to Hindry. Home.

Asterion was beginning to feel a bit dizzy. Whether it was from the loss of magic, the elation of being in love, the rather fraught last day and a half of his life, or the beginnings of seasickness, he couldn't possibly have guessed. He tried to focus on Dom's breathing, blessedly steady beside him, and stared at their hands, Dom's fingers still twined loosely with his own.

It was then that Asterion noticed a small, raised, filigree pattern, like a thin pink scar, wrapped around his own wrist. Almost a copy of Dom's, but much smaller. It didn't hurt. It didn't really feel like anything at all, and Asterion wondered what it meant. He wasn't worried. Mostly curious. But if it had come from Dom, it wouldn't do him any harm.

"What's that?" Dom murmured. He'd caught Asterion rubbing his thumb against the mark.

"Something of yours, I think," Asterion said, holding his wrist up. Dom frowned, his mouth dropping open as he searched for some words of protest. Asterion shook his head. "I like it."

"I didn't mean to."

"I don't mind. And even if I didn't like it, which I do," Asterion added pointedly, "but even if I didn't, you saved my life. I'm hardly in any position to complain."

"Didn't get your magic back though," Dom mumbled, his eyes falling closed again. Asterion hummed.

It seemed like that was true, at least for now. And maybe it was permanent. But Asterion didn't really care. It was fortifying instead of frightening to discover that there was someone he would give anything for. Someone who would love him no matter what he lacked.

"Should we ask Anders if he can take us back to Leyland Hall? You never told me what happened with Ares."

"Ares is stubborn," Dom yawned. "We can go back soon. After a nap."

"But he's safe? Well?"

"Seems to be. Sidney's brother's there."

"What?" Asterion exclaimed. "How?"

"Dunno," Dom mumbled, "we'll figure it out." And then he sank into sleep.

Asterion might have dozed off himself, but the next thing he knew, Anders was seated on the low table in front of Asterion, elbows pressed against his knees.

"Thank you for your help," Asterion murmured groggily. Anders nodded.

"It wasn't entirely selfless, as I'm sure you've guessed."

"What are you looking for?"

"Edmund Morrow is under investigation," Anders said. "His magical signature keeps popping up where I least expect it. And I've been having to move around rather quickly. I tried to speak to you about it before—"

"Before?" Asterion frowned. Anders smirked.

"At the diner. And at the bar. But you wouldn't talk to me. I'd thought, up until today, that you were working with him."

"What?" Asterion hissed. Anders shrugged.

"I know better now."

"Who's investigating him?"

"That's not for me to say," Anders said with a shake of his head. "But you may be hearing from some of my people, if we need testimony." Asterion nodded, the shock of being mildly accused replaced by the elation that he might be able to help put Morrow behind bars.

"You should talk to Jonas."

"He's already agreed," Anders said.

"Are you going to be staying for a few days? We may need transportation."

"Unfortunately, no. Once you disembark, I have some reports to see to."

"You're an elemental, aren't you?" Asterion asked. He wasn't coherent enough to be more discreet. Anders blinked at him.

"I'm a fisherman."

"Because if you are an elemental, you have more magic than me. Than Dom. Than anyone I've ever met. You could have freed him," Asterion accused. Anders at least had the good grace to look sheepish.

"Investigators aren't allowed to interfere with an ongoing case," he said quietly. Asterion rolled his eyes. The goodwill he'd felt toward Anders was fast fleeting.

"Well, can I ask you to do something for me before you go? I promise, it has nothing to do with your investigation."

～

THEY ARRIVED AT THE APARTMENT WELL AFTER DARK, AND DOM could barely stand to let go of Asterion for more than a few minutes at a time. Luckily, Asterion agreed. They showered together, and then climbed into bed, Dom curling around Asterion's back and holding him close.

"I love you," Asterion said before Dom could say it first. Dom kissed the back of Asterion's neck, and something deep beneath his blood sang in delight.

"I love you too."

They fell asleep and woke up in almost the same position. Jonas and Sidney had spent the night in the upstairs apartment, with Dom's promise that he'd drive them to the cottage in the morning. Dom could hear them now, moving around in the bedroom above his head.

Asterion turned over to rest his head on Dom's shoulder and began to kiss Dom's neck. His chest. Dom smirked as their legs tangled beneath the blankets, and Asterion pressed his hips forward. Heat blossomed between them, and the next thing Dom knew, Asterion was climbing on top of him, still wearing Dom's shirt that he'd borrowed to sleep in.

Dom let himself get lost in it. Enjoyed himself, truly and fully. Everything he had to do would still be there in half an hour. He'd spent so many years ignoring the things he wanted, afraid to take anything for himself because he'd known he was just going to have to give it away again. But now he knew that sacrifice wasn't always loss. And that devotion didn't have to be one-sided. Giving and taking were a balance. And balance was where there was the most fulfillment. The most joy and the most pleasure.

Asterion curled, sweating, gorgeous, and wonderfully alive against Dom's chest, pressing his lips to the center of Dom's throat. Dom had pulled Asterion's shirt off in the course of things and ran his fingers slowly over the bare skin of Asterion's back, enjoying touching him.

"I have something for you," Asterion said.

"Something else?" Dom murmured. Asterion laughed.

"Yes." He climbed off Dom with an exaggerated groan, and Dom tried to slide off the mattress after him. "Stay in bed!"

"We ought to get up," Dom said, as Asterion dug through the pile of clothes they'd left on the floor the night before.

"We can't go anywhere without Sidney and Jonas." Asterion said, and, as though they planned it, at that exact moment, the shower upstairs turned on. Dom laid back against the pillows with a sigh, and Asterion climbed in bed beside him. "So, you know how you marked me?"

"Yes?" Dom said, ignoring the way the memory of it made him blush. Asterion smirked. Beneath the blankets, he pushed his fingers against Dom's hand, dropping something into his palm.

"I was thinking about that. And when you wore this with the heartrender. If you still wanted it, you could..." Asterion trailed off, as Dom rolled onto his side and looked down at the silver necklace in his hand. The one Morrow had stolen from him. Asterion's ivy.

"How did you get this?"

"Kephisto gave it to me. He was gloating. But that doesn't matter. I want you to have it. If you want it."

"I want it," Dom said immediately. Asterion smiled.

"You don't have to—"

"Will you help me put it on?" Asterion nodded, and in a matter of moments, Dom felt the silver crescent of ivy fall into its spot against his chest. Above his heart.

"It looks good on you," Asterion said.

"I'm glad you think so," Dom smiled. "I don't plan on taking it off."

EPILOGUE

When the bell over the door rang, Dom was in the kitchen, hunched over the griddle with a rag in his hand. It was too late for new customers; the clock on the wall read ten thirty, and through the small window in the back door, Dom could see the glow of the streetlamps illuminating the falling snow. Dom stretched as he turned, feeling the low ache between his shoulder blades. He'd spent most of his day in the kitchen, working on pies, which they were always short on in the days before Christmas. No matter how he begged people to order ahead of time, it just wasn't December 23rd if Dom wasn't rolling out crust well into the middle of the evening.

He pulled one arm overhead, reaching up to grab his elbow, wanting the kink gone from the center of his back. Of course, it was then that Asterion swung into the kitchen.

His blue hair was long enough now to tie back at the nape of his neck, though two soft looking tendrils curled down, framing his flushed cheeks. He arched an eyebrow at Dom, and his smile turned into a smirk.

"You look pleased," Dom observed.

"Well, I finally got Maude and Dierdre out the door," he said. "Though I had to give them the last of the eclairs in the case."

"You didn't charge them, did you?"

"Of course not." Asterion reached behind him to untie his apron. Dom swapped arms and tugged on his other elbow, as Asterion pursed his lips and tossed his apron onto the counter. "Are you okay?"

"My back's tight."

"Aww," Asterion cooed. "What happened?" He came up behind Dom, pressing his long thumbs against Dom's spine. He pushed right into the center of the knot and Dom groaned.

"Oh, God, yes."

"I told you to let Nina help with the pies," Asterion chided.

"Nina can't help with the pies. She's got to make the food for all the other customers who aren't *just* coming in for desserts."

"I don't think you can reasonably be expected to be a diner and a pie shop at the same time." Asterion dug his knuckles into Dom's back. Dom groaned again, leaning forward to grip the counter in front of him. "You need to change your business model around the holidays."

"I'll do anything you say if you move your hand up half an inch," Dom mumbled. Asterion huffed, but he did shift his fingers and Dom let out a long slow breath, as his whole body, and the knot in his muscles, started to relax. Asterion kissed the nape of Dom's neck, and Dom bumped his ass against Asterion's hips.

"Maybe this isn't pie related at all," Asterion murmured, pressing against Dom's spine. Dom's brain was turning to mush; he had no idea what Asterion was talking about.

"What do you mean?"

"I mean," Asterion's mouth brushed Dom's neck, sending soft prickles up Dom's spine, "last night you might have overdone it." Ah. Last night when Dom had picked Asterion up and pinned him against the wall. Asterion's legs had wrapped around Dom's waist, his fingers tangling in Dom's hair.

"No," Dom smirked. "Couldn't have been that."

"No?" He could practically hear Asterion rolling his eyes. "I'm not as thin as I used to be." That was true too, and Dom was very pleased about it. He reached behind him and grabbed Asterion's hip, tugging him forward, bringing their bodies flush. Dom's extolations began to glow, the old magic beneath his veins interpreting the pleasure as some sort of holy worship. They still hadn't quite sorted out how it worked yet. It lit up a lot during sex, but not always. No rhyme or reason there. The vines on his arms grew and tangled more intricately together when they'd catered Thanksgiving dinner at the firemen's hall, though he hadn't noticed it at the time. Devotion and nurturing, creating an abundance, finding peace; he never knew anymore what was going to etch itself into his skin.

Asterion's single tendril around his wrist hadn't expanded. But it had sprouted new leaves, and neither of them knew what to make of that.

Asterion leaned forward and pressed a kiss behind Dom's ear, and Dom couldn't stop himself.

"Did you lock the doors?" He asked, voice low.

"Dominic," Asterion chuckled, even as he brushed his nose against the back of Dom's neck. "We ought to go home."

"Why?"

"We've been here all day. And home has a bed. And a shower."

"Are you saying I smell?"

"I'm saying I can continue what I'm doing now more effectively in a shower. Or in a bed." Asterion reached around and palmed Dom through Dom's trousers and flour covered apron. Dom bit his lip, but before he could speak, the bell above the front door rang out again.

∾

IT WAS TRUE THAT ASTERION HAD NOT YET LEARNED HOW TO properly lock up the diner. There was a trick to it: the key was old and the lock had stuck, and he might have left the whole thing alone after having flipped the sign around to "Closed" because he hadn't anticipated being so distracted when he walked into the kitchen.

"Oh, great shitting hells," he mumbled, pulling away from Dom.

"I can take care of it." Dom straightened up. Asterion's hand-print was conspicuously outlined in flour on the apron in front of Dom's crotch. Asterion shook his head.

"No. Because if you do we'll be here for another hour making dinner for someone who should have come in when we were actually open," Asterion said, being precisely loud enough for the person who had just entered to hear him. Dom scowled and Asterion winked, before pushing open the door and step-ping out to stand behind the counter. "Sorry, we're—"

Cressida looked entirely out of place in The Silver Platter. A chartreuse and black checkered cape swallowed her whole. Hot pink lining clashed so violently with the exterior fabric that it almost worked. She looked around the room curiously, holding some small parcel to her chest, and Asterion scrambled to find any words to fill the void. He'd not seen or spoken to Cress, or his mother, since they were all at Paravel. And he'd sort of thought he never would again.

"So, this is what you gave it all up for?" she asked. Asterion bristled, even though it didn't sound unkind, or even judgmen-tal. When she looked over at him, she cocked her head to the side, like a dog trying to understand human speech.

"Yes," he said. "I love it here."

He really did. It was very different from his old life, and yet all of the things he loved, all of the things he was never supposed to have wanted, he'd managed to hold onto. They'd turned the upstairs apartment into a painting studio. Asterion worked full-time at the diner, and got his hair done at Ree's salon, which she was letting him redecorate. He had Dom. He had friends. He was happier than he'd known it was possible to be.

Cress hummed. Dom appeared, stepping out of the kitchen to stand beside Asterion, his apron draped over his arm.

"Your majesty," Dom said, his voice stiff, defensive. Dom barely inclined his head toward Cress, and Asterion's heart swelled with affection.

"Mr. Silva," Cressida nodded. "Or should I say, your holiness?"

"Mr. Silva is fine." Dom's hand pressed against the small of Asterion's back, and Asterion couldn't help the fond smile that drifted across his face. Perfect, wonderful, Dom.

"To what do we owe this very surprising visit?"

"I wanted to talk to you about Paravel." Cressida stepped toward the counter. "And I wanted you to meet your niece."

She lowered her arms before Asterion could speak, and what he'd thought was a parcel was revealed to be a small bundle of newborn child.

Asterion couldn't stop the gasp that escaped his lips any more than he could avoid the tears that were pricking at the corners of his eyes. The child had soft wisps of blue hair, ears that came to long, tufted tips, and the same pointed nose that he and his sister shared.

"Gods, Cress. She's beautiful."

"Do you want to hold her?" Cressida asked. Babies didn't make Asterion nervous in theory, but the thought of holding something so precious made him immediately shake his head. Dom, however, couldn't have stepped up faster. Before Asterion could try to navigate whatever horrible thing Cressida was sure to say, Dom was reaching over the counter, and Cress was placing the baby gently into his arms. Asterion needed to sit down.

Cress seemed to feel the same way, hoisting herself onto one of the stools at the counter, while she watched Dom cradle her child. Asterion's niece. Asterion leaned against the counter and tried not to collapse. He turned to Cressida.

"Have you moved into Paravel?"

"No," she said, her eyes drifting over his face. "After Felix's little part in mother's schemes, it didn't feel right."

"Di Rilke kidnapped Dom as a favor to mother. So that mother would let him marry you." When they'd been recovering, and sharing stories of their time apart, Dom had quickly pieced together the reasoning for Di Rilke's deception. "So, are you, then? Married?"

"I am. Felix is in the car. He was too embarrassed to come in."

"You can have Paravel," Asterion said. "I have no use for it."

"Are you certain?" Cressida asked. "It's yours, if you want it."

"We may want to get a few things," Dom said. Asterion glanced at him over his shoulder and Dom gave a small shrug. It was a good thought. If the option was available then, perhaps...

"So, you're staying here then?" Cressida asked. "You're certain?"

"I am," Asterion said, without a single moment of hesitation.

"Well," Cress gave him a small smile. Small, but sincere. "Good for you." The baby yawned audibly and drew everyone's attention. Dom stepped closer, and Asterion looked down at a little pair of bright crystal blue eyes.

"What's her name?"

"Felicity. But I think we'll call her by her middle name."

"Which is?" Dom prompted.

"Aster," Cressida said with a smile.

ASTERION CONSENTED TO HOLD THE BABY, HIS LITTLE NAMESAKE, while Dom went in the back to find a spare pie. Five minutes later and pie in hand, Cressida took Aster and her dessert and went out to her husband in the idling car. Dom locked the door behind her and turned to look at Asterion.

"Are you okay?" he asked, coming around the edge of the counter, to wrap his arms around Asterion's waist

"Yes?"

Was he? Some small knot of tension he hadn't realized he'd been holding had loosened. Starting over had been full of strange things like this, unexpected small joys. He was okay. It was odd. But it was good. Dom kissed his cheek, and Asterion leaned into his embrace.

"Let's go home," Dom said. And Asterion nodded, because it would have been too maudlin to argue that they already were.

THE END

Thank you for reading *The Prince and the Silver Platter.*

The Bittergate Bay trilogy will conclude with
In the Garden of the Demigod
in early 2026.

www.ingramcontent.com/pod-product-compliance
Lightning Source LLC
Chambersburg PA
CBHW020008120726
47903CB00004B/1191